The Harrow Saga
Shadow in the Flame
Book Two

Philip Mazza

THE HARROW SAGA

FROM UNDER A TREE

BOOK ONE; SPECIAL EDITION

THE HARROW SAGA

SHADOW IN THE FLAME

BOOK TWO

THE HARROW SAGA

CHILDREN AT THE GATE

BOOK THREE

The Harrow Saga
Shadow in the Flame
Book Two

Philip Mazza

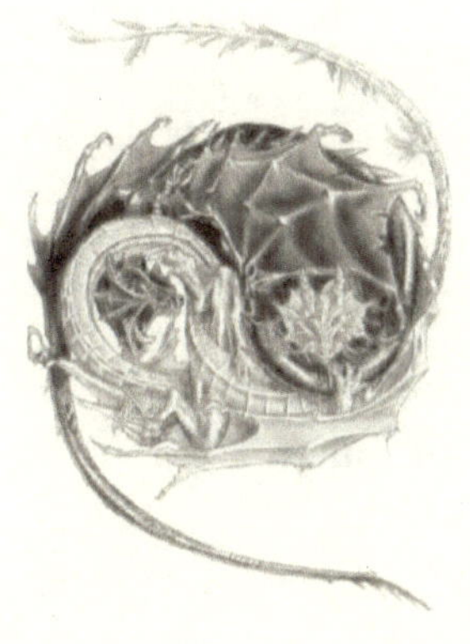

Omni Publishers of New York

Cover and book design by publisher

www.philipmazza.com

Omni Publishers of New York
ISBN 978-0-9977109-1-5
Printed in the United States of America

First Printing: December 2020

Alkar I' Aran - The Song of the Anar Ere

O with a charge like thunder does the Maker
Hurl brilliant rocks and stones asunder,

With seeds of light sowed in furrows to grow
in wonder.

O with a charge that crashes does the Maker
Stir a furious wind that lashes,

With a storm of fire that swiftly burns souls
to ashes.

O who will stand with the stones in hand?

O who will stand to nurture the seeds of the
land?

O who will answer to the Maker on his throne?

Hear it not, for the noise and quiet are of the
same tone.

About the Author

PHILIP MAZZA IS A novelist with boundless imaginative gifts - a spellbinding storyteller who has created for us a captivating world with *The Harrow Saga.* Born in New York in 1959, Philip received his undergraduate degree from LeMoyne College, where he majored in Business and later achieved his MBA. His career focused on human resources and operations, having held leadership positions for companies, both large and small. He has also served on the boards of several not-for-profits. Now a professor of business at the Madden School of Business, Philip devotes his time to his students and his writing. A writer since a young age, *Shadow in the Flame* is the second novel in *The Harrow Saga* trilogy. He and his wife enjoy travel and their cat; they continue to live in upstate New York.

Dedication

To Little Grey: On July 8, 2020, our explorer Livingston sailed off on misty waters, on a new adventure. He was our Shaer Thol.

* * *

We will forever miss our Livingston. He was a tender and loving cat who loved to chatter at wildlife from his window. We know Big Grrrr, our Drake, welcomed Livingston to his new reality as his ship came ashore.

* * *

As Harlan Ellison wrote, "For a brief time, I was here, and for a brief time, I mattered."

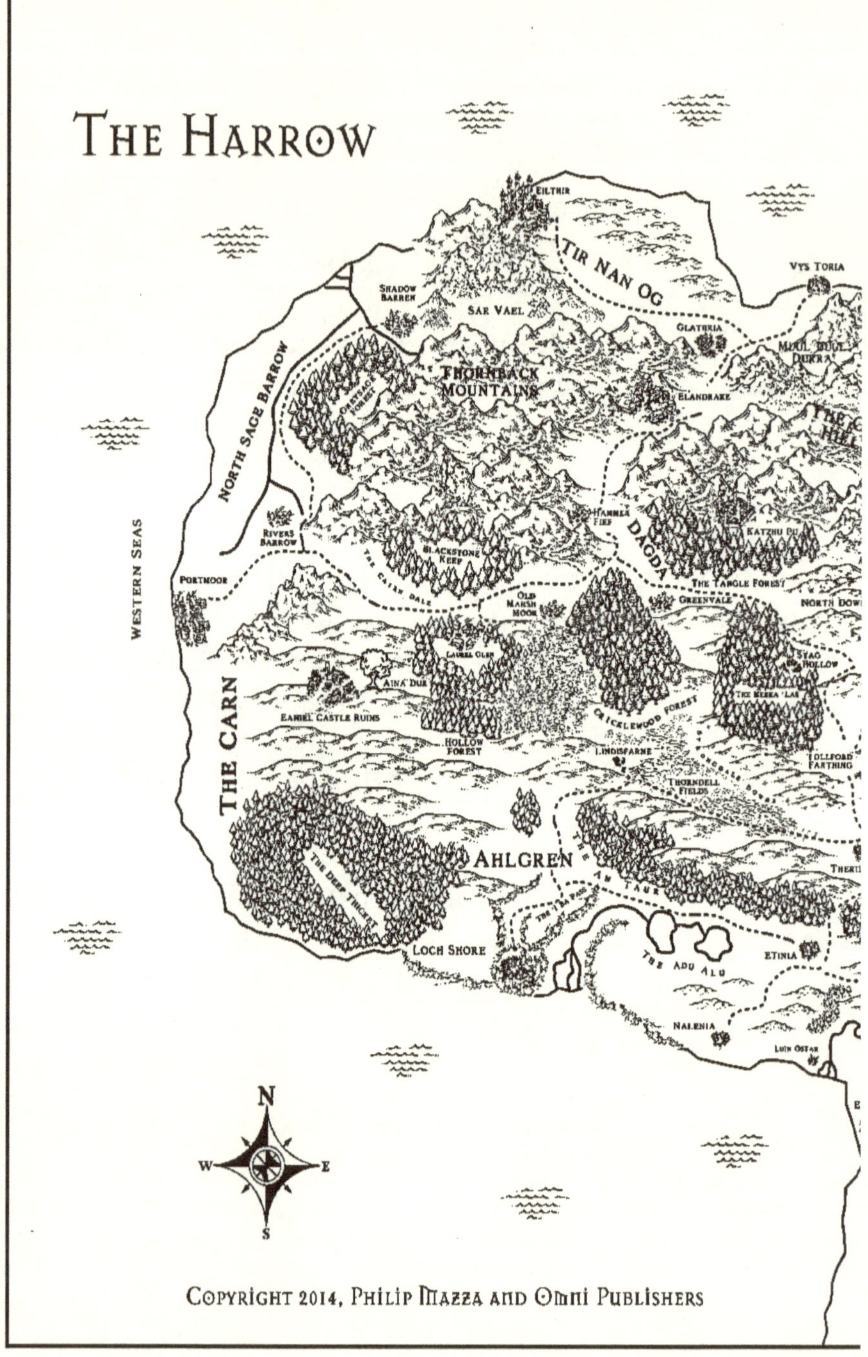

The Harrow
Eilthir
Tir Nan Og
Vys Toria
Shadow Barren
Sar Vael
Glathria
North Sage Barrow
Thornback Mountains
Elandrake
Western Seas
Rivers Barrow
Hammer Fief
Dagda
Katzhu Du
Blackstone Keep
Portmoor
The Cairn Dale
Old Marsh Moor
The Tangle Forest
Greenvale
Laurel Glen
Stag Hollow
Aina Dur
Eamel Castle Ruins
Cricklewood Forest
Hollow Forest
Lindisfarne
Tollford Farthing
Thorndell Fields
The Carn
Ahlgren
The Deep Thicket
The An Taur
Loch Shore
The Adu Alu
Etinia
Nalenia
Luin Ostar
N
W
E
S

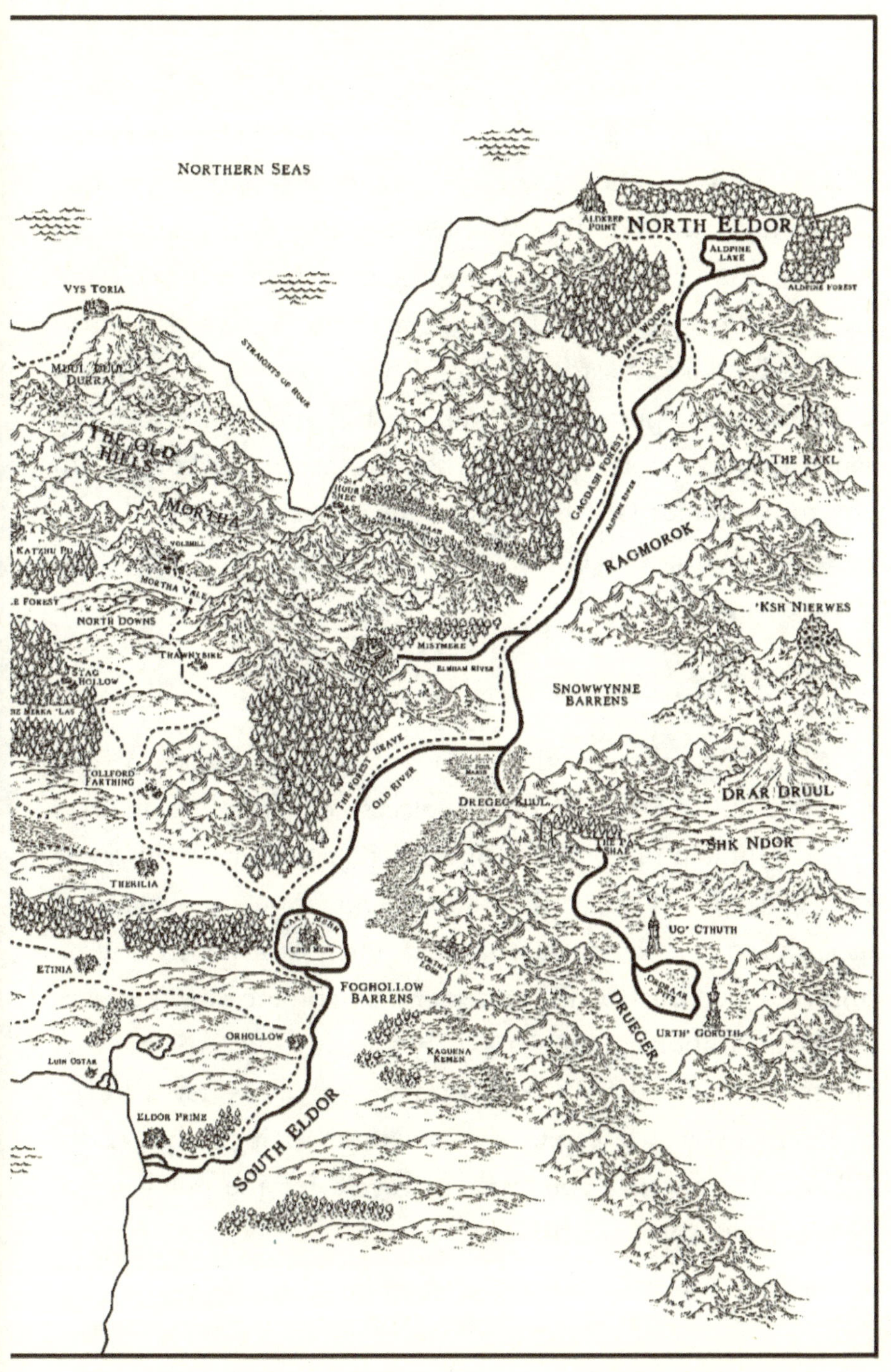

NORTHERN SEAS
VYS TORIA
ALDKEEP POINT
NORTH ELDOR
ALDPINE LAKE
ALDPINE FOREST
DARK WOODS
STRAIGHTS OF HUUR
THE OLD HILLS
MORTHA
MORTHA VALE
NORTH DOWNS
STAG HOLLOW
TOLLFORD FARTHING
THERILIA
ETINIA
ORHOLLOW
LUIN OSTAR
ELDOR PRIME
SOUTH ELDOR
CAGDASH FOREST
THE RAKL
RAGMOROK
'KSH NIERWES
MISTMERE
SNOWWYNNE BARRENS
THE FOREST HEAVE
OLD RIVER
DRAR DRUUL
'SHK NDOR
UG' CTHUTH
URTH' GOROTH
DRUEGER
FOGHOLLOW BARRENS
KAGUENA KEMEN

Author's Note: Editors have rewritten and edited my Harrow novels since 2014, and yet there were still some lingering errors that needed to be corrected. This was because they had dramatically changed aspects of the story. I have taken some time to edit and restore my Harrow novels to their original form. I have also added new material to take the story further. I want to say that editors do serve an important purpose for authors. But sometimes they can mishandle a good story. This is what has happened here. I am grateful to my publisher who allowed me to restore my novels to their original form, and I thank them for doing so. I hope you enjoy the result.

Publisher's Note: Sometimes the author uses capitalization to add weight of emphasis to objects or places, either as an indirect reference to the proper noun, or as a personification of some greater concept. The author does not use capitalization consistently, so it is fair to assume that much of it depends upon the immediate context of the statement. In some cases, the races receive capitalization when named, but again, this is somewhat inconsistent on the author's part. In many instances, races of the good and righteous are capitalized, while those of the brood are not. This has proved a continuous struggle for the publisher to attempt to create some consistency.

Rosary5

My relationship with my mother was unique. I saw her differently than others. We would have fun with one other, exchanging witty banter with each other on politics and religious topics. It's what we did. But please do not misunderstand. I loved her, as any son loves his mother.

You see, my mother was a religious person, a person of incredible faith. For her, faith provided the strength to walk through the greatest storms of life. And in her life, there were many storms. Her beloved husband, my father, fought in the European theatre during World War II, and together they made it through the Great Depression. As a young couple, they struggled at first to make ends meet, but provided for their children, putting each through college, always helping them along the difficult journey called life.

Faith was so important to my mother. It ordered her life and moved her forward in her destiny. It told her that there was kindness all around; you simply had to look for it and recognize it. Her God and her faith guided her.

In her later years, she would call me and ask me how things were, and I would often visit. We would have a beer together and talk about past remembrances. We would laugh. But as was always the case, she would turn to matters of faith.

"Why don't you say your prayers?" she would ask clutching a set of rosary beads, a smile on her face. "I raised you better than this."

"I don't pray because he just wouldn't listen," I would respond.

"I know him pretty well. How about if I put in a good word for you."

"You know something - I bet he would listen to you. You do that old woman. You do that for me."

She would laugh and I would chuckle along. We made each other laugh. It's what we did.

When I presented my mother with the author's proof of *From Under a Tree,* she was so proud of me. She smiled and immediately turned to the dedication page. She read each dedication aloud and noted that I had dedicated the book to my father who had passed three years earlier, but not her.

"How come I'm not part of the dedication?"

"Mom, the book is dedicated only to those family members who have passed. You're still with us."

"So, I have to die before you'll dedicate a book to me?"

"I suppose so. That's kind of how it works."

She hesitated then smiled. "Hmm. Ok, I'll see what I can do. I think I can make that happen," she said.

My mother had a wonderful sense of humor and was quick-witted. She never took things too seriously, and always had a great understanding of where she was in her life. But at the age of eighty-six, life was beginning to become a burden. She missed my father and told me she desired to reunite with him in the afterlife. Her faith told her this would happen.

As my mother slowly turned the pages of my book and started to read, after a few moments, she took a deep breath, sighed, and put the book down.

"Why do you write about these things? Elves? Dragons? Why can't you write a nice love story? Something I would like."

I pointed to my heart and made a circular motion.

"There's nothing inside there," I told her. "You know that. There's nothing there at all."

My mother again smiled, and we laughed.

"Just like your father always said - you're all business. You always liked strange things. You've been this way since you were a child." She paused and I knew she was thinking of my father. A tear came to her eye. "He'd be so proud of you. Come here so I can kiss you."

I did as my mother asked, and with a big smile, she pinched my cheek and gave me a gentle kiss.

That day, I spent more time with my mother. We talked about the news, about my work, about family, and about times long forgotten. She loved reminiscing.

As I left, she said, "Drive carefully. Love you."

Those words - always her goodbye to me.

"You be good, old woman. Don't do anything I would do. Love you," came my same good-bye response.

She would always smile.

It was about six weeks later when my mother began to fail. Darkness came to her quickly and thankfully so. I did not watch my mother take her last breath; I did not need to witness it. For you see, death is not always a peaceful act. A person's life force does not leave this reality easily. It must be wrestled, sometimes violently from the body.

As my mother took her last breath I sat outside her room. I composed her dedication which I would now add to my first book. When my brother came to me with tearful eyes, I knew she had passed. I smiled and showed him the new dedication. He nodded and smiled back.

My mother's wish had been granted. In the end, her faith prevailed.

Later, I started to write her obituary. It began with a simple phrase: "On August 15, 2014, Dolores B. Mazza, 86, was brought into the loving arms of her husband of 64 years, Vincent. They are now together, forever."

I do not believe in an afterlife; I do not have the faith that my mother had even though she tried to give it to me. I guess faith is not something you can easily give to someone, like a gift neatly wrapped up in a package with a red bow. It seems faith is something that must be passively received. It is something to be cherished and nurtured over time. Yet, I knew the words I wrote to begin my mother's obituary would please her, that in her afterlife my father would embrace her, just as her faith had described. It was my way of showing respect for my mother's faith.

I visited my mother one last time. My siblings were by her bedside, sobbing, while she now rested, peaceful, with her eyes closed. She was dressed in a robe I recently purchased for her, the colors she liked. In her hands, she held a set of pink rosary beads. She always said her rosary and had many strands of beads about her room, just in case she forgot where she had left a set.

It was as it should be.

As I looked around her room, I thought of how my mother was the last of her generation in our family. All her friends and relatives had already passed. I thought of her life and the fragments that now remained. There were some pictures and a few pieces of furniture. There were medical bills and legal documents. A calendar on the wall listed birthdays and anniversaries.

It was a life condensed to a few scraps of paper.

But there were the many memories, yes, the memories, the images in my mind of times long since passed. Her life was full! I thought of the obituary I would complete, and how I would attempt to capture such a rich life with but a few words.

One week after her passing, as I drove to work in the early morning, my mother remained in my thoughts. I thought of my last vision of her, of the rosary beads in her thin hands. It made me smile.

As I drove, using the left lane and making good time, I saw the sameness all around me - the same vehicles on the roads, the same runners trying to stay fit, and the sun breaking through the morning clouds. Everything was in its rightful place.

All was right in the world.

Her faith was strong enough to see a meaning in all of this, I thought. *What a wonderful gift.*

I continued making good time, making all the lights, which was unusual.

"Old woman, are you doing a good thing for me?" I said aloud thinking that somehow, she was orchestrating all this for me.

I chuckled at the thought. I knew she would try to do such a thing if she could, even from so far away.

As I made a turn and passed by a restaurant my parents used to go to on dates so many years ago, I saw a small bronze van with rust spots in the right lane. I had never seen this vehicle during my morning commute. It put its left blinker on. I slowed to allow it to move in front of me. It did so unhurriedly and cautiously.

Odd for the morning drive to work, I thought.

Suddenly a chill overwhelmed me, for there, in front of me was the small van - its license plate - Rosary5.

Rosary5!

My throat welled up as tears gently formed in my eyes.

I slowed down giving the old van distance. I could only think of my mother, the words I had just said aloud. A fog came over me as I stared ahead at Rosary5 for what seemed like forever. But my gaze was only a few moments as Rosary5 put its right blinker on and moved back to the right lane, slowing to a crawl. I could not look at the driver as I passed, frightened of what I might see. I sped up and continued down the road, looking back at Rosary5 from my rearview mirror. But other vehicles were passing the old van and it was gone from sight.

The vehicle's sudden appearance, how it suddenly brought disruption to the sameness, transformed me.

Now, as I write and look from my window, I see things differently. Even though it is winter with its cold winds and drifts of snow, I instead see birds in a bright, blue sky, dancing under the warmth of a summer's sun. I see flowers in bloom and a soft summer breeze playing with leaves, sighing gently among the trees. I see my parents walking in my backyard gardens, holding hands, looking at the flowers, talking to each other, and laughing. I see my father give my mother a gentle kiss. They turn and wave to me. I return the wave and smile, a tear in my eye. I feel the warmth of everlasting love.

I now see where before I was blind.

I understand.

Faith is a strange thing. It can grow on you.

Mom, I will write that love story you so wanted.

You be good, old woman. Don't do anything I would do. Love you.

“We are all geniuses up to the age of ten.”
Aldous Huxley

Table of Contents

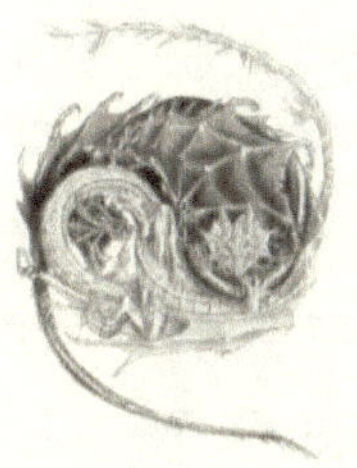

PROLOGUE

NIGHT WAS UPON THE elven kingdom of Tir Nan Og and the grand castle Kaer Tari like a black cloak. The broken moon was dim and pale. It hung over the castle's lofty spires, inundating the scene with a cloud-veiled brilliancy. For hours the Elf-King had read aloud passages from a book to Jin Dalhar, a young elf-child. It was a wondrous tale that conjured visions of a time long since passed, of great heroes, of glorious deeds. Now, the elf-child lay soundly asleep in the Elf-King's arms, without a stir. The aged Elf-King slowly closed the red leather-covered book, placing it on the floor.

A whisper came from the doorway. "Is he ready?"

It was Kala, a young female elf. She was of slight form and stature, with black hair pulled back into an intricately woven twist. She wore a strapless velvet gown of white with a glimmering belt of gold.

Dalgaes gave a nod.

Kala quietly entered the library and gently lifted Jin Dalhar from the Elf-King's lap. She cradled the elf-child who rustled a bit and opened his eyes.

"Great Grandpapa, is the story over?" asked Jin Dalhar sleepily.

"Oh, no it is just beginning. But like the story, the darkness of night has come. It is time for you to sleep. We will continue in the morning."

Dalgaes looked at the child and smiled. He lifted his aged hand and gave a slow wave. Jin Dalhar returned the smile and then snuggled into the warmth of Kala's bosom.

Before leaving with the child Kala turned to Dalgaes.

"Your presence is requested. It is Shamma," she gently said, sadness on her face.

The Elf-King's heart immediately sank upon hearing the words.

Dalgaes left his library and made his way through the marble hallways of the Kaer Tari. Along the way, as he passed courtiers they would stop and bow in deference. He would nod with a smile and lift his hand, but he kept a steady pace.

He came around a corner and to a large wooden door that led to a great circular chamber with large windows overlooking the night sky. Sheer white drapes flowing from the cool night breeze lined the walls from floor to ceiling. In the middle of the room was a small bed with white linens and upon the bed laid a cat. It was Shamma, once the high-priestess of the Tar Shor. She was old and gravely ill. Around the bed stood several elven caregivers, their faces swept in sadness.

"Her breathing has become shallow," a caregiver told him. "I fear it is time."

Great sorrow crept upon him. He approached the bed and knelt on one knee. He stroked the cat, light brown fur now matted and grey in places. Upon his touch, a great rumbling purr filled the room. The cat lifted her head.

"My Lord, you honor me with your presence," said the cat barely holding the words.

A tear came to him.

"No, my dear Shamma, grand high-priestess of the Tar Shor," he murmured, "it is I who is so honored to be in your presence."

Dalgaes gave her a gentle kiss. She returned the kiss with a lick of his face.

"Have I served well?" she asked.

"Hush now. Do not waste your strength with such a silly question."

"The great golden citadel at Katzhu Pu, will I ever see it again?" she asked. "Tell me my most gracious Lord, will I ever gaze upon its beauty and majesty?"

"You will haste to that place and there, gaze long upon the spreading scene of such splendor," he said, his voice faltering. "Flowers shall rain from the sky as it is so beautiful a thing."

He gave her another gentle stroke.

"My Lord, I will miss you. You have treated me with such care and grace. Do you think we will meet again?"

His throat swelled with sadness.

"By the Maker, we shall when the time comes," he said. "Such friendship is forever."

A smile came to her.

"Then I will welcome you at that time, as you have always welcomed me." She paused; a great purr still thundering. "My Lord, I am ready to meet the I' Ra Heru."

She closed her eyes.

With tears now running down his face, he gently brought a hand over her and whispered the sacred words "Coia a' gurtha ie' seere" which in the common tongue means *From life to death, be at peace.*

A tranquil look came over her face. The purr that filled the room began to slow to a quiet until it was no more.

Shamma, Laurn Cora, grand high-priestess to Shia Alia Ce' Tu, the Huntress, had passed.

He slowly lifted himself with the aid of a caregiver and called for two guardsmen who quickly appeared.

"She is to be given full honors of the En' Edhel as Eir Shasos and interred at Katzhu Pu within the walls of the Kaer Taraedar. The Sil' Heru and Guild Lords have decreed it so," he told the guardsmen. "The procession over the land, south to Dagda, shall be purposeful so the Ra Cath may honor her glory. In life, she could not enter the great city, but in death, she shall glorify its existence."

"My Lord, shall we prepare for your travel?" asked a guardsman.

He wiped back his tears.

"No. My days of wandering about are long gone. I am happy here in my library, with my feet firmly planted in the soil of my forefathers. When my time ends, I wish it to be here, in this place. She would understand."

The guardsmen bowed and gently wrapped Shamma in white silken sheets. They would place her upon a golden caravan as all fallen elven warriors are, and in the morning set off to Katzhu Pu.

The procession would take several days. The roadways through which the march took its way would be lined with throngs of felines, and houses crammed with spectators from top to bottom. It would be noted later, that even the great Bombadorn Roundthaler, upon hearing of the procession, would march a legion of his finest dwarf warriors under the banner of the Axe, to the great golden citadel, to join the procession and in honor of the once high-priestess.

Dalgaes made his way back to his library and returned to his chair. He looked from his window and into the waning night. He thought of the passing of his good friend Shamma; he thought of the story he had read so many times, the story in which she played a role. He knew the tale all too well and he wondered vaguely how he had lived through it all.

I have told this story so many times, but it is important not to forget . . . and if I continue to tell this tale over and over again, generations to come will be telling it and shall learn its lessons.

There was a hard lump in his heart as he looked down from his castle window. The dark city of Eilthir, with its narrow, cobbled streets glittered in the moonlight. While the darkness of night gave relief from the sweltering sun, it was always a foreboding prospect. The Elf-King knew that darkness naturally casts a spell upon living creatures, even in the best of times.

He thought of Jin Dalhar, the innocence of childhood, and the lost dreams of the past. He thought of the next part of the story he would read aloud to the elf-child. He thought of the story's darkness, its turmoil, rage, and helplessness.

He looked at his reflection in the window. He saw a wrinkled face with a white beard and eyebrows. He saw nothing but a tired old man.

Time is the darkness of night and comes before the eternity of day, he thought. *Knowing is timeless, like the darkness in the shadow in the flame.*

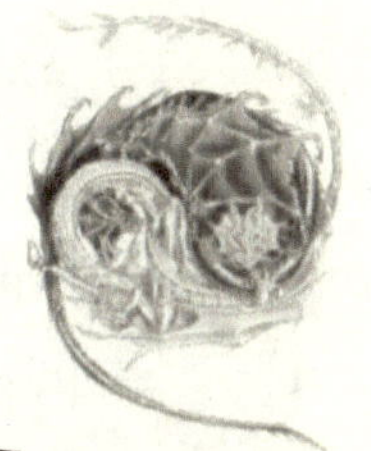

CHAPTER I
A TIME OF SHADOWS

IT WAS A TIME of shadows; when tears became the only release one could find, to channel the hurt that was flooding the soul. Darkness was all around. Thunder cracked, and lightning flashed, but water did not always pour down. And as the flashes lit the ground, every creature of the land saw them all - thousands and thousands of streaks of light, more even, more than anyone could ever imagine, surrounding places near and far. All as downtrodden as those within, some with wounds still bleeding, though healers made their way about the place, their progress could be nothing but slow. For darkness was everywhere, as was fright, rage, and anger - thick and solid.

And in such times darkness is hidden in the recesses of the mind, that if conjured, a demon surfaces like a great beast bursting forth from the depths of the sea. Once the beast appears it is difficult to return it to the darkness for it brings such a sudden force that it threatens reality. Many have tried with a vengeance, attempting to force the demon back into the dark recesses of the mind, only for the beast to rear its hideous self, unexplainable manifestations at unforeseen times. This is the true nature of all life: a raw and vile evil at its core.

The truth is that the capacity for evil and depravity easily becomes a permanent feature of reality. It is not limited to enemies, but lurks within all creatures, veiled, hidden, waiting for the right moment in time to rupture. The breaching of evil shows how fragile reality is to each of the Maker's creatures; it shows that only thoughts and deeds of good and pure intentions can restrain the vile core of existence. Yet such goodness is fleeting, only whispers in a maelstrom of shouting voices.

This is the way of this world, and for all living in this world, they will be touched by the way.

* * *

The black tower of Urth' Goroth stood malignant under the night sky now made darker by smoke and ash from the underground forges. The air was difficult to breathe, hot, and dry, making the Drueger a place where few creatures could survive for long, that is except for one evil beast, the one called the Lor Shys by the brood, or *demon worm*. As she looked upon the evil wasteland, she thought of the past.

Long had the evil creature lived there; it had been said, for ages, far more years than any living being could recall. As the brood surmised, the creature was as old as time itself and had probably been born of the fire and chaos that had first created the world. It was of an ancient race of creatures long extinct, the last of a strong, intelligent, slithering, snake-like species whose flesh consisted of course bristles, barbs, and slime. The demon worms were knowledgeable in the arts of dark magic and had scourged all the known lands until great wars gradually reduced their numbers. Their quest for dominance slowly faded.

After a time, only one of the species remained, a female, well adapted to surviving in the harsh, harsh terrain of the Drueger. Alone, it spent its time burrowing into the rock, creating tunnels and rooms, a murky and dank labyrinth of confusing and distorted passages. The brood who entered the labyrinth found themselves quickly disoriented and at the mercy of the Lor Shys. The snake-like beast would extend out an almost human face from its torso, contorted and horribly twisted, and along with two thin arms and long hands devour its unsuspecting prey whole. Its mouth and two rows of teeth on each side of its upper jaw, and one row on its lower jaw were not used for chewing, but rather to hold onto its prey and push it leisurely backward into the gullet. It was a slow and painful death for the prey, yet such a manner of death pleased the Lor Shys well enough.

Over the ages, she lamented the demise of her race and became bitter. She sought vengeance and blood against her enemies, the races of man and dwarf and elf, and she sought those who would support her reprisal. Hatred stirred, and she felt its fire.

The brood tell of the day the Szard first came to the land. He traveled as a stranger, carrying nothing with him, and speaking to no one. He found his way to the Drueger and became trapped in the demon worm's labyrinth. Frightened and confused, he looked about for a means of escape, turning, and running this way and that way, but the labyrinth's walls seemed to close in around him. He fell to his knees and dropped his head into his hands and groaned in resignation. It was then that he heard a slithering sound. He looked up and froze. The Lor Shys stood before him, silent. Exhausted, anger grew within him, filling his body.

"Leave me be," he howled, his looked fixed on her. He fiercely clenched his fists. "Leave me be I said, or I'll kill you if I can."

It is said that she became obsessed with him as she looked upon his countenance, his eyes two round black orbs, empty yet so marked by an inner evil. She was infatuated with the purity of his wickedness and enchanted by his soft voice which was desiccated and voluptuous at once. Immediately knew she could use him. He would be her bridge, to accomplish her ends, but it would take time. She would need to harness his anger.

As the Szard trembled in despair and anger she thought of a plan.

"Pretty thing you are," she told him, caressing his face. "Such smooth skin but inside you rage uncontrollably. Stay with me. I will feed you. I will shelter you. I will show you how to survive."

She lifted him from the cold stone floor of her labyrinth and brought him to her lair. She cared for him, fed him, protected him from those of the good and righteous, and the brood. Later, he served her. When she got hungry, he would bring her food, luring unwary brood into the labyrinth. She would reward him with tales from her perversion of history. She would teach him to control his anger, his impulses, and his emotions.

"In the end, one is successful and achieves a new level of power by donning an empty mask," she would say.

Over time, the two formed a bond based on similarities in their shared experiences, and the common desire to dominate and destroy. She taught him dark magic and fed him a steady diet of hate. Soon, dark magic easily boiled from his heart, drowning his soul. The darkness swelled, vicious and furious, greater than any Dark Wizard's power, like an enraged animal ready to strike. She believed he could and would bring her the revenge she sought. As she continued with his lessons, her obsession with him grew, and her emotions became confused. He sensed this, and as his powers became stronger, stronger than her powers, he began to manipulate her emotions towards him. In this madness, she became helpless. She forced her way to him and threw herself at his feet. However, her desire for him became unfulfilled, for he was incapable of such emotions; he did not aspire to such a height.

The Lor Shys had come to be his servant and would follow him in his depravity.

"I only ask for one delight," she said in tears, staring into his black eyes. "That you forever hide your face; for only I wish the pleasure to have looked upon the evilest of faces."

The Szard did so, forever donning his black robe with a large hood. Their relationship endured and strengthened. They called each other *sweetness* and *dearest* and he called her *Miss Hiss*, and their lasting bond did not weaken through trying tests to come.

Under the Lor Shys' tutelage and their mutual manipulation, the Szard became master of the land's brood. One by one the many races comprising the brood fell to his powers and were enslaved. They called him Mori Ni and feared him, succumbing to his overwhelming cruelty. The miscreants were put to work in constructing the dark tower of Ug' Cthuth, underground forges, workshops, and caves used to craft great armaments of war and house the armies of evil. The rising scepter of a kingdom of malice was forged, dedicated to the seduction and ruin of the land's races.

War would be waged, again and again, unprecedented in scale and destructiveness. Blood would stain the lands; flesh and bone would be scattered to the wind. The good and the righteous would prevail, and the great tower of evil brought to rubble. Upon each defeat, what remained of the vile brood would slowly seep back into the rock of the Drueger, waiting for another time to emerge and fight again. But through the endless carnage, no one outside the Drueger knew or heard of the Szard or the Lor Shys, their identity protected by the brood, fearful of retribution; and through this secrecy, the power of their rule and kingdom would be eternal.

Their defeats would be no small hindrance to their final success in war; their defeats would be the worst thing that ever happened to the Harrow. It was all part of a great scheme, one that was designed to be measured and last for the ages.

Victory is only gained through death, the Lor Shys would think.

Soon after the most recent defeat, brood again emerged from the rock. The tower Ug' Cthuth which crumbled under war was rebuilt and a new tower called Urth' Goroth ascended deep into the sky. New alliances were formed, and strange miscreants of evil were bred for battle. Together the Szard and the Lor Shys laid a new foundation for evil and like all things infernal, were firmly transformed into monstrous demons.

Now, and on the verge of yet another war, the Lor Shys slithered within the many secret passageways and most dark recesses of Urth' Goroth. But her movements had slowed with age.

Time creeps up on one slowly. But once it catches you it mocks your presence, your entire existence. It is both cruel, and kind for it gives one perspective. Moment upon moment - time creeps until the moments stop.

The demon worm paused to catch her breath and then continued. She was anxious and at the same time excited, listening to conversations in the dark passageways, and thinking of strategy while making her way to the top of the tower.

Time has not slowed my mind.

As she slithered her way up staircases and secret hallways, she thought of the doom to come. Such thoughts gave her great delight; they fed her very essence. And nothing gave her greater pleasure than being atop Urth' Goroth with its colossal fire, while she overlooked the legions of brood massing for battle. As she reached the summit and passed through the fire, the flames roared with even greater fury and stretched high into the night sky. She took pleasure in the warmth of the intense fire.

"Tell me my dearest, what do you feel?" came the deep but soft voice of the Szard. He saw her, a shadow in the flame.

The Lor Shys was startled by his presence, it was unexpected, but an exhilaration swiftly came upon her as it always had upon hearing his voice. She pushed herself from within the flame and slowly along the cold stone flooring and to the edge of the tower where she looked over the evil scene. She did not immediately answer but slowly closed her eyes and took a deep breath and let it out. The smell of the forges, the pungent aroma of superheated rock and charcoal, hot iron, the thousands of fires burning below, and the thick billowing smoke burned her throat and eyes. It was strangely comforting, a joyous pain and one she welcomed. Above, thunder began to echo loudly against the mountains overwhelming the sounds of hammering and the steady thumping and clanging of a marching army. She opened her eyes and turned to the Szard.

"I feel rage, my sweetness," she said. Her voice was sorrowful and tore into the night. "I feel death creeping over the lands. I feel victory."

The Szard joined her and together they looked out over the display of evil below. He raised a gloved hand and began to stroke her ever so gently upon her head, gently squeezing slime through his fingers. She clutched onto his legs.

"It is grand, is it not my dearest? Your long-sought victory is upon us," he said.

"Our victory, my sweetness – our victory," she emphasized. "It will be our victory, my sweetness."

As the thunder grew in intensity and a hard rain began to fall, the two stood defiantly upon the pinnacle of Urth' Goroth. Below, the glow of the vast army marching throbbed and flickered, like a moving beast. From where the Ordraar slime pits boiled, the brood paraded ten columns deep, a sinuous line marked by the bright sparkle of torches that stretched past the tower Ug' Cthuth and followed the Dregec Kuul river and into the choking mountain pass. Great siege engines pulled by large muugaans slowly rolled through the mud and muck that was this evilest place. Overhead, Uakor Turg swarmed in the night sky spreading a filthy stench to the hot air. The brood army continued to pour into the Foghollow Barrens, thousands upon thousands of the creatures, gathering under the banner of the Tower and command of Grimsor, Uth' Egoreyr.

"War will soon come to the Harrow," said the Szard without emotion, quite unassumingly. His certainty was disturbing as he overlooked the evil in the shadows of the night. "So many seeds have we planted. They sprout like weeds in a garden!"

A low groan awakened deep within the Lor Shys and rose to her throat. In her depraved madness, she saw the future as it burned brightly through the darkness. She looked down at her worm-like body, running her hands over the slimy flesh and bristles which were now grey. The hardship of her life and the greying of the bristles on her body angered her. Age was a fault, a shortcoming, and she did not wish to become old and haggard, to lose control. So many ages had passed and now her time was ending.

One thought flashed before her eyes: *Time is soon to pass away but not before death falls. I will see to it that blood will flow like water, tears like mist, and the whole of this place will be convulsed as by a frightful war, a war that shall expel those that are good and virtuous. Revenge shall be taken, slow, wild, and deep to the very depth of darkness. Then I shall give myself to time and I shall rest.*

She smiled.

"Horrors are coming," she told him. "To reclaim that which is ours."

"My dearest Miss Hiss, your time has come," he said. "Our plans are in motion. We need your help. Go to your labyrinth and make your way west, in the caverns you know so well."

She gave a loud hiss and flashed her teeth. "Yes, my sweetness - as we planned."

She slithered from the tower and down into the bowels of the Drueger and the labyrinth of tunnels. The tunnels were dark, low, and long, their jagged walls always cold and wet. It was a realm unto itself and she had to remind herself whether it was day or night. Slowly, she wriggled from one passageway to another, resting as needed. In places, she could hear the muffled sounds of the brood army above as they scattered over the barrens. Over time, however, sounds from the surface quieted. She knew she had entered the western lands.

The neck of the races shall be opened, and blood shall cover the face of the Harrow.

* * *

Snerv Slog was a deformed creature who hobbled within the dark, dampness of the Esku En' Urra, the mighty subterranean fortress of Urth' Goroth, not paying attention to the howls and cries of his fellow Ai di'thu. As he made his way within the torturous place, the sounds of pain were but an annoyance to him, background noise. He cared little for the torment the other slaves endured, even though he was a slave. But he was different. He was favored by the Orc Master and received food and shelter in exchange for doing his master's bidding. Because of this, he saw the other slaves as lesser beings, owing to inborn deficiencies, whose sole purpose was to toil in the darkness of the great fissure. He gradually convinced himself that he was equal to his captors, because he hungered to inflict what they had inflicted, and was provided the opportunity to do so.

As the miscreant continued to hobble along, he turned back in great joy at the hulking figure that followed, the Orc Master, Drogur Vorn.

"This ways now. Yesssst. This ways now," said Snerv Slog, gurgling out the words. "This ways to see what has growns. Most pleased youz will be. Most pleased."

Vorn smiled demonically behind the Dol Goran, a mask carved from his father's skull. Unlike Slog, he did not find the lamentations of torment annoying. There was a melodic quality to the sounds. He would stop along the way, close his eyes, and listen to the moans and screams. Something was soothing about the noise, calming.

"No. No. Master wez musts continue. Yesssst. We musts go on. Youz musts see this." Slog would say whenever Vorn would stop.

Vorn would take a deep breath as if feeding off the pain. The hulking beast would again smile looking upon writhing slaves as they wallowed in their demise. He was soulless and sadistic; his very existence was to exalt himself in the advance of evil. He not only caused pain, but he also tortured. He not only killed, but he also mutilated.

When the two came to a long stone wall at the back of the fissure, hundreds of creatures stood in formation, large, tall, with hunched backs. They were brown and had a scaly appearance, covered in slimy mud that dripped from their bodies. Mouths and nostrils were visible along with large, unrelenting black eyes on round heads. There was a stench of rot, mixed with the smells of earthy mud, but there was something else too, that sour, coppery tang of blood and decomposing flesh. Rotting body parts of slaves were scattered about the place, the remnants of daily feasts. The Ai di'thu served many purposes, the least of which was an available food source for its captors.

"Theez be the Gurtha Naur! Greats servants theyz are. Theyz desires to serves and theyz awaits yourz command," said Slog, slobbering through his words.

Vorn looked at one of the creatures and pointed.

"Zi hundur Gurtha Naur," he ordered, his words deep and dark.

The Gurtha Naur creature uttered something in a guttural tone that could not be understood. Its eyes turned bright red fire as a large flame materialized and engulfed the beast. It hunched forward and began to twitch uncontrollably, a flickering shadow in the flame. There came the dry and brittle sound of bone cracking, echoing through the fissure as the shadow in the flame changed its shape. Slowly, hideously, irrevocably, the Gurtha Naur was transformed into a great wolf-beast, a Fenri, black-furred with eyes that shined white in the darkness. Vorn burst out laughing, rocking the Esku En' Urra to its core.

"Yesssst. Shape changers theyzz be," cackled Slog.

"My corruptions," said Vorn, with an evil sneer.

Vorn then went about and set each Gurtha Naur with commands, each of the beasts changing into a different form, a different race. He would direct them to low and high places about the land. They would attack, each at an appointed time, and when they did it would be unexpected.

So did the Orc Master summon a great army of shape changers, born of stone and mud and wicked magic, concealed within the deep shadows, unleashing them upon the forces of the races. Mayhem and darkness would stir the hearts of the good and righteous. Fear would rule the lives of all.

We'll shake their reality with falseness, thought the Orc Master with a smile and sneer. *The lands will cower and bow before us, and all hope will be devoured.*

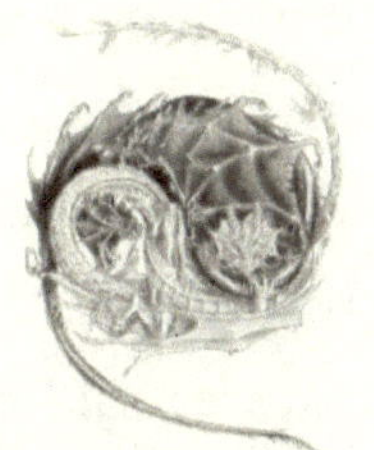

CHAPTER 2
THE GRAND DENIER

WITHIN THE WESTERN REACHES of the Ahlgren was the Deep Thicket. It was a forest thick and black with trees, brush, and woven undergrowth. The place was old, and the trees were large and broad, especially in their trunks, with misshapen leaves that refused to rustle in the wind. Dense grass matted the earthen ground, silencing the steps of the despicable creatures and malevolent spirits that dwelled within the forest's shadows. This was an evil place, a place shunned by all creatures of goodness because of the deep cold and gloom there.

But there were some, those who dared not enter the Deep Thicket, that lived near the wicked place since the soil to the east of the wood was rich and fertile. Small and large farms stretched along the landscape separated by crumbling dry stone walls as animals grazed on the lush grass. Fields were plowed and sown with vegetables, barley, or wheat. Once fields were plowed and crops planted, children were responsible for their care and protection. But in a child's life, not all the time is to be spent tending crops or other useful activities. There must also be time for play and fun, as long as one did not stray too close to the Deep Thicket.

To ensure children kept a safe distance from the forest terrible stories were told from father to son, from mother to daughter, and were often changed in the telling. These were tales of creatures living within the darkness, ferocious, and cruel, creatures said to defy the authority of the Maker, and to feed on the flesh of En' Edan, especially the flesh of En' Edan children.

However, stories alone do not always provide adequate protection because children are often fearless. They are not always aware of danger and are unaware of their limitations. They lack a clear concept of death and sometimes become indifferent to their lessons. It is for these reasons and many others that a parent's fear is seemingly eternal. It was no different for Zachary Bucklorn and his wife Kalea, a young couple with two children.

Zachary Bucklorn was an ancestor of Gathad Bucklorn, a great warrior of ages past who settled in the Ahlgren after the War of Rage. To give his demonstration of a higher character of utility, Gathad Bucklorn became a simple farmer. He worked hard and found a way to make a successful living off the land. Gathad's heirs and their heirs were also successful and as the generations passed the Bucklorn family was able to expand their landholdings, and on occasion required hired help. For Zachary and other Bucklorns throughout the Ahlgren, it was a legacy for their young, an example to others.

The Bucklorns were neighborly folks and like most farmers willing to extend a helping hand in exchange for the promise of one similarly extended in their own time of need. They were a well-respected family, pleasant and jovial, and always protective of their two children, a boy named Jurl and a younger girl named Senna.

"Keep an eye on the two of them. Something doesn't feel right," said Kalea Bucklorn to her husband as they ate breakfast.

Taking the last sip of morning tea Zachary Bucklorn smiled and lightly caressed his wife's cheek with a rugged hand.

"Always worrying woman," he said with a smile.

"In these parts, one must always worry."

Zachary gave a nod and was off to the barn but not before checking on Jurl and Senna, both of whom had started the day early and were already working a small section of field near the dark forest.

"Be careful," he shouted to his children. "Keep to your work."

Upon hearing the shout from their father, Jurl and Senna stopped their work and waved with a smile. Zachary continued to the barn. He had a long day of hard work ahead of him.

With his father out of sight, Jurl decided he would have some fun. He picked up a soft clump of soil and tossed it at his sister's backside as she pulled weeds. Senna turned at him and scoffed. She looked around and finding a nearby clump, threw it back at him. The two began to frolic, unaware of what was approaching the forest's edge.

Many creatures would find the sounds of children playing to be soothing to the soul. But some would find the noise painful, a sound that would cut through the mind like a knife through living tissue. This was the case for many in the darkness of the Deep Thicket, as the noise of the children playing nearby drew the attention of a stare, two bright, yellow eyes emerging from the gloom. The eyes followed the children, at times giving a slow blink.

Wretched things, thought the creature.

As the children played, they laughed and giggled and talked about their friends. But their words were meaningless to the forest creature, as all words of the En' Edan were. Even though it understood the common tongue it refused to allow its mind to capture any meaning. This was just one of many disciplines of the creature, disciplines under its faith.

Lesser beings, came another thought.

Jurl and Senna did not notice the strange set of eyes at first. They had caught but a glimpse of the piercing yellow and gave little thought to what was there. That was until a horrid sound came from the forest's edge. It was a deep groan, like a fiendish beast's howl, long and repeated, with no mind or soul to it.

When the children turned to face the sound, they saw the yellow eyes staring back at them. A mysterious force then grabbed ahold of them, slowly dragging them to the edge of the woodland.

They could not look away from the gaze of the yellow eyes or extricate themselves from the force that now held them. Jurl was silent, fighting feverishly, trying to stop his body from moving nearer to the forest. Senna tried to run but her legs kept a slow pace moving her closer to the murky woods. With a gasp, she struggled to stop her legs but could no longer control them. She opened her mouth in a bleating scream through the morass of emotion.

"Help! Help!" she shrieked.

Hearing his daughter's anguish Zachary bolted from the barn. Fear coursed through him as he saw the two children stumbling towards the forest, seemingly pulled by an invisible force. He saw the yellow eyes shrouded within the blackness of the Deep Thicket.

"No!"

Zachary knew of the horror. He started to run to the children but soon felt a force surrounding him, pushing against him. Suddenly, he, too, lacked strength and the ability to act or think. He could not even panic. He fell to his knees and did not move because he could not move. He did not shout because he could not shout. But he could hear the screams of his children. His mind was in turmoil; all he could do was listen to his children's screams and watch in horror.

The creature kept its focus on the children from behind the darkness and smiled viciously at the anguish he was slowly inflicting. There was a coldness to its thoughts, a distance from the world. Pain was all there was to the creature. It fed on it; it needed it like one requires water or food. There was nothing in life that it enjoyed more.

The agony of cries for help is such a soothing noise in the morning light.

The creature closed its eyes and gave a deep sigh of satisfaction.

Such delight today brings.

The children's movements began to slow. Both were now a few paces from the forest's edge. The force stopped them, holding them in place as the children's bodies began to stiffen. Zachary could see as the children tried to fight against the same force that now imprisoned him. He knew what was going to happen and wanted to turn away, but the force drove him to look.

The yellow eyes then opened and gave a slow blink and moved, and from the Deep Thicket, a thin black cat appeared. It was a scraggly-looking creature, its fur tufted in many places. One of its back legs was twisted and deformed which caused a limp.

The cat walked up to the two children who were now frozen in utter despair. It paused looking up at them with disdain.

They serve no purpose. No purpose at all.

The cat lifted a paw and spoke in the ancient tongue. "Tel' rakka ere' ena agar."

Zachary knew the words and wanted to shout, to run to them but could not.

The children grimaced in unbearable pain as their bodies stiffened. They could feel a freezing cold coursing through their bodies, as their flesh, bone, blood, and tissue turned rigid. Their eyes glazed over in grey, and their skin crackled as it shaped and molded, transforming into stone.

Unable to move, to close his eyes to the terror, tears fell from Zachary's eyes. But his sadness was soon overcome by anger. He fought mightily to break through the spell that bound him to at least speak.

"Denier! You will die for this!" he said, the words barely escaping. "You will die! I will see to it!"

The black cat turned to Zachary.

Such an annoyance.

"Tel' rakka ere' ena agar," he uttered, lifting a paw to Zachary.

Zachary's head began to tremble as a devastating pain came to his face. His lips had been sewn shut, black twine now crisscrossing his mouth.

The wicked cat looked at what he had done. Great pleasure filled his soul. He then slowly hobbled away heading northeast.

Insignificant beings. Such a waste of flesh and bone.

* * *

Some time had passed as tremendous pain shuddered through Zachary. It played with his mind and now he did not know where he was. He struggled to stand and felt the force that had held him slowly give way. He brought his hands gently over his mouth, his lips painful to the touch as he felt. He felt the coarseness of the twine, the pattern of the crude stitches. He tried to open his mouth to talk and began making panicked sounds. Near the forest's edge, he saw his two children in the field, turned to stone, like statues frozen in time. Zachary stumbled to his feet and ran to them. From behind, he could hear the screams of Kalea as she ran from the house.

A profound sadness so overwhelmed Zachary and Kalea as they came upon their children that their knees went limp. They placed their hands on the stillness that now embraced their children. The heavy stone was smooth and cold to the touch but there was no movement, no signs of life. Zachary and Kalea clutched onto each other and cried. They were so stricken with sorrow that life itself no longer mattered until Kalea saw her husband's face and his sewn lips.

"What madness is this," she said through her cries. Instinctively she knew what had to be done. "Hurry now, to your feet."

She helped her husband to stand as Zachary mumbled something to her. She held on to him from his hips and walked him across the field to their house.

"No. Don't try to speak. We must get you help. We may have lost the children, but we're not going to lose you."

Once inside the house, Kalea brought Zachary to their bed and tucked him in. She brought some cool water to him and with a soaked cloth gently caressed his sore lips.

The coolness felt good on his throbbing lips, and he gave a slight smile through the pain. He was weak and his thoughts were clouded, and he found it difficult to focus. His mind began drifting; his thoughts wandered from one thing to another. He worked to push back on the fear, but the thought of helplessness tortured him. He realized that in his current state only Kalea could help.

He caught her stare as she continued to gently caress his lips with the cool water. He made a writing motion with his hand.

"You want to write something?" she asked.

Zachary nodded and closed his eyes to the pain as Kalea left the room. She returned with some parchment and a quill. He sat up in bed and started to write, telling of what had occurred. He then ended with: *Get my brothers and others to help. It was the Denier!*

Kalea did exactly as Zachary asked and soon word had quickly spread throughout Ahlgren, about the incident at the Bucklorn farm.

Zachary remained in great pain but was able to shut his eyes for some rest. Family and friends came to the simple house to provide comfort while others sought the help of healers from Loch Shore. Fear so consumed Kalea that rational thought was impossible. She had lost her children and her beloved husband could not eat or speak; she did not know what to do or who she could turn to. But she also knew she had to be strong for her husband and children.

One by one healers arrived. Some tried to gently clip the twine only to have it instantly reappear. Others brewed concoctions of meadowsweet, bloodroot, and heather over a fire, but none were able to remedy the magic that beset Zachary or the children. Men brought firewood while women brought dried meats and loaves of bread for the family.

Kalea tried to feed her husband, but it was almost impossible. She made a hearty soup and did her best to drizzle some past his lips, but she could see the pain in his eyes.

"You must take nourishment," she said.

But Zachary could only close his eyes in agony and shake his head.

As dusk fell, the place was soon quiet, save for the sound of Zachary's painful breathing coming from the bedroom.

"What we need is a wizard," said Kalea's sister Marnie Pritchett, anguished and hushed.

Zachary's older brother Emyr Bucklorn sat stoic and emotionless, packing his pipe with a locally grown cherry leaf, staring straight ahead.

"There's no wizard in these parts. I'm afraid there is only one who can help," said Emyr Bucklorn.

Marnie knew who he was talking about.

"No. There must be someone else," she said.

"I've already sent for him," said Emyr. "He should be here at nightfall."

Kalea and her sister looked at Emyr, tearful and afraid. They knew of the man who would visit. Just the thought of him darkened their mood even more, and they did their best to block him out of their thoughts. They closed their weary eyes. The only sound they could hear was Zachary's breathing.

As the broken moon rose, the temperature dropped considerably, and they could hear the fields around them begin to wake as darkness fell. Others came to the Bucklorn home to help. Those that remained with Kalea listened for any sign of movement, waiting for the stranger. Emyr heard a rustle in a nearby tree, but it was an owl.

Soon, the man would visit, a man of the world yet a stranger to it, as it was said.

* * *

The stranger knew the land well. He had traveled its many pathways and roads, crossed its fields and rivers, and ventured high into its mountains. Over the years his travels had been distant and wide, but his past was never far away. Here was a man with a tortured past, a person who struggled with visions of darkness in his mind, dark visions that had filled his head since childhood.

He was born into a family of fishermen, the oldest of four brothers, all large and fit. Their home was a ramshackle structure of boards on the coast outside Loch Shore, surrounded by desolate-looking dunes that would glow unearthly in the night sky. As a child, he remembered peering from the front door and down a narrow sandy path that led through short grass with patches of black trees to either side. His father was always somewhere out there – usually out to sea, or maybe down at the waterline in the surf, or hidden in the dunes, or amongst the trees. In his mind, he could hear the soft blast of the surf as it crashed the shore and went racing up the tight hard sand, and he could hear the strange wind as it occasionally struck the house, sweeping in from the coast. He remembered the sound of the wind causing the front door to bang.

Indeed, he remembered many things, so many things, dark things.

He remembered the dark visions that came to him throughout his youth, visions that at times ravaged him, and provoked him to evil and sadness. They were the visions of madness and death, inescapable and horrid. And even though he kept the visions to himself, his mood and actions would reflect the vileness. As a child, he was angry a lot of the time, and this required strict discipline from his father. As he grew older, he became increasingly difficult to manage at home and learned it was best to do as he was told. The struggle to free himself from his dark visions seemed endless. Despite all this, he found solace in the hard work the sea brought.

"Hard work will make a man of you," his father shouted to him one day, over the sound of the waves crashing against their boat. "It never goes unrewarded."

He and his brothers helped their father to provide for the family. They worked the sea on a small boat, casting nets, and emptying them when they were full of wriggling fish. Each day much of the fresh catch would be sold at the market with some left for the family. It was barely an existence that was wrenched from the sea, but it was their life, mundane, and never changing. They had no concept of another way of life and had no clue that there was anything more to life but working at sea.

Throughout it all, the dark visions continued to haunt him. They were different each time, showing him something terrible happening to someone he cared about. He tried to run from them, but they always caught up with him. He would try to fight them off, but they always won.

That was, until one day a short man came to visit. He was old, peculiar, and had an odd way about him.

The stranger remembered that day; he remembered the short man, his walk, and his smile. He remembered the old man's wooden staff, polished, pale brown. It seemed to gleam in the sun. He also remembered his father's words, the last he would ever hear from his father.

"You must go with him to the west. You'll have a better life. We'll be fine here."

The stranger did as he was told.

You always do what you are told to do.

He spent a few years with the old man who he only knew as his master. At first, they wandered the land where, with the master's help, he learned many of life's lessons; charity, honesty, integrity, loyalty, and the meaning of commitment to one guiding principle – the truth of the self. He also learned to control his dark visions, and in doing so very special abilities came to him. He learned to move and transform objects by thought, and he learned to see through things to determine the truth of the matter. But the master taught him how to only use his abilities for good, that to do otherwise would be unfaithful to his purpose.

"Never use your abilities in darkness," the master told him. "Doing so will concede weakness and invite others to take advantage of you. Never show weakness."

The stranger always found the words confusing.

Together they built a farmstead deep within a dense forest. The farmstead included a house with a cellar below and a barn. The house was a sturdy frame structure with clapboard siding on the outside. The inside walls were lined with oak. They labored to dig wells, and constructed feeding and watering troughs, and livestock pens. They had cows for milk and meat, sheep for wool, poultry for eggs, and bees tended for honey. The land was tilled, fields of barley and corn grew plentiful, and fruit trees provided seasonal flowers and a canopy of ripe, luscious delights;

silver and gold and clear designs, and shapes with unknowable names, all in the peak of their perfection. Each tree bowed with the weight of its bounty bent toward the soil. Surrounding it all was a great wooden fence, a barrier designed to ward off evil, the posts of which took root and grew into great trees.

Then there came the day when the master would say that the time had arrived for new lessons to be learned. The master instructed the stranger to leave the farmstead and travel west where there was a great castle. His master told him that there he would meet with others with similar abilities and learn even greater lessons.

The stranger did as he was told.

You always do what you are told to do.

He remembered the master's last words: "To be able to understand your purpose, to distinguish between what's good and what's bad for your purpose, you should have a strong understanding of the essence of existence. To better understand yourself is to better understand others."

Several days of travel passed when the castle was in sight. The sunshine was on it and its towers and turrets were silhouetted against a green forest behind it and its stone bulwarks glowed with a light that made it seem almost to float above its terraces. Around it rose great gardens with beautiful flowers and trees, in which were stags, deer, and hares, and everything that could be desired roamed freely. The castle itself was a grand edifice, with halls paved with marble, and the walls were all bright with beautiful hangings. In its many rooms were chairs and tables of pure gold, with magnificent iron chandeliers that hung from the ceilings.

The stranger joined many others and gained greater insight into his abilities. He learned the things he needed to learn, as did the others. He learned that everyone had gifts given to them by the Maker, forged from both light and darkness. He expanded his understanding of the nature of the world, of light and darkness, and in time the image of the Mark of the Tree appeared on his neck.

Soon, the word that would place everything in context was spoken: *Wizard.*

It was a glorious time of learning and rebirth for the stranger as his dark visions seemed to vanish. But war broke out and there was great strife. An evil brood enemy decimated the land and neared places close to the castle. As they approached most of the wizards fled to safety, but the stranger and a few others remained together, for a special bond had been formed by their training. They joined the armies of the good and righteous and fought bravely on the battlefield, pushing the brood back. He and the others in the small group of wizards were called Hulnur Istare, or *Warrior Wizards* in the common tongue, and they became the dark arm of the Edainar. On the battlefield, the brood called them Fighavu Duukav, for they brought great and dire havoc.

One can only combat the darkness by using darkness. Light can only come from the dark.

He remembered when he first had the thought. It was on the battlefield. He had just killed several orcs with a spell of fire while quickly turning to slay a hurtling orc with his sword. Having withdrawn his sword from the flailing orc, he watched as the blood dripped from the blade's sharp edges. The dark visions flashed with madness but slipped away with a thought.

Never use your abilities in darkness.

There were more battles to wage and with them came a time when the stranger surprisingly met up with one of his brothers on the battlefield. For the remainder of the war, he fought alongside his brother in many great battles. But he found little glory in death and when victory was gained at the end of it all, and when there were no more battles to fight, he seemed lost, without a sense of purpose.

The experience of war affected him; it had transformed him, had influenced his perspective, for better or worse, he did not know which. When the Edainar disbanded the Hulnur Istare, the stranger became distraught as did many of the other warrior wizards. He disavowed his relationship with the Edainar and decided to return to his family home near Loch Shore and fish the sea. The place was peaceful. His brother also returned to the sea, but to the west.

Much had changed since the time he left with the master. His parents had passed from disease and his two other brothers were lost to the war. He never visited the master for fear of how he thought the master would respond to him for using magic during wartime. The Mark of the Tree once so emblazoned on his neck had faded, but traces still were there. He traveled some and rarely used his magic, only doing so to help those in need.

Few knew of the stranger's past and stories grew to fill the void. Over time he became known as a healer, one with knowledge of magic and dark sorcery, a reclusive person who kept to himself and had few true friends. This was now his way.

As time waned, the past was sometimes forgotten but never lost. It would sometimes enter his mind and continue to shape him, disturbing memories of death and blackness. Yet, he worked hard at making the present seem virtuous in his mind, almost sacred. This he learned from the master.

Now, as he made his way west, suddenly there was change. The past and the dark visions came haunting once again with the visit of a winged messenger from the north, the companion to Erol Carrick, the majestic falcon, Windthrasher.

The mostly white bird perched on a nearby tree, its chilling burnt orange eyes focused on him.

"The great Erol Carrick wishes to inform you that your brother, Skag Harwell, has been killed by the brood," said the bird, words that stirred a great unease within him. "The great Carrick expresses his deepest sympathy. He also asks for your help as darkness spreads over the land once again. What say you?"

He did not utter a word in response but returned the bird's gaze. Then, with a huge shriek, the bird spread its wings and flew off, soaring above the trees.

He followed the bird as it flew in circles, seeming to hover right above him. Then in a flash, it was gone high into the sky. The wind picked up, and a ripping coldness blew against him. Even with his hands pushed deep into the pockets of his coat, he was chilled.

Anger filled the stranger; anger for the past; anger for the present. It seemed all he knew was death, and now his family was gone. He was alone. The dark visions in his mind swelled like the waves of the sea.

One can only combat the darkness by using darkness. Light can only come from the dark.

The shadow of his past remained with him, now more vibrant and real. A sense of peace now forever lost. The stranger quickened his pace.

* * *

As Kalea stared into a candle's flame, mesmerized by a dancing shadow within it, a coldness came upon her.

"He's here," she whispered.

Everyone gathered at a window overlooking the field. In the night light, they could see the stranger looking over the stone figures of the children. They saw him place his hands on the cold, stone surface of the figures; they saw him pause, dropping his head as if a great disappointment had washed over him.

"Now. Quickly. Away from the window. Leave him be," said Emyr Bucklorn.

The family sat nervously when there came one solid knock at the door that seemed to shake the house. Emyr opened the door to the sight of a tall but bone-thin, fragile-looking thug, who, however, was far from fragile.

To the Bucklorns, the stranger appeared weak, feeble, and old, but they knew he carried wisdom and power. He had long greyish-black hair that was pulled back and hung scraggly. His face was scarred and ravaged, and his facial muscles became slightly twisted when he spoke as if he were making a physical effort every time he attempted to say something. A black leather eye patch covered his left eye which had been lost in battle. It was said the skull of the combatant rested on a large oak pole in the center of the Thorndell Fields.

"I am Ridley Harwell," said the tall man. "I was called to this place. You have asked for my help."

"Yes," said Emyr. "There's no wizard nearby and my family requires your assistance."

They look upon me as something lesser than a wizard, thought Harwell.

He looked past Emyr to Kalea who sat at the table, her head in her hands in distress. He approached her, placing a hand on the back of her head.

"The strong individual is the one who asks for help when it is most needed," he told her.

Kalea looked up at him.

"Master Harwell my children are dead," she said, "and my husband is but a step away from the darkness."

"My lady we are all but a step from the darkness. But know that your children are not in such a dark place. They are alive, frozen in time. Terrible and powerful magic was used on them, one which is beyond my abilities to reverse."

"Who can help then?"

"Only those of the Edainar have such ability and I am afraid it will be some time before they can assist. War is coming to the land again, as a voice like thunder."

"But what then are we to do?"

"Patience my lady. In time all will be sorted out. Your children will be fine if they are not moved and remain together; for this is a form of a binding spell, as best as I can determine. But come now, I need to see your husband and speak with him."

Harwell and the others went to Zachary's side as he lay resting. Sensing a presence Zachary slowly opened his eyes to the sight of Harwell. He was at first frightened to see him but regained courage at his friendly salutation.

"Master Bucklorn, there is no need for concern. I am here to help."

Zachary nodded.

"Good sir, your children are alive and must remain together. The stone that encrusts them cannot be broken. If one tries to break the stone, your children will be broken. Powerful magic was used, magic that I cannot undo. In time all will be as it once was. Please have patience."

Zachary closed his eyes, grateful for the words about his children. Again, he nodded.

Kalea gave Harwell the note Zachary had written. The word *Denier* screamed to him.

He grabbed Zachary Bucklorn's hand and tightly squeezed it. He looked over Zachary, the twine that now stitched his lips closed. He immediately knew that again such magic was beyond his ability to reverse. He closed his eyes and spoke a few words in the old tongue. With those words, Zachary Bucklorn felt a strangeness come over him.

"Master Bucklorn, I have placed a spell on you," said Harwell. "When you breathe each breath will now provide you with the sustenance you require. Food and water will be unnecessary. Life will continue for you until one with such power can be found to correct what has happened."

Zachary took a deep breath through his nose. The strangeness was again there. The air that filled his lungs seemed to strengthen him. He squeezed at Harwell's grip.

"Good," said Harwell with a smile. "You can feel it. Already you are gaining strength. But I must ask you some questions. Are you strong enough to help me?"

Zachary nodded.

"Be strong for the flood of death is upon us once again," said Harwell. "When the whirlwind of fury comes from the Maker and the senses are shaken, and the soul is driven to madness, only the good and strong shall stand." And then he spoke unfamiliar words, "Seere tu yassen lle" which in the old tongue is p*eace be with you.*

Using parchment and quill, Zachary Bucklorn answered every question Harwell asked. As the night grew longer, storms came and seemed to increase. Through the noise of wind and pelting rain, the Bucklorns and Harwell heard a bird cry out and a dog howl, like someone in agony.

"It is time for me to leave," said Harwell, his distorted face in the candlelight.

"Please stay," said Kalea as Zachary nodded, eyes widened. "We've food and warmth. Stay the night."

"I appreciate your gesture of hospitality, but I must be off."

"But the storms," said Kalea. "It's not safe to travel."

"Much greater storms will soon arise to the sorrow of the land," said Harwell, an ominous tone to his voice. "Someone with the power to help your family will come. I promise you. But it will take time. You must be patient."

He hastily bid farewell to the Bucklorns with a sincere embrace. He left the home and made his way north, into the storm.

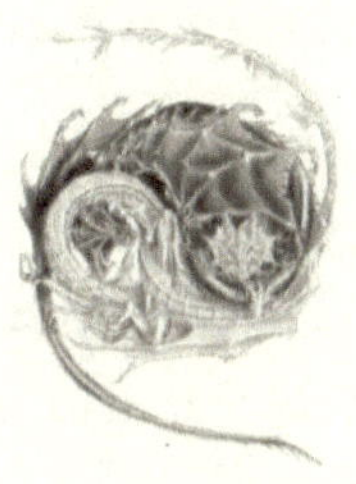

CHAPTER 3
THE MEANING OF GREY

EVER SINCE THE ATTACK on Molly, just outside the small village of Thawnybire, the company walked quietly, having abandoned their wagons and horses. Bran said there was no point in bringing horses with them, only to abandon them to die or be noticed by agents of the darkness. They left the road and turning southwards went on by narrow paths among the folded lands.

"We will hold our course for many leagues and days," said Bran. "The land will become rougher and more barren, and our going will be slow. It will be too treacherous and difficult for horses. The benefits provided by having horses would be counteracted by the necessity of finding paths in the rough peaks of the mountains that they would navigate. We do not wish to be easily tracked. We hope to escape the notice of unfriendly eyes."

Molly and Elizabeth, who adored their elven ponies Adhara and Shaula, found this extremely difficult. The pure white ponies disliked being left behind as well. But everyone understood what was required.

The journey remained slow and arduous. The girls now wore sturdy boots made of leather and several layers of clothing and a coat, and each carried a backpack of sorts, a dark green canvas satchel that stored various items. Even though they had brought with them the most basic of provisions, dried meats, bread, dried fruit, water, blankets, and clothing – enough to last for several days – there was little comfort. Elizabeth was not very happy. "Very unbecoming of royalty," she would tell the others.

Molly and the orc continued to bond as they traveled. They both seemed to enjoy nature, which at first surprised Molly, but then again, she realized that her preconceptions of what an orc should be were very different from how Ug'ghi Otha behaved. Somehow, their love of nature made them kindred spirits. They listened to the woods which were full of bird calls, and the orc spent a lot of time discussing each bird in detail. Molly knew about gardening, of course, having learned such from her uncle. But in the Harrow, even though many plants were familiar to her, there were some she saw that were unfamiliar. There were a lot of bright green ferns, but also delicate flowers with strange feathery leaves that shone like silver when the sunlight hit them at just the right angle.

"Do you know anything about plants?" she asked Ug'ghi Otha.

"I know some things," he said.

Molly pointed to a small broad-leafed plant.

"What about this one?" she asked.

"It is called Eopos. It flowers during warmer times, producing large yellow or orange flowers that are round. When the flower dies, the wind takes its seeds. It is a very meddlesome plant. In some places, it can spread almost everywhere. Also, the plant's leaves have the power to heal. When heated in a bit of water, the resulting oil is used to treat open sores."

He could identify almost every plant, tree, shrub, and grass, and describe their parts, even in the smallest of details. Molly found it fascinating and did her best to remember what the orc told her, collecting the flowers, roots, and leaves in the fields and forests. She made notes, labeled, and wrapped each collection in small pieces of cloth, storing them in her satchel. But her enjoyment in learning the flora would wane whenever the orc became too technical. "Sometimes I am long-winded," he would say smiling at her. "I guess you could say I understand plants very well." She would smile back and say, "Yes, you do."

"I learned about plants by helping my uncle in his wonderful gardens," she told him. "I'm especially knowledgeable about the best times to plant and the best times to prune."

"Prune? I do not understand the word. What does it mean?"

"It's like cutting or clipping back a plant. You do that so it can grow stronger, without overtaking those plants nearest."

He hesitated and thought. He turned and glanced back at Brows who was walking several paces behind them.

He chuckled.

"Wonder if bobbins can be pruned," he said to her.

Molly broke out in laughter.

"But where did you learn all this, about birds and plants?" she asked.

"When I was young a kuunajbor would show me things."

She interrupted. "What? Now, I'm the one who doesn't understand a word."

"Oh, I am sorry," he paused, searching for the words to translate. "A kuunajbor is an old male orc, who is near that time in life when he would be killed by the horde."

"Killed! Why would they kill an old orc?"

"The life of an orc is very different than the life of a man or even a dwarf. In the horde, an orc must serve the masses. That means he must kill many enemies in battle or provide food. Life in the horde is just that simple. But if an orc can no longer do such things, they will soon be killed by the horde, because they are taking precious resources. The kuunajbor I now speak of was called Ju'cfa Furq. He was once a great warrior but with age, he had become feeble. His skin changed color. It became a greyish tone. He could no longer fight or hunt for food, but he would help females by foraging for plants and nuts. This is how he learned about plants. Some of us helped him. We tried to protect him from the horde because we knew of his greatness, and we learned from him. But eventually, he was killed, for only one purpose remained for him."

"What was that?"

He turned to Molly, a look of calm distress on his face.

"He helped to fill my mind, and then at the end, he filled my belly. The day he was killed he became that night's meal. This is our way. As I said – an orc must serve the masses."

Molly was appalled by the horrible story. He sensed her repulsion and paused.

"My Queen, I know you are distraught by my tale. Do not be. I am not like other orcs. You must understand this. I am different. I did what I did and that is all I could do."

Molly was surprised by his last statement. She had heard it, or something like it, before. She attempted to remember who had spoken such words, or something close. Then it came to her.

The white cat!

"Can you repeat what you just said?" she asked.

He seemed perplexed by her request.

"I did what I needed to do to survive. I am not like the others. Please, you must understand."

He uses different words.

"I do but I'm asking you to repeat the exact words you said just a moment ago," she implored.

He thought back, trying to recount his exact words. He remembered.

"I did what I did and that's all I could do," he said. "Are these the words you wanted?"

She smiled at him.

So strikingly similar to the white cat. But why?

He gave her a curious look.

"It's fine. Yes, I understand. You are different from the others of your kind. We must continue with our plan."

The orc drew a deep breath and nodded.

* * *

Over the next few days, as the company journeyed south, Molly increasingly kept to herself. She kept silent on her dreams; they were her burden and her burden alone. She also attempted to find time away from everyone. wanting to continue to experiment with the Lia Fail, as she had while at Katzhu Pu. Whenever they made camp, she would take a short walk, never too far from camp, to gather firewood or forage for berries.

Bran was always displeased when she wandered off. He would have Big Grey follow her, unbeknownst to her, to make sure she was safe. He did not know of the large cat's relationship with the Lia Fail, that Big Grey was its Caedaes, but somehow, he felt it incredibly important that the cat remain close to her.

In following Molly, the cat would keep his distance. He did not want her to know he was following her, observing her, sensing her thoughts, guiding her as he continued to aid her training on the use of the Lia Fail stone. As with past training, he would gently direct her thoughts to good uses of the stone's power. But lately, he found it more difficult to guide her thoughts. Even though she no longer spoke of her dreams, he sensed turmoil in her, possibly brought about by the dark dreams. She was changing and there was a stillness about her.

After a recent meal, he asked her, "What is making you so thoughtful?"

She shrugged.

"Many things. Too many things."

Her dreams of war and destruction were increasing in frequency. She saw herself on a battlefield, and she would become enraged at the enemy who was causing so much destruction. Her anger would push her to use the stone to defeat the evil. These images would haunt her as she practiced using the stone.

I have a duty to protect all the good races of the Harrow from evil, the thought struck her.

Because of her dreams, she started to show anger during her experiments with the Lia Fail. Big Grey struggled to keep her rage under control. He thought of his meeting at Blackstone Keep when Dalgaes first spoke of his role as Caedaes.

He remembered the Elf-King's words.

"It is the word-keeper who unlocks the stone's capabilities, but only when her experiments are principled and when the use of the stone's power is appropriate for the situation. The Caedaes has insight into some of the Queen's thoughts and must fulfill his duty in perfect harmony with her. Master Purr, you must be the Caedaes to the Lia Fail, its word-keeper."

How can there be harmony with such anger? he thought.

* * *

So it came on one occasion as the company made camp in a small grove of trees and bushes beside a much larger forest, that Big Grey followed Molly as she wandered from camp to gather firewood. But this time, instead of keeping his distance in secret, he called out to her.

"Wait," he shouted. "I want to come along."

She sighed and returned his gaze. She did not say anything.

The two walked in silence through tall grasses and scrub oak and hickory as Molly gathered firewood. She would stop to pick up small branches and tree limbs. At other times as they walked, she would pull on branches from low-hanging limbs that snapped off easily. Along the way, they came to a tree that had fallen, and she spent some time breaking off branches, carefully inspecting each. When she had a good-sized bundle of wood, she set down two lengths of bundling straps and stacked the wood into a small pyramid-shaped pile on top of the straps. She used as many pieces of wood as possible, knowing what she could carry in one load. She discarded some of the smaller branches and limbs.

"Where did you learn to do all this?" asked Big Grey.

"From Mr. Brows. He taught me that the best burning wood is not only dry but dense. Nut-bearing trees like oak and hickory are hardwood and the most desirable. They burn cleaner and longer. The best wood can be gathered from living trees. If you pull on a branch and it comes off, it means the branch is dead. Deadwood found on the ground can be good too but can also be full of water. I've also learned a lot about the local plants from the orc - which ones can be used as a tea, and which ones can heal. He told me it's not enough to know which plants heal. You need to know how to make them heal."

"Did he show you which plants kill?"

"Yes. He told me which ones are poisonous, to stay away from, and which ones are safe to forage for. I have tried to teach Elizabeth, but I do not believe she's very interested."

"There is much that you have learned since coming to the Harrow. It is changing you."

"Sometimes one does not like what one becomes."

"Sort of like looking at a reflection in a mirror I suppose."

"What do you mean?"

"If you look into a mirror and you do not like what is learned from the reflection, you have one of two things that you can do. You can replace the mirror with a new one. But that is folly. A new mirror will only provide the same reflection. Or you can accept what you see and improve upon it. Molly, if you look hard enough you may just see something you like."

She smiled at him.

"I know you have followed me every time I have left camp," she told him. "I can sense your presence, your thoughts. You have seen me try to learn how to use the stone, haven't you?"

She must not know that I am the word-keeper, he thought.

"Yes," he said. "Please, do not be angry with me. I worry about you, about the weight the stone places on you. It is changing you; I sense it."

Molly looked off. She decided to tell him of her dreams.

"There are times when I want to go back under the tree and have my birthday cake," she said. "But then there are times I am angered by what is happening here, about the darkness. I see it in my dreams. I see the death and destruction that awaits. I see the misery in so many empty faces." She turned to him, teary-eyed. "I think to myself that I am the only one who can stop this nightmare and defeat the darkness on the battlefield. This is when anger comes over me like a great wind, and if I had something to hold on to, I might be able to stop myself from being blown away by it."

"Think of what I said about the mirror. Remember, having a different mirror will not change the reflection. You must deal with what you see, what is before you."

"But when anger rages within me, it is unsettling. I am afraid I may say or do something that will not do a bit of good."

"Our anger comes from our thoughts which come from what we believe. If we alter what we believe around anger so that it is closer to the truth, then it will bring our thoughts and our emotions more into alignment. Perhaps look at anger as a way to greater harmony. If you can do this, then anger becomes less about pain and dysfunction, and more about a means to an end."

"Are you saying anger is a good thing?"

"I am saying anger like all emotions can be used to good effect. Anger can reduce violence, benefit relationships, promote optimism, and be a motivating force. Anger can be good for you because in its own way it is designed to protect you, your relationships, and your way of seeing the world. In a battle between right and wrong, light and darkness, good and evil, the emotion of anger simply tells you something is wrong and that something must be done."

"Well, clearly, something is wrong, terribly wrong."

"Use your anger to show you what is wrong and what can be done. Do not ignore your anger, but also do not feed into it. Use it to motivate you to do the right thing."

She sat on the ground and wiped her tears. He approached her and began a light purr. He rubbed against her feet and put his front paws on her lap. She reached out to him and gently stroked his back.

"Did every Queen of Ahlgren experience what I am going through?" she asked.

"I do not know exactly, mind you, but something tells me your experience is not unique. A Queen of Ahlgren named Aerin used the stone on the battlefield to defeat the enemy, but there was one who came before Aerin who refused to use the stone's power. Her name was Hycis. She was of House Riorn and her brother Kern Durned was King. He ascended to the throne as a young man and reigned for several years until time brought a strangeness to him. Darkness consumed him and he became ruthless and hungered for power. He gathered great armies and stormed across the lands, conquering kingdom after kingdom. He became known as Durned the Vicious for the many atrocities he committed. Along with death and blackness, wherever he went, he had statues erected in his glory. This was the time of the Gurtha Ahtar, or War of Death.

"Hycis was sickened by the darkness in her brother's heart. She felt she had no choice and fled Riorn Castle and joined with Erol Carrick. In doing so, she knew she would have to face her brother on the battlefield. And when that day came, when she faced her brother, he taunted her, called her names, belittled, and disparaged her. In her despair, she withdrew into herself. A thread of anger began to glow in her mind, though it was anger against herself rather than at him. The anger tore through her, and it confused her. It became so consuming that she could not muster the strength to use the Lia Fail. She did not understand what was happening. It was sort of like looking at a compass, and not knowing how to read it, not knowing the right direction to take."

"What happened?" asked Molly.

"She let the stone slip from her hand. She turned and ran, refusing to face her brother. It is not known what became of her. Some say she traveled far east. Others say the Maker took her from this place."

"And what of the battle?"

"It was but one of many battles in a war. In time, Carrick and the great armies of the elves and dwarves prevailed, and House Riorn was restored." He paused for a moment, then continued slowly. "Molly, I am not wrong about this. You are not like Hycis. No. I feel you are beginning to understand your anger. You are more like Aerin who used the Lia Fail on the battlefield to defeat the enemy. You see, anger can be used to justify oppressing others, or anger can be used to bring about desirable changes. Aerin understood this. She knew the many directions before her, and understood that the stone's destructive force is sometimes required to bring about a needed change."

"Like the compass, you spoke of?"

"Yes, and like the mirror. Look at the compass and it will point you in the right direction; look hard enough into the mirror and you will see something you like. But I have a warning."

"What is it?"

"While the energy of anger can be used to combat the forces of evil and to heal the consequences, it can also be a trap for us. It is like a door we must pass through. If you do not pass through the door, you never move forward and away from anger, you never read the compass, and you stop looking into the mirror. When this happens anger is all-consuming, becoming your only companion, robbing you of every other emotion desperately needed to nourish your soul. You see, a soul will not let itself be empty. It will store the anger we feed it and in time, we become dark and soulless."

"Like her brother Durned."

"Precisely." he nodded.

She sat contemplative and unmoving, thinking about all that had been said when a strange question came to her.

"What became of the statues that Durned left behind?"

"Some are still standing, but others have been taken down and broken apart. For some, it was important to remove them from sight, because doing so invited forgetting a dark past. Others, on the other hand, see those that still stand as reminders that evil may take many forms."

"But there is a problem with keeping the statues."

"How so?" he asked.

"Some will say the statues are the most important part of their past." She stared off into the surrounding trees. "They will become monuments and will call out to many, to embrace the anger and the darkness they represent. The cycle can continue."

He looked up at her in silence. Her words were profound, yet they had the simplicity of a chilling truth. She was growing as a person, becoming more insightful. Through her dreams and experiments with the Lia Fail, she was learning about herself, about the world around her, and becoming a stronger person every day.

The two sat silently for a while, listening to the sounds of the forest, the chirping, the fluttering of wings, and the wind's quiet rustle through the murmuring leaves.

The Guardian's words then came to her as if they were blown on the winds, shaped by them.

Search for the voice that is silent . . . Search for the voice that is silent . . .

She remembered the little butterfly with a ripped wing as it fluttered about and landed on her shoulder.

"Purr," she said, "I know I cannot tell you what the Guardian said to me, you know when we were at the tomb in Katzhu Pu. But I have thought about it and thought about it, and I do not understand what the Guardian was trying to tell me."

"Sometimes it is best not to look for meaning everywhere or in everything. Sometimes it is best to wait for it, to let your intuition tell you."

"Hmmm . . . I suppose you are right. I guess what matters in life is not so much all the things that come to meet us, those things we have to deal with, as much as our readiness to meet them."

He smiled.

"We should be heading back," he told her.

She nodded with a smile when unexpectedly a look of bewilderment came to her face. Her body stiffened as her eyes darted about the surrounding forest. The Lia Fail warmed and brightened and it began a gentle throb. She quickly gripped the stone with both hands.

Within the darkness of the surrounding forest, she sensed a presence - piercing, bright yellow eyes staring at her and Big Grey. In her mind, she heard whispers, two distinct voices. Her breathing began to quicken.

Silly human child.

Yes, demented little thing she is. But she has the red gem.

And we, what do we have?

Ah, we have the looking glass.

Must be done with her.

Yes, must be done with her.

He'll be most pleased by her death, won't he?

Oh yes, he'll be most pleased.

Is he on his way?

Yes. Soon he'll be with us again.

She was concerned for their safety but wished to maintain a calm exterior. She took a deep breath.

"Yes, we must leave this place and return to camp," she calmly told the cat.

He sensed something was wrong.

"What is it? You seem troubled."

"The forest, it's a wicked place."

He looked at the murky woods.

"It is called the Forest Heave and it is very dark. Let us be on our way."

They returned to camp.

* * *

As Molly and the others proceeded on their travels south, the great Forest Heave continued to loom to the east like a secret world. It was a threatening barricade between the east and west, thicker, and darker than the Tangle, and as mysterious. As Bran led the company south and away from the dark forest, the girls were told terrifying tales about the place. It was said that no person, group, or army had ever navigated its gloom, and those who attempted to traverse its density were never again seen. Perhaps most frightening was a legend that the Heave seemed to grow over time, consuming those who entered it. The vast forest seemed to be a living creature, dark and cruel. It did not care who traveled through its blackness or near its edge. It called to travelers, beckoning them to travel inward, a journey of death.

"This forest you call the Heave, is it like the Tangle forest? I mean was it crafted by a conjurer?" Molly asked Brows.

"My Queen, no one is quite sure. As you have heard many tales about it, there is one historic note of peculiarity. Many ages ago and during a war of conquest, an army from the North Eldor attempted to burn its way through the Heave. The army intended to cut a pathway through the forest for a second army to follow. It was an attempt to gain quick access to the west and Mortha. The army had some success. It entered the Heave, burning and ravaging its way deeper and deeper into the darkness. But the foliage that had been burned was quickly repaired by the Heave; it had healed itself. The forest turned on the army swallowing it whole. A few days later, the second army approached, hoping to see a forest trail burned through the vast darkness. Instead, they only saw the trees waving in the breeze. Many of the warriors said they could hear the lamentations of the thousands of unfortunate wretches that came before them."

"What is it about forests in this place?" shuddered Elizabeth.

Brows paused and chewed on his pipe.

"It seems we must contend with a power in the Harrow's many forests, an anger we stir at our peril. Few are hospitable places."

It seemed to Molly that there were so many places in this strange land where green fields and mountains rolled into forever, where magic was in the mists, and where dark and brooding forests held secrets. But she held secrets of her own. She did not speak to others of the yellow eyes or the whispers she heard, nor did she speak of her dreams or visions that caused such trembling in her. Only Big Grey knew about her dreams. She maintained a silent pact she had made with herself and this new world. The silence was providing her safety but, while she kept her secrets, she understood that she could never be free of them.

The problem with secrets, the truly uncomfortable thing about them, is that they never go away, she thought.

The burden of her dreams and visions was difficult. But she had friends and her sister, and she knew they would not turn away from her. She found Big Grey's words to be comforting and most helpful, as she tried to better understand things and look at things differently. But it was not easy. And when she had become frustrated, strangely, Brows was always able to sense her burden, when the weight was overly heavy.

"Sometimes things happen that hurt us deeply," he would say, putting more branches on the fire, or chomping on his pipe, "and even though it is something we think we should hold on to, it is usually better to let it go. Letting go of something forces us to look at it in a different light."

A few more days passed. They continued south while keeping their distance from the edge of the Heave. They were now just a few leagues north of Tollford Farthing. Here, the land was rich, and the pine trees were scattered about and plentiful. Everyone enjoyed the breeze as it swept from the land, heavy with the sweet scent of pine and flowers that grew wild in the hills and near streams. Their travels soon brought them to a small, thickly forested area separate from the Heave, just along a ridge of a small outcropping of mountains, the last of the Old Hills.

In the distance, they could now see Tollford Farthing, a small town with gloomy wooden rooftops and stone and brick walls. Molly was told it was a dreary place, a collection of ramshackle houses and pubs, supported by blacksmithing and carpentry and farming. They decided to make camp, hidden in the dense woodland. As they made camp, sounds of a lake came upon the winds, from the east, echoing, calling, snapping, squishing against a jagged shoreline.

"I would like to see the lake," said Molly.

Elizabeth joined in.

"Me too. We could use a bit of fun after hearing about the forest and the town."

The girls exchanged smiles as they made their way to the lake area, followed by Bran, who was concerned for their safety. Big Grey also joined the company of three.

The lake area was tranquil and lovely. The small lake was lined by a series of small beaches that gently sloped into the water, each full of small rocks sitting atop dark, dirty tan sand. At the back of each beach area was an abrupt rise; a vertical cut formed by the collapsing edge of pine-covered hills. A small stream flowed from the mountains and into the lake. Above the lake's shore, the sky looked innocent, untroubled, and the water dispassionate and serene.

The girls took in a deep breath and exhaled. The air was crisp and clean, and easy to breathe until they noticed a stench in the air.

"Something is wrong here," said Molly.

The buzz of flies could be heard off to the side by a fallen tree. They came across a dead Fenri with grey fur, its nose caked in blood. Bran studied the carcass, which had been ravaged by ravens and other beasts. Big Grey lifted his nose to the air, sniffing for a telling scent.

"Not much left," said Bran. "Looks to have been killed a few days ago."

Elizabeth looked away from the unpleasant sight while Molly stood stoic, fixated on the dead creature.

"What do you suppose happened?" asked Molly.

"I am not sure, my Queen," said Bran.

He knelt closer to the carcass, looking at the nearby ground. He gently placed his hands on the dirt, patting it here and there, feeling for the slightest of changes.

"A struggle of some kind, perhaps a battle," he said. "The tracks have since been wind-swept, but I believe them to be Fenri. It appears as if the beast was chased from the east and encircled. There was a struggle, then the creature's death, and then the victors fled the scene and headed back."

"Where?" asked Molly. "What direction did they go?"

Bran stood and pointed east to the mountains.

"To the Rakl, the land of the Fenri," he said.

"Killed by his kind?" asked Molly.

"It appears so."

She knelt beside the dead Fenri and gently stroked its grey fur.

"Do you think it is Thurir's father, the King?" asked Molly.

Big Grey carefully looked over the dead Fenri. He searched for a mark emblazoned on its neck, the royal insignia of Fenri Kings.

"This beast does not have the Mark of the Fang," said the cat.

"Interesting," said Molly

"My Queen, I am sorry. Interesting? How so?" asked Bran asked, confused.

"Do you not see what is in front of us? All that remains is the physical. We know nothing of this creature, where it came from, how it lived its life, or why its life was snuffed out in this place. All we know, at any time, is what is in front of us, a body now decomposing, becoming rich food for others, a life now long passed. But all of us - we're more than the physical."

Everyone was silent. Her words caught them by surprise. These were not the words of a young person but rather the words of a thoughtful adult. Elizabeth thought the moment was very strange and it worried her. She knew something was happening to her sister, and she felt a brightness inside of her. As the sun peeked out from the clouds she smiled. A warmth came over her. She saw her sister differently. She seemed older, wiser, and stronger. Elizabeth believed that her sister would protect them.

She hugged Molly.

"What is this all about?" asked Molly looking down at her sister in surprise.

"You're my older sister and I'm so glad for it," beamed Elizabeth.

But there was something about Molly, something she had not noticed before, something that caught her eye. She reached up and gently took hold of the ends of Molly's hair.

"Look," she exclaimed, fondling Molly's hair. "Your hair, it's turning grey."

Molly was confused. "What?"

"Your hair, it's turning grey," repeated Elizabeth.

Molly looked at her black hair. She saw a few silver strands mixed in with it.

"A sign of wisdom," said Big Grey, an intent look at Molly. "It is what happens to the Queen of Ahlgren. One should never be concerned with wisdom. But wisdom does come with a cautionary view; for power, apart from wisdom is but chaos and destruction."

Molly smiled. She remembered something the Professor said.

"The Professor once told me that wisdom used incorrectly is shallow, superficial, and has its limits. He said wisdom should only be used wisely."

"And you? Will you use wisdom correctly? Will you use it wisely?" asked Big Grey, his eyes closed, his body still, in calmness.

She felt the warmth of the Lia Fail against her skin.

"I am not bothered by grey hair," she said. She turned to her feline friend. "I understand it takes wisdom to use wisdom wisely."

Ah, she is learning, the cat thought.

Molly was amazed. She heard his thought.

I heard you! she told him with her mind. *I heard your thought! It was like a voice in my mind.*

She placed a hand on the Lia Fail.

The cat looked at her.

The stone makes us one, his thought reaching out to her.

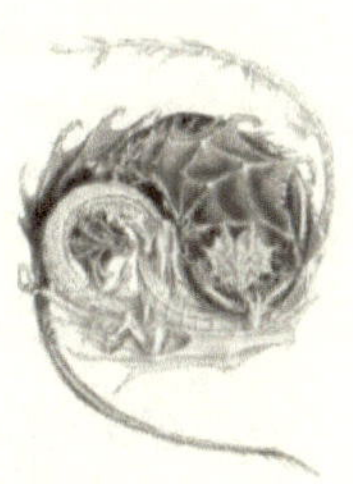

CHAPTER 4
THE OLD MARSH MOOR

I DO WHAT I *do and that's the best I can do.*

Through the crimson of his bulging eyes, the bony white cat had been witness to each creature's darkness, corruption, and distortion, their shackled monsters. He saw every creature for who they were, their true selves forever revealed. Now, as he searched for his friend, his eyes wandered about, through grasslands, then trees and thickets. All around him were signs of others who had passed the same way. But he could find no sign of his friend, and he began to wonder if he had been mistaken about which direction he had taken.

I do what I do and that's the best I can do.

The words forever sang through his mind. He shook his head, attempting to release the words once and for all, but to no avail.

I do what I do and that's the best I can do.

The words returned and punished him as they always had, but so too did a vision. It formed in his mind, a vision of his friend, the Learned One. He closed his eyes to reality and took a deep breath.

Words from his friend echoed - *Memories and thoughts define who we are. They stay in our minds and sometimes are retrieved in terrible ways. It is not up to the creature how they are brought forth. You see, there is evil in all things, waiting for an opportunity to be released onto the world. At their core, all creatures are of a despicable nature, primordial, engulfed in darkness. Over time, memories and thoughts hide the corruption and make us who we are. The Maker has made it this way, and it is the Maker who ensures a randomness of events. It is far better to not allow the past to determine who we are, but rather who we become. If we allow the past to set our pathway, then we release the darkness.*

A tender smile came to him until . . .

I do what I do and that's the best I can do.

His punishment continued. He shook his head from side to side, but the torture remained. He looked about, and his senses guided him unerringly in a new direction, to the Old Marsh Moor.

***

He had run for two days, through the Old Hills and the outer regions of Dagda and south past the Greenway until he reached the Old Marsh Moor.

I do what I do and that's the best I can do.

The words repeated through his mind as he ran, keeping pace with each stride. Over and over they sounded as they had done from the beginning of his awakening. They were his torment, his agony, but at times they were his salvation, his very existence. He did not try to understand why he was different from others; he simply acknowledged his uniqueness and followed where the events of his time took him.

He lifted his nose repeatedly, sucking in and expelling the baffling air, trying to sense his friend. But the air was filled with the acrid stench of rotting vegetation and carcasses. His flesh crawled. He imagined worms and maggots and all sorts of vile creatures, but his impulse to press ahead and unite with his friend became his strength, his resolve.

I do what I do and that's the best I can do.

The words continued when he approached the Old Marsh Moor, a wetland of heather, gorse, rough grassland, with bare rocks. It was a landscape that engendered fear and awe. The land was dominated by dramatic stone tors that towered over the sweeping expanses of the open moorland. To the south, the marshes and bogs on the high moor drained into shallow valleys as small rivers crossed onto softer shales around the land, carving themselves into deep valleys, and providing shelter for rich, damp oak woodland.

Few traveled or lived in this place. There were no roads or pathways. He, on the other hand, knew it well, having traveled secretly with his friend for years through the sleepy shades and dark corners.

He knew of one passage, one, in particular, the one way that few dared to journey.

I do what I do and that's the best I can do.

He shook his head trying to release the words, but they would not go away. There was no trying to ignore them. He sighed.

What are the words telling me?

He trembled in the cold night air, ripples of tension running across his sinewy neck.

Where is my friend? What to do? Wait! My eyes! Use them! Look with them!

He followed his thoughts and peered deeply into the marshland with his red eyes.

My friend, where are you?

Deeper and deeper he looked until he came upon a faint image in the distance. It was his friend, but there was a strangeness lurking about him. There were others nearby. He mustered what strength he had and focused on those dark images, those closing in on his friend.

Enemies? Are they enemies?

The words whispered in his mind. He was worried. There were many images near his friend, some appearing to hold instruments of war, the dark silhouettes of sword and spear.

Overhead, lightning flashed through the dark sky, followed by a boom of thunder that rocked the ground. Frightened, he fell to the ground and clapped his bony front paws over his ears, and shut his eyes. Another boom of thunder echoed far off, and heavy rain began to sting the land. The storm eventually passed, leaving only a gentle drizzle. Quiet and calmness came over him until the haunting continued.

I do what I do and that's the best I can do.

Again, the words sounded defiant. They reverberated round and round and came bouncing up over the marshes and moorland to where he stood.

Friend, I need you. I need you!

Through the rain, a faint image appeared in his mind. The outline was of an old man with a long beard and long hair, pure white with streaks of grey.

Friend! It is you!

The image brought him warmth. Then, the voice of his friend started to flow through his mind. For just that moment did his words of torment dissipate.

I must undo what I have done, his friend's voice whispered, words from the past.

He was closer. He bounded forward into the Old Marsh Moor, his surroundings dimmed into pitch black. He knew of the one passage, remembering the words of his friend.

Take the safe route, or you will hear the shout of adventure, whispered his friend's voice.

On he ran, through the passage and deeper into the darkness.

I do what I do and that's the best I can do.

The words returned, but for now, they were no longer his torment, for he would soon be reunited with his friend.

* * *

Deep within the marshland, Theor Thaken turned to view the edge of the Cricklewood forest, where the massive oaks and beech abruptly gave way to the vast, open wetlands of the Old Marsh Moor. The young commander stood with arms crossed, in a black, fur-lined overcoat that flapped in the brisk winds. He was cold, and he hated the northern lands. Indeed, Thaken hated many things, especially being far from where the action was. He knew a great battle was to be waged to the east, and he wanted to be part of it. That was what he was trained for, and in his mind what he was bred for. But he was given a mission by the great Carrick, to join with a wizard and attack a newly constructed evil tower, and like all good warriors, he would do his duty without question. As a downpour thrashed, he stood in what for him was a forsaken land, searching through the grey tendrils of dampness, looking for an old man, a wizard.

Cur Vosser, the second in command and a towering man not much older than Thaken, approached.

The man gestured to the west.

"My liege, over there," he said.

Thaken squinted through the rain and wiped it from his brows to keep it from running into his eyes. He strained to make out exactly what Vosser was pointing to.

"There. Do you see him?" he asked. "It's an old man in a brown cloak and hood, crouching over what looks to be stones of blue."

Thaken focused on the blurred image.

"Yes, I see him. Hopefully, he's the one we seek. The sooner we find the old man, the sooner we can get out of this waste of a place. But we must be careful in our approach."

Thaken did not much care for wizards. They spoke with vague references to information they felt only they were privileged to know, and they brought with them an evil side, that which led to the rise of Dark Wizards. In the south, wizards were most hated. The Sur' Edan believed them to be corrupt, and history supported this belief. Most remembered the tale of the Dark Wizard Rave Morgan and how he corrupted the Nur' Edan and its leader Tyrus Turl. It was Turl's killing of King Aelis that brought the War of Flowers, a most infamous moment in history for the Sur' Edan.

This was the history taught to him by his father who was an elite warrior himself. It was a history that shaped him and defined him, a history of distrust of those wielding magic. It was a legacy passed from father to son, a guiding path for the young man.

"Magic's a natural part of this existence," Thaken's father once said. "Wizards say only they can control it, that only in their hands can magic be properly used. Think about it. How is that fair? Would the Maker devise such unfairness?"

As Thaken grew older, he gained a full understanding of history, and he realized that even the Sur' Edan could be easily perverted, without the influence of a Dark Wizard. The time of House Riorn's Kern Durned and his War of Death was an example of this, a black mark that still haunted his people.

"History tells us that unfairness in life is limitless," he would later tell his father.

As with most of the Sur' Edan, he held to his hatred of wizards. He had no use for them, and he would have been rid of them if he could.

"Remember, if it's a wizard, he's not to be trusted," Thaken told Vosser. "A wizard's character is not fixed; he can be so many people at once. His concerns will be elsewhere, and this bias will bring about blindness to what's right."

As a fellow southman, Vosser understood Thaken's distrust.

"Yes, my liege."

Thaken instructed his warriors to break into four small groups led by Vosser. The groups would approach slowly from behind, north, east, and south, while Thaken alone would approach from the west, from the front.

Not a sound was made by the group as they maneuvered through the marshes. All that could be heard was the wind and rain. Vosser's groups soon took their positions and held, while Thaken continued toward the figure. He slowed his pace as he approached the hooded figure who huddled over warm blue stones.

Thaken stopped. Vosser and the others raised their swords.

"I search for the one who is called the Learned One," said Thaken firmly. "I am to aid his mission."

"I am who you seek," came a soft voice from within the hood.

The figure raised its head. From within the hood an old man's face appeared, bearded, his hair, streaks of grey and pure white flowed from within the shadows and down along his neck. Thaken looked at the old man's face. There was no sign of fear in it, only curiosity, and quiet dignity. He knew that face. He had seen it before, in his mind, a face he alone could imagine, a memory, a moment frozen in his mind.

This is a wizard! he thought.

"Well, I am not as learned as some, which is my misfortune," said the old man.

He slowly pushed back his hair from within the hood and slightly turned his head. A black mark in the shape of a tree revealed itself on the old man's neck.

"I am of the Edainar and you may call me Ras Amon."

* * *

On the Old Marsh Moor, Thaken, his Etinian warriors, and Ras Amon were on their second day together. The rain had ceased and the wind had died down. The marshland was bleak, featureless in many parts, wild, and unchanging, hidden by sheer clouds of mist and fog gently floating over little vales of unceasing runnels. Covering many leagues, this most forbidding and mysterious terrain was thought of as a non-place, a grim territory in which terrible things could happen. This was not a land for most creatures of the Harrow. It offered a thousand deaths and very little in the way of resources. In many places it was too deep with water and reeds, making it difficult to find the few pathways of mud and rock. And as desolate as the Old Marsh Moor was, it was not silent. Sounds began to rise in counterpoint to the rustle of cattails and sawgrass when suddenly there came a low, heartrending howl swelling to a shout. It began again, unrecognizable yet still filled with grief.

At hearing the wail, Ras Amon looked up into the mist.

"Wizard, what was that?" asked Thaken. "What creature would make such a horrible noise?"

"I do not know. It is best to not worry oneself when traveling the Old Marsh Moor. Here, worries only undermine clear thought, and clear thought is what is needed most in such an unforgiving place. If the creature wishes to make itself known to us, it will do so on its terms. Let us continue west, through the Hollow Forest, and then to the dark tower."

The conversation was short and to the point. Since their joining, few words were spoken. Everyone seemed locked in silent sorrow, a dislike of the marshland. Thaken and Vosser quietly kept an eye on Ras Amon and instructed the others to keep their distance from the wizard. Ras Amon sensed this and respected it. These were dark times. He knew that silence was sometimes a cover for concern.

As they continued west, Thaken and the others grew tired and weary of the cold and dampness. They were wet to the skin from traversing the moors through the rain and mist, their clothes clinging to them and rubbing them raw. The Etinians found the marshland smell rank and pungent, a horrible stench that got into their throats where they could taste it. Flies constantly flitted around them, landing on their faces, in their eyes and mouths. To make matters worse, they could not figure out where they were or where they were going, but Ras Amon sensed the correct direction. He and Shaer Thol had traveled the moors many times; they knew the one passage.

They soon came upon an area drier than most and patched with small rock outcroppings with cave-like recesses that provided some shelter.

"So cold. I'm chilled to the bone," sighed Thaken. "Let's stop here and make camp."

Not wanting to light fires, Ras Amon instructed the warriors to collect rocks and stack them in small piles. He then used a little magic and warmed the stones, their cold surfaces glowing a dull blue.

They ate a light meal, some dried meats, and stale bread, and they kept as quiet as possible. Some in the group kept watch while others slept, leaving Ras Amon and Thaken alone, together.

The feeling of solitude weighed heavily on each. Another day or two and they would be near the tower Drar Dukhaar. But first, they would need to pass through the Hollow Forest, a place shrouded in mystery.

"We could make our way south and around the forest, keeping close to its edges," proposed Thaken.

"Evil sometimes avoids the Hollow, but not always. We keep to our plan, through the forest," said Ras Amon. He was adamant. "Once we leave the forest, nearing its edge, we should see the tower. From there, we will hold our position and determine the best course of action. We should not be so exposed."

"Will the Dark Wizard sense your presence as we near the forest's end?"

"Perhaps. I do not know the strength of his powers, nor that of Bentgibber. But we shall know soon enough. I will do my best to mask my magic. For now, we have shelter and warmth from the cold. A good night's rest and in the morning we will be closer to the end of our journey." Ras Amon looked at Thaken and gave a wink. "Traveling where few have gone before provides needed cover."

Thaken agreed, but his brashness and overconfidence left him wary of the plan. He felt something could easily go wrong. He and his men preferred battles and open field combat over such maneuvers. His orders, though, were to follow the wizard's lead, which he would do. But now, and sadly, he realized the truth that he now faced: he knew very little about this place, spoke very little of the ancient tongue, and lacked the experience necessary to face magic.

As he looked into Ras Amon's eyes, something occurred to him. He had not planned to say it and thought it best to hide it. But it just came out.

"I'm different from you. I'd go about things differently. I know when I must learn and when I must adjust. But there's something you should know."

"And what is that?" asked Ras Amon.

"We're Sur' Edan and we don't much like you or your ilk."

Ras Amon warmed his hands over the blue stones.

"I know this. It explains your distance," he said.

"We come by our distrust honestly. History tells us many things."

"History is a strange thing," said Ras Amon. "There are moments, days and weeks, or even years when nothing happens, or nothing seems to happen. Then suddenly, from nowhere, as it were, everything happens all at once. History does not record the small moments. It will not even record this conversation or the past few days. But when we reach the tower and face its evil - then history may take note. Time is fluid. It never stops. But history, history, it stops and only when a moment tells it to. Your beliefs, those which you hold so dearly, are only formed from brief moments, what your history tells you."

"What are you saying? Do you dismiss the history of the Sur' Edan? Do you disregard the tyranny of Turl or the influence of Rave Morgan on Turl?"

"No, not at all. That was a critical moment in history. But like I said, history does not record all moments. Most go unnoticed, unrecorded, dismissed, and disregarded. What I speak of are those moments few know of. Perhaps it is a moment in time when a wizard cures a child's illness. Maybe it is that time when a wizard helps a farmer's barren land produce bountiful crops. Because history does not recall such events, only the child and the child's family, or the farmer and his family, know what happened. They look past the evil of Morgan, past the brutality of Turl. I cannot speak to Morgan, nor will I ever attempt to. At the same time, I do not expect you to speak to the likes of Kern

Durned. History only makes sense when one can see all moments."

Thaken sighed.

"I remember telling my father that history's unfairness was limitless," said Thaken.

"Very true. How did your father respond?"

"He told me I was wrong. He distrusted wizards. He said he had never seen a creature as dangerous as a wizard, with their spells and their secrets."

"Your father was strong-willed. I take it he fought in the Great War."

"He died on the Ronin Plains just before Aerin used the Lia Fail."

"I am sorry," whispered Ras Amon.

"Don't be," snapped Thaken. "It was what he loved. He was a warrior, a leader of men. All my ancestors were warriors. They fought against Stonehelm, against Rile, against Turl. They fought against the Zeph, and yes, they fought with Durned." He lowered his head. "History has its black moments."

"You should be very proud of your heritage, for it has come in a variety of shapes and forms and natures."

"I am."

"Your father's distrust of wizards - did it come from Rave Morgan's corruption of Tyrus Turl?"

"He believed magic corrupts its owner, that it has a power all its own, that it could never be fully controlled. At the extreme, he didn't understand why the Maker would give magic only to what he thought a favored few."

"Favored, eh? Hardly. I did not wish for magic. I did not ask for it. It was simply there, inside me. It was something I could not ignore or deny, something I had to deal with. For me, as with so many others, it was something to conquer. As I matured, I learned it was something I could use as a force for change. But change is never easy. What many do not understand is that magic is a burden for those who possess it."

"Not much of a burden, I'd say," scoffed Thaken.

"So, what is a burden?" asked Ras Amon. "Would you say that something is not a burden if it were lighter, or that it is a burden if it were heavier? No. As long as something is burdening a person, it is a burden. A burden is what you know, not what you have to discover. If you have one, you know it. It is wrong to look inward to see whether you have one. It is something known rather than found, and I, I know magic. It is important to recognize this fact. I am sure you know of your burdens. After all, is not war the greatest of all burdens one can have?"

"War is no burden. As my father would say, it is glory, it is privileged in its endlessness."

"Are you not burdened by the responsibility it forces upon you?"

"And what responsibility is that?"

"The responsibility for the lives of your men?"

"Wizard, you don't understand. My burden is simple - to follow orders. The lives of my men are no burden at all. Let me explain something to you - the greatest warrior is peaceful and strong, calm, focused, and not easily affected by slings to the ego. He understands that the greatest power is time, and with time comes death. He doesn't fear death, he only fears the Maker, and he who fears the Maker has nothing else to fear but life itself. He doesn't fear death, because he's spent his whole life seeing how one dies, awaiting its void. He seeks it and yearns for it. Wizard, war is not a burden, nor is the death it brings."

The two stared at each other for a long moment.

"Your second, the one called Vosser - if he were to perish in battle, would you not feel a burden, the burden of regret?" asked Ras Amon.

"Quite the contrary. I would bask in the glory of his death, his reawakening from this fearful thing we call life. For a warrior, death is but a validation of life, a finite moment, a moment of transition to a different existence. Let me ask you something- what about the Hulnur Istare, the great Warrior Wizards - do they view war as a burden?"

"I am unsure, but I would think, as, with me, their burden is magic. I have said wizards look to use their magic for change, and the Hulnur Istare are no exception. You know the truth of it. The Hulnur Istare was formed by the Edainar to counter the evil power of Rave Morgan during the time of Tyrus Turl. They fought bravely on the battlefield, to preserve all that was good while overturning all that was dark."

"At last!" exclaimed Thaken triumphantly and somewhat sarcastically. "There are wizards I can like!"

Ras Amon smiled and quietly laughed.

"Allow me to ask another question," said Thaken.

"Of course, and what would that be?"

"Has one of the Hulnur Istare ever turned? Has one ever become a Dark Wizard?"

"No. History is clear on this point. Those who have turned to darkness have not been of the warrior caste."

"Why do you suppose that is?"

Ras Amon paused contemplatively, as he seemed to reflect.

"I do not know. I have not given it any thought," he answered.

Thaken became animated.

"Well, I've given it thought, plenty of thought. A warrior's purpose is so very well-defined. It's to defeat the enemy, not merely its army, but its very existence, to cleanse the land of the darkness. The enemy's army is simply a barrier that must be first broken through. The warrior's purpose is to fulfill himself wherever death is thickest. He has no fear. Because of this, darkness cannot consume him, for he knows of it already, differently, in a different sense. There's no appeal, no draw, nothing the darkness can offer that the warrior can want. This is the same even for one of your warrior wizards." Thaken looked at Ras Amon. "Has the darkness ever reached out to you?"

"For those with the burden of magic, we know that darkness patiently awaits in the cracks and folds of everything around us. It silently slips in even during the brightness of the day. It is there when your eyes are closed or when your eyes are open. It does not call for you. It only waits for you to submit to it. And if you do, it will consume your very existence."

"Well, then wizard - you and I have something in common. We both know of darkness."

Ras Amon nodded and said, "So, here we sit after such a long conversation. What more is there left to say, what more questions remain to be asked?"

"None, I suppose."

"Ah, but there is one, one last question that remains."

"And what is that?"

"After all that we have spoken to, do you now have trust in me?"

A slight smile came to Thaken.

"I have trust, but it's only a trust in my warriors," said Thaken. "My orders were to follow your lead, and as much as I may not like that, it's what I must do." A pause, then a serious look came to his face. He struggled. "We've shared much on this dreary evening. I will share one more thought with you. I know of your history. The great Carrick told me. I know why you're here and even though I don't quite understand what you feel or why you act in the way you do; I know that what is now happening must weigh on you. For this I am sorry."

Ras Amon straightened up and looked at Thaken very intently. It was a solemn look. In this grey wasteland of bitter cold, he found a bit of light and warmth in the truthful words of the young man.

He thought of the evil he had brought to the land. A shudder of guilt ran through his bones. He wondered if he would ever be able to make it up to the races; he wondered if he would ever be forgiven.

Darkness. Foulhand.

"Thank you," he said as he looked away from Thaken.

Thaken stretched his arms out and sighed.

"Enough talk for one night. I believe it's time for some rest," he told Ras Amon.

The two wrapped themselves in their cloaks and blankets. They attempted to get some sleep along with those Etinian warriors who were not on watch. Most had a restless night, and while many slept, Ras Amon's mind was filled with agonizing pain: guilt and shame. Long had he attempted to understand the emotions that swamped him. But understanding was fleeting, like trying to embrace the wind.

He closed his eyes to the darkness of a dream, a dream haunted by death. He saw a blurred, greyish image of Foulhand moving about piles of faceless dead. There was a flash of pale skin and enormous eyes, the anguished image of the apparition. The image flared in his mind. He cried out, and tried to run, but it was too late. Foulhand leaped into the air and was on top of him, slamming into his shoulders, gripping him with dark magic.

"You cannot run from this Learned One," the image of Foulhand spoke in a mocking tone. "That's what you want to do, though, that's what all those of the Edainar want to do - run! But you cannot run, you cannot hide from what you've created." Foulhand brought his face next to Ras Amon's with a wide grin. "You cannot hide from somebody who has eyes. Oh, you can hide from yourself, and you can hide from the world. But you cannot hide from somebody who has come to know what clarity is, what perception is. For such a man, you are but on the surface."

Ras Amon tried to shout, but Foulhand clamped a hand over his mouth. He was lost in silence. He clenched his eyes tighter. As he did, he invited the image of his mentor to come to him. It was an image of the aged face of the wizard Windainn. His throat swelled in emotion and a single tear slowly formed in his eye and rolled down the side of his face. The image of Windainn smiled, then faded. All that remained was the darkness.

Darkness. Foulhand.

Rather than succumbing to the darkness, Ras Amon sought a different way out. He sought relief in a forbidden attraction that electrified his senses, as it always had - a craving so seductive he could only follow where he was led, puppet-like and numb. Like a crazed animal, in his mind, he succumbed to the craving for relief, offering no resistance. Slowly, he whispered the spell that gently pushed the pain from his mind. Over and over again, he whispered the words with a steady rhythm, shivering as the spell took hold of him. It was a euphoric feeling, a feeling of exaltation so wonderful he could not move. But he knew there was something strange about it, something wrong about it.

As he lay motionless in his ecstasy, drifting from his pain to sleep, within the darkness of the dark tower Drar Dukhaar, an eye, round and white, bloodshot, and disturbed, slowly opened. It was Bentgibber. The hideous creature snarled, choking on his drool. Something had jarred him from his rest. He recognized what it was. He had sensed the use of a forbidden spell.

The miscreant closed his eyes, and he was able to doze off again, though it was to formless dreams in which black shapes swarmed around his sleeping body and whispered ancient words into his ears. A most wicked smile came to his distorted face.

The one who uses Amin Tarn nears.

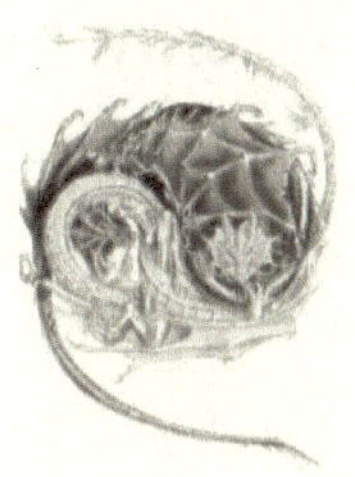

CHAPTER 5
THE HUNTRESS OF THE TAR SHOR

JUST NORTH OF THE southernmost end of the Draaklel' Daan defile was the forest called Gagdash. The forest stretched in massive swells from the plains of the North Eldor to the steep mountainside of the defile, blanketing the craggy slopes for as far as the eyes could see. It was a dark forest, shrouded in mist, green and dense with tall, straight trees that seemed to stretch to the stars. Gagdash was a dim underworld that stood like a black curtain of mystery. Few entered the thicket for fear of becoming lost and wandering until they were released by death. Yet, the forest teemed with life as this was the home of the exiled Tar Shor, the fifth guild of the Ra Cath, the Guild of Witches; for Gagdash was a sanctuary for the Tar Shor and its leader Shia Alia Ce' Tu, known as the Huntress.

Within the mountains of the defile, three female cats journeyed. They had run through the steep peaks for most of the day and were tired, especially the oldest of the three. In the distance, they could see Gagdash before them, perhaps a league away, but night had fallen, and a storm was beginning to howl from the east.

"Huntress, you are weary. Using your power to help the elven army has taken its toll on you. Let us take shelter here," said one of the cats. "We can take refuge high up into the mountains, amongst some of the rocks and within the crevices."

"No." said the Huntress, panting hard, her eyes half shut. She had a nervous look about her. "We must . . . we must get to the forest . . ."

"But Huntress," implored the third cat, "you are weak, and we worry about the Balor cats here."

The grey-striped Huntress attempted to gather strength.

"War is upon the land. The Balor scout for brood. I sense trouble and fear. We must not fear the Balor. It is the brood we must avoid. My power cannot fall into their hands. We must get to the forest and the mountain."

The two younger cats understood. They looked upon the weakened Huntress and saw a quiet determination and purpose in her green eyes. She possessed a great spirit, that was the source of her magnetism, which drew others to her. It was a spirit that seemed to radiate life and joy and hope, perhaps imposing to some, but one in whose presence one felt quickly at ease. Hers was a life of purpose and dedication to the Tar Shor, their existence, and one day their return to Dagda. But there was frailty there, too. The mind and spirit were strong, but the body was weakening under the weight of the green light's power. The years of duty bore down on the Huntress and it was beginning to show physically.

"Please, let me take the burden from you and put it on my spirit," a high-priestess once beseeched the Huntress.

"It is not mine to give," the Huntress told her. "The En' Calin Kalina is not in the power of the Ra Cath to grant, but to those for whom it is prepared by the I' Ra Heru."

She knew the burden was hers and hers alone until the I' Ra Heru would grant it to another.

It was then, just as a crackle of lightning brightened the sky followed by a thunderous boom that from the distance the snap of a twig was heard. The younger cats spun around as the Huntress rested, but they could see nothing. Another snap of a twig and a flash of lightning revealed two Balor cats, both tabby in color. They lurked below in the brush, their senses keen. As the Balor cats drew closer, the female cats became aware of their heavy breathing, and the creak of their tense bones. Their instincts took hold and their inner voice called to them.

Steady now. Stay low. Quiet.

The Balor cats approached slowly sniffing the air then suddenly stopped. They crouched on their short back legs. Their heavy shoulders twitched. Then the lead cat burst out of the brush running but a few yards in front of where the Tar Shor hid. He leaped into the darkness and onto a firbolg that was lurking nearby. The evil, dark-skinned evil creature stood and roared bent legs and arms, and hunched back, flailing about. The second Balor cat followed, and the attack was on.

The Balor cats were relentless in their assault moving quickly about the massive firbolg's body, avoiding swipes from its massive hands. The cats tore at it ripping off chunks of the evil creature's flesh and muscle and tissue. As the firbolg dropped to its knees under the onslaught the Tar Shor cats decided to make their move.

"Our opportunity has come," said the Huntress with urgency as she looked to the dark forest ahead.

The Tar Shor cats sprang away, winding in and out of the brush like smoke racing for the Gagdash. Faster and faster they ran, darting this way and that until reaching the forest and vanishing into the overgrown darkness.

The woodland was so dark at night that one could not see a tree trunk inches away from one's face. The Tar Shor cats, on the other hand, knew their way around. They were familiar with every shade of darkness and every sound. They were one with the forest, both physically and spiritually, since when they were in it, they felt at home and were instantly re-energized.

Other Tar Shor cats joined the three, running, watching, and protecting. They swiftly traveled to the mountain which rose high above the forest. They ran up the mountainside where they came to a well-hidden cave entrance hidden under an overhanging ledge with a small crawl space.

The cats entered the cave and into a chamber room with irregular rock walls, pitted and creviced, with several tunnel openings of varying shapes and sizes. The chamber was deceiving for many of the openings drilled deep into the mountain but led nowhere. But some of the openings and crevices led deep within the mountain and to a sanctuary. Knowing the ruse, the cats ran around and around the chamber faster and faster, driving dust into the air, and then one by one disappeared through the many cracks within the rock wall. When the dust settled the cats had vanished, but only from the chamber.

Now, deep within the mountain, the cats were crawling down small, cramped, long corridors that twisted through the rock and ended into a massive circular hall they called Zheu Zhullus. The great hall was almost as tall as the mountain itself and in its center blazed a large fire. The flames whirled and crackled aloft, picking out the faces of thousands of Tar Shor within restless shadows, as they sat upon ledges that jutted out randomly.

The Huntress found her place near the fire surrounded by several of her high-priestesses. She was glad to be in her sanctuary, safe, and hidden from the dangers of the Harrow. Even amongst the throngs of Tar Shor felines, her sanctuary seemed different somehow - empty and desolate. She realized that soon she and her followers would need to leave the sanctuary and become one with the Harrow.

She curled herself, surrounded by her high-priestesses

"My Huntress, why did you venture out to assist the elven army?" asked one of the high-priestesses. "I know it was many days ago. But why?"

The Huntress, aged, and weary from her journey hesitated and gathered the strength to respond.

"The Elf-King once granted me a favor," she said, almost gasping for air. "It was a favor which gave me hope, which gave all of us hope. What I did today was an act of gratitude for his past actions. I owe him this much and more. We owe him this and much more."

"Huntress, we do not challenge your motive, other than to trust in your words," another high-priestess declared.

"By your life, no evil shall ever harm us," the high-priestesses said in unison, like a chorus.

"Then trust in these words," said the Huntress with conviction. "Great turmoil is upon the land. It is darkness greater than any darkness in our history. It may enter our black forest. There is much to do. Tell all to prepare."

The words of the Huntress reverberated inside each high-priestess. They felt the deep timbre of her voice resonate to their very core. Each knew that every word the huntress spoke was true, for they also felt the danger.

"By your life, no evil shall ever harm us." The chant was strongly made.

The Huntress looked upon each of the high-priestesses, one by one, and then through the flickering shadows, she looked upon the many faces of her followers. A great sense of purpose and determination came upon her and she began to purr. Her destiny and that of the Tar Shor lit before her like a great beacon. Sensing the moment, the other cats began to cuddle about her preening her, providing her with warmth and strength. Soon, the great mountain hall roared with the sound of purr, and the Gagdash trembled under the might of the Tar Shor.

* * *

As the night wore on the Huntress slept restlessly. She slept in the bright light of the fire, surrounded by her high-priestesses. Dreams came and went within her, as they always had, dark or light, with distinction, flashes of events; for her dreams foretold the future. This night they were dreams of strange images within shadows, fleeting moments of great battles and death, of many ships on the sea, and of a young female cat with large, round eyes, deep green, emerging from the tree. Then there came images of Bentgibber, pale and twisted evil, crawling about the library within the Aina Dur, and sounds of his gurgling voice. Most frightening were the shadowy images of Tar Shor felines fighting, hurting, destroying, and killing each other.

An unknown future, the thought rang in her mind.

She woke often, her paws clenched in a tight curl and her nerves jumping, but there was always a high-priestess there for her, caring and watching over her.

"Huntress, what do you see?" whispered a high-priestess, the one called Shamma.

She was a young cat whose white fur was long and straight, with a light brown at the very end. The cat had deep black eyes and a puffy tail. She was the Laurn Cora, the grand high-priestess, and was closest to the Huntress.

Shamma gently licked the head of the Huntress.

"Is it Katzhu Pu?" she asked. "Did you see it in your dreams? Are we to return to the golden citadel?"

The Huntress was tired.

"No. In my life, I shall never again see the golden spires," she told Shamma, her words drawn out and slow. "The Si Jhys will not accept a female with power. But listen to me. The I' Ra Heru will take me from this place. Do not despair. I have seen another. Yes, another with deep green eyes. She will come from the Aina Dur and have within her the En' Calin Kalina. Shamma, you must be there to greet her. I have seen this and more."

Shamma was saddened by what she heard.

"My Huntress, there cannot be another. There can only be you."

"We are all in the spirit of the I' Ra Heru and what he determines to be best. It is only when we are in his spirit that darkness cannot touch or harm us." The Huntress smiled at Shamma. "You must submit to his will patiently and walk the path he sets forth, for it is he who determines our future moments. Do not be saddened on this day. Rejoicing in the I' Ra Heru must be your strength."

But Shamma's voice was still saddened.

"I do not understand. What will happen to you?" she asked.

"We are not forever, for we were born. We have not always existed, and we all eventually return to that first state. This is our teaching. You know this. There will be others after me." The Huntress looked into Shamma's eyes. "And there will be others after you. Moments are fleeting, as is our existence."

In her sorrow, Shamma was confused but accepted what she was told.

"I do not understand but know I must. When will the other arrive? How will I know to meet her?" asked

Shamma, barely able to speak the words and closing her eyes tightly to hold back her tears.

"You will know . . . you will know," said the Huntress smiling. She licked Shammas forehead. "But I must tell you one more thing. I have also seen a great war and evil as ripe as a harvest field. It is as I said earlier, a great darkness that will spread over the land. But great unrest will also come to the Tar Shor. Such will be a burden to you." She began to purr. "Hush now. We must sleep and gather strength for there is much to be done. Tomorrow I will depart on a journey, alone. You must not follow me. You must remain here, to tend to the others."

Shamma wanted to question the Huntress about the journey she now spoke of. But at that moment she felt a sense of finality to what the Huntress had said and decided it was best to remain silent. Her eyes blurred with tears. Sadness overcame her. She hugged the Huntress, feeling her sweet breath on her fur. The Huntress then closed her eyes.

"Shia Alia, mother of all, by your life, no evil shall ever harm us," whispered Shamma ever so tenderly as the Huntress fell asleep in her paws.

* * *

During the night more dreams came to Shia Alia Ce' Tu, frightening dreams of light and of darkness that flashed within her mind. It was as if she was running through a forest, traveling down pathways impassable, scurrying to find another pathway only to again have her journey slowed by another impasse. In time the dreams fled her, but soon became overshadowed by another vision, a vision much darker and deadlier than those before. She found herself within Drar Druul, the great mountain of fire, the 'Kish Taurn in the feline tongue, in a place where there was no light.

The darkness was thick; it was total and with a wintery cold crispness; she could see nothing ahead and nothing behind her. It began to press on her, and she found it difficult to breathe. Then, in the darkness, she could hear a sound. At first, it was faint, but it grew in intensity. She could hear the wheezing of a large beast, of unknown name and form, its breath heavy on its lips with the smell of rot and decay. Frightened, she turned and extended her paws, seeking the touch of a rock wall, a way she could escape the darkness. But there was none, only the bitter cold of emptiness. She stopped and closed her eyes and took a deep breath, attempting to calm herself when within her mind there came a whisper, ever so soft and slight, the name of the beast.

Dor Gordur.

It was a name she had not heard before, and its sound was terrifying. Again, and again, the name rang through her mind.

Dor Gordur. Dor Gordur. Dor Gordur.

The light grey cat with dark grey stripes crouched and pulled back her ears. She hissed; her instincts served her well for the great mountain trembled as within the frozen darkness the beast lifted itself high within its rock realm. She could feel the movement but could not make out the beast's form until it opened its eyes, and a piercing yellow light filled the place.

"Why do you awaken me?" asked the monster with a voice deep and full of venom.

She gave another hiss, this time stronger but instead found herself within Zheu Zhullus and cradled in Shamma's paws. The dream had ended.

I know what I must do, she thought.

But back within the blackness of the great Drar Druul, and sensing the presence gone, the mighty beast closed its eyes and returned to its sleep.

A dreamer, a sleeping fool, the creature thought.

* * *

Within the nighttime darkness of Gagdash, the black cat called Nott emerged, walking into a small clearing. She could hear the wind whistling through the dense trees. It was cool as it blew through her fur. She lifted her nose and sniffed the air. The weather was starting to change. This was the time when the sun would begin to ease more and more to the north, behind the Old Hills. The days would grow shorter and the nights longer and colder. For the Ra Cath, this was Hrive Findl, that time when the feline fur thickened, when cold winds rushed from the north with increasing frequency, and in some places when snow would fall.

A sudden gust of wind raged briefly. It brought a chill to her. She looked over the area and her ears perked, turning from side to side listening for any sound. Her head was up, nostrils flared, this time testing the wind for the scent of the Balor. But there was no sound and no defining odor in the air. Ease came over her. The place was secured.

She turned back to the darkness of the surrounding forest.

"It's safe," she called out.

A smallish cat, beige in color, with subtle stripes appeared.

"I don't like the thought of us sneaking around," said the small cat.

Nott shook her head.

"Tessia, we're not sneaking around. We're simply enjoying a nice stroll on a cool night."

"Call it what you'd like to call it, but it still doesn't make me feel any better about what we're doing."

"And what are we doing?"

"You know exactly what we're doing."

"Tessia, how many times have I told you? She's old and she's weak. Soon she'll be feeble and lame. I'm not the only one who talks about this in the open."

"In the open! Do you call this in the open? It's night and we're in the middle of Gagdash, more than two leagues from the warmth of Zheu Zhullus. I wouldn't call this in the open."

"You must stop this. Don't you understand what has happened to us? Every day we live in fear. Few of us venture from Gagdash, and clearly, we'll never see the golden city. We're prisoners here and I don't intend to stay caught for the rest of my life."

Tessia sighed and closed her eyes. There was some truth in Nott's words. But the small cat was torn up inside, torn between loyalty and love she felt for the Huntress and the torrent of despair that filled her thoughts and crowded her mind.

"We're Tar Shor. We're N'alaquel, discarded by the Si Jhys," she told Nott pointedly. "Where are we to go? The Huntress brought us to Gagdash. We are safe here."

"Are we? Are we safe? You've seen the dark clouds. You've heard the rumors, the tales of evil coming from the east." Nott approached Tessia and nuzzled her face. "I understand your devotion to her. I do. But the time has come to take responsibility for our destiny. We can't just believe and have faith in another cat, even if that other cat has the stability and wisdom of the I' Ra Heru. We must take control of our future, or it will take control of us."

"But the En' Calin Kalina, her power, it protects us."

"In her weakening state, it's becoming more difficult for her to use the power. Everyone knows this. Every priestess talks about it. Her time is ending."

"But if this is true, the power of the green light, that within Zheu Zhullus, will transfer to the next. It's how it should be. We must have faith. Are you saying we should simply abandon our faith?"

"Like you said, we are N'alaquel. The faith you speak of is elusive. It has become diluted over time. There's no use in fondly clinging with desperate devotion to its dissolving form. Abandon our faith? No. Correct it? Yes. We must begin to build faith in one another, in a new life, a life outside the dark forested walls of Gagdash. Are we to have the Guilds solely control the faith of the Ra Cath? Why do we not have a gilded throne in the Kaer Taraedar? Are we not part of the I' Ra Heru?"

"You're talking about changing our world."

"It's not about changing our world. It's about embracing the I' Ra Heru and letting him change us so that we see and approach this world differently. When we recognize our fullness with the I' Ra Heru, that we're his children, no different than those of the Guilds, then we're no longer driven to try to force the world to recognize us and offer life to us. It will recognize us, and we will prevail over the evils we see in this world right now. We will do that."

Tessia looked into Nott's eyes. There was a depth and calmness there, a calmness she could not explain.

"I may disagree and may challenge your words, but we're only two. Isn't yours a hopeless dream?"

"Ah, but with hopelessness comes strength, and sometimes, strength from others."

Nott gave a devious smile and let out a large meow. The dark forest floor, the tangle of fallen branches, and debris seemed to move. Slowly and cautiously, one by one, cats appeared, entering the clearing. There were hundreds of them. To Tessia's surprise, she now knew there were many, many more within the Tar Shor who believed as Nott did.

She was worried by the calmness of her tone. She could not understand how Nott could so easily lose her faith in the Huntress. An uneasiness came to her as the others began to circle, listening to Nott. There was a change in the black cat's tone. It was harsher, more biting, and darker. She spoke of removing each high-priestess and even the Huntress. Her words were of conspiracy and disguised meaning.

At one point Nott told the group, "Let's join in an understanding that freedom can only come to us through the swift removal of those who enslave us in this forest. I only wish there was another path, but I see none. Freedom comes when those oppressors are diminished."

Tessia was disgusted by what she heard. She slowly made her way into the crowd to blend in, then she disappeared quietly into the darkness of the forest, returning to Zheu Zhullus.

The problem is that with hopelessness comes anger, despair, or total resignation, she thought.

Inside the great hall, she made her way to a ledge where there was some room and nestled in with one turn and a wriggle. Below she could see the Huntress in her place near the fire surrounded by her high-priestesses. The cats were peacefully asleep, only the sound of a soft purr rhythmically rolled through the mountain.

Strangely, Shamma looked up at her. She met Shamma's look evenly until the high-priestess slowly closed her eyes, returning to sleep.

A test of one's faith creates doubt about it, thought Tessia. *Sometimes, instead of seeking answers, it's better to look inside and take stock of one's true intent.*

She eventually was able to sleep, and a vision of the Huntress came to her.

By your life, no evil shall ever harm us.

* * *

As the morning broke, the Huntress awoke. She cleaned herself and left the great hall and Gagdash. No one had seen her leave. As she left the dark forest's edge, the view opened to the Aldpine River and the mouth of the Draaklel' Daan. She could smell what remained of the great battle, the smell of rot and death. She continued to make her way south, running from one hiding spot to another, brush, a dry hole, and a pile of leaves. Her senses were keen and acute, ever-alert. She heard crickets, the distant howl of a Fenri, and from above, the call of a raven.

I must travel carefully; I will not falter.

She lifted her nose and lightly sniffed the air. She seemed to catch a trace of a scent, the scent she was looking for.

Elves.

CHAPTER 6
THE SAI MAS

AT THE NORTHERN REACHES of the Old Hills lay the realm of the dwarves called Mortha Vale, or Alaithlos in the old tongue. The kingdom was an expansive landmass of mountainous terrain and fertile valleys, and within the wide and jagged peaks was the heavily fortified city of Volemill. The sprawling city was nestled in the mountains that served as a natural, near-impregnable fortress few pursuers dared to enter. For ages, the dwarves of Volemill had known only peace and prosperity, and the city was generally considered to be one of the most advanced in the Harrow.

Travelers to the grand city had to first pass through a narrow gorge, where two great rocks stood on either side; great pillars of stone chiseled from the mountainside, sheer and ominous they stood, grey figures, silent and threatening. The structures were known as the Bagnar Pelaithis and each was carved in the likeness of a mighty dwarf paragon. To the west was the monument to Paragon Boidac Aldril, while to the east was the monument to Paragon Driado Aldril. Each figure sat upon a throne wearing an iron crown, with an axe in the right hand, the left hand a fist placed over the heart. At first, the imposing statues would strike fear into the hearts of any traveler, and for good reason. They stood as silent sentinels, with a foreboding stare of power and eyes that seemed to follow one as one moved. They were meant to be a deterrent for any enemy considering an attack upon the dwarven realm, and their might and majesty demonstrated the regal strength of the dwarven race who built them.

Once beyond the monuments, travelers would make their way into the deep gorge, the walls of which were so close that in some places they could reach out and touch them. The road passed beneath towering rock arches, some natural and some cut through living rock by dwarf stonemasons. It meandered through dark tunnels and over steep-walled streams, and in places, small, beautiful wildflowers blossomed. Eventually, travelers would reach the end of the gorge and come upon Volemill.

The city was a fortress, a place of great strength, curiously unsightly but massive. It was embraced by a great wall of black iron. All along the wall were defensive posts, lookouts, and iron towers that reached as high as the mountains. The vast city which stretched along the valley and up the sides of the soaring mountains appeared to be made of small square towers of stone and rock, tiered in fortified sections. It contained plazas and residential areas, and large street markets, and in places there rose great rock stacks that vented steam and smoke from underground mines and forges deep, blanketing the city with a sulfur mist. To the north along the mountainside were farming terraces linked by steps and supplied with water from mountain streams. It was a breathtaking sight, shrouded in the darkness of night.

Glaeynd, flanked by Thurir, members of his pack, and Fairfax, stood atop a hill overlooking the pass. It was shrouded in the darkness of night, a breathtaking sight. They could see the surrounding valley spread out before them, the majesty of the towering stone sculptures, and the massive city held by the mountains.

"Incredible," gasped Glaeynd as she looked over the landscape before her.

"Indeed, you now gaze upon the dwarven realm of Mortha Vale," said Fairfax, "one of the most revered strongholds in the entire known world. Its great protectors, the magnificent Bagnar Pelaithis, were crafted over a millennium by dwarf master stonemasons."

"It is true what they say about the dwarves of Mortha Vale," she said.

"And what is that?" asked Fairfax.

"They are renowned for their mining skill, as well as their superior metal-working," she said. "Their fortifications are essential to their survival and wealth."

"They are expert miners and craftsmen," said Fairfax. "Few people can match the quality of their weapons and armor. They are a proud and noble people and set a fine example of steadfastness and consistency for the other races. But they are generally emotional beings. If you upset them, they will get angry and seek retribution. If you make them laugh, they will smile and feel better. If you make them sad, they will cry and feel worse. But I am afraid something is amiss with what we see before us."

"What do you mean?" asked Glaeynd.

He spoke with worry in his voice, saying, "Curious. There is so much darkness about the city. Usually, at night, it would be illuminated by the thousands of covered lights, lamps, and lanterns of all imaginable shapes hung throughout the city. So many lights that even the valley and surrounding mountains would seem ablaze in a soft, white glow. But strangely, on this night, it seems the giant Bagnar Pelaithis watch over a kingdom of dwarves that lay eerily silent and dark."

Thurir lifted his nose and sniffed delicately.

"There are many scents," he whispered. "Strange scents. There is the smell of dwarf and a bit of magic in the air. But also fire and heat – the smell of forges far away."

His nose continued to sniff and wrinkle.

"Not strange at all, my friend," said Fairfax. "We do not have much time. Let us venture to the great wall."

"But this may be a trap," said Glaeynd. "The city appears dead."

For the moment, they stood quiet and solemn. From the north, they could see storm clouds surging down across the shoulders of the great mountains and the wind freshening. Thunder began to roll and mutter overhead. The clouds then opened and brought a deluge of slashing rain.

Fairfax turned to Glaeynd with a twinkle in his eye and a smile.

"Some things are not always what they appear to be, young one," he said. He turned from her and looked up into the rain, his face soaked along with his clothes. "We must take shelter. The night brings with it many evils. Trust me - we must be on our way to the city. Our hopes rest with meeting the Paragon. Hopefully, he will aid our journey."

They trusted Fairfax, so they quickly made their way through the pass until they stood before the great black iron wall. In places, it was pitted and badly rusted, but strong and thick, and well-formed. Its massive gates were closed and locked, and there were no dwarf guards about the posts and lookouts.

"How do we get in?" asked Glaeynd.

"I know of a way," said Fairfax.

They followed the wall for some time into the darkness, Fairfax keeping a hand on the cold iron until he felt a small door hidden within a crest of rocks. As he went to use a small bit of magic to open the door, a gust of wind swirled, and the door blew open a crack. Warm, damp, earthy air rushed at them.

"It seems the storm looks to aid our journey," joked Fairfax.

When they made their way through the door, yet another gust of wind came and blew it shut behind them, and a bolt clanged. They were on the dark and empty streets of Volemill. The buildings were shuttered and there were no dwarfs about. Fairfax raised his hand. A small fireball flared up over them. It was dim but provided enough light to help him lead them through the twisted streets.

In haste and through the stinging rain, they came upon a small iron building whose windows were shuttered. Over the door were the words En' Nahrat.

"What is this place?" asked Glaeynd.

"It is a gathering place," said Fairfax opening the door. "In today's tongue, it is called *The Box*. Quickly now, let us get out of the rain."

Glaeynd closed the door behind them as they entered the building. The place was deserted and in shambles, with empty glasses of mead everywhere, cloth napkins, and nuts and grains scattered over the tables and floor. Thunder roared overhead, rattling the flooring, and the pelting sound of rain on the metal roof, like pebbles being dropped by a giant, echoed through the hollow building.

"Dry but chilly," said Glaeynd with a shiver.

Fairfax magicked a fireball and threw it into a fireplace at the far end of the room. There was a burst of flames and in an instant, a fire roared and blazed. The room was suddenly filled with shadows and warmth.

Fairfax sat at a table near the fireplace. Glaeynd sat next to him while Thurir and his pack huddled near the fire. Everyone was quiet as they rested from a long journey, that is until Fairfax looked around the room inquisitively. He sensed a presence, unseen.

"Who is here?" asked Fairfax. "Make yourself known to us."

"Wizard, this place is empty," said a weary Thurir. "The whole city is empty."

"Is it you Bofut Highborn?" Fairfax called out to the emptiness, ignoring Thurir. "Bofut, show yourself."

Glaeynd was concerned with his behavior.

"Fairfax you are fatigued. Rest now. Thurir and I will split the watch while you sleep."

"Fatigued? Perhaps. But you do not understand," he chuckled. "There is magic here, and we are not alone."

"Magic? Dwarves have no magic, and we are the only ones here. Just look around," said Glaeynd.

"Ah, but dwarves do have magic, rudimentary mind you, but magic, nonetheless. Even our Fenri friends sensed it. Like many creatures of the Harrow, dwarves tend to be careful in their use of spells and incantations. They view magic as more of a problem, believing in using it to only achieve the most basic of needs, not wants, and only when it is absolutely necessary."

Glaeynd smiled at him.

"My friend, we are alone here," she told him. "There is no one here but us. This place and the city are empty. I am afraid our quest to speak with the Paragon may be lost."

He stroked his long beard and raised a hand. Using some magic, he brought a soft white glow to the room. Within the radiance, a faint image began to come into view. Slowly a dwarf appeared, shadowy, like a ghost, sitting near Fairfax. He was a squat man, wearing a hooded outfit, wide, flat boots, dark brown leather pants, and a shirt. Across his back hung an axe, ornate, and nearly as big as him. Fairfax recognized him.

"Ah, Bofut Highborn. There you are," said Fairfax, "within the magical shadows. I knew I would smoke you out."

"Well, if it isn't Mirandell. Come at long last to visit. But why now? Why during such dark times?" asked the shadowy dwarf.

"Bofut Highborn, indeed it has been a long time and yes, dark times are upon us all," said Fairfax. "But I am not here to make small talk with you. No. I am here to see the Paragon. Please inform him that it is with great urgency that I wish to take counsel with him."

"Why would you need to take counsel with the Paragon?" asked Highborn. He paused then answered his question, "Ah, yes, but of course. It is a favor you wish to ask. You are one to always ask for favors. What is it you wish to ask of him this time, Mirandell?"

Fairfax was irked by the question but managed a smile.

"That is between the Paragon and me. Now, please – let us not waste any more time. As I said, I do not wish to talk with you. Please inform the Paragon that I need to speak with him."

But the dwarf held steadfastly. He was relentless.

"It's always something with you wizards, is it not? Tell me what you seek?" asked Highborn.

Fairfax thought then started to laugh. This infuriated Highborn.

"What do you find so funny?" he asked.

"I find your unremitting, constant, incessant, never-ending, and interminable nosiness to suddenly be quite amusing," said Fairfax. "So, to quench your inquisitive thirst, I will tell you exactly why I wish to speak with the Paragon. We wish to free the Fenri from the darkness. The Sai Mas would be most helpful."

His response enraged the dwarf. He pointed at Fairfax in anger.

"As I thought! The Paragon has already given you the banner of the Axe and Roundthaler has joined with Carrick. You ask for too much and do not appreciate that which has already been given. Insolence! Pure insolence! You do not know what you ask for, wizard."

"Does the Paragon not know what is happening?" asked a determined Fairfax.

Highborn pursed his lips in anger.

"He knows exactly what plagues the land. The east seethes with darkness and evil intent. Storms rage in the sky and the ground trembles from brood marching to war. The Paragon has prepared for this, and he is with his people deep within the mines. His priority is the protection of his people, as it should be."

Highborn was dismissive of Fairfax. But Fairfax would have none of it.

"Ah, so the great dwarf Paragon hides like a child!" smirked Fairfax.

Highborn stood and flung his mighty axe forward in a menacing manner, his image flickering in and out.

"Do not disrespect the Paragon!" burst Highborn's words of anger. "You do not know that of which you speak. The Paragon has used magic to protect the dwarf race. He does not hide. He does what he must to protect his people! You and your kind are fools! You come here to insult the Paragon and then have the boldness to ask for the Sai Mas! How grand of you wizard, how grand indeed!"

"Bofut, let me ask you this – what if the war is lost?" asked Fairfax, his voice calm. A confused look came to the dwarf. Fairfax continued, "You seem somewhat bewildered at my question. So, allow me to repeat it for you - what if the war is lost? Then what? What will the great Paragon and dwarf race do?"

Highborn seemed stunned by the wizard's words. He again swung his axe.

"We would emerge from the mines and fight! We would fight! And if the land becomes a sea of our blood, and the low places become hills of bodies, and even if the sky rains down mountainous rocks, no enemy will ever see our backs! We would spill blood as we have done before! As we speak, our forges glow, our hammers ring beating iron into shields and swords and axes. We will fight to the last of us falls on the battlefield."

"And with that bitter end may very well come the end of the dwarf race," said Fairfax in a softened approach. "My good friend, do you not see the pathway? Give me the Sai Mas to help the Fenri, and when I am done, I will do my best to protect the great dwarf race. It is a small price to pay for the greater good. All races must help each other if we are to survive."

Highborn returned to his chair leaning forward on his axe. He sat quietly, pondering the wizard's words, looking at the others in the room. He then gave a deep sigh.

"I shall see what I can do," he said with a sigh of resignation. "I shall see what I can do."

His words seemed to linger as his image slowly vanished.

"We can only hope now," said Fairfax almost exhausted with the conversation and his emotion.

"Funny creature," said Glaeynd.

"Indeed, but he is a wise and most trusted adviser to the Paragon," said Fairfax. "He is simply set in his ways, as most dwarves are."

"What's the Sai Mas?" asked Thurir.

"It is a very precious stone, one with great powers that the Paragon has hidden for many years. Few know of its existence."

A moment of clarity struck Glaeynd.

"It is part of the Fail stone isn't it, Fairfax?" she asked.

"I will not speak of its origins, young one," said Fairfax. "Yet, it seems that it is of no matter; for if the Paragon does not help us, we cannot help him or his people."

They sat in silence, waiting for a response. They were all listening intently, for any sound other than the rain on the metal roof. No one had said anything in a while. It was a heavy silence when suddenly the room began to quake ever so slightly, and a pale grey mist filled the place. Within the mist, a shimmering glow formed, as a strange image slowly took shape in front of them. As the glow became brighter, the strange vision became clear. They could see a figure much like Bofut Highborn, a dwarf, but older, and wearing an iron crown, sitting upon a metal throne, the back of which appeared like a massive double-bladed axe. At his feet lay a mighty axe of bronze, sharp on both sides. It could only be the Paragon, Sendoic Aldril.

Fairfax stood and steadied himself with his staff.

"Great Paragon, we are honored by your presence," he said with a bow.

"Mirandell, it is so good to see you again. I am told you had an exchange of words with poor Bofut," smiled the Paragon.

"Exchange of words?" said Fairfax with a slight hesitated in thought. "Hmm . . . now let me see . . . well, I suppose you could say that. Words were indeed exchanged, but I must attest they were exchanged most respectfully. Of this, I can assure you."

The Paragon gave a bellowing laugh.

"You? Respectful of Bofut? It seems poor Bofut is no longer sport for the sage wizard, is he now?"

Fairfax again bowed.

"Paragon, my good Bofut always provides a challenge, but perhaps not as much of a challenge as in years past."

"Ah, Mirandell you are most gracious. As much as Bofut may sometimes be stubborn in his ways, and shall we say, prickly, he remains a faithful and loyal servant to his Paragon." The dwarf paused. He looked past the wizard and at Glaeynd, Thurir, and the many Fenri in the room. "I see you travel with a Lady of Mistmere and Fenri royalty. You are in good company. I am honored by your presence. I want to thank you for choosing to travel to Mortha. It has been a long time since such distinguished guests have graced this realm. I know it has been a lonely journey thus far. I am afraid that it is only the beginning of a much longer journey. You are all welcome. I will summon a great feast to be brought to you at once, with some fine ale, of course. You may spend the night, and in the morning, a hearty breakfast shall await."

"Paragon, you are most kind," said Fairfax with a slight nod. "We will not task your hospitality."

The Paragon returned the nod in an equally knowing way.

"Now, as it regards your request, as told to me by Bofut – word has reached me that you have taken counsel with the Si Jhys," said the Paragon. "It is their guidance that has brought you here today. I have met with the Elders and as you can well imagine, there is great concern over the transfer of the Sai Mas to a wizard. As you most certainly know, the Elders are naturally distrustful and fearful of wizards, and well, for that matter, anything that presents change to what is. Our ways must be preserved at all costs, or otherwise, where will we be as a race. I have reassured them that I have no desire to change our way of life and that I will work hard to preserve it. But it is difficult, especially in such dark times. A Paragon is given a great responsibility, and one that always requires great thought."

"I understand the concern, but I must also remain faithful to my calling," said Fairfax.

"And your calling is a noble one, but it can be a dark one too. It is a calling that requires great sacrifices. I know that you have been faithful to your calling thus far, but you will have to make even greater sacrifices in the future." The Paragon leaned forward against his axe. "There is so much that is unknown about the Sai Mas and there is a fear that if you can harness its power, even with the best of intentions, you may suffer unimaginable consequences. If the Sai Mas is as powerful as you and the Elders believe, when used, the whole of the Harrow will know of its master, its location. Worse yet, it is believed the stone may corrupt the one who holds it, who uses it. Mirandell, it could change you, transform you into a Dark Wizard. As a Dark Wizard, you would surely be a most formidable opponent. This is a risk we could ill afford. I am not sure the path you seek is a wise one."

Silence came over the room. Fairfax stroked his long beard while the Paragon sat upon his throne in quiet contemplation. The Paragon had spoken most gently and persuasively, but Fairfax knew that his possession of the Sai Mas would possibly provide those of the good and righteous with a powerful weapon.

"I understand the risk," said Fairfax, "and I am willing to take such a risk to protect the Harrow. Great Paragon, each of us travels a different path and even though we may not know of the destination we know that at the very least a destination awaits, nonetheless. We have few choices, and I believe we must muster all the power we can to defeat what now befalls the land. As in all things in life, the journey may be difficult, but failure is not a destination to be arrived at."

"What if it were used for evil?" asked the Paragon. "What if those who were the most committed to good were corrupted?"

The words were frightening.

"What if it were used for good? What if those who were the most committed to evil were corrupted by it?" came Fairfax's response.

"Ah, questions to answer questions," said the Paragon. "Such is the unknown, and it is its very nature that provokes fear, for we cannot begin to comprehend what it might be or what it might do. But when we are faced with the choice between the known and the unknown, between the path that is safe and certain, and the path that is risky and uncertain, we must always choose the path of uncertainty. Mirandell, do you fear the path of uncertainty?"

"I do not fear the path of uncertainty," said Fairfax, his eyes never leaving the Paragon's stare. "I do not fear it. It is the path of courage, the path of light over dark, the path of glory. I will not abandon it."

The Paragon gave a look of approval to Fairfax, then turned his gaze to the others in the room, one by one, and the eyes of each hardened, each with resolve. For a long time no one spoke, each lost in their thoughts.

The Paragon broke the silence.

"I will not abandon the path of courage either," he said, his voice strong and commanding, filling the room.

With a nod and a smile, the Paragon pointed to the wizard's staff. In an instant, it was done. There atop the long crooked wooden staff was a gleaming red stone. It was small and pulsed and glowed with a dim, eerie light, pushing back the shadows of the room.

"Mirandell, the Sai Mas is yours," said the Paragon. "Who am I to thwart such a noble deed, a most courageous act? But be warned, our friendship shall quickly wane if you succumb to the stone's burden. I do not doubt that if you or others turn to the darkness and accede to its evil ways, the forces of good will rise and defeat you. Your death shall be one of agony and a day of glory for those of the good and righteous."

"I would expect no less," said a solemn Fairfax.

"Evil may be bold, but goodness is never fearful. For you see, goodness is never a means but an end." But the Paragon was not finished. He had something for Glaeynd. "For the Lady of Mistmere, I have a gift for you."

Before Glaeynd appeared a sword sheathed in a scabbard of wood, leather, and richly overlaid with gold studs from end to end.

The Paragon continued, "I bequeath to you the Varekan Ithrun, the great light sword, forged in the hot hearths of the deep and dark abyss by none other than Troidoc Aldril, Paragon of the En' Naug during the Age of Kings. Fashioned of the finest steel, it will glow orange when in battle, and is hard enough to hold an edge along a length, yet strong enough and flexible enough that it can absorb massive shocks. It will not crack or break. Use it well, but carefully."

Glaeynd reached for the sword, removing it from its sheathing. It was light in her hands. She thought she knew the sword - it felt somewhat familiar - but suddenly she was overcome by a torrent of words filling her head, calling to her, shouting to her, pleading to be heard.

She looked at the Paragon who was staring at her, his eyes bright and green as emeralds, gleaming in the light of the candles, searching into her soul.

What is happening to me? Words repeating in my head! Not my thoughts!

Then as quickly as the words came to her, they were gone, and she could not remember them. The Paragon smiled at her as if answering an unasked question.

You will know the words when it is time, he spoke to her mind. *The Maker is with you. For now, forget this moment. But remember it when doing such comes from your inner strength.*

Glaeynd shook the cobwebs from her head. She did not understand what had just happened.

I am tired, she thought. *I just need to rest a bit.*

The Paragon kept his stare upon Glaeynd.

"Like the wizard's gift, your gift also comes with a warning," said the Paragon to the young woman. "The sword may gain its power by feeding off the soul of its wielder. Such a force can quickly corrupt, making one soulless, unable to understand the workings of the Maker. Do you understand?" Glaeynd nodded. The Paragon then turned to the others. "We are done here. My good friends - may the Maker protect you and your companions. Kydaer, kydaer," he said in the old tongue as he placed a hand over his heart.

With that, the Paragon faded, and the room was restored.

"What did he mean by his last word?" asked Thurir.

"It is a dwarf blessing," said Fairfax. "It means *in the afterlife.*"

Fairfax brought his newly adorned staff close to him, staring into the glow of the Sai Mas.

"How will you use it?" asked Thurir.

"I do not know," said Fairfax. "I do not know."

* * *

As evening blanketed Volemill, darkness also settled upon the company. A surreal feeling washed over them, one that felt like a strange dream. They were tired and dirty and ragged and felt as if they had reached the end of a long journey. But they knew it was only the beginning. They had a long way to go still.

As promised, food was provided in the warm room. The meal was simple, consisting of stewed meats, beans, biscuits, dried fruit, and strong tea. The journey from Katzhu Pu had given them a good appetite, and they enjoyed their meal, the better for it. Later, basins of water, herbal soap, and cloths for washing magically appeared. Fairfax and Glaeynd took their time washing up, scrubbing their hands and feet clean first, and then their faces and behind the neck. Glaeynd washed her long golden hair and, using a small hairbrush made of boar bristles, wound it into a firm coil at the nape of her neck, allowing it to lie free on her shoulders and back. The Fenri also spent some time cleaning. They first soaked their front paws in the basins of water and then licked their paws cleaned, drying them with some cloths. They also went about biting, scratching, and shaking to remove loose hairs, dirt, and prickly burrs from their fur.

Everyone was thankful for the Paragon's hospitality and after spending some time washing, they rested and spoke of their upcoming days. Fairfax told them that they would first travel north then east through the heights of the mountains until they reached the mouth of the great defile, the Draaklel' Daan. He warned that their path would at times be dangerous and fraught with peril, the terrain difficult to cross.

"Why do we not journey back within the mountains, through the great halls discovered by the Learned One?" asked Glaeynd. "Would it not be easier than through mountain passes?"

"It would. The Learned One has traveled the labyrinth for many years. But I do not know the way. If we were to be lost there would be no one to find us."

"Perhaps, my pack can pick up our scent from our last journey," said Thurir.

"We could simply retrace our steps," said Glaeynd, "or you could use your staff or magic to help us find the way."

Fairfax was resolute.

"My friends, the path before us will not be easy," he told them. "It will never be easy. I don't know the power of the Sai Mas or how yet to use it. And I must be careful with how I use magic. Those who live in the darkness sense when magic is used. They are drawn to it like a moth to a flame. If evil were to come upon us in the stone labyrinth, and without complete knowledge of its many passages, I am afraid we would not make it out alive. As difficult as it will be, I am most familiar with the mountain passes, and they will provide us with enough cover." He turned to Thurir.

"Our friends here know quite a bit about mountain passes. I believe they can help."

"Most certainly wizard," said Thurir, knowing no shyness. "We Ra Draug live in rugged terrain that remains largely uninhabited by the En' Edan. Our fur is thick and keeps us warm. We can see in thrashing rains and heavy snowfall, and our hearing is extremely sensitive. Our paws are rough and adapted to sharp slopes and cliffs by being flexible, so we can easily balance and jump from rock to rock. We have survived the mountains for ages. And while we have suffered considerably, long have the mountains hardened us to almost everything. They call to us with a song that thickens our fur, toughens our pads, and sharpens our nails. Ah, the mountains, the mountains give us strength against our enemies. They are our home, as they were to our fathers. You are friends to us; we'll help guide you."

"We could not ask for better friends on the journey into the Old Hills," said Fairfax

Still weary, everyone settled in for the night. They knew they would get a very early start the next morning. Members of the Fenri pack were asked to keep watch for the duration of the night and met their task with vigor, but eventually, most were unable to resist the weariness that seeped through their bones.

* * *

When everyone arose in the morning, much to everyone's surprise, the room had been cleaned and organized. They discovered several small, bundled packs of wood near the doorway and cloaks of differing sizes placed over chairs. Each cloak consisted of thick linen with long-haired pelts and dense, crinkly underfur. And there were new boots made of thick leather and lined with fur that stood in a row. The boots were higher and wider to allow the thick insert of woolen socks that were neatly displayed nearby. Picking up a pair, Fairfax ran a hand over the supple leather. They were the right balance between flexibility and support.

"Nothing like footwear so crafted by the masterful dwarf cobblers of Mortha," he said with a smile.

The soft leather soles were like clouds against the skin, insulating and enveloping, and the tread was sure and did not show wear. Even the woven straps, so fine they were almost weightless, softened the impact of the steps. Each step felt like a caress.

Thurir gave them a sniff.

"Nothing here for us Fenri," he said.

"There will be more and better gifts to come, my friend," Fairfax told him. "So many more gifts to come for you and the Ra Draug. Our journey is long, and the greatest gift awaits."

"And what gift is that wizard?"

"The gift of history."

The Fenri Prince nodded and looked serious as thoughts of revenge ran through his mind.

"I have told myself that when the time comes, history will take revenge five times worse than what they have done to my race," said Thurir.

"Remember, revenge may be pleasant to anticipate, but it is a tricky path to take. Nevertheless, your revenge shall be ours," said Fairfax.

There was also breakfast which appeared on several tables. It was simple but adequate. There were bowls of stewed apples and dishes of porridge with shredded fruit. There was brown bread cut into thick slices with sweet butter, jars of a kind of jam, and baskets of boiled eggs. When they finished breakfast, they packed away some leftovers and readied to leave. Fairfax and Glaeynd looked over the many cloaks and each donned that which best fit their frame. The same with boots and woolen socks. The mood was quiet, and what talk there was tended to focus on the upcoming journey.

As they were about to leave the room, the shimmering image of Bofut Highborn, the rotund dwarf, appeared blocking the doorway.

"Well, if it isn't my good friend," said Fairfax with a slight tilt of his head and a cock of an eyebrow.

"Spare me your words, wizard. I am here only to collect that which is mine."

Fairfax was surprised.

"Bofut, I know not of which you speak. What is it we could possibly owe you?" he asked.

"Gratitude, your gratitude," Highborn answered slowly, cynicism in his tone.

Fairfax laughed.

"Oh, my good friend. On this morning you are of fine wit and humor. I suppose you would also seek some form of repayment for the clothing and food?"

"No wizard. I do not ask for coins or gems, nor do I ask for a future service. I simply ask for your statement of gratitude because this is what friends do. It is a simple request and only requires you to speak a few kind words."

"Yes, you are correct. That is exactly what friends do."

"And wizard, are you a friend?"

A broad smile came to the wizard's face.

"You have my endearing appreciation Bofut Highborn," said Fairfax, then with a slight hesitation, "and, you are indeed a friend, a great friend at that!"

The dwarf looked at Fairfax and with a wink said, "You are to travel safely and return to this place, so we may talk of your high adventures. As we dwarves say, *ukee lat ukoon meavime* - we will see you again sometime."

Fairfax lowered his head and placed both hands over his heart.

Highborn lifted his axe high into the air and with great power brought it swiftly down. The room shook violently, and flashes of light illuminated the walls. His image shimmered and then disappeared.

They left En' Nahrat with Fairfax and Glaeynd wearing their new cloaks and boots, while the Fenri bore the bundled packs of wood. They made their way through the narrow, empty streets of Volemill heading north. Eventually, they came to the northern reaches of the great black iron wall and stood before a door. A wind swirled, and the door opened. When they had passed through the iron archway another gust spun. The door closed, and a bolt clanged reverberating through the mountains now before them. They let the sound sink into their consciousness.

Glaeynd turned to Fairfax and spoke no words. He returned her look with a slight smile.

"Now we search for the door which is open," said Fairfax.

* * *

The mountains sat before the horizon steeped above the land, interned into a dark morning sky. Past the black iron walls of Volemill, they started their journey north into the Old Hills. Fairfax told them that if all went well, they could expect to see the mountains of the Rakl in a few days. They followed a cobbled road until it became a muddy pathway that branched out in several directions. This was the place called Malle Carak. If a traveler took the wrong pathway, they were doomed. Fairfax knew this well and he stopped the company.

"We now inhabit a space, where others have walked, as we do today, thinking their thoughts, and swayed by their passions," Fairfax told them calmly. "But they are gone from this place, as utterly as we shall someday be gone, like ghosts. This is the tension we need to hold as we continue our journey. The past is there only to learn from."

He looked at the many pathways before him and chose one of many that led north. It was a broken pathway of rock among the bowers of stunted foliage. They went along the path as it narrowed among the land, folded and waved from hills and valleys to the vast jagged mountains of the Old Hills. They held their course north for many leagues as the terrain grew rougher and more barren. With the help of the Fenri, they kept away from dwarf villages, making wide detours through the bleak country. There was no let-up in the steady, yet exhausting pace as they plunged into valleys and climbed up steep stone and rock. Heavy mist covered the mountains and at times heavy snowfall made sight difficult.

As they trudged forward Fairfax led the way, and with him went Thurir. Glaeynd followed with the other Fenri.

This was the first part of their long journey to the Rakl. The days were dreary, and the snowfall seemed unending, and despite the clothing provided by the Paragon kept Fairfax and Glaeynd well clad, they did not feel warm. Along the way, they would find a small hollow or a place where scrawny brush could be gathered and formed into a barrier against the wind and cold. Here they would light a fire and rest and try to sleep.

The journey through the mountains was hard. In just a day or two Fairfax and Glaeynd were weary, but the Fenri remained strong. Each day the terrain looked much the same as it had the day before. The mountains towered over them, closing in, rising higher and higher, and the land was quiet, save for the sound of the wind. The pathway narrowed and, in many places, led them to the edge of sheer falls and rocky crags.

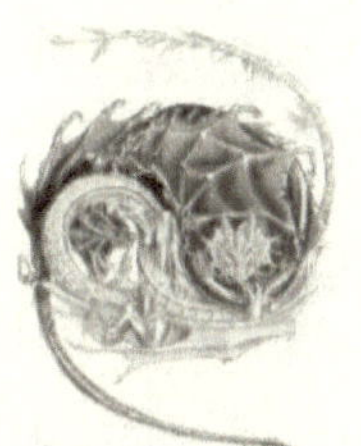

CHAPTER 7
THE MOUNTAIN PASSES OF THE OLD HILLS

TIME PASSED SLOWLY FOR them. After many days of battling freezing winds and sleet thrashing in their faces, they found themselves at a pass that narrowed and curved east. They were now several leagues south of Huur Shec and the weather was changing. The wind suddenly fell as the swift-flowing clouds dissipated breaking way to the sun. As everyone lifted their faces to the sun's glow, Fairfax stopped the group for a brief moment of rest.

"The warmth is a great welcome," said Glaeynd throwing back her hood as her golden hair fell about her shoulders.

"The sun is always welcomed in the mountains, and its rays in particular, for the air is still and the warmth exquisite," said Fairfax. "But we must press ahead. Our journey is not nearly ended. We now must make our way east. I am afraid the mountains will grow larger and the passages more dangerous."

"Time seems to fail us," sighed Glaeynd.

Fairfax turned to her and placed a hand on her back.

"Perhaps, but we cannot fail time," he said.

"In the mountains, time is a feature of nature that passes in its own unique way," said Thurir as he started eastward. "The frontier shifts swiftly from the past to the future. Our future lies to the east, to my homeland."

More days passed. Ever forward they trudged, the towering shapes of the mountains pressing down on them. As they continued, alternately ascending and descending through jagged rock for several leagues, they reached a place where the path grew, and a small clearing appeared. To the south, many tall peaks rose before Glaeynd, their great mass fighting back the red glow of the sun's light, casting large swathes of darkness. She knew what was beyond them and it called to her.

At first, she hesitated to look, looking away, far away, trying to keep her eyes ahead, but her beloved city of Mistmere was whispering to her, beckoning her to look. It was as if the city wanted to be seen, to be remembered, to be understood, and she was not sure she could stop herself from trying to catch a glimpse of it.

Fairfax sensed her anxiety.

"Try as you might, you will not see it, you will not see what it once was," he said. "You cannot see something that is already changed. Just looking at it does not change it back to what it was. A different viewpoint will not have it turn out differently than what has already occurred. If you continue to seek that which is gone, you will have no future. My dear lady, do not look for something, just see where you are. Let the future come to you."

She nodded. She knew she had to focus on the situation at hand and not on her memories of what was. She closed her eyes tightly for a brief moment, then opened them, resolved not to seek out a look at her city.

"There! Straight ahead!" roared Thurir with excitement. "You can make out the shapes through the misty darkness."

Fairfax and Glaeynd turned. Far off in the distance and through the deep and feathered veil of a dark mist, they could see the tall, snow-covered peaks of Ragmorok. Farther beyond, stood a taller and darker mountain whose gloom was stern and stark.

"The long reach of Ragmorok, home of the Ra Draug, and deeper into the blackness, the heights of the evil 'Ksh Nierwes," said Fairfax.

'Ksh Nierwes. thought Glaeynd.

She cringed at the name, a name that came from the tales of the wicked place, tales widespread and frightening. It was a shadowland away from the light of the sun and the goodness of the world. It was a place of horror and despair, a place of sadness and madness, of death and destruction. It was a great mountain of unfeigned mystery and darkness, home of the Lok Tumu, black ajatars.

"We will keep our distance from such cruelty," said Fairfax. "It is for the Rakl that we make our way. But let us not look too far ahead. There remain many leagues yet to travel. We must first clear the Old Hills and reach the waters of the Aldpine. As we travel, we must do so quietly and swiftly, and we must be careful to avoid the men of the north."

"One never knows where the loyalties of the Nur' Edan lie," said Thurir.

They continued their journey, carefully walking along a path that twisted and turned as it wound its way along the vast mountainsides. A little way down the path they stopped. Ahead, as far as the eye could see the skies were changing. Mushrooming dark clouds formed and were rapidly moving towards them in heavy, changing forms, as flashes of lightning tore through the sky. The wind swirled and stung bringing with it a brutal stench.

Fairfax recognized the signs and brought his staff forward.

"Quickly now! Up against the rock!" he shouted. "An evil comes for us!"

Everyone filed behind Fairfax with Glaeynd nearest him. They clutched the mountainside, clinging on with fear, and peering up at the black sky when a most horrid sight emerged. It was a massive black ajatar hurtling down from the darkness, beating its great leathery wings with a noise like a deafening gale. The beast's wings were as wide as its body was long; sweeping waves of air as the creature came upon them. With its forelegs outstretched and its sharp talons extended, the demon reached for the mountainside. A mighty sound roiled like thunder as the ajatar landed alongside the mountain, sinking its talons into the enormous rock. As it clung to the mountain and steadied itself, the creature folded its wings like a great bird.

Fairfax held his staff steady and brought his right hand behind and around Glaeynd. He could feel her tremble.

"My lady, be calm," he told her. "Remember, at times, if you take matters quietly, it will be better for you."

"What are we to do?" asked Glaeynd, wrapped in fear and indecision.

"Be calm and wait for the paths to reveal themselves."

At first, she did not understand what he meant until she determined to heed his words. She closed her eyes and imagined a soothing scene.

Be calm.

Wait for the paths.

Be calm.

Wait for the paths.

Be calm.

Wait for the paths.

In her mind's eye, a path revealed itself. It was a glittering trail within the tranquility of a garden of apple trees and yellow flowers. Before her, the path split into several directions, one of which was dark, and gloomy. She looked down into the darkness.

No. That is not a path to be taken.

She looked down another direction, a different pathway, and saw light and shadow playing on the leaves of the trees, and the sound of birdsong drifted up to her. It was a scene of such beauty that she felt a sense of calm descend on her.

She let out a deep breath. She was still terrified, but not as much as before. Now with confidence and an understanding of the paths before them, she opened her eyes and looked at the hideous beast who was staring down at Fairfax.

"I know this fiend," Fairfax told them. "It is the Tura, Mori Mengel, the leader of the 'Ksh Nierwes hive and its demons. Let me handle this."

The ajatar was ancient, stooped, his once shiny scales now tarnished and dull. He smelled of smoldering ashes and rot. But he had a remarkable feature: he had just one eye, a fiery orange one, while the other was a black stone. Slowly, ponderously, he raised his head.

"Ah, if it isn't my good friend, my magic-bearer," said the ajatar, a crooked smile on a leathery face lined with gashes. He again steadied itself, rock and stone falling onto the path. He brought his long neck down to the passage and against the rock, his head now only a few inches from Fairfax. "So tell me, what brings my magic-bearer to these parts?"

"Well, if it is not the Tura," said Fairfax in disgust. "Mengel, you are far away from your hive of blackness are you not? We pose no threat to you. Now, leave us be!"

"Was this your doing, magic-bearer?" said Mengel, a deep and booming voice carried on a wave of stench-filled breath and steam. "It was you magic-bearer, wasn't it now? Tell me. You can tell me, my magic-bearer. It was you who brought the damnable white army here with their flying insects to kill one of my own, at the defile?"

"I have no idea what you are talking of. We have no concern for your wickedness, at least not at this moment. I have already told you; that we pose no threat. You are a most evil creature, a degenerate, rejoicing in awful acts. Be off with you and leave us be!"

Mengel lifted his head in laughter. Wisps of smoke and flame came from his jaws and nostrils.

"It's true enough magic-bearer - I do take pleasure in my deeds, righteous as they may be," said Mengel, "just as you find joy in yours. Funny how that is. Let's stop with the word games, shall we." He snorted. He snapped his huge, coiled tail around the mountain causing rocks to tumble around everyone. "I'll ask only once more - did you bring the damnable white army here?"

"Contemptible beast! I do not know what you speak of! Do not toil with us!"

Mengel shifted slightly, still hanging onto the slope, his talons crunching on rock and stone. More rock shattered the cliffs and landed on the walkway. In reaction, Glaeynd pressed herself more against the mountainside. He saw her movement and again shifted a little. He sniffed the air, taking time to take in all the scents.

"A curious smell," he said.

He moved closer to her and growled, blowing soot across her face. She kept her gaze fixed on him, a hand on her blade Varekan Ithrun, but she promised herself she would not follow the dark path.

"Ah, I see there's a lady from Mistmere with you," he told Fairfax. "Her smell is distinct. Sweet soul she be. And - what's this? She carries a dwarven sword. It would be such a pity if she were to vanquish in my fire. But then again, my magic-bearer, you know, my fire frees the soul! Does it not?"

Fairfax now gripped his staff with both hands. "Leave us be monster!" he shouted at the beast.

Mengel simply laughed.

"Oh, but there's more. I smell Ra Draug. I wouldn't think my magic-bearer would be seen with the likes of such vermin. But why? Hmmm . . . let me guess. You're most likely heading east to the land of dogs, aren't you, my magic-bearer? Perhaps to try to take back their sad mountain kingdom."

"Vermin! Dogs!" shouted Thurir as he moved alongside Fairfax. "Such words have no meaning coming from a despicable brute. I know your kind. You ruin everything that touches your existence. I pity all those in the service of darkness!"

Mengel again raised his head in laughter.

"I think I've hit a nerve with my Fenri friend," he said. "You say my words have no meaning to you, but clearly, they evoke emotions. You pathetic thing - the light you believe in, the light you so revere, blinds you from the truth. Flea-ridden wolf, I serve who I please and when I please, and even though on this day, I may have no taste for Fenri vermin meat, for it is sour and sinuous, you can have your worthless mountain. It matters not to me." He paused with a smirk. "Oh, wait. I'm mistaken. So forgetful I am in my advanced years. My Fenri friend, it is no longer your mountain. Is it now? How sad for you."

Thurir roared and stepped forward, brandishing his fangs.

"Stop!" Fairfax shouted at Thurir. "This is neither the time nor the place!"

"What's wrong, my magic-bearer?" chortled Mengel. "Can't control your little pet?"

With a snarl, Thurir heeded Fairfax's words and took several steps back. Fairfax then brought his staff closer to Mengel, almost touching the beast's nose with it.

"Ah, what's this, my magic-bearer?" said Mengel taking a sniff at the staff. "A new toy sits atop your wooden stick. It's all bright and red. What a pretty thing it is. Hmmm . . . be warned, my magic-bearer. A child should always be careful when playing with a new toy. Some toys are unsafe, especially if a child doesn't know how the toy works. I fear this new toy of yours may be dangerous to the point of being lethal. It would be such madness if I lost my magic-bearer, now, wouldn't it? But then again, maybe you wouldn't be lost to us. Ah, maybe, just maybe, your use of your shiny new toy would change you. Eh, my magic-bearer? Now I ask, wouldn't that be something - my magic-bearer turned, changed, living a different life, rejoicing at screams bellowing through pain, putting darkness to where there was once light."

An angry smile came to Fairfax's lips.

"Do not tempt me so, sly worm," he said. "I am not weak like your kind, nor subject to every trifling word and whim. As much as it would please me to use my staff against you, for it would be quick and such a treat, it would also be wasteful of my time, futile in every way. There is not enough of you to quench my thirst for goodness. Your life means very little if nothing to me."

"And your life, my magic-bearer, your life and the lives of your companions," said Mengel, his voice growing shrill, a fire coming to his one eye, "do such small and petty lives have meaning to my magic-bearer? Perhaps. But for me, such lives are insignificant. They're nothing to me. You see, it doesn't much matter what you do. Let me help you, my magic-bearer. Let me free you and your companions from the misery you cannot escape. Please, my magic-bearer, let me help. Let me free you, all of you. Let me take your souls."

Mengel lifted his head and took a deep breath.

His fire, thought Glaeynd, *it will destroy us!*

Her eyes widened in fear when suddenly, a deluge of words filled her head. She remembered them. They were the same words from Volemill, from the Paragon. They called to her and shouted at her. Instinctively, she reached out to Fairfax with her mind, touching his mind with hers, barely a brush. But there was no response. Whatever it was her instincts were trying to do it was too late.

Mengel released his breath, exhaling a long and powerful fiery geyser from his lungs. The explosion of flames barreled down at them, but Fairfax had swiftly lifted his staff and called upon his magic that shielded them from the vicious flames. When Mengel stopped, the ground beneath them and the mountainside had been scorched black. In some places, the scorching heat had transformed the rock into shards of glass.

"Ah, my magic-bearer, it seems you do know how to use your toy. Shall we see how powerful it is?"

Mengel took another breath, this time deeper. Fairfax again lifted his staff, but before Mengel could release his fiery fury, there came a screeching cry from the sky. A streak of red came tearing through the dark clouds that were now dissipating. It was Moondancer. Seeing the red ajatar, Mengel turned to Fairfax.

"My magic-bearer, there will be another day, another time to play," he snarled with a cold smile. "Remember, fire frees the soul."

Mengel sprung from the mountainside, hastily taking wing far to the east, back to his hive.

But Moondancer did not take chase. Instead, he circled high above as the sun started throwing its crimson rays about the land. He gave one more shriek before flying north.

Fairfax sighed with relief and looked up at Moondancer.

"Thank you, my friend," he whispered.

Glaeynd looked at Fairfax. She wanted to speak to him about what had happened, about the words in her mind, about how she reached out to him. But as the Sai Mas now glistened in the sun, something told her that he knew what had happened.

He looked at her and gave a wink.

"My lady, the path before us is clear," he told her.

She smiled.

* * *

Since their encounter with the treacherous Mengel, their journey had been especially punishing, along twisting and narrow mountain passages of the Old Hills, rough and slithering downward paths. Eventually, they came upon a hollow with a stream littered with tumbled rock. To the north, within clear view, was the mouth of the Draaklel' Daan Defile as it emptied into the Aldpine river valley; to the south, one could see the vast fruit orchards and the white stone of Mistmere. Before them, in the distance ahead, lay a small, thickly wooded area. From where they now stood, Fairfax stopped the group to survey the forested landscape ahead.

"At long last, we have cleared the wretched maze," said Fairfax. "We have but a few more leagues until we reach the Elmham river valley." He pointed to the woodland. "But first, we must make our way through the forest yonder."

He was hopeful his words would keep everyone focused on their journey. But worry quickly came to him. Upon greater inspection, he, Thurir, and his pack gave witness to a most disturbing sight to the north. Below, within the defile, they could see where a great battle had taken place. Several large pyres of brood smoldered, and near the mouth of the defile lay the charred remains of what looked to be a black ajatar.

"So, this is what Mengel spoke of," said Fairfax.

"What army could've done this?" asked Thurir.

"I suspect it was, as Mengel said, the great army of the White Star," said Fairfax as his eyes probed deeper into the scene below. "But there is something else."

"What?" asked Thurir. "What is it?"

"Magic. Magic was used, and its signature is one I have not felt in ages."

"Whose magic?"

"I am not certain exactly," said Fairfax. He had a suspicion but kept his thoughts to himself. "My friends, we may very well have a mighty ally on our side."

While Fairfax and the Fenri took note of the defile's devastation, Glaeynd could no longer refuse Mistmere's whispers.

My Mistmere calls to me.

She gazed south upon her beloved city and its surrounding plains, and her thoughts turned to her father, her brother Goselthout, and young Twain Boggans. But these thoughts vanished quickly from her mind as she was confronted with a terrifying sight.

But what is this?

She saw throngs of brood pouring from the city's walls and onto the river valley. They took an assault formation, their sights set on what looked to be the elven army's rear flank as it marched south.

"Look!" she shouted pointing to Mistmere.

Fairfax and the Fenri turned to the call, to where Glaeynd was pointing. They could just make out the rear flank of the elven army as it marched south while the city spewed forth its evil brood in the chase. Fairfax leaned on his staff.

"So many goings-on and so much evil about," he sighed, concern on his face. "May the Maker guide us."

Glaeynd turned from the sight in profound sadness and sobbed. The haunting reality of losing her family and Mistmere was a recurring nightmare. Now, it seemed all she had left were fragments of memories.

"Can we not do something?" she asked Fairfax with tearful eyes, trying to be strong. "Surely, we now know the stone you possess is a most powerful weapon. Can you not use your staff as you did against the ajatar?"

Fairfax reached out to her. He gently stroked her hair.

"My friend, I am sorry. You see, the magic I used to protect us from the demon's fire was mine. Granted, it was not much, a speck, but it came from my hands and not from the stone. The beast was mistaken. He is ignorant in such ways. We must be careful. Once the power of the Sai Mas is used, its existence will become known to the darkness. We cannot give them any hint of our whereabouts. Our path remains to the east."

"But Mengel knows of us, he knows of our location," she said in frustration, her tearful eyes now of anger. "Surely, if he knows then the darkness is soon to know. What good is the stone's magic if you refuse to use it?"

"He is selfish and cares not for others in his dark realm," said Fairfax. "He hardly cares for his kind, let alone the darkness. He bows to no master. And magic, well, magic has a way of never working out the way you want it to. I am not of the warrior wizard caste, the Hulnur Istare. I use magic most carefully, and only when it is necessary. I know your heart aches, but the past is behind you. Magic cannot easily undo what has already been done. Your father is under an evil spell, easily turned to the dark ways of the brood. He is no longer your father, at least not the man you once knew. There is little you or anyone can do. You must trust in me, in our path forward."

She looked into his eyes and saw her own. It was most wonderful, for their eyes were as those of one person, and this gave her strength. She felt safe with him.

We are connected. You know this, he told her with his thoughts.

Yes. But how? What does it mean?

I do not know, but I am sure there is a reason why we are connected in this way. Do not speak of this to anyone. Have trust in me. There is still time for you and Mistmere - time enough to heal the wounds and reveal purpose. My lady, something tells me you have much to do yet.

She gave a short smile but quickly turned her attention to the woods east of their viewpoint. Her Rhiorsnan training heightened; she sensed something or someone watching them from afar.

"What is it?" asked Fairfax. "What does your awareness tell you?"

Her eyes darted back and forth trying to pierce the darkness of the wooded areas around them.

"I do not know," she said. "I am not sure."

Thurir lifted his nose to the air and sniffed.

"There is no strangeness, other than from the valley below, my friends," said the Thurir. He then scowled as he surveyed the brood pouring from Mistmere. "Yet, another evil army enters the fray. Is there nothing we can do to help the elven army?"

Fairfax shook his head.

"They do not need our help," he said pointing to the elven army. "Look, for they have brought the full power of the White Star to this place."

They stood in awe as they heard tremendous horns sound and saw several wings of the Vilyarok break away from the massive elf army in preparation for an airborne assault.

"I fear this brood attack is but a diversion to other things," said Fairfax. "There is nothing we can do here. The White Star surely does not require our assistance. We have little time. We must stay focused on our mission." He looked up as the sky darkened. "Let us now make haste to the forest. When we clear the woods, we shall travel north along the Aldpine River, then cross the mighty waters and make our way to the Rakl."

The journey may be difficult for you, Fairfax reached out to Glaeynd with his thoughts. *I will do my best to help.*

She responded with a brief nod and a thought.

Your strength will help to guide me.

As they hastily made their way into the pinewoods, creatures stirred whispers in the mist that started to creep in with curling fingers.

* * *

Within the darkness of the forest, yellow eyes appeared, flickering like candles in the wind. Glaeynd sensed their presence. She strained her eyes trying to detect any movement, but the eyes were clever and went unnoticed. All the group could see was the illusion of shadows. But there were sounds, whispers only the creatures could hear, three voices of the mind. And they spoke to each other.

Who are they?

Do not know. But they are different.

Yes. Very different.

Some tall, some short.

Some furry, some hairless.

Some young, some old.

Creatures of different forms.

Together. Strange.

Yes. Very strange.

But there are so many of them.

So many different ones.

Some with fur and teeth.

Long teeth.

And the old one.

Yes. The old one.

Something different about that one.

Different, they are all different.

The old one carries a stick.

Stick! Stick with a red gem atop.

Red gem?

Yes! Red gem!

We must be on guard.

Yes, on guard for red gems.

He looks for red gems.

He always looks for red gems.

What should we do?

Wrong question.

Yes. Very wrong.

Need to ask again?

Yes. Ask differently.

Very differently.

But what question to ask?

Think again.

Yes. Think hard.

Oh! What would he have us do?

Yes. That is correct.

That is the right question.

Yes. What would he have us do?

Now, think.

Always think.

What would he have us do?

Think hard.

Think. Path the way.

Yes! That is it. Path the way.

We always path the way.

And consequences.

Always consequences along a path.

Yes. Consequences.

Path the way.

Think. What would he have us do?

What would he have us do?

Think. Think hard.

Yes. Think. Path the way.

Do nothing. Let them pass.

Yes. This is a path.

Kill them. Kill them.

Oh! How fun. Kill them.

Indeed. Much fun.

Killing is grand.

Most grand indeed.

He likes that.

Oh yes! He likes that very much.

A good path.

Need another path.

I have one. Tell him.

Oh! Good one.

Oh! Another path before us.

A good path for us.

Yes. Tell him.

But which path?

Yes. Which path do we travel?

Think.

Think hard.

Yes. Think hard. Consequences.

Always consequences.

Yes. Think of consequences.

What to do now?

Look. Always helpful.

Oh. Look.

Yes. Looking is good.

Looking helps, doesn't it?

Yes. Looking helps.

Many of them.

So many of them.

Different them.

Fur and long teeth.

Young and old.

Stick and a red gem.

Too many of them.

Yes. Too many to kill.

And the red gem

Yes. The red gem. Not good.

We could vanquish.

He would not like that.

No. He would not like that.

Not at all.

What was another path?

Do nothing. It was do nothing.

Oh yes. Nothing. Not sure.

Nothing?

He would not like nothing.

We would suffer for that.

Yes. He would make us suffer.

Suffer long and hard.

Yes. For doing nothing.

He would make us suffer.

We do not wish to suffer.

Nothing does not work.

What is left?

I think it is this - tell him.

Yes. Tell him.

He would like this path.

Indeed. Always good to tell him.

He would be grateful.

Yes. Most grateful.

I think this is the best path.

Yes. The best path.

Indeed. Desirable path.

We shall speak to him.

Yes. Speaking is good.

We must speak in a voice only he can hear.

Together then we shall speak.

Yes. As one. Always.

The creatures joined and spoke as one, one loud voice of the mind. Their master was far away, but he heard the voice, gave a most terrible smile, and slipped away into his darkness.

***

On its march south to the citadel city of Chyh-Mehm, near where the Old River bowed eastward into the Snowwynne Barrens, the elven army was caught somewhat by surprise as brood swarmed from Mistmere attacking the White Star's rear flank. Dalgaes did not expect brood to occupy the city, and their sudden attack appeared as a strange and desperate maneuver. But he knew there was no choice but to engage them in battle. Under his direction, the White Star recoiled and quickly surrounded the brood. The battle was ferocious and bloody as elven warriors fought with a vengeance.

"My Lord, we must continue south to join with Carrick," implored Col Shas. "This is but a small commotion. The evil is vastly outnumbered and plays a game. Let a legion of our finest handle this while we continue south."

Dalgaes watched as the battle started.

"No. We must cleanse the land of this evil," he said. "We have little choice. We cannot move forward and allow such a menace to scar the land. Let the sky erupt with the Vilyarok. Let us quickly dispense with this foolishness. Carrick will understand our delay."

Col Shas raised an arm and motioned with his hand, signaling the order to release the Vilyarok.

The winged archers filled the skies above the demons as the rear flank of the White Star surrounded the brood attacking it on all sides. Elven archers and the Vilyarok discharged showers of arrows against the brood, but the brood protected themselves with shields raised high and without breaking the line. They formed a wedge and began to slash their way into the White Star with brutal force. Then, from behind, rode Rhiorsnan guardsmen into the Elmham River valley. Led by Goselthout, the Rhiorsnan charged in support of the brood and into the White Star as brood archers on the flanks shot arrows with new vigor.

The Rhiorsnan entry into the battle was yet another surprise. Col Shas swiftly ordered more elven warriors to join in what quickly became a brutal action. Brood, their bloodlust raging, swung their blades with a new dexterity and strength. All around, the screams of the elven warriors could be heard above the clash of metal and splitting of bone. The White Star had lost momentum on the battlefield and suffered large losses, that was until more Vilyarok were released. The army's massive numbers finally overwhelmed the brood as the demons were cut and stabbed with elven swords and spears till the soil flowed with blood. When the brood had finally been decimated, and the battlefield was strewn with the dead and dying, the victors began to pull apart great heaps of flesh, to separate the living from the dead. There was carnage of every conceivable kind.

As Dalgaes walked the battlefield, amongst the dead and wounded, he came upon a dying Goselthout. He ordered that leafy branches from surrounding bushes be gathered and placed under the head of the weakening warrior. A surprise was expressed in Goselthout's failing eyes. He held out his hand to Dalgaes, who grabbed it and held it tightly. But Goselthout's firm grasp soon became weak.

"Son of Kraneth of the Mists," Dalgaes said to Goselthout. "Why? Tell me why!"

Goselthout tried to answer; silently he attempted to mouth words but could not. His eyes closed, and his hand became flaccid. Death gripped his soul.

"Why do you think they turned?" asked Col Shas.

"How the many who were once against unrighteousness, against those of evil tempers and works, can turn against all that is good and honorable? I do not know the answer to such an abomination."

Dalgaes stood and looked at the white-stoned city of Mistmere in the distance. A terrible feeling came over him, a feeling that Kraneth had been condemned to death by the wicked evil that had overcome him, and that his breath would soon be choked from his body.

"Send a battalion to Mistmere and secure it," he ordered. "Rout any evil that may remain. Show no pity in doing so. Provide order to the citizenry."

"What of the Lord of Mistmere?"

"I fear that soon he will be with the Maker," he said in a whisper.

The great elven army of the White Star continued south.

* * *

"Grand vizier … grand vizier … where have you gone?" shouted a panicked Kraneth, his words echoing through an empty Ewellinoth.

He was confused, verging on delusion because no news on the status of the combat with the White Star had arrived. He stumbled about the immense great hall as if it were in darkness.

"Where are you, vizier? What word do you have? Have we repelled the enemy? What of my son? What of Goselthout?"

From behind the great throne of carved crystal, the Cryuk Avhro, appeared the pale and gaunt Grimshade, stroking the fur trim on his leather coat, and holding the royal scepter.

"My Lord, all is well," said the vizier, an evil smile on his lips. "Please come to me and take your seat on the throne. All is well."

Kraneth made his way carefully through the tangle of columns in the big hall, his attention fixed on his throne. As he approached it, Grimshade offered Kraneth his arm to lean upon as the old man walked. He aided him into the chair and presented him with his scepter.

"It is mine," said Kraneth grasping the royal scepter with greedy and cruel hands. "Tell me of the battle. I am sure victory is ours. The glory belongs to us."

Kraneth's breathing was effortful, his chest rising and falling in huge, swift curves. He looked over the empty darkness of Ewellinoth. He felt alone and lost, his mind wandering, searching for something, but he did not know what he was searching for. He was tired, so tired, and he longed for the past. Delirium set in, and within its swirling maelstrom of madness, a vision came to him, of a young Goselthout and Glaeynd playing in the great hall.

"Yes, my Lord. The battle is won, and the glory is all yours," whispered Grimshade, deceitful words. The evil vizier was aware of what was going on outside the city's walls. But the truth did not serve him. "You have been victorious today. A great victory on the battlefield has been achieved. Soon a great celebration shall be held in your honor. Now, it is best to rest."

"Rest, yes, I would like to rest," said Kraneth in a meek voice. "I can now rest for the battle is won."

Grimshade stroked Kraneth's hair, and, speaking as if to a tired child, said, "You have done well today. Now close your eyes and sleep. A great celebration will be held in your honor tonight, and tomorrow, more battles, more victories."

Kraneth obeyed at once. He closed his eyes and as he fell asleep, the words of a song softly fell from his lips.

On the battlefield we are ready to die, our brave souls
We die daily only to wake, broken bodies no longer whole
With certainty do we strike the enemy, a beast to tame
Brutal and forceful, sword and arrow twist into our frame
And as we perish again, still we do not deny our name
It is never lost to us because the Maker tells of our fame
We fight, by the Maker, hearts and minds stirred
Give us the faith to live and die for his word

Kraneth of the Mists was at last at peace on his throne, relaxed now, drifting to a place of dear and distant memories. He was not thinking; he was scarcely feeling when something seemed strange. He felt a sharp coldness along his neck, followed by a burning sensation deep into his flesh. An unfamiliar fear about the unknown came to him as he felt the strength in his body fade. His eyes burst open in terror, and he gasped for air. He shuddered in pain as he felt the warmth of his blood flow from his neck. Just as he realized that this was his death, images of Goselthout and Glaeynd as adults flashed in his mind then faded.

With little strength left, the white stone scepter slipped from his grasp. The crystal globe from atop the staff shattered into tiny pieces on the marble floor. Grimshade grinned a darkest and nasty grin and took a shard of crystal and slipped into the darkness. He would later ride a horse northward, into the shadows of night.

The Lord of Mistmere had served his purpose.

CHAPTER 8
THE HANU EN' NNARD

"HO THERE, HALFAST," shouted the old tinker with his scratchy voice to his friend across the road. "We'd be heading out. Give my best to the wife."

"Tinker man, I reckon you be off to your next stop," said Halfast as he waved goodbye. "Safe travels Rudigar. Remember to try to find that teapot the wife's been looking for."

"Teapot? Well, I've plenty of those," said Rudigar pointing back to his wagon that was full of pots and pans and other goods. "If she didn't like any of the ones I have then I'd say she's mighty particular, isn't she?"

Halfast shrugged his shoulders.

"I do as I'm told," he shouted.

Rudigar laughed.

"Always best to do what the wife tells you to do," he shouted back.

He snapped the reins and the wagon slowly started down the cobbled road. Fastened to the wagon with rusty hitching hardware and wood was an old brown horse with a grey mane and tail. As far as Rudigar could tell, the horse was not of the Ure Rokko, for he did not speak, nor did he display an ability to reason. But Rudigar always told others that the horse spoke to him, with his eyes.

He had come by the horse some years ago, a gift from a tall, thin man with an eye patch, he met outside the city of Orhollow. In those days he peddled his trinkets from a small pushcart, and he was seeking a horse after purchasing a dilapidated wagon to renovate. When he happened upon the man, the man told him he no longer had use for the horse and happily gave him to Rudigar.

"He has seen better years," the man told him. "I have no longer use for him. He will work hard for you. But treat him with care for that is how we should treat all creatures. His name is Baru."

Feeling uneasy about such a gift, and without the man's knowledge, Rudigar slipped a piece of iron into the man's satchel, enough to forge a sword. Rudigar then went about repairing the wagon, substituting new wheels and axles for the old and replacing a few boards. With the wagon restored and now having a horse, Rudigar was able to widen his reach and earn a respectable living.

* * *

Rudigar and Baru departed the village center, vanishing into the distance, now at an amble and with the clinging and clanging of pots and pans. Their destination was the Aldpine River valley in the east. From there they would go south, staying close to the Dark Woods and away from the Rakl and its wicked tower Ur' Morir.

"The mountains hold their secrets tightly. They only reveal them to those willing to explore the dismal terrain. That is not us. No no. We are not so adventurous in our old age, are we now?" Rudigar asked Baru.

He again snapped the reins and tsked Baru to a steady pace.

"And the drums, the drums beat, strong and rhythmic, for the Ra Cath. Dark days old friend, yes, dark days. People are afraid to buy anything in such times. Black clouds and tales of wickedness spread like a fire in the dry grass. We'll have better luck to the south, in Mistmere. More safe land in the south. Plenty of riches there and far from the Rakl."

Baru gave a faint neigh and trudged along with some difficulty as the road became muddy. In time, they were on the road heading south, approaching the Gagdash, still many leagues from Mistmere. Their travels were quiet, almost beguilingly pleasant. Rudigar would have felt the voyage was ideal if they had not come across a peculiar sight, a man sitting alone by a fire near a river. He thought nothing of it at first, but this was the north, and he wondered if the person was a hunter or perhaps a bandit.

But bandits don't travel by day, he thought, *and they travel in prides, groups of many including youngsters. Probably a hunter. Plenty of game about these parts.*

He dismissed the strange sight as perhaps nothing more than a chance to make a deal.

"Stranger, can I be of assistance to you," he said as he pulled back on the reins to stop Baru. "Lots of wares and goods for sale. Good quality merchandise and at fair prices. Of course, we can talk about such details when the time suits us. Do you have a name, stranger?"

The man looked up from the fire, his face pale, hollow eyes, blank and dull, with a high forehead. He wore a long black leather coat with brown fur trim. Rudigar thought there was something different about the man. He looked impatient as he sat there alone, not the kind of man to sit and wait.

"Names are unimportant, kind sir," said the stranger, his voice haunting, almost unnatural, yet somehow soothing. He started to gently stroke the brown fur trim of his coat with his long, pale fingers. "However, you can be of great assistance. You see, there is something you have that is of value to me. It is something I most desperately need. I make haste to the north, but unfortunately, my trusty steed failed some leagues back. I am afraid that without your assistance, without your kindness, I may not make my destination on time."

Rudigar looked confused and uncertain.

"Good sir, I'm unsure of what you ask," he said. "Of course, I'm most glad to be of assistance. I'm always happy to make a sale, that is if you think I've something in my wagon that can be of use to you."

"But you see, you most definitely have something that is of use to me, in fact, great use to me," said the stranger, a captivating sweetness in his voice. He stood and smiled and invited Rudigar to sit with him. "Please join me by the warmth of my fire."

They spoke for some time. Sadly, though, Rudigar did not know that evil would soon befall him. As storm clouds loomed overhead, a sorrowful bargain was struck. It brought with it darkness and pain.

With an eerie peacefulness, night slowly shrouded the land. The river's melody was calming, and the air was still. Rabbits milled about, attracted closer to the fire by a curious scent in the air. They cautiously peered through long grasses on their way to Rudigar's wagon, which sat dark and silent off the road. They lifted their noses in the air and sniffed. They followed the odd scent past the wagon and closer to the fire, where they discovered blood on the ground and Rudigar's body, his throat slashed open. An unexpected sound then penetrated the eeriness startling the rabbits. Their ears pointed forward, fixed on the sound. It was the sound of Baru galloping off through the grasses to the north - his rider, the pale and gaunt stranger, Gurandurm Grimshade.

* * *

Sunshine breaking through the morning mist sparkled and shimmered as Grimshade and Baru approached Aldkeep Point from the south. They were still some distance from the massive city which appeared like a mirage in the haze. It dominated the landscape with a deep sense of foreboding, a grimly and shadowy uprising against the sky. Grimshade could not see the city gate but knew the pathway he was now on would lead him past several ravines and forested lands and to the gate. He was familiar with this land since the North Eldor was his home, and he, like those of the Harrow, understood how much its people had suffered through the years and at the hands of others. History had not been kind. The people of the north had been betrayed and used by their leaders, first to secure power and then to keep it. They had been led into wars they did not always understand and had seen their land destroyed. But those were memories of a different time, and this was now. He could feel a newness in the air and hear it in the birdsong and the rustling of the trees. It was a freshness of a new time soon to arrive, for the north would soon be reborn and he would be part of it.

Grimshade dismounted Baru and looked into the horse's eyes.

"Sad beast, old and grey," he said stroking Baru's mane. "You have done well bringing me here to this place. But what to do with you."

You are not of the great horses, he thought with a shade of pity. *You do not speak. No. You are just a slave to the rigors of this life, with little understanding of the many layers of this existence. Perhaps a blessing, if such a thing could be. But there is something about you, your eyes. It is as if they talk to me, in an unknown language.*

He stroked Baru's head. He was surprised by how soft the horse was, and how he seemed to enjoy the attention. There was a glimmer in Baru's eyes, and it stirred him, a slight smile coming to his pallid face. He had made the decision.

"You were born into servitude," he said looking into Baru's black eyes. "Your blood is not good enough and of no use to me. You are weak and tired and of no threat. On this day, there is no need for me to end your life. Spend your last days staring at the trees, at the rocks, at the birds, and wondering when it will all end for you."

He slapped Baru's backside sending the horse off riderless. He watched as the horse galloped away. When the horse was out of sight, he picked up his few belongings and made his way down the road to the city.

Ahead, the forbidding Aldkeep Point perched high atop the northernmost edge of the Harrow, clinging rather precariously to the craggy and treacherous coast of the Northern Seas. The massive fortress city was encircled by extremely steep drops and was only accessible from the mainland by a bridge to the south. Its imposing towers and bastions were bathed in shadowy darkness, while its weather-beaten ramparts snaked along granite-hewn contours resembling a line of broken teeth.

Grimshade made his way down the road, through treed terrains and clearings, until he found himself at the bridge. He took a deep breath and set off across the bridge and through a large stone gate. He could feel a bit of the tension rise in his shoulders, and his stomach began to churn. He had thought he would feel excitement at entering the city again, but instead, he felt despair for he knew what was ahead of him. He knew all too well what the city had become.

Within the city walls, dilapidated terraced structures lined the narrow streets and alleys as the city's dregs quietly went about their way, sullen-faced and withdrawn. Poverty was everywhere - in the worn-out clothes, fireless hearths, the dank, musty smells of the place. There was the stench of rot and decay, of bloated loaves of stale bread, of sewage that had risen from broken pipes and slithered into houses. It burned to breathe. The rank went to Grimshade's throat. To keep the stench from overwhelming him, he got a rag and wrapped it around his nose and mouth, tying it behind him. He tried to breathe shallowly.

A thin man, feeble and unclean, in ragged clothes, appeared out of nowhere and stumbled towards Grimshade.

"Stranger, got a silver to lend?" asked the dreg. "A silver for a bit of bread?"

"Avo skator," said Grimshade in disgust, a wave of his hand. "Avo skator!"

The man understood the phrase and shrank away as quickly as he appeared.

Grimshade clutched at the rag covering his face. As more dregs saw him, he quickened his pace. He only wanted to make his way quietly in this place until he reached the center tower. But it seemed like with each step, more and more dregs were taking notice of him. He was getting pushed and jostled as he made his way through the sea of bodies.

Such misfortune, he thought. *A once rich and proud place, now impoverished, distressed.*

He remembered the city in its former glory. It was so full of life, magnificent, a beautiful and fabled place of vast riches, and the resources that other realms could only dream of owning. However, ages of brutal warfare by the Nur' Edan and its many tyrannical leaders brought Aldkeep Point and the North Eldor to a stage of sorrow. For this was a land whose people had always been slaves to tyrants like Shade Stonehelm, Adr Rile, and Tyrus Turl. These tyrants were able to unite the many Nur' Edan clans through brute force. But the thirst for power can never be quenched, and as each tyrant sought to expand their realm, they faced inevitable defeat and the ruination of their people.

Indeed, history tells an unfortunate tale, that over time one master is simply replaced by another. As the Nur' Edan so suffered under the rule of tyrants, they soon suffered greatly under the rule of the many stewards put in place by their Sur' Edan victors. Wealth was squandered, the fertility of its land stripped, its quarries mined for others, and its ship timber simply used as firewood. Intense squalor compounded by wretched diseases once inconceivable prevailed. Hopelessness abounded in the eyes of the elderly who begged for death, and in the eyes of orphaned children who yearned for life. All this was but an act of destruction that was in the nature of a protest for the thousands of Sur' Edan lives lost in battle.

In only a few years, the Nur' Edan became a homely and uncultivated people because of their isolated situation. All that remained was strife and calamity, and they could not have been more miserable. They had never known such hardship and misery. It was a time of great trial for them. The only thing that kept them going was the hope of a better life. They yearned for their fathers' fields, orchards, and gardens to be returned to them, for the great mines of mineral wealth to be exploited, and for the vast forests of hardened timber to be harvested for the homeland. The only solace that remained was their shared love for the past, a time when they were as one, a time of plenty and happiness, full of festivals and celebrations. They spoke of those days often and longed for their return. But, alas, such was not to be.

Times change and change comes slowly and with caution. One must be patient.

As Grimshade headed into the heart of the dying city, making his way through the throngs of traders, beggars, and nameless dregs, a small boy came to him and tugged at his coat. He stopped and knelt to one knee, pulled the rag down from around his face, and looked at the boy. He took his hand and gently wiped dirt and soot from the child's face.

"What is it, little one?" asked Grimshade. "Do you have a name?"

"I am Tolan."

"Tolan. A nice name indeed. And from what clan are you?"

"The Inceni."

"Ah, the Inceni," said Grimshade with a scowl and lifting a clenched fist. "Very proud warriors they are."

He reached into his satchel and found a large, thick piece of bread and gave it to the boy.

"For me?" asked the boy.

"Yes. For you, a proud Inceni."

"Thank you."

"Remember to eat it slowly young Inceni warrior. Make sure you chew."

The boy's face brimmed with joy for a moment. He had never seen such a thick slice of bread. He looked up at

Grimshade with hesitation and asked, "Can I share some with my sister?"

Grimshade stood and patted the boy upon his head.

"It is yours, Tolan, to do with as you please. I think sharing it with your sister is very noble. Yes, very noble indeed."

With a smile, the boy ran off down the lane and into an alleyway.

Grimshade pulled the rag back up over his mouth and nose and turned north. He narrowed his eyes on the center tower in the distance which stood fair and high, with a ragged banner flaunted to the sky. He made his way to the tower and as he approached guards at the tower's gate recognized him and allowed him to pass.

Once inside the tower, narrow winding stairways led through many timbered rooms, many connected by secret passages. He climbed and climbed countless stairways until a doorway appeared, guarded by two Nur' Edan brutes. He stopped at the door. Acknowledging his presence, one of the guards nodded and gave a stomp of his foot, making a sudden, dull thud sound that echoed. The sound was a signal. The door slowly creaked open and he found himself looking at a rather large, sturdily built, formidable man.

"Is it time?" asked the man, gruffly.

Grimshade's stare was unnerving.

"It is time."

* * *

The man was named Vrong Kav. He was darkly skinned, with smoldering blue eyes, a badly scarred face, and a mane of long black hair. Exceptionally tall and strong, few men of the Harrow had such a brutish appearance. In battle, he overpowered most men with his strength and skill, and his endurance allowed him to fight with unfailing ferocity long after most would have collapsed in exhaustion. It was often said of Kav that he was almost impossible to defeat in hand-to-hand combat. He only needed to have his back to the wall so that he could not be surrounded, before engaging and killing opponents by the score. But he was more than a brutish warrior. He was a talented commander, strategist, born leader, and even thief. He spoke several languages and was able to recognize, or even decipher, ancient writings.

"It's good to see you once again," said Kav clasping Grimshade's forearm. "I hope your travels were pleasant."

"Oh yes. Very pleasant. We have much to do," said Grimshade.

They walked across the room and to another door that was locked. Kav pulled on a length of chain from around his neck, which up until now was hidden underneath his shirt, and revealed a key dangling from a lone clasp. The key was small with a round stem, the teeth end squared off. Using it, Kav opened the door. A smell came from the darkness, the smell of dust and abandonment. As soon as light entered the room, they saw in the back a filthy blanket covering what appeared to be a body lying on the floor. The body stirred a small movement beneath the cover. More movement and a man's face showed, much of it hidden by the blanket. The man turned and squinted into the light.

"The time is upon us," Grimshade told the man.

The man threw away the blanket and revealed himself. He was malformed, his head badly misshapen, his spine contorted, and he was without legs. What remained of his torso was deformed like his skull. His skin was a sickening combination of white, grey, and yellow, and his clothes were torn and tattered, stained in areas where open sores oozed pus and blood.

Using his muscular arms, he dragged himself across the room to Kav and Grimshade. He looked up at them with hollow, soulless eyes that sunk into his bulbous head, giving the appearance of the vaguest semblance of sentience. But appearances can be deceiving, for here was a man, deformed and distorted, of the vilest kind, intelligent and evil, but not mad.

"Have our plans been set in motion?" asked the man, his voice, dark, deep, and cold. He took a gasp of air. "Does my army await?"

"Yes, my Lord. Everything is moving forward," said Kav. "We've already sent word. Your army will arrive very soon now."

The man gulped as spittle and other secretions dripped from his mouth. He sputtered, "The steward? His guard? What of them?"

"Let's just say they all have a wonderful view of the seas," said Kav with an evil snicker.

A twisted smile came to the man's face.

"What of my people?" he asked.

"They're just now understanding what's happening."

"Good. Lift me," said the man, his words gurgling in his throat as he choked on fluid and gasped for air.

Kav reached down and lifted the man bringing him to a place outside the room where there was a table and chairs. He carefully placed the man on the table as he and Grimshade sat in the chairs.

"I have something for you," Kav told the man.

He reached into a shirt pocket and removed several coins and placed them on the table. The man picked one up and looked at it.

"We have already begun to mint currency in your likeness," said Kav.

"This pleases me," said the man.

But Grimshade was also bearing a gift. He reached into a pocket and revealed the mirrored shard from Kraneth's staff. He placed it on the table and slid it over to the man. The shard sparkled even in the room's darkness.

"For you," he said.

The man's eyes lit up with pleasure as he reached for the shard. He picked it up, its mesmerizing beauty seeming to pierce his very soul, refracting images deep in his mind, terrifying images of war, death, and destruction. It was difficult to discern but a twisted smile came to his deformed face.

He turned to Grimshade, drool dripping from his mouth.

"Gurandurm, this is a most generous gift," he said. "But we have much to discuss."

"Yes, Lord Drow."

* * *

He was first known as Drow Kullas, the last of Nur' Edan royalty, a direct descendant from the line of Tyrus Turl, and of the Regnes clan. Unlike others born of Nur' Edan royalty during the reign of the conquering Sur' Edan, Drow's life was spared. The steward at the time took pity on him, due to his incurable deformities. It was thought he was of little or unsound mind and condition, and incapable of living to adulthood. But even though his life was spared, the lives of his mother and father were not. The steward's guards, known as the Tironian, brutally killed Drow's parents for illicitly bearing a child and took the infant Drow to an orphanage where he was harshly mistreated.

Life at the orphanage was indeed cruel for Drow. He was beaten and ridiculed by his caretakers and isolated from the other children. All seemed lost in a pit of blackness, that was, until one day, a wealthy widow who often visited the orphanage happened upon where Drow was kept. She instantly became fond of the poor deformed boy.

The widow's name was Muraly Mallor. She was a lady from a good family, with excellent understanding, and most amiable character. She was tall, elegant looking, with pure white skin which was envied by the dark-complexioned Nur' Edan. She always wore an elegant black dress, with sleeves looped up, and a sash around her waist.

Her face, careworn, nonetheless bore traces of fine beauty for which it had once been distinguished.

In her younger years, Lady Mallor married an enterprising man from a good family. He had amassed considerable wealth, through commerce and trade, but unfortunately met with an untimely death at the hands of disease. She vowed never to love another man again and set herself against all worldly things, and lived a life of great austerity, but was determined to put her bestowed wealth to good use. She helped to fund renovations of village buildings and helped to feed those most in need. She was well-liked by those in her village, known as someone who was of a kind and generous spirit.

Unable to bear children of her own and without direct heirs, she decided to adopt a child and raise the child as her own. With each visit to the orphanage, her affection for Drow grew. She saw how he was mistreated and would scold his caretakers, and she would reprimand those who made fun of him. Unlike so many others, she looked past his grotesque deformities and came to love the quiet dignity with which he bore his fate. She wanted to make his life better and adopt him, even though his caretakers considered him an imbecile and a burden. When she expressed her desire to adopt the boy, his caretakers advised against it. They told her the burden of care would be too great for her. But she felt the boy wanted to go on a long journey, and she wanted to go with him. So, she took him to her home in a small village east of Aldkeep Point. He would become the child she could never have.

It was the Lady Mallor who taught a growing Drow to read and gave him a considerable amount of instruction.

She filled his young thoughts with awe and reverence of the Maker; a love of everything good and wholesome; she possessed him with just notions, of it being his duty to do good things for others. His childhood and period of young adulthood with the widow was a happy time, and the villagers embraced him with great fascination. It was a time of learning and discovery, a time when everything he learned and experienced underscored the importance of the values taught by the widow.

But she knew she would not live forever. She needed to plan for his protection upon her death. She knew that he would struggle without her and that he would not be able to face the challenges and uncertainties of the future alone. She did not want him to die a shameful death in some dirty alley. He needed to be looked after properly; he needed the right guidance to make certain his struggles would help him to make his way in the world. So, she went back to his past and made her plans.

When her death came, Drow's world was shattered. Being unable to lay claim to her wealth because of his bloodline, the widow's riches were taken by the steward, and her house was destroyed by the Tironian. All that remained was the widow's name. So, Drow took the surname of Mallor, which means *ill-omened* in the old tongue.

The steward at the time was most surprised upon hearing that Drow had grown to young adulthood. He issued orders to bring Drow to Aldkeep Point to be publicly humiliated and then killed. But the widow's plan was in motion. A chieftain of the Cornovel clan called Kaian, with an allegiance to the Regnes, took Drow from the village before the Tironian could imprison him. The Cornovel protected him and were constantly on the move, from one place to another, to places unknown by the steward and the Tironian.

Over the years, as Drow became older, a terrible kind of anger overcame him and filled his heart with anguish. It was not the anger that burned and twisted in the gut, nor the anger that lurked in the mind, but a different kind of anger altogether. It was a quiet, still anger, and it came from nowhere in particular. It was the kind of anger that eats away at the soul, leaving a hollow sensation behind, anger that seems to have no cause or reason. He knew only one thing about this new anger: it was dark and it sustained him. Those around him, his protectors, fed into this darkness. They surrounded him with hatred, and it swept him on.

The last of the Nur'Edan royal bloodline, Drow started to think of ways to regain power. His vision of the future became a dark tunnel and he snarled at those who subjugated the Nur' Edan. His people had been wronged. They had been betrayed and humiliated. He vowed they would never again be disgraced, that they would never again be shamed by others. He vowed to show them, to show them all. He had never felt so strong, so in control, as he did then. So, Drow plotted his vengeance. He would make the Nur' Edan great again. He would make them respected and feared by all.

He would tell others, "I cannot run but I can draw a bow as well as those who enslave us. They force us to live in the shadows. But know that shadows are rarely what they appear to be. We will wait there, within the depths of the darkness, waiting for the time when we may emerge and break through the gloom. And when that time comes, we will shine a light of death on those who committed abominations against us."

His name grew glorious in the ears of the Nur' Edan as he and Kaian united the chieftains of what clans remained. It was in the remote forested lands and mountains of the North Eldor, where plans were hatched and executed either by suggestion or possession of receptive, proud clansmen. The clans came together, and their groups grew in numbers, small bands who were fearless and who operated in secrecy. They harassed the Tironian at every opportunity, playing a role in the slow subversion of the steward's rule. There were no real battles, only small skirmishes - too quiet all-in-all, however effective, with a constant sense that there was a looming battle ahead.

"This moment is all we have, so we must make the most of it," said Drow. "Let us take our time with their death, for a slow death is most painful. Let us revel in their pain."

Larger clashes with the Tironian soon broke out, and while the Sur' Edan would send reinforcements to support the steward, in recent times many of the Tironian were recalled to the south as there was concern over the darkness to the east. With this, fighting in the north increased, as did the dead and wounded, and the Tironian grew weaker and unable to maintain any semblance of control.

Sensing weakness in the Sur' Edan and Tironian, Drow's thirst for revenge and power consumed him and drove him to seek an alliance with the darkness. An envoy from the Drueger visited with him at one of his many encampments, a man who once hailed from the North Eldor, one of the Silara clan. The envoy became a firm friend to Drow and the two struck a secret bargain. It was widely understood that Drow would go along with the dark brutes of the Drueger and their conquests in return for his being brought to power in the North Eldor. The envoy's Nur' Edan name was Trynt Morain, but everyone called him by the name given him by the brood - Gurandurm Grimshade.

* * *

Tolan and his sister were sitting on the street slowly nibbling on the crust of bread given to them by Grimshade when a haggard man stumbled up to them.

"Where did you get that?" he growled reaching down for the bread.

But Tolan jerked it away.

"It's no concern to you!" he snapped. "I'm of the Inceni, a great warrior, and if necessary, I'll fight you over it!"

"Well by the Maker," said the man angrily, raising a hand to slap Tolan across the face, "I should beat you . . ."

But the man became distracted by screaming and yelling in the streets as crowds of dregs hurried by in waves.

"I'll deal with you and your sister later," he barked at Tolan.

The man followed the crowd to the city center, where it stopped, as thousands gathered pressing forward, pushing, heaving in front of the great central tower. Tolan and his sister tried to get through the throng of dregs, but there were too many and they were forced to stand still, unable to move in any direction. They could not see what was going on and asked others what was happening. But no one responded. A hush then came over the crowd and then a rustling and a murmur. Many of the dregs looked up at the towers and pointed, while others started a cheer.

"What is it? What do you see?" shouted Tolan.

"Want to see it boy?" asked a tall man with a large grim smile. "Want to see it?"

Tolan nodded.

The man reached down and picked him up, placing him on his broad shoulders.

"Look up at the towers boy," said the man. "The towers! Do you see it?"

There, high above the streets of Aldkeep Point, from the many smaller towers around the center tower, hundreds and hundreds of bloodied bodies of men hung from ropes tied around their necks, their bodies swinging rhythmically. Each had been slowly tortured with the maximum amount of pain and anguish until death ended their suffering.

"It's a revolution boy," said the man, brutality in his voice. "It's a revolution! Let the steward and his guards swing in the wind!"

The viciousness of the sight was dark and made darker when the steward's body, which hung from the center tower, suddenly split from the rope and fell to the street below. The dregs quickly surrounded the body and continued the desecration.

Tolan had never seen such horror and it frightened him. But there was something about the mad fervor that now took control of him.

Ah, the Inceni. Very proud warriors they are. The words of the stranger rang through his mind repeatedly.

He pulled himself from the man's shoulders and onto the street. His sister could not see much but knew something very wrong was happening. She was frightened.

"Let's go home," he told her, sensing her fright. He took her in his arms, and they fled the commotion of the streets for home.

As more of the bodies fell to the street, the crowd grew and pushed forward, forcing those closest to the bodies to trample on them. The bodies were slashed and stabbed until they were unrecognizable as men and were covered with spittle. A few in the crowd brought a wooden pole. They found the steward's body and tied it to the timber and paraded it through the streets, as the crowd jeered and threw stones at the body.

The parade found its way to the entrance of the main chamber of the keep, to grand wooden doors that had been sealed for ages with thick pine timbers and metal strapping. The crowd tore at the timbers and metal with their hands, giving voice to a wild, and savage cry of rage. When the last timber and piece of metal was removed from the doors, the crowd fell silent. Then there came a sudden loud thump that shook the city. The large doors slowly groaned open on frozen hinges as a bright light shone out from a great hall.

Down the length of the great hall, stood a thing of nightmares, the Hanu En' Nnard, a large throne made of bones, blood, and death. The bloodstained remains of those who had dared to challenge the throne's many occupants were piled high, rows of skulls lining the top of the back of the throne and along the bottom, while skulls sat at the ends of both armrests. The bulk of the throne was made of small bones, vertebrae, and pelvic bones placed in geometric patterns. On either side of the throne were walls, tall and wide, made of the thigh and other large bones stacked in great quantities. It was a thing of evil, a grisly testament to the power of those who sat upon it, a mockery of life, a symbol of unrestrained power, of the pain and suffering of others, a perversion of all that was good and natural. And all who gazed upon it felt a chill run down their spine, for it was a throne of death.

As the dregs peered into the shadows of the great hall they saw Nur' Edan clan chieftains standing alongside the aisleway leading to the throne. They were a formidable sight, each armed with great swords and clad in their finest armor. Then there came another loud thump that shook the city and the startling sight of Drow Mallor on the floor of the hall's entrance. He had not cleaned himself and was still wearing his soiled clothes. He looked out at the teeming crowds who fell silent, then he turned and dragged himself down the long aisle, past the chieftains each who knelt to a knee as he passed. When he reached the foot of the Hanu En' Nnard, he pulled himself up the stairs and onto the throne, pushing himself upright, as Grimshade and Kav appeared from behind.

"I am Drow of the Regnes, the last of the line of Turl and I am your leader,". said Drow, raising his voice through the gurgling fluid in his throat. "I am unkempt, wearing clothes like you, soiled and torn. I am older now. My once powerful arms are less so now. My back muscles which were once sturdy have atrophied. I have barely enough strength to pull myself up. Yet I do, and I do so, fed from our hatred of our oppressors. You know who I am. My mind is the same. My determination is the same. I have brought us to this time, where the blood of Tironian bodies fills our streets. Their ashen faces and their eyes stare at us, as though imploring help, or mercy. But there will be no mercy, for no mercy was ever shown to us.

"The evil that surrounded us for so long is no more. Know that in their deaths we will be freed, that never again will our people bleed. We shall never forget the terrible cost we paid, and never forget how much we have lost. But do not fear, for we will learn again how to mine the rich ore, to cut the large timber, to conquer those who dare to enslave us, so corruption again will never arise. This is my plan, to bring a storm of fire to the south, and when the storm passes there will come a new day, a day when we will rise from embers. With you, my people, I am again one! We are again one! Rise Nur' Edan to victory! To victory! To victory!"

The crowd erupted and responded with applause and cheers.

"Hooray! Hooray!" they shouted. "Hooray for Lord Drow! Hooray for a storm of fire! Hooray for the Nur' Edan!"

When the crowd had quieted, Drow proclaimed deification for the Lady Muraly Mallor and that a great edifice would be constructed in her honor. The crowd erupted in adulation as there was tumultuous rejoicing in the streets. All celebrated Drow as master of the Nur' Edan. Music was played and there was dancing all night. The dregs never forgot the importance of their ancestry and still believed in their superiority. They cared little for war and death but feared much more to live in cowardice and servitude to others. They saw themselves as a race of warriors, builders, and conquerors. The lesson of history was a cruel one: it was better to conquer than be conquered. It was only a matter of time before they would conquer the whole of the Harrow.

The next several days were a time of great excitement in Aldkeep Point. Drow, along with his general, Virl Voracious of the Cornovel, led thousands of the great warrior clansmen, both young and old, through the streets of Aldkeep Point. The people of the city cheered and waved as the mighty procession made its way through the streets and there were great celebrations.

Before long, the time came when the army marched out of the city, ready to face whatever enemy awaited them, and Drow told the throngs of warriors, "Now is the time to inflict vengeance on the foe even if it means death. And if this is our fate, then let us embrace the darkness of the unknown than cower under the calamities of enslavement."

They marched south, representing the strength of a reunified Nur' Edan people, and the other races of the Harrow would soon learn to respect their resolve. And within the mass of warriors, there was one who marched, confident and bold, a young boy – Tolan of the Inceni.

CHAPTER 9
THE GREAT CONVERGENCE

NIGHT WAS APPROACHING AND the White Star began looking for a place to camp. Dalgaes chose a place west of the Old River, several leagues from where the river branched into a maze of shallow, narrow, winding channels flowing southwest from Mistmere and near where an outcropping of mountains met the Forest Heave. The area was large enough for the army of the White Star while also providing several defensive positions. As the elven army made camp several lookouts spotted brood east of the Old River, small groups of enemy forces in what seemed like random positions. Dalgaes did not know what to make of the brood formations and asked Col Shas to have a wing of the Vilyarok fly a reconnaissance operation.

"Put Tirn Elen in charge. Exercise caution," he told Col Shas. "There will be no engagement. Make sure Elen knows this."

After only a short time, the reconnaissance party returned. Tirn Elen approached Col Shas and Dalgaes. Like all elven warriors, Elen was tall and muscular with shoulder-length hair, a strong face, and determined eyes. But unlike other elves, his was scarred, with a gash that ran across his jaw showing the mark of a blade, and a puckered scar on his cheek. It was obvious he had been in many fights, and more obviously he enjoyed it.

"We have not seen such movements before," said Tirn Elen. "The evil flows from the Dregec Kuul but in small groups. No more than five or ten. They splinter off in haphazard patterns across the flatlands. Some groups wade through the marshlands while others hold firm, close to the Old River. There was no mishap." He paused in concern. "What is most curious, the wretches did not look up at us or attempt a defense. It was as if they did not care about our presence. Their focus was to the west, to the Heave."

Dalgaes nodded and dismissed Tirn Elen.

"They could cross the Old River and attack from the north," suggested Col Shas. "We should leave a few legions near the forest, to guard our rear flank as we make our way south to Chyh-Mehm."

Dalgaes reflected for a moment then said, "That may be what they wish us to do, to spread us thinly across the land. Their goal is to enter the west and through the Thorndell. That is how it has always been. And the only way to get to the Thorndell is through Chyh-Mehm. We must remain alert. It could be a trap set by a clever opponent."

"Clever? Brood?" laughed Col Shas.

"Evil prowls for the unsuspecting whom they may devour. Staying alert means we must never underestimate our opponent. We should never minimize the impact of their willingness to overcome past failures. Evil learns from its pain. We must be careful that such a tempting exposure may be a trap. Remember, it is always better to miss an opening than to risk rushing into a snare. Have Tirn Elen keep an eye on the brood's movements. In the morning we will maintain our march south to join with Carrick."

The night continued its tranquil course, creeping calmly over the land as the elven warriors went about their tasks in silence. They made their encampment, erecting their tents and making fires from whatever wood they could forage; Vilyarok horses were corralled and given great care; scouts and defenders were dispatched along the vast parameter of the encampment. The smell of roasting vegetables was strong on a gentle breeze, as the warriors prepared some drink and food; spearsmen, swordsmen, and archers sharpened their weapons. Several legions maintained a defensive posture on nearby hills, while other elven warriors kept their sights set on the brood east of the Old River.

Outside the largest tent, the one bearing the banner of the White Star, Dalgaes sat alone by a fire near a small outcropping of tall pine trees. He was deep in thought as he sharpened his sword with a specially carved stone. He thought of the upcoming day, going over the terrain in his mind, and how he would march the White Star to Chyh-Mehm. He thought of the strange formations of the brood and wondered what they were up to. There was a disturbing calmness about him as he and the others prepared for the next day and possible battle.

Then, from the corner of his eye, he caught a glimpse of a cat. It sat beneath a pine tree and he could see the glowing green of its eyes from within the dark shadows of the night. He recognized its coloration, shape, and size. Soon, there came the deep rumble of a soft purr, a sound he also recognized. He looked away from the cat.

"My friend," said the cat. "It is good to see you again."

He remembered the voice and took a deep breath. He closed his eyes as sadness came over him.

"Shia Alia . . . Huntress of the Tar Shor . . . night brings its dark rule," he said, eyes still closed. "As I thought. It was you at the defile."

He could not look at the cat since it reminded him of a painful moment in his past, a time of profound betrayal. He knew it would bring back sad memories. Still, there was a bit of gladness in his heart to hear her voice, which sounded like the gentle rippling of water.

She makes her presence known during such troubled times, he thought. *If she continues to show her magic, others will question how she escaped the Ra Cath. Then, all eyes will turn to me. They will know that it was I who crossed the Ra Cath and the Si Jhys.*

He opened his eyes. He took his sword and plunged it deep into the ground.

"You required my aid, and I was glad to give it," said the Huntress. "I remember when you did the same for us, when you gave us shelter and food, first at Elandrake and then at Gagdash, with such generosity that you did not even choose to reveal who offered such gifts. It was the most difficult time for me and the others of the Tar Shor. I wanted to help my En' Edhel friends, a way to repay you for your kindness and generosity."

He took another deep breath, still not looking at her as she sat under the pine tree.

"The Guild Lords were misguided," he told her firmly. "The Ra Cath extermination of the Tar Shor was an abomination. One does not destroy that which one does not or cannot understand. The unknown must be embraced for it to become known. I simply went about correcting an injustice."

"And in doing so you shattered the oath of the En' Edhel, the oath to abide by the decisions of the Si Jhys, regardless of the right or wrong of the matter. It is an oath of generations, sworn by your forefathers."

"It is my secret and my secret alone. It is what I must live with."

"We are forever grateful to you and your people." She paused as sadness for him crept across her face. "I know it is difficult for you to gaze upon me. I know how trying it has been for you, what you have carried lo these many years. It is the burden of being everything we imagine that we are not. My heart goes out to you, and I know any words of comfort I may have can never replace what you have lost."

He was silent. He lifted his sword out from the ground and started to again sharpen its edges. As he sharpened the blade of his straight double-edged sword, he looked to keep his mind active, on something other than his haunting secret. He sometimes refused to accept the reality of his actions, preferring at times to blame the Si Jhys and others.

If not for their decision, I would not have been compelled to defy the authority of the Ra Cath Guild, an entity I am obligated to defend, and in doing so compromise my honor. Everyone has secrets, I suppose.

"We live with our secrets, carefully so. Do we not, Huntress?" he asked.

"Yes. Sometimes in comfort and sometimes in pain."

"I did what I believed was best for the Harrow and its future," he said. "I knew my decision would forever haunt me and indeed it has. I have often painfully revisited it and have kept it hidden when I would have liked to shout the truth out to the world. But is the guilt and the fear, the uncertainty of being found out that strikes at my soul. What we fail to realize is that we do not keep secrets; our secrets keep us. Like small voracious bugs, the secrets we keep slowly eat away at our lives."

"Those same secrets also eat away at relationships," she said. "Sometimes it is best to stop running from a truth and start running toward it. The person who runs from a truth, ventures to dark places where one does not want to go. Running from something, denying it, never makes it go away."

Anger started to grow inside of him and as he sharpened his sword, his strokes became quicker and longer along the sides of the blade.

"And what will embracing the truth of a matter do?" he asked her. "Will it make the fear and anguish go away? The guilt? The uncertainty?"

She was silent.

He closed his eyes and gave a deep sigh, full and large, to calm himself.

I must control my impetus, my emotions at all times, he thought.

He stopped sharpening his sword.

"Tell me - why are you here after all this time?" he asked, his voice calm, but his mind still in turmoil. "Why Huntress? Why now at this moment in time? Is not my past torment enough?"

She continued to be saddened by his words. She realized that even after so many years, he struggled to conquer his worst enemy - his inner being, his self. She knew she could not help him, although that was what she wanted to do. But time was now precious for her. There were dark matters at hand that needed to be tended to.

"I do not wish to anger you or remind you of your suffering, my friend," she said apologetically.

"I require no such reminder."

"I understand. But I am here for one purpose, and it is not about the past, but rather the present. We know of the emergence of Dark Wizards and the Librarian. We have heard the marching of man, dwarf, and elf, the drums of Katzhu Pu. Your presence and that of the White Star in the east tells me the great armies of the Harrow will meet as one. A sad foreboding has seized my visions. I have seen great death and destruction, the burden born of something evil, something greater than that which you now face, a demon, unlike others. It lay dormant within the Drueger, a mountain beast of Drar Druul. The darkness that prowls the land, that which resides within the dark tower knows not of this menace, nor how to awaken it. But understand if the demon is awakened it will be most terrifying. In my dreams, I heard a sound, the demon's name - Dor Gordur."

He looked up into the surrounding trees and took a deep breath, to keep calm, and clear his head. His thoughts turned to the affairs of war and what she had told him.

"I have not heard of such a fiend," he said. "The evil sounds formidable enough. But what are we to do? Are the Si Jhys or the Edainar aware of this terror you speak of?"

"The Si Jhys cannot see into the depths of blackness as I can. However, the wizards may know of its existence. But I am uncertain of this. My concern is the Librarian who has been released. He knows of the ancient texts. He may have the power to awaken the demon."

The Librarian! An uneasiness entered his thoughts. *So many wrongs in this world.*

"Also, I wish to tell you I will soon leave this realm," she said gently. "My journey here is complete. This too I have seen. But there will be another, one who shall come from the Aina Dur. She shall possess great power and lead the Tar Shor."

He looked down at his sword and again started to sharpen it, striking sparks that shot and danced about.

If she is to leave, perhaps I should look upon her one last time, to say a final goodbye, he thought. *So many years have passed; perhaps she is correct; perhaps, as she said, it is time to stop running from the truth and instead run to it. Maybe it is time to face my betrayal, my guilt, my fears, and risk learning to feel again. It is time to turn and face the truth that has so plagued me.*

Just as he peeked over his shoulder to gaze upon her one last time, she was gone as if she had never been there.

I will never see her again.

He felt a cooling, soft breeze in the air. He paused, listening to the whispering winds. There were no voices from the camp, no popping sound from the fires, and no snort of horses from the Vilyarok. The strangeness of the calm was unsettling to him, and he listened intently for something, anything at all. But no sound came.

He was left with his secret thoughts; thoughts which would have to remain his forever. He lowered his head and sobbed deeply from his chest.

My Huntress, even though I could not look upon you one last time, know we are and have always been as one. I should have told you this. I have always tried to do what was right. May the Maker bless you. By your life, no evil shall ever harm us.

* * *

The Huntress ran, keeping low to the ground, stopping periodically to sniff the air. She would make her way west, past Katzhu Pu, and to Blackstone Keep. Her journey would be arduous and long, exhausting, and dangerous. She would travel over mountains and plains and pass only an occasional village with a few scattered homes, and sometimes for hundreds of leagues the only break in rock and forests would be a small river, low, and flowing quietly. It would be in these places where she would rest.

The White Star's encampment was now several leagues away when she stopped to rest in some dense underbrush. After catching her breath, she lifted her nose to the air. There was a peculiar scent, but one familiar to her, from ages past. It was a foul, sour odor, one only learned Ra Cath could detect. She looked to the south, to the darkness of the forest, the Heave.

The Soran Cath, she thought. *They live in the woods like wild beasts. They eat everything in filth. They speak foul before their fathers.* Her eyes bolted around. *I do not have much time.*

* * *

As morning sprung, Molly's group passed Tollford Farthing. Their travels now brought them across fields and farmlands and over hills. When they came to a road they stopped, listened, and if they heard no sound they crossed it quickly. If the road ran their course, they would not follow it, for fear of being spotted. They would look around diligently everywhere, avoiding trouble. Where they could, where Bran thought it safe, they would stop to rest. When night approached, the company knew that they would look for a place to camp, and were fortunate to find places that provided cover, a rock outcropping, or a burrow within a hillside. They would rest at a variety of places, making camp in wooded dells, sheltered by alder, birch, and ash trees, and on one night they found shelter in a large cornfield. They cut up the green corn for bedding and slept well. The girls did not care much for such travels, but along the way, they continued to gather courage, rooted in their belief that they were on a great and noble quest.

They continued their way east, passing north of Therilia, hugging the tree line of a forest where the Old River joined Lake Mehm. From there a storm arrived. Clouds that had built up over the mountains moved across the lands releasing great downpours of rain. Through it all, everyone was able to see the Old River to the east and the blurry tree line of the Forest Heave to the north. To the west they could make out Carrick's great army as it approached, the army's line extending for leagues, back past Therilia and on to the Thorndell Fields. They could see the army as it took various positions along the plains south of Lake Mehm. So too did they witness the Balor Guild of the Ra Cath, thousands upon thousands of feline warriors as they made their way to the lake region.

The girls had never seen an army, let alone one marching; they had never seen such vast numbers. Masses of soldiers, horses, and great implements of war passed in the distance, one endless stream of might in the cold dampness. It was quite a spectacle. Elizabeth was enchanted by the sound of the drums, the bagpipes and the trumpets, the teams of horses, the banners, and the flags. She could not take her eyes off the massed troops. She was fascinated by how the armies moved as one and felt as if the winds carried the smell of victory. But Molly was saddened by what she saw because while the sight of the massive armies marching was incredible, she knew it meant war, and war meant death. She clutched the Lia Fail in solace, and it warmed to her touch.

"Is this all because of me?" she asked Brows.

"Do not burden yourself. Sometimes war is necessary and sometimes it is not. Sometimes there is no choice in the matter. In a fallen world, war is required to bring peace. Of surely, war is an ugly thing, but not the ugliest of things. The makings for what we will soon see have simmered for many ages, the ingredients for such an unappetizing stew coming together at one time. No. This war is not your war, nor is it of your doing. Understand?"

She hugged the bobbin and they continued, now moving north.

As they endured more travel, it became increasingly clear – the girls did not like traveling by foot, for it was very slow and it took a long time to travel from place to place. But Brows pointed out that such a mode of travel permitted relatively direct routes, whereas animal transport demanded that the characteristics of the beast be taken into consideration, typically forcing a gentler but more circuitous route. Traveling by foot also required stamina and a willingness to get dirty.

They would take time to rest, and this was appreciated by Brows who would take the opportunity to not only catch his breath but provide the girls with more history about their strange new home. As they entered the eastern lands with the woods of the Heave looming nearby, he spoke of geography.

"You must become familiar with the terrain of this land," he told the girls. "I am not sure how it is back at your home, but here there are parts of the land that act as natural protection. Rivers, lakes, and mountains provide natural barriers while vast open fields are places where battles occur. But there are places of monolithic loneliness, of the great empty spaces that lie in between here and there. Many of these places remain unexplored or uninhabited. We may venture into some of these spaces, while others cannot be navigated.

He pointed to the forest.

"That place, the forest that you see, is an example. As was discussed before, the Heave is a place no one enters. Unlike the Tangle, it is a lifeless place, dark, and swollen with despair. The forest is so dark it is difficult to discern whether it is day or night because the tall forest trees trap the light. No creature can live in the Heave, and it has never been traversed. It is considered an enemy to all."

Molly looked at the forest. It was a murky blur of trees, so dark and dense that it was as if the air was filled with solid shadow. It was impossible to make out individual trees, and she had no way of knowing who or what lived there. There was no movement in the forest, even though there was a slight breeze. She felt nervous about the place, without knowing why.

"Because of the Heave, Lake Mehm and its island city is the only gateway between east and west," he said as they moved on. "Every major battle fought over the ages has included the lake and its city. By holding the lake territory, the forces of good protect the western lands from invaders."

Bran was listening intently.

"Your geography lessons . . . have you talked of the Pas Shae to the east?" he asked Brows.

"No. Why would I speak of such a frightening place," said Brows. "It is a wilderness, deep with desperation and filled with the sludge of suffering. Why would I ever speak of it?"

"Because historian, that is where we travel," said Bran, his words short and to the point.

Brows was aghast at what he heard, and he wondered if he had heard correctly. But before he could ask why such a venture was required, Bran stopped the group. He had to say something so he cleared his throat.

"I feel as if I ought to speak to the nature of our journey," he said.

"Speak to the nature? What is this craziness?" said an annoyed Brows. "There was no talk of the Pas Shae at Katzhu Pu,"

"We cannot simply walk into the Dregec Kuul," said a determined Bran. "The place crawls with brood. And we did not speak of a plan before because it was left up to me, and I have now decided on one. We will cross the barrens and then the marshes and make our way to the Pas Shae. From there we will enter the Drueger from the north."

"This is stupidity. How do you propose we navigate the marshes?" asked Brows.

Big Grey sensed anger in the bobbin. It was a hot, stinging, prickly anger.

"Cooler heads are needed to guide us," warned the cat with a pointed stare at Brows. "We are all in this together. We need to keep our wits about us."

Brows saw the cat's gaze. He took a deep breath to try to calm himself.

"Perhaps the orc can help," said Bran. "I believe he is familiar with the marshes."

Bran and Brows looked at Ug'ghi Otha.

"Yes. I know of the place," said the orc. "A friend I know can help us. He lives in the marshes and can sense the safety of the ground underfoot, those narrow pathways through the foul. But it is a wicked place and difficult. Some would say the darkest of places in all the Harrow. Few survive such a journey. But it can be done if one is careful."

"Good. Once we are through the marshes, we will make our way east," said Bran.

Brows could not believe what he was hearing, even though he was a little calmer. He shook his head in bewilderment and astonishment.

"It is at a time like this that one wishes he could be somewhere else," he said.

Bran now became agitated at the bobbin.

"Historian, how did you think we would enter the hive?" he asked. "Did you think we would go up to the gates and knock? Did you think the darkness that lives there would open the gates for us and welcome us with open arms?"

Still shaking his head, Brows ignored Bran and sighed. He turned to Ug'ghi Otha.

"You mentioned you have a friend in the marshes," Brows said to the orc. "What kind of creature lives in such a place? Surely, it must be unnatural."

"Precisely," said the orc with a smile.

Brows scoffed, "Start off wrong and we will not survive. I think we venture into the impossible."

"You are a historian. I think you have forgotten what history teaches us about survival," said Bran.

"Remind me then," said a sarcastic Brows. "What does history teach us about survival?"

"Survival is but a dream, but as with all dreams all things are possible."

While the talk worried Molly, she recognized that her destiny would be fraught with places of evil and suffering, places that lured good souls to darkness. It seemed suffering was this land's due. There was an unearthly look about her face, and a melancholy determination in her eyes, which told the working of a spirit within her, that was recently awakened. She gave a singular smile of recognition of the impending difficulty. She was prepared.

"I am sure the plan is a good one," she told Bran. "I trust you and have no reason to question your ability."

"Thank you, my Queen. I am most grateful for your support," said Bran.

Brows grumbled something under his breath. He was not happy.

Molly looked at him and then at the others.

"I think we can all agree that regardless of the direction our journey takes us, it will present some unpleasantness," she said. "However, no matter what happens I know we will be fine. Now, I think we have all been looking forward to a bit of a rest."

"Yes, my Queen. We will make camp here before continuing our journey," said Bran. "I want to review the brood movement to best plot our path forward."

They quickly made camp while Ancorbow looked for a place that had some cover where he could fish. He was familiar with where they were and knew of a few places that provided cover along the Old River, hidden from the brood's stare. A campfire was prepared for dinner and soon Ancorbow brought back a fresh catch of fish from the river.

After dinner, as the light was fading, Bran and Ancorbow left the group. They made their way to the Old River, to the forested place where Ancorbow had fished, where they could better study their surroundings. It was a ridge made of enormous tree roots and covered by a canopy of green branches. From here, they could see the Old River snaking over the land, sparkling in the receding light.

"This place offers us good protection. It conceals our presence," said Ancorbow.

"Yes. There are many such places along the river," said Bran, "some we will consider when we keep pushing north."

The two surveyed the Foghollow Barrens before them. Both were familiar with the land, but it had been quite some time since they had journeyed this far east.

Bran pointed to the south then north.

"The dark peaks of the Drueger rising in the distance and the marshland before them," he said. "And there, the ruined city of Gortha Losh and the black Dregec Kuul. Have you been to these parts before?"

"Yes. But these are places one does not often visit," said Ancorbow. "It has been some time."

"Little has changed in this wretched land – cold, dark, isolated," said Bran. He pointed east. "And look, look at the evil. Look at how they slither and crawl, their malicious intent clear in their cold, dead eyes. They are coming for us."

They saw black shadows of brood marching westward from Gortha Losh, toward Lake Mehm, with slow and steady steps. The monsters hissed and snarled, drooling with hunger, their claws extended and teeth bared. Bran then pointed north where they saw another brood army spewing from the mouth of the Dregec Kuul. Each army occupied a different place along the Old River's eastern bank.

"We can get to the marshland easily enough as we are west of the river," said Bran, his mind reeling through options. "We can cross north of the brood positions. But before we can venture into the marshland and to the Pas Shae, we will need to find a way to avoid the brood."

"You think they will pursue us into the marshlands?"

Bran turned to Ancorbow, a hardened look across his face.

"Such evil is ravenous to consume good," he said. "We will need to find a way to go unnoticed."

"If we are so vulnerable, then we should look to enter the marshes under the dark veil of night," said Ancorbow. "That should provide us with some protection."

Bran returned his gaze to the east.

"Yes. I think it is best to continue north, away from the brood, a short trek, perhaps a few hours to where the Old River meets the marshlands. From there, we can cross the river and make our way through the marshes to the Pas Shae, north of the Dregec Kuul and the evil brood passage. Let us return to camp. We will make our way north. Tomorrow we will use the day to rest, and when nightfall arrives, as you have said, we will pass into the marshes."

They returned to camp and told everyone of what they had witnessed, of two dark armies massing across the wasteland. Bran made it clear: it was important to continue north, that their journey into the marshes would be difficult and dangerous.

"Is there a plan to avoid the brood in the marshes?" asked Brows.

"We hope that the darkness of night will help," Bran told them. "But only the Maker knows."

"May the Maker be with us," said Brows, a look of despair on his face.

So much gloom and darkness, thought Molly. *So much lack of hope. Is everything pointless and empty?*

She had a thought, remembering something the Professor once had told her.

"One can only conquer hopelessness by daring to seek possibilities," she said with clarity.

They broke camp and continued north.

* * *

Rain, hail, sleet, and snow fell over the land as the morning wore on. Amid the gloom, there was a vast movement across the Harrow, the Ra Alye', or great convergence. Under the pounding thunder of galloping hooves, three great armies of the good and righteous marched under the banners of the Fist and Axe and Tree. They came from the Thorndell Fields, descending on the island city of Chyh-Mehm. At the front, in the foremost ranks of the grand and mighty army rode Erol Carrick on the magnificent Warsinger while above, the great falcon Windthrasher soared gracefully. Alongside Carrick rode Bombadorn Roundthaler followed by the Shyr Shar, a legion of the most ferocious Nalenia warriors and archers. The great army followed, a mighty host reckoned at three hundred thousand, led by Waywyn I'Kinillel and Ranagul Dithil, and Entur Donduin.

On the plain south of the island city, the mighty army marched carefully arrayed in hundreds of columns. Within the mass of warriors stood great wooden siege engines, catapults, battering rams, towers, and flamethrowers pulled by huge woolly beasts. As the army settled into position Roundthaler gave a wave of his arm, directing a legion of men from the Eldor. The legion made up of warriors on horseback and archers separated from the larger army and marched to a position farther south of Chyh-Mehm and west of the Old River just behind a large area of grassy hills.

As Carrick's legions began to occupy strategic positions on the plains, a fourth army under the banner of the Claw, the Balor Guild of the Ra Cath, quietly marched to a place just north and west of the island city. There they held a position hidden by the city's tall stone walls, without wavering, patiently waiting for the moment to be as one, to form the extraordinary force known as the Kyr Thysaer.

As the four great armies took their positions, a fifth army, the elven army under the banner of the White Star led by the Elf-King himself, continued its march from the north, from near the Forest Heave. The vast elven legions marched south, still some leagues northeast of Chyh-Mehm. As they marched, they continued to watch the small bands of brood to the east, as the evil flowed from the Drueger.

As Dalgaes once said, "Wherever there is good, there must also be evil. Wherever there is life, death must follow as its shadow."

And so too did a shadow stir over the land, great darkness, for never had there been so large an assemblage of evil brood upon the land, as come together to answer Urth' Goroth's call. From the devastated city of Gortha-Losh, a great brood army under the banner of the Tower had emerged. At the lead was an Urur Maw called Rotghoul, and he rode a giant muugaan and was followed by column after column of cu sith, fachens, trolls, firbolgs, and orcs. From Gortha-Losh the brood continued its slow march westward and was several leagues southeast of the island city and east of the Old River. There Rotghoul waited for the enemy, for Carrick himself, while from the north another evil army stirred, this one much larger. Here, a mass of brood seethed from the Dregec Kuul and onto the plains. This large army, also under the banner of the Tower, was composed of a multitude of legions and was led by Grimsor, Uth' Egoreyr, or Great General. Parts of the enormous, wicked army were slowly making their way south and to the Foghollow Barrens, while small groups broke away and marched south of the Ug' Foul Marsh to the Old River, toward the Forest Heave.

The land trembled and quaked as the massive armies set in motion. Ripples ran through the ground of the Foghollow Barrens and into the city of Chyh-Mehm in ever-rising waves of sand and dirt and rock, breaking under the hooves and feet of the marching armies. Above the armies, an immense dark mass spread across the sky like a cloud and transformed itself into a figure gigantic and strange. It foretold of the horror to come, of an awesome power that would come from the skies.

* * *

Elban Miragrin was standing outside his tent, stunned by the breadth and complexity of what he now saw. The army encampment appeared to stretch over the whole horizon of view to the west. The scene was vast, with rows upon rows of twinkling campfires and low, white tents by the thousands, like stars in the night sky. Men moved about purposefully, sharpening swords and arrows, some talking and having a morning meal, others tending to the great horses, and others preparing the many siege engines. The young man moved his gaze eastward. There, he saw the immense brood army moving about many places, beginning to slowly position its numbers toward the west in full battle array. The army was darkness incarnate, its sheer size frightening, reaching far into the distance, to the base of the snowy, white-capped mountains that was the Drueger.

A voice startled Miragrin.

"What's your name?" asked an aged warrior with a voice scratchy like the sound of wind in dry leaves.

He was short and stout, his face hard, his teeth grinding together within the tangle of a beard. It looked almost as if he was shaking, fighting some terrible battle within his mind. He carried knives sheathed in the front and a shorter sword sheathed to his back.

"Miragrin, Elban Miragrin."

"Hmmm . . . not a name I've heard before and I've heard plenty of names."

"And your name?" asked Miragrin, looking down at the old warrior.

"I'm called Sark Gruelor. Some call me other words, many of which shouldn't be repeated for they're foul and hurtful. But it's no matter to me what I'm called, as long as I'm called on to fight and kill. Where do you herald from?"

Miragrin was careful with his response. He knew how some, those narrow-minded, held prejudice against those from Portmoor.

"From the west," he said.

"Hmmm . . . the western lands. Many beautiful places there. Many dangerous and sad places as well. Take a place like Portmoor. Very sad place, a hive of vagrants and half-witted, half-bred fools. Brood did us all a favor by taking it from the land if you ask me. I say good riddance to them all." The old man itched his beard and laughed.

Miragrin became angry.

"Old man, you shouldn't talk of a place in such a way. I'd be careful if I were you," he snapped.

With surprising speed and deftness, Gruelor drew his sword, placed it against Miragrin's wrist, and with his other arm grabbed the back of Miragrin's neck. Miragrin found himself being pulled closer to the old man, whose face was now inches from his own. The stench of Gruelor's breath was horrid, a foul mixture of rotting food, tobacco, and something else that was indescribable. Miragrin tried to turn away but could not.

"Do you feel my blade on your wrist?" scowled Gruelor as he tightened his grip on Miragrin's neck. "It is called Anda Maeg and it obeys my every command. With one quick slash, I can end your life, and watch you bleed out on the ground like every beast I've killed. Don't ever voice such irritation at me boy. Do you understand?"

Gruelor then pushed Miragrin to the ground who was stunned by the swiftness, ferocity, and strength of the old man.

"You're from Portmoor," said Gruelor. "I know this because you ride Sarannth, the grand Ure Rokko steed of Skag Harwell." He reached down and offered a hand to Miragrin who gladly took it. "You may hear ugly remarks and witness or be the target of intolerance, but always, always be proud of who you are, no matter what your heritage. Such things are only caused by ignorance or fear. Stand tall. Be proud. Refuse to tolerate disrespect."

Miragrin brushed the dirt from his pants.

"Isn't that what I did?" he asked.

The old man laughed.

"Hardly. I had to pry it from you, forcing your anger. Remember, anger is but an expression of inner turmoil. It's a weakness. Let this be my first lesson."

"Lesson? What do you mean by lesson?"

"You, you're the one to be with the great Carrick, to fight by his side. He asked me to teach you some things. Why you of all the warriors, I don't know. You're gangly and young. Too young I say. But who listens to me? Huh. Have a bit of food then rest some. I'll return to continue your schooling, young Miragrin."

The old man walked away, fading into the maze of white tents, men, and horses.

Those nearest to Miragrin snickered at the encounter, relieved they were not the target of the old man's feigned wrath. They knew it had been a deliberate performance, intended to create a shared experience. The same thing had happened to many of those who looked on.

"You know of this man?" Elban asked the others.

There was boisterous laughter now.

A large warrior stood. His form was sizeable and justly proportioned.

"Know of him?" said the warrior, sarcasm in his voice. "Everyone knows of Gruelor. He can be your best friend and your worst enemy."

"More like your worst nightmare," another growled.

"But who is he?" implored Miragrin.

The large warrior became serious. He paused to stare at Miragrin, his expression thoughtful.

"Sark Gruelor? The old man? He's to be your mentor, as he's been for so many in the past. He's a master swordsman, as renowned as any who've come before him. He fights with knife and sword and will train you to adapt his training to that weapon with which you're most comfortable. He possesses enough skill to defeat the mightiest of the brood. When I first met him, I didn't care if I lived or die. I was a hapless soul. I would fight any person or any group of persons. It didn't matter to me. Nor did it take much to provoke me. I wasn't of good mind. Then that old man came to me and taught me many things. He shaped me into a fine warrior, and the same will happen to you. To this day, I don't what he saw in me, or why he chose me. But I'm thankful he did. You now look upon me, here, in what I've become. I ask you – what do you see? Do you laugh at me?"

Miragrin shook his head in response, the large warrior's face fierce in its intensity.

The warrior continued, "The old man said you're to be with Carrick. He doesn't know why, and I don't care much. In the end, you're no different than any of us." He waved to the others who now gathered near Miragrin. "You're of flesh and bone. You can die at the hands of the brood, no different than myself or any warrior here. I only hope you're ready to learn your lessons."

"How long will it take?"

"As long as necessary. No more questions. Do as you were told. Get some food and rest. You'll need it."

Miragrin stood watching as the warrior and the others walked away, his mind in a whirl. When he had first been told he would be traveling with Carrick, of course, he had thought it a great honor. But now, as he looked at the many warriors about the campsite, he realized that something more was at stake. He would have to prove himself worthy of being a warrior, and that meant learning from the best.

* * *

When Gruelor returned he had several knives in one hand and with the other, he dragged a long sword alongside. The sword was unique, fashioned of black metal, and so sharp were its edges that it easily furrowed the hardened ground behind the old man. Those around Miragrin shrank back having seen the sword before.

"Look. He brings the great sword," the large warrior remarked to the others.

"Will the boy be able to lift it?" asked another.

"Doubtful," the response was quick. "No man can lift that sword. Much too heavy for the wielder. Only one has ever used it. No one else has the strength."

Gruelor stopped in front of Miragrin and looked up at the young man.

"Turn around," he told Miragrin.

Miragrin did as he was told. Gruelor took the knives he was carrying and placed them about Miragrin's garb, sliding them between his garment and his flesh, and into his boots and trousers.

"There now. You've many weapons you can use when you need them," said Gruelor. "But there's one weapon, one of the mightiest of them all which you'll need. It's been used before, in many battles, but only by one man."

Gruelor reached over with his other hand and now using both hands and with a grimace of great strength, dragged the long sword forward, facing Miragrin. Miragrin saw the strain on Gruelor's face as he moved the sword and found it strange.

Why can't he lift the sword? How heavy can it be? But if he can't lift it surely I won't be able to either!

He looked at the sword. It was magnificent, like nothing he had ever seen before. But it was not the fancy hilt encrusted with gold and jewels that set it apart. No. The sword was quite plain and of a simple design that appealed to him at once. What made it so remarkable was the long razor-edged blade itself, for it was as black as pitch and as wicked looking as midnight.

"Let's see if you can lift it. Take the sword in your hand," demanded Gruelor.

Miragrin reached down and grabbed the hilt with both hands. It was cool to the touch. He closed his eyes not wanting to view his failure, and slowly, ever so slowly, lifted the sword. Surprisingly, it was light in his hands, easy to lift. He thought he knew the sword - it felt somewhat familiar - but he was taken from these thoughts and drawn to the roar of a great battle in his mind.

Miragrin imagined hands, fingers, and arms flailing through the brood as the blade found targets with zeal. It was a wrath-filled rage that was also precise. To him, the creatures were mindless, inept animals. As he swept the huge sword deftly through a wall of foul flesh, he saw it dripping in bloody gore. The brood began to fall like weeds, and Miragrin soon found himself stumbling over their shattered remains.

There came a cheer and his mind cleared.

"He lifts it," the large warrior whispered in astonishment. "By the Maker, he lifts it."

Miragrin opened his eyes.

"Whose sword was this?" he asked.

A smile came to the old man's hardened face.

"The blade is called Zi Gurut and it was the sword of your master – Skag Harwell," said Gruelor.

Hearing the name of his master saddened Miragrin. He had come to think of Skag Harwell as a father, and the loss of him had been devastating. He missed his master's company and his sage words. He stared at Gruelor as confusion set across his face. Slowly, his fingers released the sword to the ground.

"No . . . I can't," he told Gruelor.

The old man was angered, deeply angered by Miragrin's action.

"There's no time for emotions, no time to grieve. Your master would've been displeased at your sadness. I've much to teach you."

"I can't use his sword. I'm not him. I'm not the man he was."

Gruelor bent to a knee and using both hands slowly brought the sword to his side, the strain of its weight on his face.

"He was one man, only one man. And you, you are no different, only one man. The sword decides its wielder. Now, take the sword."

"I cannot wield such a sword in battle."

"The sword doesn't make the warrior," said Gruelor, "it only extends the fighter's will and strength. It does this by becoming one with its wielder. Do you understand?"

Miragrin nodded and asked, "But why were you given the sword? Why didn't my master keep it?"

"He was done with war, done with leading men to death, done with all killing and all that went along with it. He was set on being a different man, a man he was more comfortable with. He was going to do the right thing. So, he returned to the sea. He left part of him in the blade and knew there would be another, one who'd have the strength to wield the blade in battle, to protect the innocent, to lead good over evil."

"But it will change me, won't it? As it changed my master."

"Oh, it's true, you're not your own until the blade belongs to another. But you've little choice now. Refuse the blade and it'll be an insult to your master's honor. Just look around you. Every man here has tried to wield the blade and failed. Given the opportunity, they'd gladly accept it. You see, he's within the blade and you. The blade senses this. That's why it chose you. This is who you are now. It's your time."

With those words, confidence grew in Miragrin despite his still-perplexed expression, confidence born of having been through an ordeal and survived. He thought of his wife Mora and their two children. He thought of the destruction of Portmoor and the darkness that spread over the land. Now, he realized that there was a reason why he was here, at this place, at this moment. There could be no better way to avenge his master's death, than by using the black blade.

He reached down, now lifting the mighty sword with only one hand, and gracefully swung it over his head. A cheer rang through the army. In days that passed, he learned many more lessons from Sark Gruelor, and a great warrior was born.

* * *

During the day, the wintry mix of precipitation lessened over the plains. The proud sun was dull and subdued by murky clouds which slowly thickened. It was at that time when three dark figures emerged from the evil brood army that had amassed at Gortha-Losh. They neared Lake Mehm and came to a halt just east of the Old River, where the river made its way south from the lake and into the South Eldor. They were evil shapes mounted on wicked beasts. At the lead, was the Urur Maw named Rotghoul who rode a frightful muugaan. Behind him were his lieutenants, two large orcs, one called Gorbak and the other Durgrut, each upon great beasts of unknown origin. They waited quietly, watching as Carrick and Roundthaler on horseback, continued to position their army across the plains.

Carrick eyed the three demons warily, his hands together, one on top of the other, resting on the saddle horn. He gave a silent order to his men to halt all activity. He stared ahead at the three fiends, his face betraying no emotion as the great falcon Windthrasher, perched on his shoulder, gave a mighty screech.

"Emissaries," said Roundthaler. "Ha! Do you think our friends offer a truce?"

"We shall listen to what they have to say," Carrick told him. "Have Straya join us."

"Is that wise?" asked Roundthaler.

Carrick did not respond. He kept his eyes fixed on the dark forms across the river.

Roundthaler sighed. He turned to the Shyr Shar and motioned for its Ohtar Tari, or warrior-queen. There amongst the fierce warriors upon a chestnut-colored horse named Nassor was the Nalenian female named Straya. She had ascended to the throne of the small city-state in Ahlgren as a child, the result of the death of her mother. A beautiful and powerful woman, her face was well sculpted with large, deep brown eyes, and flowing brown hair twisted into a single long braid extending down her back. Her body was lean and golden, and it glistened under the hazy skies, her muscles rippling like water in a mountain stream. She was dressed in a short brown leather dress with attached steel armor parts and a short metal overskirt. Her boots were black leather and came up to her knees.

She was known as a ferocious fighter who showed no mercy to any rival and who killed, as it was said, simply for the pure pleasure of the act. A necklace of teeth and small bones strung on braided threads of her hair hung around her neck, the artifacts of those she had vanquished in battle. The sword she wielded with such deadly skill was named Megil En' Gur, *Ajatar Killer*, as it had been used in past battles by her mother to slay the deadly beasts. It was a magnificent sight to behold - long, straight, and pointed, its handle highlighted with protruding steel carvings of ajatar wings and heads. Its blade was razor-sharp and sparkled as if it had been wrought with the dust of a thousand diamonds. And even though it had been through countless battles there was not a single blemish or hint of deterioration on its surface. Megil En' Gur was a true work of beauty, a weapon, it was said, that fed from the emotions of its wielder.

She nudged Nassor up into a trot and drew up alongside Carrick and Roundthaler. The three crossed the Old River and stopped before the brood emissaries.

There was a moment of silence, followed by the sound of a great snort from Carrick's majestic black steed Warsinger.

The great Ure Rokko horse lifted his nose and sniffed the air.

"I smell the filth of the soulless," he said in disgust.

Rotghoul's muugaan roared, pounding its front feet in anger.

"Silence foolish creature," threatened Rotghoul, his piercing orange eyes studying the Ure Rokko from within a black leather mask and helmet. He was a menacing presence; a tall, muscled, and thickset body garbed in studded black steel plates with a long black cloak of armor weaves. "Hold your tongue or I shall rip it out!"

Windthrasher gave a mighty screech in defiance as Warsinger stomped and snorted and swished his tail.

Carrick curbed Warsinger firmly, pulling his head up.

"Easy now, my friends," he whispered to Warsinger, then back at Windthrasher. "Remember, we are here for a purpose."

"On this day the forces of good offer peace or war," he told the brood emissaries. "Crawl back to your desolate land and from these plains or face the cut of our sword. The choice is yours. We care not that which you decide."

Rotghoul laughed still struggling to restrain the agitated muugaan.

"We choose that which will purge the weak from this land," said the beast, the words gurgling from his throat. "Only the dead will see the end of this war and you Carrick, you and your horse, and your winged friend will be among the first to see its end." He then gave a large smile and said, "Our master demands that you lay down your arms. In return for such obedience, we will show great mercy to your kind and only kill but half of those souls on this plain."

Roundthaler spat on the ground.

"Master? Master?" he shouted. "Ah, so you grovel at the feet of another! You and your ilk are but mere puppets, performing all sorts of antics before spectators, none of which is done of free will, but rather as guided by your master who pulls your strings. Sniveling little puppets, the lot of you, all the while your master hides! Perhaps your puppet master is sly enough to keep out of sight, but all the lands know he's there, directing movements. Let your master show himself! Or is he too frightened? How pathetic! What a pathetic lot you are!"

Rotghoul moved closer and stared down at Roundthaler. He opened his mouth and snarled, long, thick strings of saliva dripping from his teeth.

"So, the fat dwarf from Mortha speaks. He talks of puppets, does he? Who pulls your strings, dwarf? What of your puppet master? What of the one you call the Maker?"

"Insolence! Insolence!" Roundthaler's vehement outcry echoed over the plains as he raised his axe. "The Maker has let you live this long only because of his infinite patience. I pity you. I do. In my pity for you, I believe it's my life task to fix you, and the way to fix you is to have you meet your death!"

"Did we hit a nerve, little fat one?" laughed Rotghoul horribly.

"Be careful with your words," said Straya sternly, drawing Megil En' Gur.

"Enough! Enough with the words!" said Carrick lifting his hand to calm the Nalenian warrior and the dwarf.

Rotghoul smiled and chuckled, his orange eyes turning to Straya.

"Ah, so there's a female amongst you," he said. "Now we know how weak of an army is before us. In our realms, females are only good for breeding and providing us with pleasure. In their old age, they're slaughtered. Flavorful meat for our pallet they become." He wiped the drool from his face, a wicked smile emerged as he stared at Straya. "We've no time for you or your words, female. You're weak and insignificant to us."

Straya was enraged.

"Wretch!" she shouted, clenching her teeth. "You dare speak to me in such a manner!"

In a single motion, she took a concealed dagger from her right boot and flung it at Gorbak cutting his throat. The orc flailed, attempting to stop the bleeding but to no avail. He fell from his beast with a thud and crumbled to the ground in a mass of blood and death.

Stunned by Straya's unexpected action, Rotghoul and Durgrut backed off their muugaans by several steps. Straya dismounted Nassor and ran to the dying Gorbak. She hovered over him, twisting her dagger free from his throat. She then pried apart his jaws and carved out one of his crooked teeth using the dagger. She notched the tooth and hung it on her necklace. Straya wiped the blood clean from the dagger, returning it to her boot. Gorbak writhed in pain then gasped his last breath.

She turned and looked up at Rotghoul.

"Foul one, your demise will come soon enough," she sneered. "It'll be a lonely, painful end, then an eternity of torment and suffering."

Rotghoul glared at Carrick.

"I've attempted to make peace with you," he told Carrick in anger. "Now, the time for your death approaches."

He spat at the ground, and with a grunt and roar, he and Durgrut turned their beasts and rode back to their brood army.

Roundthaler dropped and shook his head in disbelief.

"Woman, must you always provoke?" he said to Straya as she returned with the first spoil of war. He then lifted his head, a big smile across his rugged face. "But I see your aim remains unforgiving."

"Dwarf, my aim was off. I wanted the Urur Maw's eye for my necklace! But for now, a tooth from an orc will do just nicely," she chided. She mounted Nassor and slapped his haunches with her hand, causing the horse to buck and jump. "And this I promise you - I'll get that eye! Let's get on with this."

She pulled the reins, turned Nassor around, and rode to the Shyr Shar.

"She is a most impetuous creature," sighed Roundthaler.

"Yet, she has stirred their emotions," said Carrick, keeping his eyes on the brood army. His voice was unwavering. "She has done as I had expected. The trap is now set. We will have her bring the Shyr Shar across the river. The brood will fall victim to their lust for blood.

Column after column will move to the river to assail her and the Shyr Shar, to seek revenge for the orc . . ."

". . . then we will release the Kyr Thysaer," added Roundthaler, "cutting the wicked vermin in half."

Carrick nodded.

Roundthaler lifted his head into the misty air and looked into the darkened sky.

"Ah, my friend it is a good day for a battle," he said. "But what of the ajatar and the White Star?"

"He is where he needs to be, keeping a watchful eye over things," said Carrick. "As for the White Star, they may have met with unexpected evil forces along the way. Our friends may be delayed but we'll fight on."

"There is a risk without the White Star's Vilyarok," said Roundthaler.

"My friend, life is full of risks; what fun would it be without such risks?" said Carrick. "Dalgaes will be here when the time is right."

He kept his stare on the battlefield with a calm eye, all the while grasping the small leather pouch holding Gallia's white crystallized vial. In his mind, he saw the plains littered with the dead and wounded, bodies clumped in dark masses of twisted bone and flesh. The leather pouch warmed in his hand.

This vial will take you to a place where you will need to be. Gallia's words haunted him.

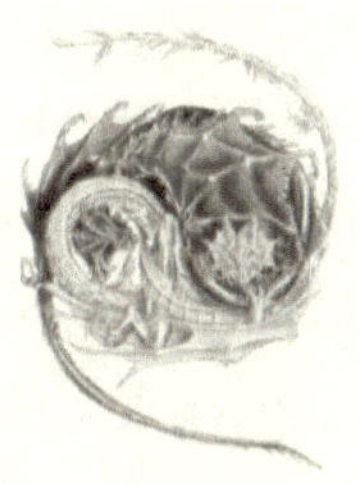

CHAPTER 10
THE BATTLE FOR CHYH-MEHM

NESTLED WITHIN THE NORTHERNMOST reaches of the Thornback, rising with stark abruptness, lost in misty cloud cover, loomed the great mountain called Sar Vael. It was so immense, its flattened peak so impossibly high, that only those few winged beasts, those with great strength could ever reach it. Now, only Moondancer stood atop the great mountain, his great leathery wings unfurled in their awesome span. He peered through the misty clouds, looking east then west, making out the dark figures of the armies in the distance. With his keen vision, he also saw the small groups as they made their way over the land. Carefully, he focused on the Old River and the Forest Heave.

The Queen and Princess make good time, he thought. *The land is difficult but the man from Dunhollow leads carefully. And the black demon, he has returned to his hive. All is as expected.*

He then saw something unexpected.

What's this? Men marching from the north. I must keep an eye on them. Unsure what this means. Could mean many things. I will keep a watchful eye on them.

He stretched his wings high into the air; his sharp-edged red scales shimmering in the brightness. From his vantage point, he surveyed the skies deeper to the east, and past the Snowwynne Barrens, looking for black ajatars and their Dark Riders. Then he saw a cloud, then another, and another! Lightning flashed; thunder rolled.

War is soon here, and the sky may be a mass of black and grey. Will they come? It does not matter for I will be quick and ruthless with my revenge.

To the south, he gazed upon the great armies now converged on Lake Mehm. He gave a mighty flap of his wings and stretched his neck high into the air and gave a howl of rage.

A clash of races will soon occur. Bring death so that we may bring life!

* * *

By early afternoon, there was a smell in the air, like damp earth. It was the smell of war and reeked like a grave - decay, ruin, dank and musty. Carrick felt cold in his bones; he felt fear and anxiety surrounding him, feelings he had before but never liked. It was as if his stomach was a clenched fist. He took a deep breath. It was time.

He knew the brood army had become agitated. There was no ignoring the tension now. He released Windthrasher to the air and rode Warsinger forward like the wind and called out to the Shyr Shar who now formed a line of battle with swords and spears raised. Near him was Straya upon Nassor.

"Mighty warriors of the Shyr Shar, who is your queen?" he shouted in a strong voice. "Who leads your army? Who is the finest fighter among you? Who is your beacon during the darkest of times?"

"Ohtar Tari! Ohtar Tari! Ohtar Tari! Ohtar Tari!" shouted the Shyr Shar, their shouts becoming stronger and louder. "Ohtar Tari! Ohtar Tari! Ohtar Tari! Ohtar Tari!"

The noise was deafening.

Then, he lifted a hand, and slowly the roars were quieted.

A deathly silence came over the plains. Around the army in the woods, birds were beginning to call; somewhere within the walls of Chyh-Mehm dogs started to bark. Above, Windthrasher circled high, his large wings extended, gliding on the winds.

"War! War! War!" came his harsh call. "War! War! War!"

Carrick pulled up on Warsinger's reins. The massive horse reared up and clawed the air, braying loudly.

"Warriors of the Shyr Shar, to assail the great and admitted evils that you will soon face, be strong!" he roared, his arms to the sky. "Be strong! I see the fear in your eyes, but fear not, for on this day it is your strength that will prevail on the battlefield! Know that when sword and shield clash, when spear and arrow break bone, fear not death; for, there is nothing to fear in so normal, harmless, and beneficent a thing as death! Embrace it! Embrace it and bring it to the enemy! Let the river now before you flow with their blood! For only their blood shall appease death! May the Maker give you the strength to prevail!"

He reached into his shoulder harnesses and swiftly brought forth the twin blades, the fire swords Eligor and Ravenscar. They glistened and quivered like lightning in a storm, and in a powerful stroke, he brought the fire swords together over his head in a perfectly controlled motion. The land trembled as the fire swords clashed and sizzled like furious hot metal, blasting a stream of white fire that shot up into the sky, reaching into the heavens.

Straya came alongside him. She drew Megil En' Gur from its scabbard and raised the blade high into the air. Then, with a forceful motion, she brought the formidable blade into the white fire of the fire swords, its steel now a scorching flame. With her sword now ablaze, she turned to her mighty force with rage and fury upon her face.

"Warriors of the Shyr Shar, I ask - who will follow me into the darkness?" she screamed. "Who will follow me into the unknown? Who will follow me into the thickest of night, where light cannot shine?"

In the brilliance of the swords, the army thundered and cheered, as in one voice, "We will! We will! We will! We will! We will! We will!"

Her warriors' hearts were primed and ready for battle, but she was not yet finished. She raced Nassor along the battle line, clanging the fiery Megil En' Gur against the swords and spears of her Shyr Shar warriors.

"Death now! Death now! Death always!" she howled. "Death now! Death now! Death always!"

Again, and again, the chant came from the vast army, "Death now! Death now! Death always!"

She raised Megil En' Gur to the battlefield and gave one last scream.

"Today you shall see death! But do not fear it, my warriors! For you shall spit in its face and reap a harvest of skulls!" she yelled. "Skulls for the Shyr Shar! Skulls for the Shyr Shar! Skulls for the Shyr Shar!"

The fierce Shyr Shar warriors could no longer be restrained. With a mighty shriek, they surged over the river and onto the plains, led by Straya and Nassor.

Seeing the Shyr Shar crossing the river and charging forth, Rotghoul's anger and lust for death got the best of him and he began to rally the brood for an attack. He raised his arms to signal an advance, and the brood responded with a bellow. Their bloodlust was strong, stronger than any desire to live.

But the orc lieutenant Durgrut warned Rotghoul.

"Uth' Egoreyr wants us here," he shuttered. "He said we wait for his word. He said not go to river."

Rotghoul knew of the battle strategy, but that did not mean he would follow it. He spun around and reached out with his massive arm and knocked Durgrut off his beast and to the ground. As he stared down at him he spat on him, the thick green spittle streaming down Durgrut's face.

"I command this army and not the Uth' Egoreyr," Rotghoul told his lieutenant as anger consumed him. "You can tell him that yourself at our victory celebration! And the female, she'll get her share. She'll be mine to devour!"

The hulking beast then roared out an order and the brood charged forward in a broken and irregular array. The dark army now began to spread itself over the plains and westward.

Reacting to the oncoming enemy Straya ordered the Shyr Shar in attack formation. The treacherous onslaught began. The Shyr Shar charged forward on their warhorses, the pounding hooves making the ground quiver. Then came the deafening sound of metal clashing upon metal as the two armies collided. The Shyr Shar warriors were relentless, carving into the brood, slashing forward, ripping through the demons. The fallen brood bellowed out in pain and anguish as blades came down upon them again, and again, each time bringing more of them to their death.

Straya slashed at the chests of orcs and firbolgs and fachens, cutting open arms and legs, and tearing into shoulders and necks. She savored the feeling of their hot, sticky blood running down her arms, and the hissing sounds their wounds made as they gushed blood. She had never felt so alive, or so free, and she craved more.

"Bring me more!" she screamed. "Bring me more!"

I'll give her what she wants, thought Rotghoul.

He ordered another column of brood into the fray when suddenly a cu sith flung itself at Straya knocking her from Nassor. But she held her ground and with a powerful thrust of Megil En' Gur speared the black beast's head. A swift twist of her wrist and the demon's head split apart. More and more columns of brood pushed forward, and the Shyr Shar started to take losses. Now on her feet, she kept slashing forward, mutilating brood that dare approach her.

From the riverbank, Carrick and Roundthaler looked upon the slaughter.

"Now?" asked Roundthaler.

Carrick drew a big breath.

"Patience," he said softly. "Patience my friend."

The roar of the Shyr Shar warriors was like the howling of jackals on the hunt. The din of battle echoed across the land, the sickening crunch of shield against shield, followed by the screams of the dying as spears and blades found their way through flesh and bone. This was a battle where there would be no quarter given, no mercy shown. This would be a battle to the death.

Rotghoul was becoming impatient. He felt victory was nearly in his grasp. He ordered more columns of brood into the battle and ordered their great siege engines to advance, pushed, and pulled by great beasts. Soon brood catapults began to thud, some launching large rocks while others fiery cauldrons. Horses keened terrible sounds as they were struck down by stone and fire, and many Shyr Shar warriors fell as arrows whistled a deadly tune through the air.

Carrick carefully watched as greater numbers of brood neared the river, attacking the Shyr Shar. This played into his strategy.

"Now?" asked Roundthaler again.

Carrick gave a resolute nod.

Roundthaler raised a hand, and the order was given.

A legion of men from the Eldor who had been positioned behind a grassy hill south and west of the Old

River began to charge the brood. To support the charge, Eldorian archers released a torrent of arrows making the sky black. The brood army now had two fronts to defend. It began to separate and spread over the plains. Carrick knew it was now time to unleash the ultimate fury.

"My friend, our patience has been rewarded," he told Roundthaler. "Raise the banner."

Roundthaler gave the signal, lifting his axe high into the air. In response, a solid red banner with a black claw was lifted into the sky, and then another, and another, and yet another, and so on; banner after banner leading west and north of Chyh-Mehm.

"See! The banners of the Claw are raised, calling for the Balor army," cheered Carrick's warriors. "See! They go speeding west. Soon the Kyr Thysaer will be as one!"

When the final banner was raised, a low-pitched, thudding sound came from the distance. It was soft at first but grew louder and louder, a mighty thumping of drumbeats that rolled and rumbled over the ground.

Dum – dadumdum – dadada Dum – dadumdum – dadada Dum – dadumdum – dadada.

Soon, the thunderous sounds of the drumbeats were joined by strains of bagpipes echoing far off in the distance, from the north, from the golden city of Katzhu Pu. The sounds joined and synchronized from across the land, as if by magic. The drumbeats strengthened, pounding like a heartbeat. The throbbing filled the whole of the Harrow as cats everywhere began to revel in the sound and whirl in excitement. The fury of war filled their feline hearts; the passion for victory silenced all other feelings.

On the battlefield, Carrick's army continued their cheers and stomped their feet. They knew what was about to happen. The cheering grew in intensity as the drumbeats grew louder, more urgent, while near Chyh-Mehm masses of Balor cats collected, packing themselves tightly together, paws raised high in rhythm to the thunderous beat. The ferocious Kyr Thysaer was forming.

As the drumbeats tolled across the lands, the brood stopped their attack, now frozen in fear. They began to slowly retreat, circling around and around, terror striking their hearts. Seeing the enemy's dread, the Shyr Shar and Eldorian warriors raised their swords in the air and started to slowly withdraw, shadows receding into the gloom of the battlefield. They backed away, so slowly, so solemnly, in pity of what would soon befall their enemy.

"They come! They come!" Durgrut shouted at Rotghoul. He swallowed against the lump of dread in his throat. His gaze flew to Rotghoul. "Not go to river! I told you! Not go to river! Now must run north to the Uth' Egoreyr!"

Rotghoul became riled with an unmoving, nameless fear. He began pushing brood back into formation.

"Get back in line! Back in line!" he shouted.

But it was too late as there came the booming crescendo of drums and bagpipes releasing the fiery beast, the Kyr Thysaer. Faster than one could imagine, the throng of Balor cats now as one, with fur ablaze, sped from north of Chyh-Mehm and onto the plains. From the battlefield, all that could be seen was a massive cloud of dust that grew closer and closer, as the ground trembled and quaked.

Tormented by the approaching horror and filled with a terror immeasurable, the frightened brood collapsed upon itself. Then in one horrible moment, the Kyr Thysaer was on them, crashing and slicing through them like a strand of mist. Durgrut was torn apart while the severed brood went clattering. Rotghoul shrieked in despair as the mighty Balor beast turned and sliced through the brood again and again until blood soaked the ground.

Having decimated the brood, the Kyr Thysaer withdrew from the battlefield, returning to its camp north of the island city.

The wounded and dead brood lay on the ground in charred heaps of blood, bone, and flesh. What brood remained alive were quickly slaughtered, delivered from their misery by a swift slash of a warrior's blade, that is, except Rotghoul who fled north pursued by Straya.

He stumbled across the battlefield, trying in vain to flee the deadly scene. But he was slowed by several injuries and was quickly overtaken by Straya. Using her foot, she forced Rotghoul to the ground.

"Now who's the weak one?" she snarled.

Exhausted and weakened he gasped for air but mustered enough strength to spit at her. The green slime ran down her strong face.

"I don't fear death," he wheezed. "Kill me, female. Be done with it."

She looked at him without pity.

"Demon, I am not here to kill you," she snickered. "Killing you would be a kindness you do not deserve. And it would be messy and inconvenient. No. I am here to take my prize."

With that, she took a small blade from within her dress, grabbed his lower jaw holding his head steady, and carved out one of his eyes. He did not scream. Instead, he gave a slight heave of his chest and bellowed a deep groan.

She looked over the eye. It felt wet and slippery. She took loose strands from her necklace, and wrapped a few around the bloodied eye, adding it to her collection.

"Crawl back to your hive and bring me more of your kind," she cackled with an evil smile.

He whimpered, then struggled to his feet and with a hand over his bloodied, empty eye socket, staggered away, heading north.

* * *

As night fell and the fight ended, Carrick and Roundthaler rode through the battlefield to view the aftermath. The butchery was unspeakable. Brood were strewn about the plains where they had fallen, their eyes frozen open in death. Orders were given to set large pyres across the field to burn the bodies. The stench of death soon filled the air, as clouds of thick fetid smoke rose from the fallen, drifting over the blood-stained ground.

Roundthaler looked into the dark skies.

"Why do you suppose no black riders joined the battle?" he asked.

"They choose wisely. This was not the battle to end all battles."

Roundthaler understood. It was over this grim scene that he decided to ask his friend another question, one that he knew would cause apprehension. It was a question he had wanted to ask for some time now, one that worried him, but it was a question that danced in his mind, in his ears, in his eyes; it made its way through his memories. Now, amongst so much death, strangely it seemed to be the right time to ask the question he had long dreaded.

"Even though we were victorious today, we could have used our friend. He would have been most helpful. Why have you not called for his aid?"

Carrick turned to Roundthaler, his face hardened in anger.

He knew the person Roundthaler was speaking of; there was no need to mention the man's name since his deeds were long remembered amongst many. There was but one man about whom innumerable stories could be told, a great warrior and leader of the Mur' Edan, of the clan of men who lived in the northern wastelands of the Crag, the place called 'Shk Ndor. For over the wastelands did the man and his people barely survive, forever in battle with a demented variation of brood known as the Ru Gwaith. Indeed, Carrick knew this man well; he knew of his anger and rage, and he knew of his sickness.

Carrick had so much he wanted to say in response but sensed Roundthaler was not yet done.

"Speak. What is on your mind?" he said. "Out with it."

"Carrick, we need him," said Roundthaler. "You know this. We need his decisiveness, his cunning. We need his ruthlessness. We need his strength and his resolve. Can you call upon him, so he may join with us?"

"He cannot be controlled," said Carrick in a terse tone, turning from Roundthaler.

"This is true."

"He's most vicious."

"Again, true," came Roundthaler's quick response, a voice that had taken on a deeper tone. "But his acts reflect war. They reflect the trials of his people, the oppression, the death."

"He is too emotional," said Carrick turning back to his friend. "His anger and aggression are based on a delusional viewpoint that everyone and everything exists simply to kill him."

"Yes! Yes! I know!" exclaimed Roundthaler. "We all know! But he comes by this naturally. Everything in 'Shk Ndor existed to vanquish him and his people. Carrick, his anger is pure and raw, but it is completely justified. He is no more than an expression of his life, of the struggles of the Mur' Edan. By the Maker, war is but a deluge of dark rain that poisons the land, bringing those that fight one step closer to the death of reality. He has already seen his reality die, thousands and thousands of times over. He has lived death, felt its certainty, and has welcomed it. But he has also watched in horror as it has refused to take him, instead leaving him an outcast, a failure. These emotions have driven him to the edge of madness, yet he never gives in.

He does not retreat from his punishment or let go of his obsession. He endures. He waits. And he hopes. Do you not see? It is this strength we need, now more than ever. And it is his anger and desire for brutality that we also need. Please consider calling upon him."

"His anger gives him a reason to do violence," said Carrick looking at Roundthaler, "to satisfy an aggressive urge he would never feel justified in following without the presence of the anger." He sighed. "I understand your arguments. Allies are important, in life and death. I will consider your request. But know that his mere existence pains me."

"Thank you," said Roundthaler. "That is all I can ask of you, my friend."

The two continued through the fields of broken bodies of the dead and dying brood. The cries and howls were haunting, piercing through the dust.

"What madness is this?" lamented Carrick.

"It is war, my friend," said Roundthaler with vigor, "and it is most glorious."

* * *

Nighttime darkened and the temperature dropped considerably. Molly and her group had traveled far and now found themselves across the Old River on the Snowwynne Barrens. They were but a few leagues from the mouth of the Crag, the Dregec Kuul and its pass. In the distance, they could hear the evil army as it poured through the passage, a steady and deep rhythmic thumping echo that shook the ground. The brood rabble snaked southward from their hive in four columns. It seemed to be an almost endless flow of darkness and misery.

They found an outgrowth, dense underbrush with trees and tall shrubs. Bran and An Van Au used their knives and swords to carve a path into the thicket and then a shallow in its center, while Calen Ancorbow kept watch. Dried grass and weeds were gathered and set around the inside as it would make for fine bedding material. When all was settled Brows reached into his satchel and removed four small round stones, Urnu Ondo, or *heat stones* in the common tongue. He carefully placed them near each other and immediately they began to glow a dim orange and gave off warmth. Everyone huddled around the stones, They passed around pieces of bread, dried meat, and dried fruit. No words were spoken as everyone enjoyed the warmth and meal. It was then that the girls realized that, aside from the steady thumping of the distant evil, there was no other sound from the forest or river, just the deadly beating of the moving army. The land seemed to be holding its breath. They never felt more alone or more afraid.

The steady sound of the brood force was nightmarish and difficult to ignore. But they were tired and sleep was calling. Bran would take the first watch and the others would follow, except of course for the girls and the orc. Just before the girls were ready to snuggle in their beds of grass, Bran took Molly's hand.

"My Queen, I wish to show you something," he said.

She nodded and they left their sanctuary and ventured out into the blackness of the night, into a nearby outgrowth. Little light came from the broken moon for the clouds were thick and dark and deepening. Some of the clouds were lit red and purple from below, from the torches and fires of the marching brood army. And as the wind came from the east it brought with it the odor of sulfur, unmistakable, strong, and piercing.

Molly covered her mouth and nose with her hand as the steady thumping of the army became louder, the ground trembling. She and Bran dashed from the outgrowth and came upon a small grassy ridge. He motioned her to stoop as they climbed the ridge and neared its edge. There they found some rocks. They knelt behind the rocks, straining their eyes ahead and into the darkness of the mountain range.

"Look, it is the Dregec Kuul and the evil army of the Crag," whispered Bran.

She could not see the mountain pass for the mountain range was so imposing. It was severe and spectacular, with canyon after canyon, toothy rim rock ridges, a rugged area, and steep in grade. It appeared like a curtain in the night separating the flat lowlands and the Drueger, and its length was as far as the eye could see and to the horizon.

Then, as she brought her eyes north, she could make out the torches and the dark images of the brood with their massive armaments of destruction spewing from the mountains through a narrow opening carved by the Dregec Kuul. It was a passageway. To the south of the pass, she could see countless stone lookouts forged from the mountain, and within each, fires, and the faint images of brood. To the north was the river of filth and sludge called the Dregec Kuul that drained into the Ug' Foul Marshes. Stone armaments lined the river, where orc and other brood watched.

"Follow the foul river to the marshes," he told her.

She did so, following the Dregec Kuul into the marshes where she saw a small road, north of the river, and then she followed it back to the mountain passage. She could barely make out what looked like a small, forested area between the river and mountains, a densely packed mix of tall pines and willows. And she saw a small outcropping of rock just west of the small forest.

Bran was watching her eyes.

"You see the Pas Shae," he said, "but not all of it, for what you cannot see is a marshland deep with water and death that welcomes one to the wicked place. It is the only way to enter the Crag unnoticed. Few have traveled through this place, though. No army has conquered it and even the brood avoid it."

She remained silent. Her eyes returned to the steady drone of the marching army, the countless dark images, and the shadowy figures of a haunting nightmare. The army was massive with great machines of destruction and overseen by powerful and terrifying beasts of all shapes and sizes. She thought of Erol Carrick, a person she had yet to meet, and his armies. She closed her eyes to the frightening images of her recent dreams of war, battlefields, and immeasurable death.

Their souls will endure great hardship and face mortal danger, she thought.

She opened her eyes and looked at Bran.

"What did you see my Queen?" he asked.

"I saw a land laid to waste; the death of many innocents," she said with a pause. "But tell me about this place, the Pas Shae. Why does the brood avoid it? Why do they not patrol its roads? Why has it not been conquered?"

His dark brows drew together in a hardened look. He politely held out his hand to her. She grasped it firmly as he gently cradled her soft hand.

"It is a small, horrible land that is never been subjugated," he said. "Even though it is not under the control of the Crag's evil, it serves a deadly purpose. You see, those brood considered flawed who try to escape cannot take the passageway of the Dregec Kuul because it is watched by those loyal to the darkness. The demons can only flee the Crag through the Pas Shae, a place neither man nor brood ventures.

"My Queen, that small swath of land you see, the Pas Shae, has been left to its own despicable devices, to the vile creatures that live there. They are called Nnar' Vasa and they are four times the size of an orc but more man-like. They roam the place seeking food and consume only orc, but they do not eat their victim's flesh or meat, preferring instead to let the bodies rot, leaving only joints and bones. Then they crunch on the bones and feast on the marrow.

"But the Nnar' Vasa is not the only evil that lurks in that horrid place. No. There is the Dree Dunn der. They are four witches, each having two faces, but wield no magic. The sole source of their power is the frightening words they utter, angry words that captivate, that if you listen to their rage will entrap you in their agony. Those who have listened to the witches succumb to a most terrifying madness. They flee back to the Crag and roam the northern desolation of the Drueger as bandits, the ones called Ru Gwaith. They are outcasts within the brood and are without fear. They seem to transform and take on a hideous physical appearance. It is not known the evil that consumes or controls them. They are very dangerous and are led by the one called I' Mor Ba. He is most treacherous. The Ru Gwaith have been in an unending struggle against a race of men who also inhabit the forsaken place. They are called the Mur' Edan and are led by a man just as dangerous as the Ru Gwaith. He is known as I' Ereb. Long have they fought. I am afraid of what we may find there.

"My Queen, in past battles, not even the great Carrick dared venture to the place. The Nnar' Vasa, the Dree Dunn der, the Ru Gwaith – they are not brood. No. They are much worse. They are En' Rauko. You must know it is unheard of for any creature, let alone brood to pass through such lands. We have no choice and must be careful."

"But Ug'ghi Otha says he knows the way."

"Yes. That is what he says. It worries me. I am most mistrustful of his intentions."

"I understand."

"Showing caution is important as is being careful with your words."

"Yes. Saying the wrong words is clearly unwise, but so is saying the right words in the wrong way," she said. "If it is such a horrid place then why do we go there?"

"We must travel where the brood will not," he said. "If we try to travel through the Dregec Kuul passage, and as you can see, there is brood that watches from so many lookouts. They will easily find us." He gently lifted her hand and gave it a soft kiss. "I know you are worried. I know all this is frightening. You are wondering so many things. You are wondering where we are going, and what will happen to us. You are wondering if you made a mistake even coming here. You are wondering, most of all, if you will ever be able to find your way back home. I want to tell you something. You may not understand it and you may not like it. But I want you to know it because I need to say it."

"And what's that?" she asked demurely.

"Sometimes, when one seeks answers, one finds none or at least none that are enduring. And sometimes, when one is given an answer, it may not be the one expected, wanted, or needed. But there are still things to be said and understood, important things, things like trust. Trust is a journey, not a destination. And to travel the journey, you must leave the path, and travel down different ones. You must trust those that lead you, even when they make you doubt yourself. You must trust that they will take you down those new paths safely and help you to see things you never would have found on your own."

"You are most wise," she said. "I hope I have not given you the impression that I do not trust you. I do. I trust your strength, your intelligence, and your ability to make the right decisions. But I also trust that you will listen when asked, and when asked to make a choice, that you will make the one that is best for everyone. It is a lot to ask of anyone, I realize, especially when this world is not always the safest or most welcoming place."

He smiled at her. They had an understanding, and he felt a bit better about having spoken his mind. He still was not sure exactly how she would use her power, or if she would use it at all. And he had yet to understand the scope of his power, the ring he wore. He knew they would need to work together to make it through this, and that they would need to lean on each other when needed. For now, he trusted her, and he had a sense that she trusted him.

"Oh, and one more thing," he said. "I wish to speak to something the bobbin raised. Regarding any past discussion of our route, you must know that evil hides in all corners of the Harrow. It is sometimes best not to talk of plans, of such things. At the same time, one cannot be frightened to live life, to continue an adventure because of what may occur. We are unable to anticipate everything. To have talked about the Pas Shae would have been but a waste of precious time because there was no other course of action. My Queen, you need not be afraid for I am with you. Our destinies are entwined. The shards make us as one."

He knows he cannot escape our common fate, she thought. *There is no escape, not now, not ever. We will face whatever comes and come out stronger than we were before. That is our bond, that is our trust.*

But something worried her. She looked at him. He returned the look but could not quite read her face, but he could tell she was thinking hard about something.

"Is something amiss?" he asked.

He knows me. It is the stone.

"Have you faced the creatures you spoke of? Will we need to fight?"

He narrowed his eyes in purpose.

"No, I have not faced such evil before," he said. "But you have the Lia Fail and I have a shard of the famed stone. Together we may be able to avert such an occurrence. If not, we will ensure that the battle shall be to our favor."

She smiled at him. She was in such a strange place and she trusted him now on some instinctive level, to take care of her while there. She trusted him to keep her safe, she trusted him because of who he was, because of what he said, because of the ring he wore.

Yes, we are on the same path, she thought.

But she also understood that she would have to take the lead at times, to make difficult decisions.

I have already made many.

She was hardening to the reality that she now faced; she could feel the warmth of the red stone against her skin.

We must do what is necessary.

"Such strangeness," she whispered.

Oddly, her thoughts went to the white cat, Shaer Thol, who had mysteriously left the group during the confusion of the orc's attack on her.

Why am I thinking of him? Something curious about him. Something too curious, even for this place.

A sudden shudder went through her, as though something had briefly stirred deep within her. She held her breath, the feeling of warmth and fullness taking her by surprise.

Curious, yes. But maybe a good kind of curious.

"What do you think has become of the wizard's white cat?" she asked him.

He was surprised by the question.

"My Queen, I do not know, other than I am sure he is much wiser than we think and will find a way to survive. A wizard would always keep wise company. Of this I am certain."

She looked into his eyes.

"I suppose," she said taking a deep breath. "I am tired. Let us return. We have much ahead of us."

They made their way back to the underbrush, and tall shrubs, and rejoined the others. The thicket of bushes and trees was large enough to hide their location from the river's shoreline. Bran positioned himself to look to the east. He wanted to keep an eye on what was happening across the barrens.

"This place gives us cover but we are in the open nonetheless," Ancorbow told Bran as he looked about. "We are vulnerable in every direction."

"Yes, but there are vantage points," said Bran. "We can see anyone or anything that may approach."

"And if we are attacked?" asked Brows. "What then?"

"We have swords and arrows," said An Van Au as she crouched unloading her pack in a shallow swale in front of an eastern-facing ridge. "That should do the trick.

Anyway, it has been too quiet for my liking. I would prefer a fight."

"We will look to avoid confrontation but, if necessary, we will fight back," said Bran with firmness to his voice. "We will use the tools we have."

"The stone?" said Brows. "Are you saying we will use the stone?"

Bran gave a stare at the bobbin.

"Whatever is necessary," he said.

"So much for avoiding confrontation," muttered Brows under his breath.

Bran was angered.

"You always have something to say," he told Brows.

Brows saw that Ug'ghi Otha was intently listening to the discussion. He remembered the advice given by Fairfax to the group, to keep knowledge of Bran's ring from the orc. He would be careful with his words.

"If any part of the stone is used," he said, "then the whole of the Harrow will know of our whereabouts, and that includes the darkness that grows from the east. You are not the only one who has experience in these matters. Let me suggest something."

"And what would that be?" asked Bran.

Brows quickly drew a long knife from its sheathing hidden in the back of his pants and threw it to the ground, perfectly splitting a small nut in half. Everyone gasped at this unexpected prowess.

"Now that I have your attention," he said, "I suggest that if we are attacked, the girls, the Ra Cath, and the orc make their way to the marshlands while the rest of us fend off the assailants. We should be able to give them plenty of time." He looked at Molly. "No need to use the magic of the stone. No need to call the dark tower's attention to our location. Sacrifice is about life poured out in death."

Molly slowly closed her eyes, not wanting to think of such an occurrence.

"Where did you learn to wield a knife in such a manner?" asked Ancorbow.

"One does not survive in this place as long as I have, without the ability to defend oneself from those who would silence history's lessons."

"Most impressive historian," said Bran with a smile. "We will do it your way. You talk of sacrifice, well, sacrifice is a warrior's perfect redemption."

"Thank you," said Brows.

"We will rest today, and into the night, and then through the daylight tomorrow," Bran instructed the group. "Tomorrow night is when we will look to cross into the marshlands. While we are here, no fires will be lit, we will only use the stones for heat. We will use the blankets that we have packed and huddle for as much warmth as possible. We do not want to give away our position. We must be still. We must be quiet."

Everyone carefully followed Bran's direction. They said nothing as they quietly unloaded their packs. They rationed their food with the utmost care and sipped their tiny portions of water. The girls snuggled in one blanket with Big Grey nestled between them. The orc made a bed of branches and leaves. He gave his blanket to An Van Au saying his thick skin would provide adequate protection from the cold. Bran, Ancorbow, and An Van Au took turns on watch.

There was so much to talk about, but silence was required. Molly was left only with her thoughts. She closed her eyes to the sounds she had heard earlier, the constant sounds of battle - the clash of metal on metal, the drumbeats of the Kyr Thysaer which rose to a deafening thunder, the deep rumbling of the ground as the great feline army carved into the brood, and the screams of agony of the wounded and dying. Never had she heard such sounds, and it was most frightening. She gripped the Lia Fail stone which warmed to her touch. She thought of her dreams.

There are many sides to war - the distorted faces of men, the teeth bared with ferocity, the hideous yells, destruction, and death - but also the glory, the brave deeds, and the acclamation of all that is good. Such a difference, such a division. It shapes you, your awareness, your understanding of the past, and your perception of the future.

She opened her eyes and turned to Elizabeth who was asleep, serene, and peaceful. She smiled at the sight of her sister when she felt a stare on her. She glanced down to see Big Grey, the cat's eyes piercing and dark.

What have we gotten ourselves into? she thought, questioning the cat. *Others are talking about sacrificing their lives to save me.*

It is your destiny, came his response.

She gave a slight nod. *I understand.*

I am afraid many have already sacrificed their lives today. You heard the sounds of war. And there will be many more lives lost. They fought for what they believed in, to defeat once and for all the darkness that is a blight that covers this land. These things are never easy. But remember – do not fear, only believe.

Believe? Believe what?

Believe in yourself because within you lies all the hope and dreams of the future. Believe in yourself because you will become what you believe. Do you understand?

It is difficult in this place. There are so many differences - war and death to bring peace and life. Just another difference, another division. Understanding all this is difficult.

He settled against her.

Everything in life is difficult but its difficulties are not evenly distributed, his mind's voice told her. *Many difficulties prove to be hardships for us, while others prove to be good. Regardless, both the good and the bad remain with us in vivid ways. Each is a reminder of how life can turn, and how it can change. What we are doing, the difficulties we now face is a change, a change for the good and no good ever comes without some difficulty. This is your time, your time to show what you are capable of, what you were born to do, and what you can achieve when you put your mind to it. There is no other person who can do what you can do. This is your time. This is your place. This is what I meant when I said this is your destiny. Do not fear, only believe.*

His thoughts somewhat put her mind at ease, just as she hoped they might.

But I do fear. I fear what could happen if Elizabeth and I become separated, she thought.

Do not worry. She is stronger than you may think and able to deal with almost anything.

How do you know?

She is here, is she not? She has been by your side, every step along the way. To be on this journey with you takes great courage and strength. It is her time, her place as well.

If we are ever separated you will look after her.

Of course. But do not worry.

She gave another nod and asked, *Will you hear all my thoughts?*

No. Just when I need to.

He reached out with outstretched paws and gave a silent yawn.

Let us rest. We have tonight and part of tomorrow, then there is a long journey ahead of us.

She was glad he was with her. She closed her eyes, and despite her anxiety she soon fell asleep, being weary.

He turned to An Van Au who was resting, eyes closed.

Can you hear me? he whispered in his mind to her.

The young girl, hair flowing to her sides, opened her eyes, round and clear. No thoughts were returned, only a smile. She then yawned widely and closed her eyes to sleep.

* * *

The cold night air was filled with the howls of wicked brood and with the beams of their torches lighting the massive fortress Drar Dukhaar. The dark tower soared high into the western sky, a twisted tower with battlements and smaller turrets overlooking the Carn and North Sage Barrow. These were lands once fertile with fields of flowers and berries, large tracts of pasture lands, and glorious trees, but now they lay barren and desolate. The ground was no longer rich in nutrients and instead dry and cracked, and some areas were sand or hard rock. Only a few splotches of grass dotted the landscape, along with some thistle bushes. And the Aina Dur, the majestic tree, stood barren of leaves, burned, its vital essence forever locked in death. The winds sighed through its branches, a silent lament for what it once was.

This was now the kingdom of Mauldragw Foulhand and the Dark Wizard delighted in the decimated view. His message to the western lands was one of judgment, punishment, and destruction. From atop the tower, the red-robed evil could see the night sky of storm clouds to the east.

Soon the whole of the Harrow shall be judged, he thought.

There was a tug on his robe. It was Bentgibber groveling at his feet, large and round eyes beaming up at him. The slimy pale abomination pressed against his legs caressing them like a gentle breeze and then took a deep breath.

"The stench of death!" he sniggered. "Isn't it wonderful?"

"Ah, Librarian," whispered Foulhand, a large hand gently rubbing the creature's bulging and hairless head. "Come up here and view our creation."

The gangly and vile creature crawled up his leg.

"Librarian, look out over the scene. Tell me what you see?" he asked.

Bentgibber looked towards the east and grinned widely bearing jagged and sharp teeth. Before him was desolation, ruin, and despair as far as the eye could see. In the somber blackness he could make out, far off into the distance, the campfires of armies, alone and forsaken. But fear soon gripped him. He pushed away from Foulhand and recoiled in anguish, for in the distance he saw something else, a single, bright aura at the edge of the Hollow Forest.

"No," muttered Bentgibber on trembling lips. "It cannot be."

"What is it, Librarian? What do your sage eyes see?" asked Foulhand, surprised and quizzical.

Bentgibber shuddered, and tripped over its legs, collapsing to the cold stone floor. He covered his eyes in indignation.

"Curse these eyes of mine. Curse them!" he cried out. "It cannot be! The Learned One! I see the Learned One! His presence screams to me like how a child screams as if hurt when certain persons take hold of them."

Foulhand whirled back to the east, his eyes ablaze with indulgent disdain.

"It cannot be! I killed him. I destroyed him in the fire of Drar Druul. The Edainar fools do not have the power to bring back the lifeless."

"But I see him!" cried Bentgibber. "It's him! He's out there! He's coming for us!"

Foulhand stood defiantly overlooking the east, his hands clenching the cold stone battlement, his eyes searching for clues and answers.

"Let him come," a tormented whisper, ever soft, came from his lips. "Let him come."

* * *

Gazing up into the night sky, Carrick could sometimes see the twinkling of stars through the dense cloud cover and thick smoke of pyres. The stench of burning bodies fouled the night air as a reminder of what had happened. Still, a strange peacefulness crept about the place. The battlefield before him was quiet as silent men went about preparing for the next day. In the fires that speckled the plains, haunting shadows lengthened across the scarred land. But in his mind, he would shatter them - he had no part in them. He had waged battle before and he would do so again.

The shadows of night were everywhere. And now, alone outside his command tent, he found himself staring into his campfire, hypnotized by a dancing shadow in the flame. He thought of the White Star and its delay in joining his army and wondered what had caused the delay, and if a great calamity had befallen the elven army. He realized it would perhaps be best to plan future battles without the White Star's aid. He began to map out his strategy, of where he would deploy his many battalions and how he would use the Kyr Thysaer. Suddenly the flames of his campfire began to dance and swirl, leaping higher into the night sky. He drew one of the fire swords and glanced about the darkness.

"What magic is this?" he said. "Show yourself so I may force you from this place."

The flames continued to dance and jump, changing intensity from point to point in a way that began to form the shape of a face, the face of an old man. He recognized the image.

"Theo? Is it you?"

The flames swirled and grew, changing color to a deep red and forming the image of the Professor.

"Erol, my good friend, I am here but I do not have much time. There are many ravens about my house. They keep watch of my every move. Listen to me. There is a brood army north on the plains. It is an army larger than any you have faced. They march from the Drueger and through the Dregec Kuul. Some make their way to the Heave but remain east of the Old River in small encampments. This is strange for the brood. You must take some of your armies and engage them at the Dregec Kuul."

"But Theo, why would I do that? I would lose the tactical advantage I have here south of Chyh-Mehm. They should come to me."

"This is not about a tactical advantage. My nieces make their way to the Crag. The oldest carries the Lia Fail. But with so many brood at the Dregec Kuul, they have no alternative but to enter the Pas Shae. You must engage the brood quickly to distract them from my nieces as they cross from the Old River. If the girls are captured all will be lost. Ask our Ra Cath friends for help."

"How do you know all this?"

"I watch from afar. I can sense things at a level different from the visual or physical sense." The Professor paused briefly as if hesitant to continue, and then said, "I know you visited with Gallia, I know of the vial, its contents. Erol, you already know your fate. You will be honored for generations, a leader of great strength and great authority, and more besides. You must ride fate. Only by surrendering to it can you begin to have some control over your own life.

"My friend, our days in the Harrow are no more. Our time in that place is done. A new generation is needed, and that generation is now with us. The young man, the one who rides the steed of Master Harwell, the one who Gruelor trains – he lifts the black blade. Keep him near you. He has the strength to wield the fire swords." The fiery face of the Professor then looked over his shoulder. "I must leave you now. The ravens come for me. Remember, to the north, engage the brood. A distraction is needed. It is the only way."

As the campfire slowly diminished, the flickering image of the Professor disappeared leaving Carrick quietly alone in the shadows. He thought about what the Professor said and became saddened by the thought of his fate in a reality without the Harrow. He wondered what would happen to the Harrow if it were to fall under the sway of evil. He thought of Elban Miragrin and the great horse, Saraanth, and Harwell's black blade.

There were so many memories flooding at him like a tidal wave of emotion. He remembered when an aged Urm Riorn gave him the fire swords, and the words the aged ruler spoke. "The swords are heavy, but the weight is not physical, rather, it is spiritual, for the swords present the wielder with great destructive power. It is this power that brings destructive urges. If you cannot control such urges, if instead, you act on them, in the end, the weight will consume you, and you will walk through the land spreading death. There are no exceptions to this. Do not become an abomination."

He remembered his response. "I will contain the darkness within me, within us all."

The swords are heavy and the burden great. If it is to be Miragrin then I must speak to him those words that were spoken to me by Urm Riorn.

His thoughts turned to the girls, closing his eyes to images of them. He remembered them, having once met them at the Professor's country home.

Children bearing so great a burden. If they are like their uncle, then they are strong.

He opened his eyes and understood.

What is reality but that which is?

He knew what he had to do; he needed to heed his friend's words and visit with the Utine Heru, the lead Balor Guild warrior of the Kyr Thysaer. He thought of a plan but would need assistance.

As he looked into the night sky, the light of the broken moon barely breaking through the dark clouds, he felt no emotion. He called for Warsinger, and as soon as he mounted the great horse and had traveled a short distance from camp, a strange feeling came over him. He slowed the great horse and glanced back to see Roundthaler standing near the fire, a look of concern over his face. He halted Warsinger and the horse reared up on its hind legs.

"Do not worry," he shouted to Roundthaler. "I shall return!"

With a wave to his stout friend, they were off into the night.

CHAPTER 11
THE UTINE HERU

THE GREAT CARRICK AND Warsinger traveled west, hugging where the northernmost hills of the South Eldor crept upon the Foghollow Barrens. To the north, Lake Mehm was a dark and wonderful void, speckled with the shimmering lights of the great island city of Chyh-Mehm in the distance. The city rose high into the air above a silvery fog, heavily fortified, with strong ramparts of stone, reinforced with earthworks and trenches. One lone gate faced south with two massive towers on either side. From the gate, a narrow stone roadway led into the city; tall and narrow buildings were built close together on either side. The city was dense with people and activities. Four massive towers stretched into the night air and where the ramparts joined. The city was sufficiently close to the shore to be supplied from the surrounding area, but sufficiently far enough from the mainland, so remote and fortified, to be nearly impossible to capture. It was said Chyh-Mehm was impenetrable, a fortress built to withstand an assault from any direction.

Over the ages, many battles had been fought to claim the city for it held a strategic position through which marauding armies could easily gain access to the western lands. Yet even through the many battles, the city's walls remained pristine, slightly weathered, and discolored, with a few cracks and some moss, a revealing testimony to the city's perseverance.

Carrick and Warsinger were soon past the grand city, finding their way near the reaches of the An Taur woodland, close to where the great feline army made its camp north and west of Chyh-Mehm. As they crested a hill, they could see the immense army of the Ra Cath, a feline clowder, thousands and thousands of Balor warriors sprawled out over several leagues. They were arranged in tight groupings of interwoven and complicated circle patterns known as Ta Mellan. It was these intricate formations that allowed the Balor to quickly form into the Kyr Thysaer on the battlefield.

As Carrick and Warsinger approached the vast feline army, they saw a great cat at its center, sitting proudly, alone, dominant, and unmoved. The cat was large, tall, long, and rugged with a solid bone structure. His coat was heavy, long-haired, a glistening white with subtle black streaks, and a bulky mane around the neck area. Large, well-tufted ears were wide at the base, tapering to a point. His face was long with a squarish muzzle; his eyes were greenish-gold, large, and expressive. Streaks of red war paint marked his face and body.

This great feline was the mighty Samson Beleg Balor El Tar, the Utine Heru, High General of the great Balor army, and direct descendant of Ra Carathor, the Prime

Heru and first Guild Lord. He was the strongest of Ra Cath warriors, a feline of incredible power and superior brilliance, about whom there were many grand stories.

When the Balor warriors saw Carrick and Warsinger, they instinctively formed a defensive wedge, the cats crouching with their ears back, ready to fight.

"We are allies, not enemies or strangers," Warsinger told the cats in a deep voice. "We seek counsel with the Utine Heru."

Some of the cats hissed at them, so Carrick then cautiously placed one of the fire swords, Eligor, in his hand. It began to emit a faint white glow.

A large black feline warrior stepped forward.

"Let the En' Edan pass," he told the other Balor warriors. "He is of the Tree."

The cats quickly reformed the Ta Mellan.

Carrick dismounted Warsinger and they carefully made their way through the Balor cats and to the center of the clowder. As they neared the large, muscular cat, Carrick bowed and knelt to one knee in deference. The cat's nose twitched, and his ears stiffened.

Carrick spoke in the feline tongue, expressing reverence for the great feline race and admiration for the great cat.

"Nostale lle ar' seere Ra Cath," he said humbly. "Ra nostale a' i' cora Heru."

Warsinger knelt to one knee, the great horse's other front leg stretched out along the ground.

Many of the Balor cats started to close in around, sniffing at the two.

The majestic cat did not move, his eyes narrowing as he looked upon the great Carrick. He gave a large smile, showing two perfect rows of small, sharp teeth.

"Ah, Carrick cestal. Ur nostale Carrick. Ur nostale En' Edan," he said, feline words of respect for Carrick and the En' Edan. His voice was low and rough, his inflection slow and dignified. He gazed up at the great Ure Rokko stallion. "E' ur nostale Warsinger. Ur nostale Ure Rokko."

The great cat raised a paw and rested it on Carrick's knee. The night breeze played with the cat's silky fur, a shimmering wave of white, and Carrick could feel the warmth of the huge paw. He was well aware of the cat's enormous strength. He also knew the cat was quick, intelligent, and forceful when necessary.

"Carrick, there was a great victory today," said the cat. "War is here and splendor shall be made of it."

From behind, three Balor cats emerged. Carrick recognized two of them, Lil' Man and Chumsey, but he did not know the other cat who was called Tane Brelaak. Brelaak was slim and of good form. His fur was the color of faded sandstone with rich dark-chocolate highlights, and his tail was straight and pointy. As with the other two, he was a master scout for the Balor.

The three stopped and sat; their faces stiffened. They fixed their gaze on Carrick, their ears perked up and alert.

"We shall not force our enemies to beg for peace, nor shall we force them to beg for mercy," the large cat told Carrick. "Our enemies shall only wish for one thing: death eternal. And we shall grant their wish. This is the way of the Balor. Gurtha ilya."

Carrick gently placed a rugged hand over the cat's paw and lowered his head in respect.

"E' gurtha ilya. I' alkar e lye," he said in the feline tongue, meaning - *death for all . . . the glory will be ours.*

The cat gave a slight nod and a slow blink of his eyes.

"What brings you to the Kyr Thysaer?" he asked.

"I am here to request a favor of the great Utine Heru. Soon, I will deploy a small group of warriors to the north. They will make their way to the Dregec Kuul. Their mission will be to distract the brood as they stream from the wicked place. My request is this: I ask that at a point in time the Kyr Thysaer sound its drums but not join as one. I ask only for the drumbeats as this will certainly be enough to aid in the distraction I seek."

"Distraction? Why the need for a distraction?" the great cat asked. "E' ushtar ro diukavraca vionuk. We are not an army of distractions or skirmishes."

"Our friend the Professor has had a vision. He asks that I engage the brood, those positioned to the north, in a distraction of sorts, to aid his nieces as they make their way to the Pas Shae."

"Ah, yes – a Queen of Ahlgren again carries the Lia Fail," said the cat. "Such power in the hands of youth and innocence is not misguided. This I have seen and more."

Carrick was about to speak when Lil' Man stepped forward with a look of concern.

"My pardon, but I heard you speak of the Pas Shae. That's no place for the girls. Why there?" he asked Carrick.

The Utine Heru turned to Lil' Man, anger in his eyes.

"Qui ar' te beleg! Qui ar' te beleg!" he scolded, his voice low and menacing. "Silence and patience! Remember, she is a Queen of Ahlgren. She is no longer a human girl. How the En' Edan proceed is their concern and not ours."

Lil' Man bowed his head and returned to the others.

The great cat looked at Carrick and shook his head.

"Oban Pan sometimes requires restraint and conviction," he told Carrick. "But I understand his worry. I know he is a dear friend to both ladies of Ahlgren. But the reality is clear: there is no place in the Drueger that is fit for those of the good and righteous."

"We recognize the danger they will face in their journey," said Carrick. "But, with so many brood marching from the Dregec Kuul passage, it is feared they would certainly be spotted as they cross the marshlands and through the Pas Shae. Unfortunately, the Pas Shae is the only way to enter the hive and avoid the mass of brood. Some form of distraction will help to focus the brood's attention elsewhere and help to provide them safe passage."

But as Lil' Man listened, he was becoming more impatient. Anger got the best of him as it sometimes does.

"This is folly!" he said. "There's no such thing as safe passage through the Pas Shae! You know this. Sometimes, you En' Edan can be so reckless. Surely there must be another way!"

The Utine Heru became perturbed with Lil' Man's outburst. He closed his eyes and took a deep breath.

"Qui ar' te beleg! Qui ar' te beleg!" he roared, the ground trembling violently. "I do not wish to say this again to you! Understand?"

Lil' Man crouched in fear, his ears pinned back.

Even though agitated, the Heru's face was thoughtful. He understood Lil' Man's concern and sought to diffuse his emotions. He took another breath.

"Oban Pan, when there are few choices, commitment to the one path is required," said the great cat, his voice now changed, softened. "Just as there are but a few paths at the foot of the mountain, in the end, they all lead to the top."

Lil' Man gave a bow but remained frustrated. He was frightened for the girls. Maybe he could have managed it differently, but his motive was to keep his friends safe.

"The Utine Heru is most wise," said Carrick.

"So, our good friend the Professor still makes his presence known, even from a great distance," the great cat chuckled. "He always finds a way to impart his knowledge. But Carrick, one cannot simply stop Val Shas. When the drums roll, we can only dream about the moment we are one. There is only one destiny for the Kyr Thysaer - to join as one and fight! That is what we do! War is glorious! Oht e' aglareb! Oht e' aglareb!"

"But it is not my intention to pull the great Kyr Thysaer into this battle."

"I understand. But after our victory today surely you know the brood is angered. They will throw themselves at your – what you call distraction - with all their might.

And this may very well provoke the Uakor Turg. If this occurs and without the elven army and its Vilyarok, the brood will control the skies. Your distraction could very well lead to a battle you may be ill-prepared for. You will need the whole of the Kyr Thysaer unless you have another strategy."

"My Utine Heru, what I know is that we need to direct the brood's attention to the south, and therefore aid the Professor's nieces. Your wisdom is always most welcomed."

The great cat turned to Tane Brelaak.

"Nimbreth olwen!" he instructed Brelaak in a demanding tone. "Nimbreth olwen!"

Brelaak ran off and soon returned with a roll of birch bark, presenting it to the Utine Heru. The great cat took the roll and spread it on the ground. Using one of his claws he drew a map of the eastern lands on the bark.

"There may be an alternative, one that creates the distraction you require while also thinning the brood," said the cat, pointing to places on the map. "Send your small group north to harass the brood at the Dregec Kuul pass as you have already planned - some cavalry and archers. But consider using a second force as well. Tonight, bring this second force to those fields south of Gortha-Losh, at the Kaquena Kemen. There, position spearmen first and then archers, with cavalry flanked in the fields, to the east and west. Then, when all is in place have your small group in the north attack under the cover of night. As they attack, the brood at the Dregec Kuul pass will defend and the brood positioned north of Gortha-Losh will look to enter the battle for their bloodlust will be roused. Perhaps they will not enter the fray, that is if they are more disciplined than in times past. But you and I know that is doubtful. When they have turned their attention north that is when you signal those at Kaquena Kemen to attack. The brood will have no choice but to turn their attention south and defend their position. As they do so, lift the banners and the drums will sound. We will release the Kyr Thysaer to the southernmost flank of the despicable horde. This will create more discord and maintain the diversion as the northern brood will surely maneuver south. That is when the Claw will cut off its legs. Our attack will serve to slow or halt any advancement upon your army. The brood will be forced to regroup. This should give the ladies of Ahlgren the time they need to enter the Pas Shae."

"What of the Uakor Turg? Your earlier fear may have merit."

The large cat looked into Carrick's eyes

"I' sgiathatch raama. Let the En' Carad fly!" he said unwaveringly and fearlessly, his lips curled, his glorious whitish fur seemingly becoming ablaze. "The red one looks over us, does he not? And knowing the Queen makes her way to the Drueger, he will join the battle, eager for the encounter."

Carrick bowed.

"Yes. I' sgiathatch raama," he said.

"Make your preparations for tomorrow night. We shall do the same. Oh, and Carrick, there is more I must say. We know that the evil brood positions itself near the

Heave, in a most erratic pattern. This is disconcerting. The reason for such action remains unknown."

"Nostale lle," said Carrick. "Thank you. Yes, I have been made aware of such movements by the Professor. This is disturbing information. But I do not know why. Why would they position themselves near the forest? They cannot enter its darkness."

"We do not know. But when one does not understand something, it is sometimes best to try to guess the meaning from the context. Rather than focusing on that part you do not understand, listen to the message as a whole and see if you can make out the probable general meaning."

Carrick paused in thought for a moment.

"The Utine Heru is most wise. I will give this mystery more thought and counsel with others," he said. "But my Heru, I have one more request. But I hesitate, for I do not wish to encumber you with what is my burden."

"Burden? The I' Ra Heru tells us this: 'Let me take up what is a burden to you, what is suffering to you, what is difficult to you. For your burden may be a blessing to me.' So, what is it, Carrick? Tell me of your burden so it may be a blessing to me," said the majestic cat.

"The man who lives in 'Shk Ndor, he who is of the Mur' Edan," said Carrick, hesitation in his voice. "Can you send some of the Balor to seek him out? Roundthaler believes he would be of help."

The cat paused. He sensed Carrick's trepidation as if he were unsure of something. He let his eyes gaze into Carrick's.

"And you Carrick, what do you believe? Do you believe the man will be of help?"

Carrick returned the Heru's stare. There he saw images of war and battle, of death and destruction. He also saw courage in the cat's eyes, the kind of courage that is displayed not only in one instance of danger and heroics but as an act that forms a pattern in a medley of good works.

"My Utine Heru, I do not know what I believe, if the man can help or not. I only know two things - the pain the man harbors, and that Roundthaler would never lead me down a wrong path. It may not be a path I would choose or a path that would seem to make sense to most, but in the end, it may be the right path."

"I understand. We will do as you ask," said the cat with a smile. "I believe somewhere within the man's tortured soul there remains a spirit that has not yet been extinguished. But know that our scouts have brought us horrific word. It is believed the man's people have all but been exterminated by the Ru Gwaith. It is said that he is all that remains of the Mur' Edan, that he lives in the far reaches of 'Shk Ndor with a female of the En' Edhel as his companion. We are told they have a child together and are protected by the eagle and a Ra Draug loyalist. I cannot guarantee the Balor will find him, or for that matter, if they do, be able to convince him to join you."

Carrick bowed his head, sadness for the man.

"My Heru, I am most grateful," he said.

"Also, we will send a few of our finest to tell the Queen and Princess of the plan we have discussed. In this way, they will be ready. Our Balor can more easily escape the brood's attention than the En' Edan."

Hearing this, Lil' Man spoke up.

"Let me go to them! I wish to help!" he implored.

"Sinome ta! Nan' il lle Oban Pan," said the Utine Heru. "Master Grey is with the Queen and Princess, is he not? You are needed here! Do you understand?"

"Yes, my Utine Heru," sighed Lil' Man with a bow, displeased with the response.

The great cat turned to Chumsey and Tane Brelaak.

"Auta a' tanya yamen' ar' kwentra sen iant twun, e' quell inyas. Kwentra sen en' I' ohta. Kwentra sen en' I' ohta," he instructed the two. "You will venture north to where the Old River meets with the Heave and pick up the scent of the ladies of Ahlgren. You will join with them and advise them of what has been discussed here." The cat added, "Make your way at once. Tul're dome. Tul're dome. Travel day and night with haste. Know, that in your actions there can be no room for error. Understand?"

The cats nodded.

When the Utine Heru turned back to Carrick, Lil' Man gave a glance to Chumsey and Tane Brelaak. The three ran off into the blackness.

The great cat took a deep breath. A grim look came upon his face.

"Now, I have something for you, a favor for me, Carrick, something very important to me."

Carrick wondered why the Utine Heru would need his assistance.

"Of course, my Heru, what can I do for you."

"Our scouts pick up strange feline scents to the north. Some Tar Shor may be hidden from us. If it is the Tar Shor, their survival is viewed as problematic. If you or others gain witness to the despicable feline creatures, our enemy, I know you will act accordingly and on behalf of your ally, the Ra Cath."

Everyone in the Harrow knew of the Ra Cath's hatred of the Tar Shor, of the blood that had been spilled in what was called N'alaquel, or *feline cleansing.* For most of the races, including the En' Edan, the purge was an internal matter, and it was the rule not to discuss such affairs. Carrick did not want to upset the great cat. He would be careful with his words.

"The Professor once told me that one cannot look upon a battlefield as endless, for if one does one is already defeated. I hope you know I will always do what is best for the Harrow. Nostale lle, my Utine Heru," Carrick told the great cat. "Nostale lle. We shall take our leave now."

The cat's jaw tensed, and a hardened look came into his eyes. He knew Carrick's words were measured. He knew the sentiment, for the other races were cautious with the Ra Cath. They understood and feared the power of the Kyr Thysaer and would never dare face its might.

"Yes Carrick, what is best for the Harrow," said the cat with a bow, and then offered Carrick words of safe travel, "Varna lema Carrick. Varna lema."

Carrick and Warsinger made their way out through the Ta Mellan and rode quietly back to their massive army, where Roundthaler awaited their return with the greatest of interest.

* * *

As Lil' Man looked on, Chumsey and Tane Brelaak met and plotted a journey to join Molly and Elizabeth. They would leave immediately, especially knowing how erratic the weather was to the east.

"Come with us," Chumsey told Li' Man. "The Utine Heru may not know of your absence. Others can cover for you."

But Lil' Man was against this. He would not make the trip. Instead, he would follow the Utine Heru's instructions and remain with the Kyr Thysaer.

"I cannot disobey the Heru," he told them.

"But you should be with the girls," said Chumsey. Tane Brelaak agreed.

"No. As the Utine Heru said, I am needed here. But with your help, I can be close to them."

"What do you mean?" asked Chumsey.

Lil' Man began to quickly preen himself, lapping at his tabby coat with his long tongue, pulling at it with his teeth. He grimaced as he tugged at his thick fur, showing off gleaming white fangs. He revealed a small tuft of orange fur that he gave to Chumsey.

"Give this to the older of the two. Her name is Molly. She's the Queen of Ahlgren. Tell her to keep it with her, always."

Chumsey nodded, placing the tuft of fur in a small leather satchel around his neck. He and Tane Brelaak then fled into the darkness of night. But not before Chumsey turned back to Lil' Man.

"I'll give it to her. I will," he told his friend. "She'll like that."

As Lil' Man watched his friends run off into the distance he could only think of the girls and how much he missed them and how he now worried for their safety. There was something about being away from them that made him realize how much he had come to rely on them. They had become an important part of his life and he felt as if he had lost a part of himself without them.

* * *

With Carrick gone, the Utine Heru briefly convened with his Balor lead warriors. Together, they outlined in finer detail the plan to assist Carrick. When the meeting was completed, the great cat returned to his place at the center of the clowder, alone amidst the great Kyr Thysaer. He looked upon the vast circles of the Balor army and thought of his younger days. Images of Katzhu Pu and the great statue of the I' Ra Heru, the mighty father feline creator of the Ra Cath, came to him. The statue depicted the I' Ra Heru as an enormous and commanding feline, with long golden fur, streaks of white and blue, and blackish horns that protruded from his strong and well-rounded shoulders.

He thought of the great stories about the feline creator, as written over the ages by the many Ra Cath clerics, and he reflected on their teachings. Theirs was a complex faith that embodied an understanding of the trials of survival. It spoke of times of discord and of times of harmony, of how the glory of war and death sometimes leads to peace and tranquility. It was taught that the essence of the I' Ra Heru filled all Heru felines, that he was the source of all redemption, the embodiment of all that was good, the true meaning of life, and the reason stars shine at night.

But understanding the I' Ra Heru's teachings was something many of the Heru felines struggled with, including the Utine Heru. He felt ashamed and could not bear others knowing that he had been so foolish as to think he could fully understand the I' Ra Heru's teachings without the guidance of his essence. He would have liked to pretend that he had understood, but that would not have been true. It was this struggle that he kept secret.

He took a deep sigh and closed his eyes to the darkness of thought. He thought of a kyerma, a prayer, one he had remembered as a young cat. It went like this:

Our Father Creator,
Bring us your noise,
Bring us the wind and rain and chaos of the storm,
For, in the aftermath of the storm,
A quiet is born.
Our Father Creator,
Bring us your noise,
Bring us the wind and rain so we may have balance,
For, in the aftermath of the storm,
Noise becomes quiet.

From noise to quiet; from quiet to noise.

He took yet another deep sigh.

Tuulo' raumo a' seere; tuulo' seere a' raumo, he thought. *From noise to quiet; from quiet to noise.*

But he struggled, struggled with his faith and the purpose of his life. At times it tried to unmake him. He did not always understand why there had to be so much death, why so much blood had to stain the land, and why he had to be part of it.

But the I' Ra Heru is merciful. I must take comfort in his mercy and rely on his grace more fully. Doing so helps to recognize that this life is a spiritual journey. We are living out the I' Ra Heru's experience that true faith is learned obedience. Is this how he wanted us to live?

A tear came to his eye.

He repeated in his mind - *true faith is learned obedience, true faith is learned obedience, true faith is learned obedience.*

He tried to clear his mind but could not.

The problem with obedience comes when it is excessive when real concerns are not voiced. Does such obedience deliver lasting change?

Again, he closed his eyes to the demons of his struggle.

I look to thee I' Ra Heru for guidance during these troubled times. I look to thee with abundant faith, for the sustenance to help me prevail. Your teachings talk of noise and of quiet; of the right and the wrong choices; of the many paths each brings.

He looked up into the night sky.

Oh I' Ra Heru, I do not understand why you present such noise, the kind that only brings death and destruction. I do not understand why it must be this way. Will a deeper faith in you lead me to better understand our existence?

He looked upon the thousands of Balor warriors.

Do I serve a purpose that does not exist? If so, what a monumental waste that would be, all the lives I have deceived. Show me, your servant, the way and provide me with me an answer. For the sake of the Ra Cath!

Then a slight smile came to his face, born of a sudden thought. It was bold and powerful and struck at his core. In this, his quiet struggle, he always managed to conceal his doubt, his waning devotion, until one word always came to him, repeatedly.

Faith. Questioning beliefs is not the same as doubting faith. Belief and faith are different. It is when you have doubts that the dark ones can gain a foothold and lead you down the wrong path. Faith, faith is everything and it is all there is. It is forever with no beginning or end!

He thought about what it was like whenever he looked up at a tree and how it made him feel that he was part of something bigger than himself, and how it felt to have peace wash over him. It was then, when he looked up at a tree, that he knew he could finish the journey, that he knew he had a purpose.

In the branches, he could see faces, the faces of those he loved, and this gave him purpose. He thought about the battles he had fought, and those who fought by his side, and this gave him purpose. He could see the faces of those he had lost but also those that he had saved, and this gave him purpose. He could hear the sweet songs of the birds in the morning and the symphony of the creatures in the night, and this gave him purpose.

Alone at the center of the clowder, an understanding came to him. He gave a great roar, a raw sound that started deep within his body. It was a howl of emotion that cut through the silence of the night, shaking through the ground and bodies of the Balor warriors.

In response, the whole of the Balor began to roar, a deafening chorus that echoed across the land. A fearsome look came to the great cat.

Faith is forever, it is everything in life. You need it to take the first step of a journey and you need it for the final step, the one that takes you into the darkness of the unknown. After all, faith that the quiet will come from noise is all we have as we face eternal darkness.

He gave one last, mighty roar, so powerful and with so much force that his breath stirred the dust, several leagues away.

* * *

"Ah, there he is," bellowed Roundthaler as Carrick and Warsinger approached from the shadows. "Where were you off to? How about sharing a pint of mead with your old friend? What a celebrated day this has been!"

Carrick dismounted Warsinger and smiled at his friend.

"A pint of mead sounds good," he said, the words muted. He looked away from Roundthaler, off into the distance.

They stood near a fire that was roaring away, to get warm as the night was turning cold. Roundthaler sensed concern in his friend's eyes as he poured him a pint.

"What is troubling you?" he asked handing Carrick the drink. "I trust you know me well enough that you can share anything with me without fear of judgment. I sense it is something serious."

Carrick took a sip of mead and gazed into the fire. It was warm and mesmerizing as the flames rose many feet into the air. Glowing ash particles, lighter than air, danced into the night sky like yellow-orange fireflies.

"You know me all too well my friend," he said gathering the strength for the words he would speak. "There is so much to say. It makes it difficult to know where to start."

"Well, it is good to start at the beginning – not always of course, but usually to start with what is immediately at hand."

"Very well then. My friend, this war shall be our last together. A vision of the Professor came to me. Soon I shall leave the Harrow, never to return. For me, the end has come, here on these lands, in this place, and in this moment in time."

The gruff dwarf scrunched his eyes, taking a large gulp of mead.

"Aye, we knew this time would arrive," he said. "Carrick, I do not pretend to understand what you and the Professor are all about, where you come from, or even this world that is all around us. I am a simple creature; I am but a warrior who revels in the rigors of battle and the merriment of drink. There are few things in this life I know. I know the seasons reflect the passing of time, that death follows battle, and that friendship is our dearest help in troubled times. You have been and always shall be a dear friend. How can I not be saddened by your departure? There will never be another like you. And I have been most honored to have known you as a friend."

He reached out and strongly gripped Carrick's forearm in friendship, pulling the tall man close to him.

"I may be sad, but I cannot be unhappy," he told Carrick. "I am thankful for the time we have had. We applied our trade using the sword and axe as our tools. I ask you - is there a nobler trade?"

Carrick looked down at his friend for a long moment. He remembered how close they were as warriors in battles past. Much had happened since he first arrived at the Harrow. Great wars had been waged and long agonies endured. Nevertheless, he still thought of him not only as a wonderful friend but as a brother as well.

"You know how much your friendship has meant to me," said Carrick. "It has never faltered nor grown cold; it has been a great blessing. I shall always hold it dear to me. I too am not saddened, but in leaving this place there are, shall I say, regrets."

"And tell me, what regrets could the great Erol Carrick have?" said Roundthaler. "Surely, there were no wasted days in this place, no wasted moments in time."

"Just a couple of things I could not change; things beyond my control," sighed Carrick.

"Her, you talk of her, do you not?" said Roundthaler with caution. "You speak of the Nalenian warrior-queen, Merira."

"Yes. I regret her loss."

"What iss that word you En' Edan use," said Roundthaler with hesitation. "Ah, yes – love. You had a love for her, and the daughter you had together. This love is something we dwarves have no use for. For us, the closest we have is what we call uavliia, or in your tongue *utility*."

Roundthaler's words brought a smile and chuckle to Carrick.

"Yes, I loved her deeply," he said looking down at his friend. "I also regret something else - that you are unable to wield the fire swords."

"Enough with these regrets," came Roundthaler's swift response, like the rushing of pent waters. "No, my friend, you should have no regrets, no guilt whatsoever. The warrior-queen was a free spirit and a great fighter. She lived for battle and if no battle was handy, it was her delight to start one, much like her daughter, your daughter, Straya. You continue to burden yourself with her death. The time for that has ended too. And, as far as the fire swords go, well, well, much too heavy a weight for my stature to lift. You should have no regrets, only pride in the way you have taken care of this land. I mean there is no reason to look back, wishing you could change things. If you have no regrets, you stop wishing you could rearrange your past, and you start looking forward to whatever is up ahead. Now is the time to look forward, beyond this place."

For a moment Carrick wavered. He was distressed and again looked away from his friend peering into the night and at the flickering campfires of his vast army in the distance. He knew he would always have his regrets, like flames in his soul. But there was so much to do before the end. He knew he had to prepare; his time had come, but he did not know precisely when or how it would end. He had but one wish now and it involved his dwarf friend.

"Bombadorn, your words are spoken with grace," he said, returning his look to his friend. "You can bring clarity to confusion, a joy to times filled with utter sadness, and hope to the hopeless. And it is because of such grace that I now wish to ask something of you."

Roundthaler paused in concern, then spoke. "Of course. Anything for you."

"Will you look after Straya for me? She is much like her mother and I fear for her. She could use your guidance and wisdom."

There was anguish in Carrick's words, a hidden sorrow, and Roundthaler sensed this. Then, a rather surprising thought came to him.

"You have not told her, have you?" he gasped. "You have not told her the truth of the matter – that you are her father."

Carrick shook his head.

"Her mother and I knew that being the child of the great Carrick would be too much of a weight, especially for a female Nalenian warrior, one who would eventually be queen and lead the Shyr Shar. This is a secret that must not be shared. It must continue to remain between us."

"Carrick, but she should know. A child should know who their mother and father are."

"She is better off. She knows who her mother was and that is all that she and her people care about. That is their way." A deep sigh came from the innermost recesses of his heart. He gave a tepid smile and again asked his friend, "You will look after her for me?"

"Aye, I shall," said Roundthaler with a hint of reluctance. "Reckless she is, and truth be told she does not need looking after. What she needs is to learn a bit of self-discipline and I am not sure if she can. But my friend, I will promise you that I will do my best to show her the ways of a true warrior – courage, and selflessness even in the face of danger or death. This is my promise to you until I take my last breath."

"Thank you," said a solemn Carrick.

Roundthaler gave him a lighthearted slap to the back.

"All right, all right, enough of such sad talk," he said. "Now, how about another swig of mead?"

Carrick turned to his friend, his look staunch and determined. They smiled at each other and took a slug of mead.

"There is more to tell," said Carrick. "We do not have much time. Send word to ready a regiment for tomorrow. We shall put Thondras Çendri in charge. They will march north to meet the enemy. Also, we will need to send others to the Kaquena Kemen."

"What's this? Only one regiment? And the Kaquena Kemen? What are you talking about, my friend?"

"In that same vision, the Professor told me of his nieces, one of whom carries the Lia Fail. We need to distract the brood to allow the Professor's nieces time to enter the Drueger. They will enter through the Pas Shae. I have taken counsel with the Utine Heru who will aid with the distraction. And Bombadorn, two more things. The brood moves some of their forces near the Heave. We know an army cannot traverse through the thick forest. But I do not understand why they position forces in such a manner. Think about this for me. Your wisdom would be most helpful. Oh, and one last thing, the young man named Miragrin who rides Saraanth, he is to be by my side."

"The Lia Fail! By the Maker! And another battle!" exclaimed Roundthaler in delight.

But he quickly calmed himself. He thought of the stone's enormous power, and how it could turn the tide of an entire battle. But he also knew of its burden. It was no trivial object to hold.

"The Professor's nieces must be most courageous," said Roundthaler. "To carry the burden of the stone into the Pas Shae, such an evil place." He then thought of the brood positioning near the Forest Heave. "And the blackness of the Heave – is there no darker place? But I do not understand. Why would the foul slime look to be near the forest?"

"I do not know, but no good can come of it," said Carrick. "What I do know though is that we must help the Professor's nieces."

Roundthaler was concerned, but he gave a smile. He trusted Carrick and was glad for their companionship. Then, he thought about the request he made of Carrick.

"Dare I ask? What about the friend we spoke of?" he said. "Have you given it more consideration?"

"I have, my friend. The Utine Heru will send some of the Balor to 'Shk Ndor, to contact him on our behalf."

"In the end, all things have a way of working out for the best," said Roundthaler. "Aye! Another day of battle. Victory shall be ours! One should be so lucky, eh Carrick!"

Immediately, the two made their way to the command tent.

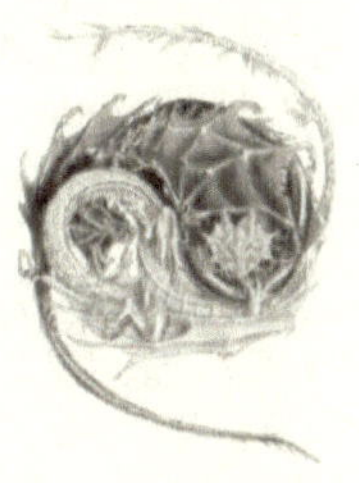

CHAPTER 12
STRAYA

IN THEIR COMMAND TENT, Carrick and Roundthaler were reviewing maps of the Foghollow Barrens and Crag, drawing up plans for the upcoming battle, when Thondras Cendri entered. He was an imposing figure, tall and muscular, in his armor of silver scales that reflected prismatic beams with every motion. An elegant helmet, surrounded by a crest of horsehair, encased his head, barely restraining long black hair and a beard. Warriors were inspired by his near presence and yet quite intimidated, for he was a man who lived by the sword and knew little of gentle hearts and tender feelings. He was feared as Carrick's enforcer and was known as one of the most dangerous men in the Harrow. Fluent in the old tongue and friend to Skag Harwell, he was able to handle himself in any fight and had a dark reputation as a savage killer.

From behind their table, Carrick and Roundthaler looked up at the commanding enforcer.

"My dearest Thondras," said Carrick.

"My liege," said Cendri. He removed his helmet, revealing a rugged face, scarred, battle-hardened, with eyes that were as black as the distance between the stars. "You called for me."

"Thondras, soon you will lead a small regiment of Basi Basu on a covert action to disrupt the brood at the Dregec Kuul." Carrick was bold.

"Basi Basu - warriors from the southernmost mountains of the South Eldor," muttered Roundthaler. "Solitary, quiet ones they are, but viciously powerful on the battlefield. Almost like us dwarves. My kind of folk."

"Prowess and discipline, a refusal to ever surrender," added Carrick.

Cendri stood motionless and without expression, directing his attention to the maps.

"My liege, show me your plan," he said.

Carrick reviewed the details of the strategy, the terrain and how the warriors should attack, and at what intervals. He explained how the Kyr Thysaer would assist.

When Carrick had finished, he looked up at his enforcer, and with bluntness asked, "Do you wish to know the reason for this mission?"

"My liege, when I am asked to do your bidding," said Cendri, "the reason matters not."

"My good Cendri, know that I am sending you and the others to certain death, for I do not expect the brood to spare your lives."

Cendri was quiet and still. He looked into Carrick's eyes, a hint of a smile hovered on his lips.

"My liege, but you are mistaken. Death will not grip my soul on this battlefield. No. If death is to have its way with me, it will do so when I am by your side. Then and only then can death have its way with me. And when that time comes, when I am by your side, and death reaches for my soul, it will be my pleasure, my privilege to give it willingly."

Suddenly, there was a commotion outside the command tent, drawing the attention of Carrick, Roundthaler, and Cendri. Straya burst into the tent with resolute steps, brashness, and a careless and jaunty air. She was agitated.

"I hear rumors, men talking of battle," she said. "And I see warriors preparing for an engagement. Tell me. Are we marching on the brood tomorrow?"

Roundthaler took hold of one of Cendri's massive arms.

"Come Thondras, let us leave these two alone," he told the warrior.

Roundthaler turned to Carrick with a smirk of annoyance at the impertinence of the interruption.

"I imagine you have much to discuss with this young lady," he told Carrick. "Please remind her that even in times of war, there is a decorum to be followed."

"Decorum?" she said, a curled lip in anger. "During war?" Foolish dwarf, there's no such thing!"

"It's a pity," Roundthaler told her. "Still, so much to learn at your age."

He shook his head and he and Cendri quickly left the tent before Carrick could protest.

Straya stood before the great Carrick, fully armored. The flickering shadows of the torches that had been placed at intervals around the tent played against the tight muscles of her stomach and thighs, while the steel of her armor glowed brilliantly.

"If we march tomorrow, I lead the charge with the Shyr Shar," she demanded. "I'll be the first to strike the hive."

Carrick was angered by her approach, but he knew his anger would get him nowhere. He needed to focus on the task at hand and get her to focus as well.

"What you hear, what you see, are the cravings for battle," he said, his voice firm. "And while there is a plan afoot, you and the Shyr Shar will not be part of it. Our strategy is different."

He repositioned several maps that were on the table, unfolding a large and crinkled one of the Foghollow Barrens that he set before her.

"Let me show you. This is a different battle, not the kind you and others so lust for," he said pointing to the vast wasteland on the map, the Dregec Kuul passage, and its gates. She leaned forward. "We intend to disrupt the brood in the north with a small group. I am confident that at first they will be confused by this, but they will quickly call for those brood positioned in the south to enter the battle. When this occurs, we will have some of our forces engage those at the southern flank. Those of the south will have no choice but to turn and fight, anger seething in their bodies. As the conflict unfolds on two fronts, there will be more confusion and fear in the brood." He again pointed to places on the map. "This will be to our advantage for we will then strike with the Kyr Thysaer. The Ra Cath will storm again and again."

She seemed perplexed at what she heard.

"But why such a tactic? I don't understand," she said, pausing in thought. "You look to draw attention away from the gates. But why?"

"I have my reasons, and they are strong," Carrick stated emphatically. "With time, you will understand why we are taking such measures. You must exercise patience. You must do what the brood cannot."

"And what's that?"

"Restrain your emotions."

She was annoyed by his response. She was, after all, impulsive and transparent - far too impulsive to be anything other than transparent. She poured out her feelings with startling candor when she held anger, defiance, or resentment. She was wayward and fitful in her moods; this was her bane. But she did not want to anger him and feared she may have already done so. She took a deep breath to calm herself. He could sense her becoming less tense.

"If I may then – what of the White Star?" she asked, her voice now calm, but cold. "Were they to join us on the battlefield?"

"I am sure Dalgaes and Col Shas will be with us. Regardless, we will take the fight to the darkness, and this time, without you or your Shyr Shar."

She took another deep breath. She had to trust him. She looked at the maps and then up to him. He returned her gaze. Her eyes were striking, a brilliant dark brown, rich, and as she stood before him, he could only be reminded of her mother, Merira, the great Nalenian warrior-queen.

He smiled at her.

"You remind me so much of your mother," he told her, gently staring into her eyes. "Your height, the color of your hair, your eyes, so much like her."

She returned his smile.

"I'm often told I resemble her," she said as she sat in a chair across from him. She raised an elegant dark brow, and her voice became softer. "I am told you knew her, that you fought many great battles together, and that you taught her of battle and leadership."

She stared at him, her anger now gone, replaced with an inquisitiveness that surprised him. She leaned forward in her chair.

"I'd like to learn more about her. Tell me, what did you know of her?" she asked.

Memories of Merira danced endlessly in his mind. He remembered the time when they first became close. It was after a long, hard-fought battle and during a victory meal. Their spirits were high, and food and mead flowed freely. He fed her fruit and they laughed, and he took his hand and gently caressed her face, so soft and fair, so open, so beautiful. With this touch, she then forcefully took him and kissed him. He tasted her sweetness in every way he could. He continued to feed her fruit and he licked her lips after each bite until she kissed him again. He was driven senseless with desire. That night, the two became such intimates as man and woman rarely are, both united in a common cause, war and victory, but also desire and passion.

He remembered every bit of her, her touch, her scent, of things that were young, healthy, and vital. She smelled like warmth and life. He held his memories of her deeply etched in his mind, embracing the terrible ache in his heart he could not deny at her loss.

As he looked at Straya as a vision of Merira appeared. It was a vision so clear, so vivid, that only with difficulty could he restrain himself from the pain of sadness. Then, in an instant, the vision had vanished, and he was left staring at Straya, who found cause to smile at him. He quickly collected himself.

"I knew your mother very well. Together we shared many things. I learned from her, and she from me. She was a ferocious fighter, very cunning on the battlefield, and she was a great strategist. She was a woman of strong thought, broad opinions, great strength, and grace with all; a woman who was fearless in the face of terrible odds. Hers was the greatness of character, not name, nor position.

"She was entirely feminine in her bearing, but still with a great gift of wisdom and courage. She was also a woman of great integrity whose love for the Maker, life, and happiness was ripe with vitality and exuberance. She knew the key to winning a battle is to avoid what is strong and strike what is weak, and this means knowing your enemy. To do this takes knowledge, and reasoned thought. Not emotions, raw and fevered. She was all this and more because she learned to control her anger and her emotions.

She was very special to me and a good friend." He paused staring deeply into her eyes. "Your mother lived her life as though each day was her last. There is no better way to live."

He then turned away from her, and from his memories of Merira. He gazed into the flickering flame of a torch only to be reminded of Merira's demise. He fought mightily to contain his emotions.

"And when she died, when she died that day on the battlefield," he told Straya, "it was a death unlike any other, for it tore a hole through my very existence and I, I have never been the same. I am haunted, even to this day, that I was unable to prevent her death. Do you have any idea how I grieve? Do you?"

There was no emotion to his words, just a flat recitation, as though he had spoken the words countless times. She was quiet, gazing at him. She could feel his anguish and distress, and it made her sad, a sadness rooted in his emotions, but also a sadness deep within her as she remembered the few cherished moments she had with her mother. She fought these emotions silently for a while before gentle tears welled up in her eyes. Deep within her hardened exterior was a warm heart, an emotion she rarely showed to others.

"I am sorry," she said choking back tears. She swallowed hard a couple of times. "I did not know how close you were to my mother. I wish I had known her. I wish I could have fought by her side. I wish I could have learned from her. I was only a child when she died and I have often thought about what would it have been like, to have had a mature conversation with her."

"You are so like your mother," he said looking back at her. "You are like her in every respect but one: you have yet to learn how to control your emotions. Without control, they prevent you from anticipating problems, and from thinking clearly about future pathways. You must learn to stop and think of how best to deal with a problem, of the many pathways before you, and to do so without emotion. If you can do this, the best course of action will unfold before you. It will become as clear as the light of day and you will be able to carry it out. This is the discipline of self-control; this is what you require to be a successful leader, to properly succeed your mother."

"You can teach me," she said with great enthusiasm and anticipation in her voice. "Like you taught my mother."

"Alas, I cannot," he said softly. "I am from the Aina Dur, and my travels are such that I barely know my whereabouts until it is time to attend to it all. But even though I cannot be with you, there is another who can. You see, it is not about the teacher, but rather it is about the student. If the student is open to learning, the student will learn many things from many teachers."

A warmth came to his features, the warmth of a tenderness that was fatherly and she felt it. It was an incredible emotion, an emotion she had not felt before, one which she could not describe.

"I have asked Roundthaler to mentor you," he told her. "He will watch over you, teach you the ways of battle and war, of leadership, of peace, and this place."

"The dwarf commander from Mortha?" she questioned with a sideways smile. "A dwarf teaching a warrior-queen of the Shyr Shar. That's plain silliness . . ."

He rose a hand to cut her off.

"This is where you fail. Control. You must control your emotions, you must control your feelings, or they will control you. Roundthaler cannot teach you everything. There will be some things you must learn for yourself, through failure. But he will be a good teacher and you will learn much. I am going to tell you something. Remember that you may not always understand everything, but you must know that the Maker is in control, and he has a plan for you. It is my only hope that you live this plan, that you live your destiny. Roundthaler can help point the way. It is about the student, not the teacher." He then added, "It is what your mother would want."

She shut her eyes. She was aware of her shortcomings. She realized she needed to control her emotions, to try to remain calm and unruffled. She thought about his gesture and it humbled her. She opened her eyes, averted her gaze, and rose from her chair.

"I don't know what to say, other than to say thank you," she said as she stood before him. "I will heed your words and do my best to learn from many teachers."

She wiped tears from her face, hoping he would not think badly of her showing such emotion.

He smiled.

"I sense you are already learning," he said.

She left the tent as Carrick sunk into his chair. He knew that he would again see his daughter on the battlefield of the Foghollow Barrens, for what could very well be the last time. He closed his tearful eyes to a vision of Merira, a raving warrior, riding her steed, screaming a fierce battle cry, circling the sword Megil En' Gur high into the air as she charged into battle. He took a deep breath, and he could smell her skin and feel the warmth of it.

I so miss you my love and the lessons you taught me about life. I miss you by my side.

* * *

Upon returning to her command tent, Straya spent time thinking about all that Carrick had said. She knew he had great wisdom to share, as would Roundthaler, and she felt better already. But, in some ways, she knew much would be up to her. In her mind, and as Carrick said, it would come down to her ability to control her emotions. But it was this inability that freed her from the grip of logic and emotional constraint, that made her cold, providing an alternative to the dominant cultural view of women as unable to fight on the battlefield. It was the bold fierceness that was the way of a Nalenian warrior-queen. It is what made her mother; it is what made her.

Then there are my words. My inability to control my tongue goes together with my inability to control my emotions. Harsh words serve me well with my kind but wear thin with others - small incidents, nasty arguments, offhanded comments, and tantrums. I see this now.

She wished she could somehow turn her emotions on and off when the time demanded such.

I must learn. I must practice. Even mix them, all for the sake of victory on the battlefield. I must be methodical - calculating - in my plotting. I will prove my worth to Carrick. I will show him I can be the warrior-queen my mother was. I will show everyone.

She disrobed and prepared herself to rest for the night. She crawled onto the bed and slid herself beneath its soft sheets and woolen blankets. The air in the tent under the nighttime skies was not cold, but neither was it warm. A small fire at the center provided the necessary heat and light.

She closed her eyes when she heard someone enter her tent. She was not frightened, she knew it was only Verno Cralan, one of her strongest warriors. She opened her eyes to Cralan who stood at the tent's entrance, a large figure before her. When he took a step forward, the light flickered against his body, highlighting his strong build. His face was expressionless as it often was, with narrowed eyes, furrowed brows, and fierceness to his frown.

"My Queen, I'm here to warm you," he said.

She started to think it was time for her to begin her new journey.

"Not tonight Verno," she said, quiet words from her lips. "Tonight, my thoughts will keep me warm. In the future, I'll let you know if I'm cold. You may leave,"

He looked confused for a moment then left the tent.

Alone in her bed for the first time in many nights, she allowed her thoughts to drift. She remembered the feel of Carrick's words, strong, forceful, but at the same time compassionate. His words rained down on her.

"She knew the key to winning a battle is to avoid what is strong and strike what is weak, and this means knowing your enemy.

To do this takes knowledge, and reasoned thought. Not emotions, raw and fevered."

As the night wore on, the time fell heavily upon her and she found it difficult to sleep. She could not stop thinking about Carrick and her mother. Something about him seemed so familiar and she was determined to speak with him again.

He can tell me more about her, and in doing so I will learn more about myself.

* * *

Chumsey and Tane Brelaak made their way north, running wildly in and out of outgrowths west of the Old River. They briefly stopped in places to try to pick up the scent of human children, then they would start again, perhaps running in a different direction, toward an unseen place. They avoided closeness to the Forest Heave, a place tainted by the Ra Cath in strangeness. As they ran, they could make out shadows of brood to the east, strangely positioned on the barrens, shadows slowly creeping west. At one point the two cats stopped and bolted along fallen logs and up a sturdy tree, where they lifted twitching noses into the cold night air.

"We're closer, much closer," Chumsey told Brelaak, pointing a paw north to a large area of trees, shrubbery, and rocks that cradled the river. "I sense something in the air. There are scents, many scents, too many scents."

"Yes. I smell them as well."

"The scent of the Nur' Edan, light, almost elusive, but it's there, far away. The scent of the En' Edhel, stronger, closer."

"The Nur' Edan? I don't understand," said a concerned Brelaak. "Why do you suppose they are so close?"

"I don't know, but we must stick to our plan," said Chumsey. "We can advise the Utine Heru of this when we return." Then his nose caught something in the air. "Wait. There. There. Do you sense it?"

Brelaak's nose quivered.

"Yes. It's different, with a sweetness to it. I hadn't sensed it before. It's very strong, isn't it? Very close. What is it?"

"It's the scent of human children," said Chumsey. "They may be hidden there, within the trees and bushes ahead."

"Yes. I see it," said Brelaak.

But to their surprise and horror, they saw two brood slowly making their way from the barrens across the river and in the direction of the outgrowth.

"Why do they cross the river?" thought Chumsey aloud.

"Perhaps they also sense the human children. Do you think they sense them? We can attack and kill the wretches," said a defiant Brelaak.

"We must be careful. If the human children are there and if we kill the brood so close to the river it'll attract the attention of other shadows. More will cross the river. Maybe we can lure them to the west, near the Heave, and let the forest have its way with them."

They looked at the Heave. In the still darkness of the forest, from its mysterious depths, no sound sounded, not even the wind itself, yet there was something about it, for it was as if the silence were a noise. They knew the many stories. The forest had stood there in silence, in the sun and the rain, and the snows of the dark season. It was old when the world was born, old when the races first climbed from the ground. It was older than time itself. But they also knew that it would swallow those that neared its darkness.

They devised a plan. Chumsey would lure the brood away from where they suspected the girls were and to the west. There, Brelaak would then lure them closer to the forest, close enough for the forest's evil forces to engulf the creatures.

"The night will help us," Chumsey told Brelaak. "There'll be confusion. They'll think two cats are one. But you must be careful. Stay clear of the forest's edge. Too close and you'll be gone."

"I know," said Brelaak, his voice trailing off as he ran to a position near the forest's edge. "And you, you stay clear of their blades."

With his friend positioned, Chumsey ran as fast as he could toward the two brutes as they made their way to the outcropping. Closer and closer the small cat came, until the two hulking, dark images, clearly came to life as orcs. These were orcs specifically bred for battle. They were much larger than men, their skin hues shades of sickening green, with long, black hair braided in orc battle fashion. He could see their small tusks and sharp teeth, implements of war and death that could easily shred an enemy apart. They each carried long swords, pitted with rust, but with a sparkle of deathly sharpness at the edge.

As Chumsey got closer to the two orcs, he focused on the lead. He raced past him and reaching out with a paw tore a deep cut into its ankle. The beast roared in pain and stumbled. It got sight of him and swung its blade down, narrowly missing his tail. As the blade struck the ground, he staggered a little, then darted back and forth racing to the west, luring the orcs away from the outcropping. He kept running to Brelaak, dodging the mighty swings of the orc's swords. But he was tiring and Brelaak saw this. So, Brelaak hurried to his rescue, hurling himself at the orc's other leg and gashing its ankle with his claws. The wounded orc fell to one knee in agony.

"Drepa avhem!" howled the beast. "Drepa avhem!"

Chumsey knew the tongue, *kill them, kill them!*

He quickly ran off unnoticed by the orcs as Brelaak ran toward the forest's edge. The orcs saw Brelaak and were on the move again, chasing after him. They were at the forest's edge when Chumsey heard a swish and thwap of an arrow as it flew past. The arrow missed the orcs and lodged itself into a nearby tree of the Heave. The tree seemed to moan, breaking the unnerving stillness of the forest as it became alive with movement and sound, spiraling vines and oozing green sap. Its large branches and vines stretched out with tendrils and snatched the nearest orc, squeezing it with its bark and leaves. The orc struggled. The beast tried to use its sword to tear at the vines, but its efforts were useless. In a matter of seconds, the vines and branches of the tree had dragged it into the darkness of the Heave.

Brelaak circled past the forest's edge again, looking to lure the remaining orc closer. The dim-witted orc yielded to its lustful rage, oblivious to the danger, and followed him to the Heave where a large tree root lifted itself from the ground and upended the beast. The orc stumbled as more roots sprung from the ground in all directions, wrapping around the beast.

Brelaak ran from the forest and to his friend. They watched the orc who was frozen in fear, held motionless by tree roots as thick vines swiftly wrapped around its ankles, while a branch crashed down upon its head. The orc was quickly overwhelmed. The long, thick green vines then lifted and flung the beast high in the air and into the forest. There was a sound from the darkness, almost like a deep moan, then silence as the Heave again became still.

The cats looked at each other, then looked to the brood east of the river. The death of the two orcs at the hand of the Heave had gone unnoticed by the other brood. Their plan had worked.

"An arrow. Did you see it?" said Chumsey. "It came from the outgrowth."

"The human children must be there."

"We must proceed with caution," said Chumsey. "The others with them will protect them at all costs."

They slowly moved toward the outcropping, keeping low to the ground with ears flattened back. Chumsey stopped and dragged his paw over the ground pulling up dried leaves and moist soil. He sniffed at the leaves and dirt.

"What is it?" asked Brelaak.

"As I thought. The scent of human children. They are there."

They moved closer, now slower and slower, closer and closer to the ground. There came another swish of air and thwap of an arrow, this one sticking into the ground right at the tip of Chumsey's nose. He froze, closed his eyes, and took a deep breath.

"Halt, or the next one will be through your heads," came a whispered voice, that of An Van Au.

"We are here with a message from Samson Beleg Balor El Tar, the great Utine Heru, High General of the Balor," said Chumsey with a slight tremble to his voice, his eyes staring at the arrow nudging against his nose.

Molly and Big Grey joined An Van Au and looked out at the two cats. Molly squinted through the darkness at Chumsey.

"I remember you," she said. "You are a friend of Lil' Man. I saw you with him at Katzhu Pu, with the Guild Lords."

"Yes. He is Chum Sey Balor El Ta, of the warrior guild," said Big Grey. "But I do not know the other, the brown one."

"Who travels with you?" asked Molly.

"I'm Tanus Bre Balor El Tar," said Brelaak. "I'm also called Tane Brelaak by many. I too know Oban Pan. My friend here is correct. We've only a message to give. An important message at that."

"We must be cautious," Big Grey told Molly.

She nodded.

"You may enter to speak with us. But know we have others here who will protect us from harm."

"We understand," said Chumsey.

The two cats entered the outgrowth hideaway, crawling through the thicket of bushes and over a variety of large rocks, coming to an open space that was larger than the cats had imagined. Above, clumped trees provided a dense canopy cover.

Molly and the others slowly emerged from the shadows when Brelaak was surprised by something he saw. He crouched, his panic-stiffened tail lashing vigorously from side to side.

Orc!

"Gulguthra! En' Rauko!" hissed Brelaak at Ug'ghi Otha. "What's this creature doing here!"

Ug'ghi Otha grunted and took a step forward, but Bran pushed him back.

"Quiet. Both of you now. We cannot give away our cover," said Bran. He looked at everyone. "Quiet or we die."

The looks on the faces of the others shifted to him along with their eyes. His stare was piercing to the point of rendering everyone motionless. His words were a reminder of the cold, hard reality of their situation.

"Calm yourself, my friend," Chumsey told Brelaak. "The orc is here to help. He's a friend of the Queen."

"How can a Queen of Ahlgren befriend such a monster?" said Brelaak, his tail swatting anxiously.

"I know this is difficult for you to understand but trust me," said Chumsey. "He was at Katzhu Pu."

"He entered the sacred city?"

"He did."

Molly stepped forward and bent to a knee before the cats as the Lia Fail dangled from the necklace around her neck. It glowed softly, even in the dark.

"You must have trust in others," she said with an outreached hand to Brelaak who sniffed at it. "He is a friend who will help to guide and protect us through the wilderness." She smiled at the cats. "I promise that no harm will come to you, proud warriors of the Balor."

There was something about her voice, a calmness, that made everything feel right. Brelaak was reassured by her words, and he and Chumsey bowed before her.

"My Queen," said Chumsey.

"My Queen," said Brelaak remorsefully. "I did not know about your friendship with the orc. It is just so very strange."

"No. No apology," she said with a twinkle in her eyes. "You have nothing to apologize for. You are most brave in coming here, and with so much evil about."

She continues to grow as a person, thought Big Grey. *She is growing into her role.*

Upon hearing the cat's thoughts, Molly turned him.

One grows when one has an incredible teacher.

Big Grey gave a slow blink.

He sniffed at the two cats, his sense of smell invaluable, as with all Ra Cath. He recognized Chumsey's scent. He trusted him. However, he did not recognize Brelaak's scent and stared into the brownish cat's eyes.

They looked distant to him, but he sensed no malice. Mainly, Brelaak looked worried, sad even. At least for now he had his scent for future reference.

"Tell us your message," said Big Grey.

"Tomorrow night, the armies of the En' Edan will attack the brood from the south, said Chumsey. "They'll look to draw their attention away from the river, away from this place, so you can enter the Pas Shae."

"Will the Kyr Thysaer be joined?" asked Big Grey.

"Yes. The Utine Heru will call on the mighty Balor to be as one," said Chumsey with determination in his eyes. "The great clowder will form. It will be Val Shas."

Bran looked in thought, arms folded.

"Such an attack will certainly bring the Uakor Turg to the skies," he said.

"The Heru said if that occurs, the En' Carad will fly," said Brelaak.

Molly remembered her conversation with Dalgaes at Blackstone Keep.

"En' Carad. Moondancer," she whispered.

"The last of his race, the red one," said Brows. There was no mistaking the definite firmness in his voice.

"But if he's to fight others, there's only one of him," said Elizabeth. "It won't be fair."

Brows took Elizabeth's hand. He looked into her eyes. He saw concern and fear.

"Of all, he is most powerful; he is the one most strong, the one who inspires fear in others," he told her. "No need to worry about our red friend."

"Then, our plan is strengthened," said Bran. "We will venture into the marshlands tomorrow night and will do so when the battle is engaged. Let us rest for now and be quiet. I will take the watch with Ancorbow. For the others, try to get some sleep. Be careful with our food and water rations. The barrens of the Drueger offer little." He looked down at Chumsey and Brelaak. "Will you stay with us, or return to your army?"

"We'll stay the night," said Chumsey. "Tomorrow, we'll help you as you enter the marshes."

Molly stood.

"Thank you both," she told the two cats. "You are most brave."

Again, Chumsey and Brelaak bowed.

"My Queen, I do have something for you," said Chumsey. He reached into the small leather satchel tied firmly about his neck, revealing the small tuft of orange tabby fur. He presented it to Molly. "It is a gift for you, from Lil' Man. He wanted you to have this to remember him by."

Big Grey took a sniff of the fur and began to purr in delight.

"It is from him, our little friend," Big Grey told her.

Molly took the tuft of fur from Chumsey and smiled. She carefully looked to wrap it around her necklace above the Lia Fail but had difficulty doing so, until Brows pulled a thread from his frayed shirt cuff and handed it to her. She took the thread and tied the fur to the necklace.

"He will be with me, always," she said softly, lips quivering with a tear slipping down her cheek. "Will he fight with the Ra Cath?"

"Yes, my Queen," said Chumsey. "He will fight with cunning and all his strength for the death of the great oppressors, for renewal of the Aina Dur, for a nobler future by the arms of those of the righteous. He does not beg for war. No. He lets war come to him, for he is a Balor warrior bold."

"I refuse to lose him to war. I refuse," said Molly, her voice trailing off into sadness. "He will be with me always."

She could scarcely speak as emotion welled up within her. The others were deeply affected upon seeing this. They gathered around her, and whispered words of comfort to her, for they knew the upcoming journey was soon to take a more serious path.

* * *

When it was time for rest, Molly, Elizabeth, and Big Grey snuggled for warmth. But while Elizabeth and Big Grey found sleep easy, Molly did not. Try as she might she could not sleep; her mind was in such turmoil and excitement. There was strange oppression in the air - an indefinable heaviness like that which sometimes precedes the coming of a storm.

She thought back to her meeting with the wizards of the Edainar, to her words: *We should not mistreat the orc. He wants something I have, something I control, something I know I can use in time to help everyone. It occurred to me that if we make the orc our friend, he could help us. He could lead us to his master.*

She stared at Ug'ghi Otha who sat with his head down, veiled in darkness. Over the many days during their journey, she had befriended him. For as much as she needed Ug'ghi Otha to believe in her mission, it became clear to her that he needed her. She could tell. But was her intuition correct? Or, was it guiding her down a perilous path?

All I have are my instincts. What are they telling me? Are they wrong?

She would go over what had happened and what could happen, again and again, trying to reaffirm her instincts. She would think about her plan; she understood there was a level of deceit to it, even an amount of treachery.

My plan is sinister. It is hidden in the undercurrents of secrecy and dishonesty. He will lead me to his master, so I may use the stone to defeat the evil. But what does he think? Does he have a different plan and if so, what is it? As with me, does his kindness mask a veiled motive? No matter. I must continue with my trickery. He must deliver me to the darkness. It is something he needs to do. I can sense it in him. He does so willingly but it is a struggle for him.

Molly thought about this, about the struggle she sensed in Ug'ghi Otha, and about her need to bring the Lia Fail to the orc's master.

But for Ug'ghi Otha, he could only think about his Queen, about watching over her, carefully, about protecting her, so he could deliver her and her jewel to his master. He trusted her. After all, she was the first one who had ever expressed sympathy for him, telling him how sorry she was for how he had been treated.

He looked up as if sensing her thoughts, staring back at her, his eyes penetrating, sending chills through her.

He remembered her words to him: *This place has misunderstood you and treated you badly. I will stand by you, against those who have mistreated you, and we will show them your strength.*

Her words were comforting and encouraging. But at times he found himself torn between succumbing to her kind words and his determination to see the journey through to the end. It was becoming a difficult dance between two realities; he knew of the darkness at the end of their journey. He thought about how it all could end for her.

Would she choose to fight using the stone, his thoughts whirled, *or would she submit to my master? Either way, it will mean her doom.*

He understood her choices were few in her reality, for the path in the road forked in two directions.

She will either be a hero or a traitor to her people.

As he thought of her possible fate, he realized he also faced a similar dilemma in his reality.

We are alike. We face the same decision. I do not know which direction she will take, and at times I am unsure of my direction.

He began to doubt his resolve as his mind replayed her kind words repeatedly. *This place has misunderstood you and treated you badly. I will stand by you, against those who have mistreated you, and we will show them your strength.*

Then he thought, *I am not a brutish warrior orc. I am different. I am different.*

He left her stare, returning his eyes to the earthen floor.

But she kept her gaze on him and sighed. Soon, she would succumb to sleep and her dreams. They had become more frequent and more vivid, dramatic, and full of emotions. At one time, she had become afraid of dreaming. Now, she started to embrace the night and her dreams; she was starting to draw strength from them. She eagerly looked forward to them, thinking of each as a piece to some large puzzle.

Gone were the dreams of the theater and frightened boy, replaced with recurring horrid visions of battlefields and war. In these new dreams, she stands alone in the middle of a blood-soaked battlefield littered with heaps of mangled limbs and corpses of fallen warriors. A million lifeless eyes blankly gaze at her. The land reeks of death. The stench is overwhelming and, in the dusk, vultures circle, black shadows against a fiery sky that quickly turns dark amidst storm clouds. A blustery wind howls. She clutches the Lia Fail which beats and thumps red like a heart. She can see her breath in the frozen crisp air as snow blankets the battlefield, drifting by the winds, covering the countless eyes and mounds of bodies. The Lia Fail becomes cold.

She continued to keep her dreams to herself. But somehow, Brows would always know when she was troubled by one of her dreams. He would try to get her to talk to him about her dreams, but she held steadfastly and never confided in him as to what she saw or how she felt.

They are my burden.

She only asked Brows for comfort, perhaps a bit of tea or another snuggle in his blanket. For his part, he would use the moment to tell another tale of ages past. As a historian he was a wonderful storyteller and filled his tales with gripping details, some handed down over the generations, while many were wholly his invention based on interpretation of historical accounts.

Whenever he spoke of the past, which seemed to be all the time, his words rolled forward like a melody, dancing up and down with images. There seemed to be no end to the number of stories he knew, and this pleased her for his tales were a diversion from her dreams. And while she listened to his chronicles, she would sometimes think of her dreams, of the puzzle pieces, and what they meant.

Molly took a deep breath and recounted one of his stories. She closed her eyes and at long last fell asleep.

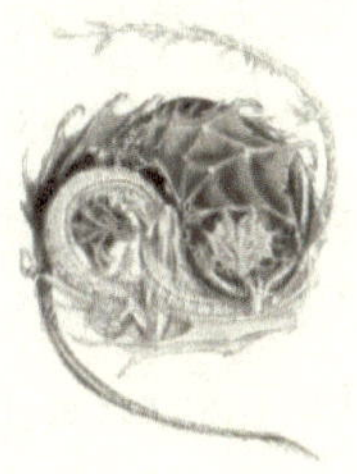

CHAPTER 13
A FLEETING GLIMPSE

THEOR THAKEN AND RAS AMON crouched low behind some brush, looking west upon a deadly vista. Over the Carn and Hollow Forest, the red sunset was retreating, casting shadows of blood and darkness over the landscape as the evil tower Drar Dukhaar loomed defiantly. The tower seemed to defy the very laws of nature, and within its dark recesses, things foul and distorted lurked. It was as if the very darkness itself was alive and waiting to consume anything that entered its domain.

A wind started to howl and brought the stench of death and destruction in sickening waves while in the distance amidst the night's shadows legions of brood scoured the land for any life force to destroy. The town of Laurel Glen was in flames amidst a land that had been stripped of its vegetation. Gone were the fields of lavender and gardenia, the rich farmland, and much of the vast green forest had been stripped of any life. Near the dark tower were the charred remnants of the sacred tree. Its leaves and most of its branches and limbs were gone. But the massive trunk remained, from which one could make out a bud and shoot, taunting its destroyers with a speck life. The sacred tree, once a symbol of life and hope for all the races of the good and righteous, was now a reminder that no matter how dark and cold the world could be, there was always the possibility of new life and growth.

"The Aina Dur," whispered Thaken. "It lives!"

"The evil cannot burn deep enough into the tree to kill it," said Ras Amon. "Over time, new bark will form to protect its internal structures. There is hope. But wickedness has brought an everlasting fire to the west. There are countless brood here, far too many for us to fight. Somehow, we must take the tower and rid the land of Foulhand and his minion Bentgibber."

"Does this Bentigbber wield magic?" asked Thaken.

"He wields a most powerful dark magic, one rooted in the many histories of many places."

The brash Thaken thought for a moment.

"Learned One, as you've said, we're outnumbered," said Thaken. "I have but a legion of Etinian warriors, and please do not take offense, but you are only one against two who possess dark magic."

"Your frankness does not offend me. But do not fear for we will have a good plan." Ras Amon turned back to look over the Old Marsh Moor. He sensed a presence following. "We are not alone in our quest."

"Who looks to join us?"

"My senses tell me it is a good friend, someone who can be of great assistance."

"Then, we should wait for your friend to arrive," said Thaken. "We will need all the strength we can muster."

"No. We cannot wait," said Ras Amon. "I do not know how far away he is. I think it is best to devise a plan and take advantage of the night. We have been fortunate as we have gone undetected by the evil."

"If it is a plan we need, I say we storm the evil fortress. Our Etinian blades will cut them down."

"Patience young Thaken," said Ras Amon. "You must learn patience. A warrior without some patience is a dead warrior."

They resumed their silent gaze out upon the gloomy scene before them. In the deep silence of the evening, the wind grew stronger, whipping over the land and swirling the black ash of burned villages and vegetation. The devastation was heartbreaking. What was once a place teeming with life had become nothing more than a vast wasteland, mere piles of rubble and ash.

Seeing the devastation, a thought came to Ras Amon.

The ruins of Eaniel!

Near the tower Drar Dukhaar, he could make out the ruins of the ancient Eaniel castle. The ruins lay among long grass and brush. Many of the stones had been used in constructing the evil tower, but not all. Most of the boulders remained largely forgotten. He then looked north at a rock outcropping heavily encrusted with moss and weeds. Another memory came to him.

"The dark passages," he whispered.

"What are you muttering about?" asked Thaken.

"I think I may have a plan, or should I say I think we have a plan. Do you see that ledge of rock up ahead, but a short distance from us? Within the rock is a hollow that leads to an underground tunnel. The tunnel goes to the ruins of Eaniel castle just outside the dark tower, most likely ending beneath one of the large boulders. With the strength of your warriors, I am sure it can be moved. What matters is that the ground may well conceal my magic, making the Dark Wizard and Bentgibber unable to detect it as I approach."

"Castle ruins? Tunnel? How do you know all this?"

"It has been said that in ages past an ancient race of creatures lived in such tunnels, a labyrinth of underground cities and roadways. The race has long since perished. When Eaniel castle was constructed ages ago, it was done so to take advantage of the tunnels, as a means of defense and escape. In time, the castle was lost to war. Here is what I am thinking. First, deploy a small group of your warriors south of the tower. Advise them to wait until a signal is given. We then will make our way to the tower with some of your men using the underground tunnel. When we leave the tunnel you give a signal to the others. When they hear your signal they will attack with arrows, then fall back deeper south and attack again, and so on. This will draw some of the brood from the area and improve our chances. Then I will face the Dark Wizard and Bentgibber. Always best to cut off the head of the snake. What do you think?"

Thaken gave a smile

"I'd say it's a plan."

"And may the Maker be with us all."

"Wizard, the Maker may be with us, but it will be our swords and your magic that will bring us victory."

"Perhaps," said Ras Amon. "Perhaps you are right Thaken."

Thaken issued his orders and a group of Etinian warriors took positions south of the tower. Ras Amon, Thaken, and the remaining few Etinian fighters headed to the nearby rocky outcropping. They ran through the night, through the burned vegetation. The wind was strong. It brought smoke and the pungent smell of death, and it tossed singed branches and brush around them. When they came to the outcropping, they climbed the brief slope of rock and stone and searched for a hollow, eventually discovering it hidden beneath a few scrub bushes and large boulders. It was a small and narrow opening and tight but they managed to enter it and down into the labyrinth tunnel.

The darkness of the tunnel seemed to swallow them. Ever so carefully they moved forward, with Thaken leading the way. But Ras Amon found his mind wandering. Something was affecting him. He became dizzy and stumbled but struggled onward, thinking about his encounter with Foulhand.

I must match his power. I must destroy him. I will ensure we enter the abyss of death together. This is my chance at redemption. My pain will end.

He then thought of his friend.

Shaer. You helped me to heal. I am forever grateful.

When they came to the end of the tunnel there was no dark glow showing them the end, only a dim string of light from around the edges of the hard, cold surface of a large rock.

I am ready.

***

Two of Thaken's warriors pushed and lifted the rock aside. Thaken and Ras Amon slowly made their way across the ruinous terrain. They crouched as they moved forward, stealthily, making as little noise as possible. They were a few paces from the westernmost approach to the dark tower, near its open gates when Ras Amon turned back to Thaken and gave a nod. Thaken made a whistle like a bird - pu-wee pu-wee - a signal to his warriors positioned south of the tower. At once the warriors began to shout with rage and filled the night sky with arrows, striking at the tower and brood. The demons responded with arrows and spears. The warriors fell deeper south, attacked again, and fell back further, each time drawing more and more brood from the tower in pursuit.

"Now!" said Ras Amon.

Ras Amon, Thaken, and the other warriors dashed through the gates and entered Drar Dukhaar. They clung against the cold stone wall and looked about. There were no brood; the plan had worked. Ahead of them was an iron door, and from behind it, they could hear the wailing of those within the black depths of the tower's dungeon. Thaken took a step toward the door with a sword in hand, but Ras Amon held him back.

"No. Now is not the time. We are here for those who stand atop the tower," he told Thaken.

He led the group up the tower's stairs, slowly, hugging the outer wall as they ascended. Closer and closer they came to the top of the tower where there was a wooden door. He turned to Thaken and gave a nod. Cur Vosser flung himself through the door and onto the stone floor as he, Thaken, and the others rushed through. Swords were drawn and he extended his hands and staff to weave a spell, but there was a horrific flash of yellow light and everything went black.

* * *

Darkness. Absolute. Cold.

"Let's kill them!" Bentgibber's sniveling voice echoed through Ras Amon's unconsciousness.

"No," said Foulhand, his voice deep and calm, calculating. "They are our friends. Pets if you will. Yes. We will keep them as pets, toys for our amusement."

"Yessss! Yessss!" came Bentgibber's gurgling giggle in a most wicked tone. "Pets they are for us. The fun we will have with them. Great fun, indeed! But . . ."

"But what?" asked Foulhand, his cavernous voice reverberating.

"But he's unconscious. No value to us in this state. We can stomp on his body, but we will not see the pain on his face. That's no fun, no fun at all!"

Foulhand laughed.

"Patience. He will awaken and when he does, you will have all the fun you can ever desire."

"See pain on his face? Here his howls of agony?"

"Yes, and so much more. Soon his pain will be so great that he will be in a constant state of misery. He will only have one request of us."

"And what will that be?"

"Death."

They laughed and the sound slowly faded.

Ras Amon struggled to open his eyes, to flee the darkness of his mind, but he could only feel coldness and hardness, and a shuttering pain that burned. The warm blanket of unconsciousness felt increasingly troublesome to his fading mind.

Then a thought: *I am not dead!*

* * *

Stiffness. Pain. Sharp. Hard cold against my face. Stinging. Arms and legs cold. Shivers. Feel of metal against my skin. Ice. Shackles! I am bound!

Ras Amon fought the dark waters of his unconsciousness, battling madly against the cold gloom that threatened to pull him down to his death and the urge from his body to succumb to its demands. He worked to gather what strength remained and finally was able to open his eyes. But consciousness brought to him a harsh reality. He was laid out on a stone floor, his head against the hard coldness.

In front of him, dim light and stale air ran through a small gap between a large iron door and the stone floor. He slowly raised his head, twisting as much as he could to see where he was. The place was dark, damp, and windowless. It was a dungeon. Then a thought came to him.

My staff! My staff!

Hurriedly, he patted the cold stone floor around him searching for his staff, until he saw remnants of it, shattered pieces reduced to charred black scraps and ashes. He reached deeply into his tired and battered body, sensing for the strength of magic. But there was none.

I do not have the magic to repair it.

His eyes quickly moved on as a pungent smell filled his nostrils. It was the vile smell of excrement. He realized the floor was littered with urine and feces. He then heard a strange rustling noise from above and looked up to the ceiling. It seemed to heave and swell with ripples of blackness.

Bats!

Hundreds of black bats covered the ceiling, hanging upside down by their feet, so close together, that at first sight, one could not tell if the ceiling were stone or alive. He could see their tiny faces twitching, with an occasional high-pitched squeak piercing the air.

But there was something else in the room, it lay to the far side. Through the dark shadows, he saw a pile of bodies.

The Etinian warriors!

They were still clothed, but most of the bodies had their heads ripped off, others their arms, and still others were but torsos gnawed in half. Bloodied body parts and bones littered the area, some of which still had chunks of flesh clinging to them.

Such a dreadful and unbearable place!

He awkwardly pulled against his shackles when he heard the moaning sound of a restless soul from behind.

"Thaken? Thaken is that you?"

It was. Thaken worked to clear his head.

"What's happened? What is this place?"

"I am afraid we are in a bad way," said Ras Amon struggling to look behind him, where his friend lay.

Ras Amon heard Thaken fighting against his restraints, tearing the flesh at his feet and hands. He heard the clanging of shackles and chains. He then heard Thaken gasp in dread. He closed his eyes to the terror that Thaken now witnessed.

Thaken was staring at the decapitated head of his close friend, Cur Vosser. The neck was still bleeding and there were drops of sweat on Vosser's brow. His eyes were open, his lips parted and twisted in agony. In his moment of death was the look of inconceivable terror.

Ras Amon grimaced at the thought of Thaken looking upon the mangled bodies of his warriors.

"Do not weep at what your eyes tell you," he told Thaken. "There is no time for sorrow. Remember what you said - for the warrior, death is not a burden."

Thaken remembered his words choking back tears as he stared at the heap of bodies.

"I would bask in the glory of his death, his reawakening from this fearful thing we call life," he said.

"We must find a way out of this morass as quickly as possible," said Ras Amon, stopping abruptly with a violent cough. He recovered then continued. "I am afraid we do not have much time."

Thaken spoke roughly as he became enraged.

"What is this? I ask you. What treachery is this that is been unleashed upon such fine men?"

"It is the treachery of the Dark Wizard."

An uncontrollable fury came to Thaken. He slammed his fist on the cold stone floor, then brought his forehead to the same coldness.

"I will exact revenge," he said, his voice trembling both in fear and anger. "It will be revenge like no other. I swear to the Maker."

"Yes, but not revenge filled with reckless abandon. Only time will exact revenge. First, we must find a way from this place."

"What about your magic?" asked Thaken.

Ras Amon closed his eyes to the sad reality.

"I am afraid my magic has been undone. I will need time to rest."

Then suddenly there came a brilliant flash of red light from the other side of the dungeon door. Ras Amon instinctively closed his eyes as shock waves reverberated through the dark place. The massive dungeon door came unhinged and broke apart, debris blown into the air by the explosion. His shackles and chains flew off, as did Thaken's. And the bats that hung from the ceiling dropped to the stone floor each in a convulsive state of death.

An eerie silence reigned, apart from an odd, yet familiar voice.

"To him, to the forest, we must go," came the voice in a deep, powerful, and peculiar tone. Then it changed becoming meek and mild. "I do what I do and that's the best I can do."

A burst of warm and musty air came rushing through. Ras Amon could feel the warmth. He slowly opened his eyes. In front of him stood the thin, white cat with his long neck and large round red eyes. The cat chirped a few times and nuzzling up to him started to lick his face.

"Shaer Thol, by the Maker," he said. "It is you. You have found me. You never fail to amaze."

The cat smiled as a deep rumbling purr started to echo in the dismal chamber.

"I do what I do and that's the best I can do," he said, softly rubbing his head against the wizard's face.

Ras Amon could feel the tremble of the cat's purr and it gave him strength.

He lifted himself with some difficulty for his muscles were sore. There was a pain in his head and he felt a large gash on his forehead. He turned to Thaken who was on all fours, shaking the cobwebs from his head.

"Quickly now," he said stepping through the bat carcasses and helping Thaken to his feet. "There is little time. Let us leave this place."

Thaken saw the strange cat.

"What is this creature?" he asked.

"Creature? No, not a creature," said Ras Amon hurriedly, hardly trusting his weakened voice. "He is our savior and a good friend."

Thaken looked down at Shaer Thol who let out a pitiful meow. The white cat rubbed up against Ras Amon's legs.

"I do what I do and that's the best I can do," he told Ras Amon with quickness and vigor to his voice.

"Yes, we must be off," said Ras Amon.

Shaer Thol scurried through the doorway.

"Your staff?" asked Thaken. "Where's your staff?"

Ras Amon paused. "It is no more."

"Where will we go?"

"As my friend said, we will make our way to the forest, the Merka 'Las, to a place near Stag Hollow."

"Why? What is there?"

"Another friend and the strength we require. The strength of wisdom. Trust in me."

Thaken nodded. He had learned to trust the wizard, even though it seemed the wizard worked in mysterious ways.

Led by Shaer Thol, they fled the dungeon, past the unconscious bodies of the Librarian, Dark Wizard, and several brood. They ran down the stairs, from the tower and eastward. The air was thick with smoke as they ran through the burned fields, their feet kicking up ash. They headed to the edge of the woods and as they neared it a bolt of light crashed in front of them creating a large hole in the ground. The force of the strike threw them to the ground. Thaken lifted himself and hurried to help Ras Amon who lay stunned and flattened out.

"What was that?" asked Ras Amon.

Thaken turned to see Foulhand and Bentgibber from atop the tower, the Dark Wizard's hands aglow.

"Evil from the tower," he said. "They attack us."

Ras Amon tried to lift himself with Thaken's help but stopped when a sharp, throbbing pain burned through his left leg. He screamed in agony. He was sure it was broken. Thaken looked to lift the wizard to his feet while Shaer Thol purred, trying to help Thaken by pushing up on the wizard.

"Leave me," he gasped. "Both of you now. Leave me. I am too feeble to go on. Get yourselves to the Merka 'Las."

"I do what I do and that's the best I can do," said the cat sternly.

Thaken again turned to the tower. He saw the Dark Wizard lift his hands preparing to unleash another bolt of magic, one surely that would kill them. He threw himself upon Ras Amon and the cat, hugging them tightly.

"I will protect you from this evil," he said.

He closed his eyes fully expecting his death. But from the forest, an orange streak of light crossed over them and crashed into the top of the tower. The blast scattered rock and stone. He did not know what had happened and looked at the forest. There, he saw a tall, thin man with long greyish-black hair and wearing a black eye patch. The stranger lifted his hand and from it came another orange streak of light that crashed into the tower, this time sending Foulhand and Bentgibber into the earthworks below.

The stranger beckoned, motioning them to the forest.

"Quickly now," he shouted. "We must hurry."

Thaken pulled Ras Amon to his feet.

"Do you know this stranger?" he asked.

Ras Amon looked at the man while catching his breath and forming a small smile on his face.

"His name is Ridley Harwell. He is of the Hulnur Istare."

"Warrior wizard," whispered Thaken.

He helped Ras Amon forward as the two hobbled into the forest followed by Shaer Thol.

* * *

The Librarian's lungs ached from the dust and ashes he had inhaled as the tower fell around him. It was different for Foulhand - there was no physical pain because his essence was of pure evil, but the blasts of magic from Harwell had drained much of his magic leaving him tired. Each slowly rubbed their eyes in weariness, minds racing with unformed thoughts.

Bentgibber staggered to his feet.

"What happened?" he asked his master.

But instead of a response from Foulhand, a mysterious deep voice came from the shadows.

"Happened? I will tell you what happened," said the voice. "You were made fools of. Fools! Both of you!"

Foulhand tried to lift himself but there was a heavy weight on him. His eyes focused on a most hideous face looking down at him, slimy and contorted, barely human-like. He could feel the creature's cold, slithery hands working themselves over his face.

"Ah, it is you, Miss Hiss," he said.

Slime dripped onto his face as the demon worm crouched over his form. She displayed her huge teeth, ready to clamp down on him.

"Why shouldn't I take your head from you as I did with the Etinians in your dungeon?" she asked.

A look of disgust passed over his face.

"This is my realm," he told her lifting himself. He cocked his head to the side and smirked. "You have no power here."

She was quiet. She used her circular muscles to slowly lengthen and push her segmented body away from him, small bristles on each segment helping her to grip the soil. When she was some distance away, she turned and faced him.

"You are more the fool than I thought," she told him, her words capturing his attention. "You talk as if this place is your domain. It is not. It is his. You are here only through his grace. Do not ever forget that I am of him. Where I am, he is. We are one. So, do not play power games with me unless you are prepared to face his wrath. He brought you back to this reality and he will easily remove you from it."

"My words, they were misguided," he said with a sigh of frustration. "We are thankful for any help you can provide."

"Why should I help idiots?" she asked with contempt in her voice that stung. She made a sound of distress, a wordless whimper, then growled. "You had a simple task to perform, and you failed him, both of you. You know you did. Do you think you should be punished?"

Bentgibber sprang to her side, slobbering in fawning adoration.

"Oh my, oh my! No! No! No punishment. No pain for us. We are but your servants and will not turn aside from your commands."

She reached down with her long fingers, stroking the abomination's hairless and swollen head.

"Ah, my Librarian. Your words are soft and poetic upon my ears, and your glances, so sweet," she said lovingly. Then she turned to Foulhand with a changed voice, irritated in disappointment. "Tell me, how did the wizard and the man escape?"

He did not answer other than to stare at her with the slightest hint of repulsion.

"Oh! Oh! A white cat," Bentgibber said trembling, slathering his words. "It was a white cat, Miss Hiss. A white cat with magic. Strange and foul creature it was."

"Ra Cath?"

"No, my Miss Hiss. No. Ra Cath no. It was strange, though, very strange. Skin and bones. Skin and bones. And white, I say. White. Its fur was white as snow, and its eyes, its eyes as red as blood. Red as blood. No Ra Cath this one. No. This one has magic more powerful than Ra Cath. And from the forest, lightning. Magic from the forest, bold and bright. Orange it was. Powerful magic. Magic made the tower rubble."

She thought and immediately knew who had helped Ras Amon and Thaken. She became incensed.

"A Tar Malal and another wizard," she said in disgust. She took a deep breath, anger flickering in her eyes. "Did you not feel their presence? Did you not see them?"

"We only saw the one wizard with the Etinians," said Foulhand, his voice dark and grim. "If we had known of the others, things would have been different, and the discussion we are now having different as well."

"Do not talk to me about how things could have been different. Do you not understand the concept of time? We can only live in the moment. There is no past and no future. What is done is done. The wizard and man are not here under our torturous ways, are they? No. They have escaped. And your failure to recognize the presence of others is a problem. Isn't it now?"

"Should we send brood after them?" asked Bentgibber. "Please! Please! Let me send brood after them. Let me do this for you. I can conjure madness in the brutes, a most savage madness. Miss Hiss, let me do this for you. Let me make things as they should be."

"No, my friend," she said with a fondness in her voice. "I know where they travel. They will be dealt with in most unpleasant ways, with great pain and suffering. But due to your incompetence, I will be unable to feast on wizard meat." She slithered closer to Foulhand, and baring her teeth, said to him, "Do you know the power one gains from feasting on the meat of those who possess magic? Who should I feast on now? Huh? Maybe you?"

He maintained his stare. He would not be intimidated by her.

"I care not the meat you wish to devour," he said daringly.

"Send me one from your horde," she snarled, retracting her almost-human face into the shadows of her worm form. "I will feast on it later, after my primary meal."

She howled, a howl that rose from the depths of her tortured soul, then slithered off into the night, toward the forest. Darkness and gloom filled the recessed trail of earth behind her.

Foulhand squinted his eyes in the deepening darkness, watching her enter the Hollow Forest. Rage filled his essence, for he could not abide by the creature.

He looked down at Bentgibber with anger in his eyes.

"Choose your allegiance now, Librarian," he said, "but choose wisely because that decision will be irrevocable."

The Librarian returned the look in confusion.

* * *

Harwell led the three hurriedly but cautiously through the Hollow Forest when they came to an area of dense brush. There was no sign that they had been followed, but as they made their way through the forest, they could hear the wails of brood from the tower as they brutalized those who had escaped imprisonment when the tower collapsed. They paused to listen to the sounds of pain and suffering and then continued on their way, a feeling of deep sorrow in their hearts.

Ahead, they saw a sense of brightness in the night. It was the end of the forest where the land sloped away eastward into the misery of mudflats steaming, small creatures swarming in search of food.

"The Old Marsh Moor," sighed Harwell. "It is a cheerless land. Our journey will be slow and gloomy, but we are cold and tired. Let us first find a place to rest."

They saw a thicket and made their way to it. Once they had entered, they found a small clearing large enough to offer shelter. Harwell helped lay Ras Amon down on the damp forest floor and watched as the Learned One's eyes darted from tree to tree, cocking his head to one side and listening to the sounds of the marshes in the distance. Very little stirred. The wildlife had ceased most of their calls and cries, as if knowing of the group's presence, save for the wind playing a plaintive cry through the tall sedges and grasses.

"It is much too quiet, my friend," Ras Amon Told Harwell with pain-filled words. He looked up at Harwell. "Why are you here? I do not understand."

Harwell placed a hand on his friend's forehead. He could feel the fever.

"My friend, you must rest . . . quiet now . . . I must heal you," he said.

"Yes, yes, of course. But why? Why are you here?"

"The land has been ripe with talk, talk of war, disease, and hate. I was summoned to help a family who had been placed under a wicked spell by the Grand Denier, the disgraced one of the Ra Cath. It seems the Grand

Denier escaped his imprisonment at the Deep Thicket and makes his way north. I was journeying to the Merka 'Las, even against my best judgment, to take counsel with our friend, hopefully, to find a way to release the spell and help the family. But to the west, I saw a horrible sight. I saw the Aina Dur ravaged by fire, and a dark tower looming gaunt and frowning in the sky. My instincts drew me to it. I do not know why. Then I saw your escape and entered the Hollow Forest for cover."

"The Grand Denier . . . the Soran Cath . . . what is happening . . . what is happening?" said Ras Amon, the words barely sound. He closed his eyes in terror, arms outstretched, his long fingers clawing into the soft ground.

"My friend, it is raw evil unleashed, raw evil," said Harwell. "We will prove our courage, as we have always done."

"We must make our way to the Merka 'Las," said Ras Amon. "But I am tired."

"Hush now," said Harwell. "No more words are needed. We can rest a bit here before venturing through the marshes, then on to the Merka 'Las. That will give me time to heal your body."

Ras Amon felt himself slipping into unconsciousness. He would sleep, he thought and closed his eyes to darkness. He fell into unconsciousness, falling into a black pit of oblivion.

"You say you can heal him. Can you?" Thaken asked Harwell.

"Yes, but it will take time and patience," said Harwell.

"You spoke of this Grand Denier, of the Soran Cath," said Thaken. "But you, you are Hulnur Istare, of the warrior wizard caste. Why not . . ."

Harwell interrupted, "It matters not what I am. We all are what we are." He pointed to the surrounding forest. "Keep your thoughts and senses focused on the forest. We may have escaped the wrath of the darkness, but they will be after us."

"Of course, yes," said Thaken. He did as Harwell instructed, turning to peer into the shadows of the forest behind them. "But I do not look forward to crossing the marshlands again. We will be exposed. Is there another route we can take?"

"The marshes may not give us cover and it will be slow going, but it provides the same to all. The sooner we can get to the Merka 'Las, the better off we will be. There is no shorter way."

"Will they follow us into this forest you talk of?" asked Thaken.

"Doubtful," said Harwell. "Evil will not venture into the Merka 'Las. They know better than to enter the woods."

"Why?"

"You will understand when we arrive," Harwell told Thaken. "I must tend to our friend here."

Thaken nodded returning his gaze to the forest.

Harwell reached out over Ras Amon's broken body with open palms, magic streaming from his hands. Slowly he guided his magic over each open wound, broken bone, and failing internal organ. As Ras Amon wallowed in the dark pit of unconsciousness, the stinging and burning sensation of his bones mending became intensely sharp, while his muscles became warm and relaxed. His wounds were rapidly disappearing as energy surged into him. After a moment, he started to ascend from the darkness, and with a gasp of breath awoke. He tried to push himself forward, but it was difficult. Harwell quickly took his friend by the arm, helping him up.

"Slowly now, easy. You are healed but there remains freshness to your wounds," Harwell told him. "You will feel a tingling, numbness in your bones and muscles for a bit. Your magic will return but it will take time. Show patience, my friend. Patience."

Shaer Thol was glad to see that Ras Amon was improving. He arched his back and rubbed up against his legs. Ras Amon looked down at the cat and smiled.

The cat returned the look.

"I do what I do and that's the best I can do," said Shaer Thol with a caressing air. "I do what I do and that's the best I can do."

"Yes. I am here with you now. We can never be separated," said Ras Amon. He gently stroked the white cat who arched his back with a lifted tail. "We will go to the forest and see our friend. That will make you happy."

"I do what I do and that's the best I can do," purred the cat.

Thaken was pleased to see Ras Amon on his feet.

“I’m glad you are feeling better,” he said. “Gain your strength so you and I can return to the dark tower and face the evil once more. We will rise above the clouds and soar upon the wind. We will find the light and banish the shadows!”

“It is a great gift to have you as a friend,” Ras Amon said with a smile.

But a strange feeling came upon him. He looked down at Shaer Thol and saw the fur on the cat’s back and tail rise. The cat’s ears dropped, and his eyes began to bulge.

“Darkness is here!” said Thol in a deep bellow.

Ras Amon realized right away that something was very wrong.

“No!” he shouted.

Harwell looked up, but it was too late. The Lor Shys had crept up behind Thaken who was unaware of the danger. Her massive jaws swung open with rows of jagged fangs that clamped down on his head. She then twisted his head away from his torso in a terrible sound of bone cracking and muscle rupturing. He did not know his fate; he did not see it coming. Harwell and Ras Amon could do nothing but watch in horror as the Lor Shys killed Thaken.

“I see your death,” she hissed to the others. “I see death everywhere You cannot escape death. Death will happen. Death is like life. It is inescapable.”

Harwell lifted his hands toward the demon worm, but she had vanished into the forest’s darkness, leaving Thaken’s torso wriggling and jerking uncontrollably on the ground.

Ras Amon closed his eyes and fell to his knees in great sadness and anger. He would never be able to forget the terror he had witnessed.

"By the Maker," he wailed, pounding his fist into the soft ground. His world seemed to fly out from under him. "This is my fault. I have failed him! I have failed everyone!"

"Sadness is not something that we should choose to endure," said Harwell. He placed a hand on Ras Amon's shoulder and gave a gentle squeeze. He bent down and whispered in his friend's ear, trying to soothe his anguish with words long remembered. "Cry out your hurt. But know our names will be revenge, our wishes will be destruction, our vision the suffering of those who have wrought madness."

"Those words – the way of the Hulnur Istare," Ras Amon whispered, a determined stare at Thaken's body.

"It is an eternal challenge to endure the disciplined living code of the Hulnur Istare," said Harwell. "The words are a reminder of our way - alertness, harsh self-discipline, the destruction of enemies, and cultivation of allies. They bring us comfort."

Shaer Thol looked up at Harwell and gave a soft yelp.

With a steadying hand from Harwell, Ras Amon stood, a tear from his eye falling on what remained of Theor Thaken.

"We cannot leave him like this," he told Harwell. "I do not have the magic to do what is proper. Will you help?"

Harwell closed his eyes and lifted his hands. A soft white glow erupted from his palms as, before them, a tomb, hewn from surrounding rock and stone was slowly, yet perfectly fitted and shaped around Thaken's body. Flowers of white and yellow sprang from the ground, ivy trailed and twined, and atop the tomb, a small fire flamed.

Ras Amon spoke words of praise: "Here lay a young man from South Eldor. The allurements of power his great land could tender were in the request to unsheathe his sword as commander of those so brave. But the metal of such a man is not poured in that mold. No place in this realm could tempt him from that path of duty that led him to draw his sword for the good and righteous. His mighty character now unfolds itself to the unknown. Let the unknown fear his bravery." He paused and turned to Harwell, a look with great clarity of purpose. "Thank you, my friend. But we must be off. I am sure he awaits our arrival."

"We must be careful with him," said Harwell, his voice low and firm, trepidation in his eyes.

"Of course. With him, one must always be careful."

Ras Amon felt Harwell's apprehension, and he understood the magnitude of what they would soon experience, and reluctantly, hesitantly, he nodded his head.

They then made their way into the vast marshland.

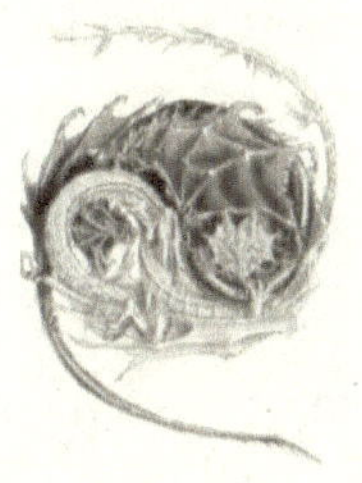

CHAPTER 14
OF MANY BURDENS

THE MORNING CAME WITH a small amount of snow, and for Bombadorn Roundthaler, it was a beautiful sight over the land. There was even a freshness to the air, crisp and keen, producing a sense of excitement. But then something in the air had changed. He could feel it in his bones. His instincts took over. He took a deep breath, and gritted his teeth, anxiously reaching back for his axe, for high in the white sky there was movement. He squinted to make out shapes, to see what was approaching more clearly, but the distance was too great.

"The winding horn!" he shouted. "The winding horn!"

A warrior sprung forth from a nearby tent. He held a curved horn, black and polished, that had been harvested from a great beast. The warrior looked at Roundthaler and, seeing the dwarf's hardened stare, put his lips to the horn and blew with such force and power that the whole surrounding plain resounded. The horn blast signaled the command to combat. Hundreds of thousands of warriors grabbed bows and arrows, swords, spears, and shields, strapped on their armaments, and charged from their tents, ready for battle.

So too did the great Carrick emerge from his tent. He stood by Roundthaler and they both looked to the sky which seemed to move, to swirl in vast waves of light. Carrick placed a firm hand on the fire swords as the horn continued to blare.

"Carrick, the sky pushes and turns toward us," said Roundthaler. "Can't be Dark Riders. No foul stench about. What is it?"

"I do not know, but we must be ready for anything."

High into the sky, in the distance, the movement continued toward them, now slowly descending, getting closer, as archers stood ready with bows drawn. Then there came the swooshing sounds of wings filling the crisp air, becoming louder and louder still, until from within the blanket of falling snow, hundreds of elven archers and cavalry on winged horses appeared above, coming swiftly upon them.

"The White Star! The Vilyarok! They're here at last!" said Roundthaler grabbing at Carrick's arm.

A great cheer rose from the warriors who had gathered to defend their positions. Carrick turned to his army, smiled, and rose a fist high into the air.

The Vilyarok continued their flight, now splitting off into varying formations and landing at positions south of Lake Mehm. Within moments, there came an unnerving sound, the galloping thuds of horses. As if appearing in a dream, Dalgaes and Col Shas emerged from within the falling snow, leading the vast White Star. It was an impressive sight, thousands, and thousands of elven riders, all in uniform, some with banners, others with swords and spears, but all heading toward Carrick and Roundthaler. As the elves neared, Dalgaes raised a hand and the army stopped.

"I hope we have not missed too much fun," shouted Dalgaes. "It would be a shame to miss a good fight."

Dalgaes and Col Shas dismounted their great steeds. They were joined by Tinnfierl and another elven warrior named Alder Fane. The four approached Carrick and Roundthaler, who were now joined by Straya.

Dalgaes and Carrick clasped forearms warmly.

Carrick looked over his elven friend, a tall man in flowing white robes with long black hair.

"It is good to see you, my friend," he said. "I have missed you."

"It has been too long since we last spoke," said Dalgaes with a smile. "Time may pass but friendship is forever."

Carrick smiled, a gleam in his eye, a hint of the vigorous kinship they enjoyed.

"Aye, and too long since we last proved ourselves in battle," said Roundthaler.

Hearing Roundthaler's words, Dalgaes chuckled.

"My small friend, your sight is always set on the fight ahead. I am pleased to join with you in battle once again," he said, reaching down to Roundthaler, the two clasping forearms heartily.

Roundthaler lifted his axe into the air.

"Small? Small you say? Perhaps. But the power of my axe is immense," he said, then gave a slight bow in deference. "My Lord, I am always at your service."

"Thank you, my friend. Thank you. And we are at your service."

Roundthaler looked up at Col Shas.

"And you, my fine, young warrior, it is good to see you," he said. "My, how you look like your father, as I remember him, ever so dearly. May the Maker bless his soul."

Col Shas smiled and gave Roundthaler his forearm in greeting.

"This is Alder Fane," said Tinnfierl with precision and erudition, his long auburn hair flowing in the breeze. "He is my regent to the White Star's Roch Cuar, our mounted archers."

Alder Fane took a step forward and bowed. He was tall and more muscular than most elves, and one could tell that he possessed considerable physical strength. Unlike Tinnfierl, Fane wore a hooded, white-toned cloak, the traditional archer garb of the White Star. A large bow was slung across his back, and he had a brown, leather quiver of gold-tipped arrows.

Dalgaes looked past Carrick.

"And who is this?" he asked. "Is it the Nalenian warrior-queen of the Shyr Shar? The Ohtar Tari? You resemble your mother. Are you as ferocious as she was?"

Straya was cautious, a glance at Carrick.

"My Lord, ferocious, when needed, but always learning," she said.

"Good. Good," said Dalgaes with a slight nod. "My father always told me that learning is something one can only do willingly."

"We must talk," Carrick told Dalgaes. "There is much to be discussed and we have mead to drink."

But Dalgaes raised a hand.

"Oh no, my friend," he said. "Today we will not drink mead. No. There is Rootweal to share."

Roundthaler's eyes grew wide and round.

"Rootweal you say! What are we waiting for!"

* * *

They entered Carrick's command tent. Additional chairs were brought in and set around the center table, where maps were already unfurled. Also, entering the tent was Entur Donduin, the small, stout man from North Sage Barrow, dressed in black. Around his grey-black hair was a red headband. And joining them was Ranagul Dithil, another dwarf commander, and Roundthaler's second-in-charge. He was a formidable force, a squat man with a long-braided beard and heavy, powerful arms, wearing layers of animal skins and a leather hat, with a short sword tucked under a brown leather belt.

Casks of Rootweal were provided as were salted meats, fruits, vegetables, loaves of bread, and a large, warm pot of stew. Dalgaes went around the table, pouring a glass of Rootweal for each person. The beverage had the color of red silk and was a smooth, full-bodied wine.

Roundthaler did not waste any time. He quickly gulped down the drink.

"Ah . . . just as I remembered. The sweet, sweet taste of a forest meadow alive in the glad light of the sun," he said, then asked Dalgaes, "Another pour, good sir?"

Dalgaes smiled and obliged with a generous second pour.

"Made from the finest petals of the Aglarond flower," he said.

"From the Sar Vael valley?" asked Roundthaler.

"Where only the brightest red flowers are grown."

"Aye, I have always wanted to travel there, to just lay within the vast fields of flowers, the wonderful feeling of the sun warming my face, sipping on a glass of Rootweal," said Roundthaler. He paused, his thoughts wandering to the image in his mind. But then his tone became harsh, almost a snarl. "But, alas, something always gets in the way - war and battle and death."

Everyone grew solemn at his words.

When Dalgaes finished serving the wine and was seated, Carrick raised his glass and made a toast.

"May the armies of the righteous defeat the forces of darkness and bring peace to the Harrow," he said, his voice firm and confident. "To building a peaceful world."

"To building a peaceful world," did everyone say with the same firmness of voice.

They started to eat in silence, passing dishes of food around the table in a never-ending circle. The silence seemed to stretch on forever until the last dish was passed around and Carrick broke the silence. He was interested to hear about the White Star's journey.

"My friend, tell us about your travels," he said to Dalgaes. "You were delayed. What did you experience?"

"The Draaklel' Daan was riddled with brood," started Dalgaes, shaking his head, "I do not know how, but they were waiting for us."

"They were just sitting there, waiting to greet us as we came entered the defile," added Col Shas.

"What of the defile's En' Edan?" asked Carrick.

Dalgaes looked down, a sorrow to his voice, "None survived the brood. All that remained were bodies, faces frozen in terror, eyes twisted in fear. The killing was complete; the madness rampant, devoid of shape."

"Except for a boy," said Tinnfierl.

A slight smile came to Dalgaes. He remembered the boy.

"Ah, yes. There is a boy. I am afraid the last of the defile's En' Edan," he said. "His name is Mas Tajae. He referred to the brood as clickers. He has been brought to Tir Nan Og where he will be safe and well-cared for. He is now of the family of the En' Edhel. I fear this land is no place for any child."

"Thank you for helping him," said Donduin.

"It was a difficult battle. They had the high ground and for a while, there was little if anything we could do," said Alder Fane, "until we released the Vilyarok. Things turned in our favor, but the outlook quickly changed when an Uakor Turg appeared."

"Dark Rider, a demon neither dead nor alive, trapped in a world of eternal darkness," said Roundthaler, his voice filled with concern.

"A most difficult battle for the Vilyarok," said Tinnfierl. "Not only did we lose many fine Vilyarok, but we also lost column upon column of Roch Cuar to the worm's fiery breath . . ."

Fane interrupted saying, "Until, by some form of a miracle did the beast fall in a smoldering heap. Some say they saw a flash of green light that fell the beast, but others say they saw nothing."

Carrick turned to Dalgaes. There was an intent expression on his stately face, a look of curiosity in his eyes.

"Green light?" he asked Dalgaes. "Was there a green light?"

"The beast was felled, the battle won," said Dalgaes, firm in his return gaze to Carrick. "That is all that matters. In battle, that is all that ever matters."

Carrick did not speak. He maintained his stare, intense, suspicious, trying to assess the Elf-King's physical response. But Dalgaes remained unmoving.

Sensing the uneasiness between the two, Col Shas looked to divert the conversation.

"But there is more. We faced the brood again," he said.

"Where?" asked Roundthaler.

"Mistmere. They poured from the city like blood from a wound and caught our rear flank by surprise."

Dalgaes turned from Carrick's stare.

"We turned and struck, mightily," said Dalgaes. "But there was decay about, for the brood was joined by the Rhiorsnan. I do not understand why they fought with the evil. But as with any decay, the treatment is not a matter of choice. You must cut out the decayed tissue, and that is exactly what we did. We were again victorious but took losses. We left a battalion behind to cleanse the city and provide order."

"What of Kraneth of the Mists?" asked Roundthaler. "What of the Lord?"

"I do not know. I fear he is lost. His son Goselthout was killed in the battle."

Roundthaler muttered, "Aye, decayed tissue removed."

"But there is more strangeness about," said Col Shas. "The brood acts oddly. They take strange positions on the barrens east of the Forest Heave, across the Old River. They cluster in small units. They move over the barrens in random and unique patterns. Some cross the river. They near the Heave, then circle back and reposition east of the river. Very strange maneuvers for them. They usually mass in large numbers."

"We have noticed the same," said Carrick.

"What do you suppose it means?" asked Dalgaes.

"I do not believe it has any meaning," said Roundthaler. "There is no understanding madness. Best to simply ignore what a mad beast does and deliver it from its misery by lopping off its head."

"But there has to be a purpose to such positioning, especially near the river and the Heave," said Tinnfierl intently staring at everyone, his eyes searching for any meaningful interpretation. "There must be a purpose to what they do."

Roundthaler shook his head.

"There is no meaning to the action of such brutes," he said, his voice sorrowful. "These are wicked times, and, in wicked times, there is only one question to ask."

"And what is that?" asked Tinnfierl.

"What is the one thing that can uphold, refresh, and strengthen the righteous under such melancholy circumstances?"

There was silence. Carrick stood to respond.

"The answer is simple," he said. "The one thing is faith. Only faith can inspire and encourage us. It is the substance of things hoped for, the evidence of things unseen. It is the faith in the Maker, that all things can be good. We walk down his path and follow in his steps. Our efforts shall not be in vain but shall be rewarded a thousand times over."

With those grand words, everyone cheered. There was merriment all around as Carrick remained still, confident, and bold. Then a warrior entered the tent.

"My liege," said the warrior. "Visitors are here. They wish to meet with you."

"Who?" asked Carrick.

"There are two visitors," hesitated the warrior, clearing his throat in such a way that all knew the visitor was of significance. "My liege, they are of the Ra Cath."

"Please allow our friends to enter," said Carrick.

The tent flaps were drawn back as the Utine Heru and Lil' Man entered. Upon seeing the Utine Heru everyone stood and bowed in reverence. Another chair was brought into the tent and placed at the table. The large, tall, long cat jumped onto the chair and sat, as Lil' Man took a position on the floor, to one side of the chair. The great cat carefully and contemplatively eyed everyone around the table. He knew many but some were new to him.

"Ah, cestal friends. Please sit," the great cat's voice was deep and strong. "Ur nostale En' Edan. Ur nostale En' Edhel. Ur nostale En' Naug,"

All responded in unison saying, "Nostale lle ar' seere Ra Cath. Ra nostale a' i' cora Heru."

Everyone then sat.

The white, long-haired, bulky-maned cat smiled. He surveyed the food and drink on the table.

"A gathering with such fine delicacies, and me, me without a proper invite," he said with a hint of sarcasm.

"My Heru, we apologize for the oversight," said Carrick. "Our friends from the White Star have just now joined with us."

The cat gave a large laugh.

"Well, I am here now as well. Am I welcomed to feast with my cestal friends?" he asked.

"Of course, my Heru," said Carrick.

Carrick rose and slid a plate of salted meats to the cat who, using his large paws to hold the food, bit off several chunks.

Dalgaes also stood and presented the cat with a rather large bowl of Rootweal.

"My Heru, for your pleasure," he said.

The cat's greenish-gold eyes grew large in enjoyment.

"Is this what I think it is?" he asked. "Can this be the nectar that few have experienced?"

"Yes, my Lord." replied Dalgaes. "It is our finest vintage."

The great cat laughed and laughed and clasped his paws at the bowl of red wine. He looked up to the heavens.

"Mela i I' Ra Heru. Mela i," he said in the feline tongue, a statement of blessing to the Father creator of the Ra Cath. He looked at Carrick and Dalgaes. "Please, sit and enjoy."

They both did so.

The Utine Heru leaned forward and lapped at the wine. He stopped briefly to lick one of its paws in a disconnected way, but then returned to the wine.

The greatness of Rootweal was that it somehow appealed to many palates. For the Ra Cath, the taste was different, not sweet, but rather nutty with a hint of mint.

Roundthaler cocked an eyebrow.

"Ir is from the Sar Vael," he told the Heru.

"I have not been to the Sar Vael," said the Utine Heru as he cleaned his face with his paws. His eyes drifted closed, and a purr rumbled from his chest.

"Neither have I. Maybe one day we can journey together when this madness is over."

"Ah, my good friend from the Old Hills. You have my solemn word. When this madness ends, and it shall one day, you and I shall walk together through Dagda and the Thornback and into the Sar Vael. We will stroll through the fields, we will taste the freshly made wine, and we will feel the warmth of the sun as it gently shines down."

Many around the table began to lightly chuckle.

"Stroll?" stuttered Roundthaler in an uncomfortable tone. "Stroll you say?"

The great cat looked at the others with curiosity as their chuckle turned to boisterous laughter.

"No disrespect, my Lord," again Roundthaler said stuttering. "But did you say stroll? Stroll?"

It finally dawned on the great cat that what he had said was disparaging to Roundthaler. He knew he would need to apologize for his words

"Ah, my friend. I forgot. A momentary lapse in my understanding of the situation," said the cat, finally understanding the frivolity. "How could I forget such a thing? Eh? Please forgive me. The mighty En' Naug do not shall we say, with delicate breath - stroll."

"I should say not! It is well known that we dwarves do not stroll," said Roundthaler.

"No. No. They saunter," said Col Shas over the merriment, his words eliciting more laughter from everyone.

"Saunter? Saunter, you say? Nay, we dwarves stride! Stride!" countered Roundthaler. "We stride with a purpose to our footsteps."

"Yes, a real feeling of power that builds with each step," said Col Shas. "It is a walk with a sense of grand importance, a sense of being at the very center of all things."

The laughter raised to a crescendo when Carrick raised a hand. He smiled gently at his dwarf friend, but then his expression turned to a serious one.

"The commander of the En' Naug army takes to jesting well," he said. "He has a good strong ego and innate self-worth that allows him to be kidded with. He likes to think of himself as sensitive, and, of course, he is. This is what makes him such a great leader. But now, my friends, as much as we would like to talk about a journey to the Sar Vael and how our dwarf friends *stride*, we must focus on where we are now, and talk of the path forward."

"Indeed. It is time to be serious about the matter before us," said the Heru in a deliberate and fierce tone. "We, the races of the good and righteous, have to be at it. If we all keep strong, we will get the work done. Many battles, both large and small, remain to be fought. But we have to be at it!"

Roundthaler stood and swung his mighty axe up and down into the center of the table with a thud - enough power to startle everyone without shattering the table.

"Aye, be at it! Be at it!" he said staring into everyone's eyes. His message was clear.

A cheer rose. Carrick motioned for silence once more. Everyone quieted down, focusing on Carrick.

"Never have we amassed such a large army and never has the dark enemy done the same," said Carrick. "The darkness we soon face will be brutal in their ways. They will have no regard for life, ours, or theirs, and will only want one result - the doom of the Harrow. This will be a war to see who is stronger, darkness or light. This will be a war to see who is stronger, the corrupt or the righteous. This will be a struggle of power over who will command the Maker's creatures. After we have said all we have to say on the field of battle, there can be no instruments of death for evil to call upon. We shall truly see how strong we are. We shall see what we are made of. We shall see how we survive. My friends, one thing is clear to me. It is this: it is all on us. There are no others to aid in our destiny."

Everyone nodded, tapping open hands on the table in approval.

"But there may be some assistance," said the great cat. "I have been told the Si Jhys have seen a vision of the White Knight,"

"Nim Dagora," whispered Dithil.

"Born of flesh and bone, joined with the Anar Ere, the great messengers, the spirit kings of the Maker, before the time of kings and during the time of great upheaval," said Donduin.

"With all due respect to my friends, I have always thought the White Knight to be the subject of fables, not history," said Carrick, his tone carefully dismissive. "I must remind everyone, and as I have often said, the blood spilled in battle will come from those living and not from one born otherwise. Our fate, the fate of the good and righteous, is solely in our hands."

"Here, here," said Roundthaler. "Only we can win the battle in front of us. That will be a test of determination and grit, integrity, and solidarity. We must be prepared for this. But, if a spirit were to assist on the battlefield, aye, I would not refuse it."

There was some laughter and more tapping on the table.

Carrick continued, "We have been victorious in the Draaklel' Daan. We have been victorious at Mistmere. And we have been victorious in the first of what will surely be many battles for Chyh-Mehm. But let us keep in mind, that this evil army is consumed by a fire we have not experienced. It is being led by a demonic entity that is incarnated as darkness deep within the Drueger, and by Dark Wizards, both to the east and the west. And I am afraid, there may be other black forces at play, forces we have yet to encounter. But we should remember that the evil army now before us on the Foghollow Barrens is much like the brood armies of the past. They remain arrogant. They enjoy displays of evil power, and they are ruled by an insatiable emotion for blood and death."

"Aye, the mad beasts cannot help themselves. Their thirst for blood is something we should not deny. Carrick am I correct?" asked the dwarf.

"Yes, my friend. They remain thoughtless killers, vicious and powerful monsters that wish only to devour their enemies. Their natural savageness, their heightened physical abilities, their disregard for their welfare, along with new weaponry and armor, may seem overwhelming, but their emotions are their weakness, their fundamental flaw, and it is deep and unforgiving. In their soulless life, they are controlled only by their emotions. They are but a headless mob without thought or reason. This is their weakness, and this is what we can attack.

"But as the great Utine Heru has said, there are many battles ahead, and battles of varying sizes. One will occur this evening. Many of you are not aware, but we have small groups throughout the land on noble journeys. One small group requires our help, a distraction shall we say, to allow it to continue its noble quest, a quest to explore and exploit the darkness, deep within the depths of the Drueger."

"Aye, and we must protect this group in a way that does not give away their location to the wicked scum," said Roundthaler, now lighting his pipe.

"A diversion," said Dalgaes raising a hand to his chin in thought. "You plan a diversion. Those you speak of must be close by."

"They are," Carrick told them. "The distraction, or diversion, must give this noble group enough time to enter the Drueger without being noticed by the thousands of brood who are near. Some of you may think that such a course of action is folly. Perhaps it is. But with the help of our Ra Cath friends, we have sorted out a plan."

The Utine Heru jumped onto the table.

"Indeed, but it will be much more than a simple distraction," he said, his tone bold and bright. "Our action will begin tonight, under the veil of darkness. The En' Edan will send a small group of cavalry and archers to harass the brood to the north at the Dregec Kuul pass. To support this small group, others of the En' Edan have been placed in the Kaquena Kemen fields, south of Gortha Losh. When the small group attacks the evil at the Dregec Kuul pass, those in the Kaquena Kemen will also attack, first led by spearmen, then followed by archers. Cavalry will flank in the fields, to the east and west."

Roundthaler took large puffs on his pipe and continued to explain the plan. "When the order is given for those in the Kaquena Kemen fields to attack, the brood in the south will turn to defend, while the brood to the north, their lust for blood and carnage roused, will become confused, with some storming south."

"And the trap is sprung," said Dalgaes, a sly smile over his face.

"Yes, we play to their weakness – emotion," said Carrick. "Their bloodlust will get the better of them. They will believe they have no choice. Confusion will mount and the brood will split, some north and some south, or they may all turn to defend our attack from the south. We do not know. It will be a battle on two fronts."

"But it matters not what the putrid scum decides," said Roundthaler. "For when they are beset with confusion, we will lift the banners, and the mighty drums will sound."

Everyone's eyes widened in astonishment.

"The Kyr Thysaer will be released?" asked Donduin.

The great cat narrowed his eyes.

"It will be the moment we are one!" he said, his voice booming in the confines of the command tent. "We will sweep the southernmost flank of the despicable horde, then blaze northerly. More discord will arise, and the distraction will continue. I fully expect the brood will flee in fear, but the Claw will cut off its legs. The Ra Cath attack will slow or halt any northward advancement. The brood will be forced to regroup if they can."

"And that noble small group I told you of," said Carrick, his eyes crucially focused, "with the greatest of courage, will get the time and cover they need to continue their journey east."

"What of the Uakor Turg?" asked Col Shas. "What if they fly?"

Dalgaes turned to him.

"That is for our Vilyarok," he told his Jhaer Tystalaes. "That is when we play our part."

"Aye, and I am sure the red one will be glad to join in the fun," said Roundthaler with more puffs on his pipe.

"I am glad the White Star is now with us," said Carrick.

"What about our Roch Cuar?" asked Alder Fane.

"Not in this battle," said Carrick. "But if it turns out to be a full-out battle, then yes, your help will be needed. He looked at Roundthaler and the great cat. "We believe that this plan should be enough, and the brood, already once defeated here, most likely will retreat and cower to lick their wounds." He turned to Dalgaes and Col Shas. "We will need the great White Star intact, for future battles. And the Vilyarok, we will need them to keep a watchful eye on the strange brood positions near the Heave."

"Consider it is done," said Dalgaes.

Carrick stood with a raised glass of Rootweal, a friendly gaze to those at the table.

"To building a peaceful world," he said, then using the cat's words added, "Let's be at it."

Everyone cheered at this. They continued for some time, enjoying the food and drink before each went separately to their armies, to prepare for the evening's battle. But Carrick asked Dalgaes to remain. He wanted to speak with him. Dalgaes had a sense of what he wanted to discuss, for as he looked upon Carrick, he saw an intense stare.

* * *

Now alone, the great Carrick and Dalgaes sat near each other. Carrick maintained his sharp stare, a hint of suspicion in his eyes and Dalgaes could feel it.

"Tell me about the green light?" asked Carrick.

"As I have already said, the beast was felled," said Dalgaes returning the stare, but rather less intently. "We were victorious. What more is there to discuss?"

Carrick was suspicious. He decided to take a different approach.

"When I met with the Utine Heru, I asked for his counsel and his aid. He gave both freely. But in return, he asked a favor of me."

"A favor? And what was that?"

"He told me that his Balor had picked up the scent of the Tar Shor, their sworn feline enemy. He was very clear with me. He told me that if we were to see any Tar Shor, he wanted me to, as he put it, act accordingly and on behalf of the Ra Cath."

"How did you respond?"

"How do you think I responded? I chose my words carefully. I told him I would always do what is best for the Harrow. But I do not think my response pleased him."

"I should say not," said Dalgaes turning from Carrick and reaching for his glass of Rootweal.

He held the glass at its base between his thumb and forefinger and swirled the red liquid around, releasing its sweet bouquet. He looked straight ahead, wanting to avoid meeting Carrick's eyes. He held his breath. He did not blink. But Carrick kept his stare on him, and he felt it, almost as if he were trying to reach inside him, looking for the truth.

"We need the Ra Cath in this fight," said Carrick. "I need to know what you know?"

A look of anger came to Dalgaes as he turned and looked at Carrick. But it was anger brought about by fear. He bit his lower lip, confronting the burden within himself, the burden that had so plagued him.

"Need to know! Need to know!" said Dalgaes, his anger growing stronger and more intense. "So, the great commander of the En' Edan needs to know something! Well, that is so grand!" He took his glass of Rootweal and threw it, the red liquid splattering against the tent's wall. "Carrick, I will tell you exactly what you need to know. Nothing! That is what you need to know, Carrick - nothing! Absolutely nothing!"

Carrick jumped up flustered. He had never seen his friend so agitated, and a slight fear came over him. But within the Elf-King's anger, Carrick sensed the truth he sought. His friend's words, his tone of voice, and his body language had all betrayed a lie. It was there, right in front of him. He was hiding something he had done ages ago.

With both hands on the table, Carrick leaned forward to Dalgaes as if to intimidate him.

"She lives. Tell me. She lives. Doesn't she?" he asked with soft but firm words. "Your anger is revealing. It tells me she lives, and you, you, helped her. Oh, the burden you have lived with; the weight so heavy."

Dalgaes stood and moved to leave, a hand ready to open the tent's flap. He turned to Carrick, his face hard and serious, his eyes full of rage.

"Burden? Burden? You of all people should not talk of burden," he said. "Carrick do not lecture me. It does not suit you. We each have been burdened from birth. We demand more from ourselves than we can ever hope to achieve. Even you Carrick, the great commander of the En' Edan, even you are burdened with seemingly unfair responsibilities." He paused. Then with the faintest grin on his face, almost an evil grin, said, "Burdens are strange things, are they not? Some are quick to come, but last only a moment, disappearing in thin air. But others creep up on you silently and never end. Yours is of this tortuous kind, the fact that you have a daughter who does not know that the great Carrick is her father. So, my friend, do not ever lecture me about burdens."

Carrick fell into his chair, dismayed and overwhelmed. Dalgaes pulled back the tent's flap door but did not leave. Instead, he looked down, his anger now fading like a breeze-blown mist. He released his hand from the flap.

What have I done? he questioned himself. *He is a friend. One does not treat friends in such a manner. What have I done?*

He took a deep breath and met Carrick's eyes.

"But how did you know?" asked Carrick.

"I just did. Your love for Merira was boundless like the sea, and her name sacred to you. And when she was taken from you, when you were left with only memories, you changed. It was as if there was nothing left to live for until you saw the child. And then your eyes came alive. It was then I knew that you were a part of the child and the child part of you."

Carrick looked away from Dalgaes as memories of Merira stirred in his mind. He remembered her face, the way she smiled at him, the way she touched his hair. He saw her eyes as they left him, and he could feel the emptiness that had replaced her presence.

"I cannot speak of it," he said softly. "You understand that."

"Of course. We live in difficult times," Dalgaes told him in a hushed tone. "It is easy to lose oneself in the emotions of war. They fade and flitter away like clouds over a distant landscape. You become numb surrounded by the horrors. Hateful actions and words become quite respectable. My words were hurtful, words that caused you pain. For this, I am sorry."

Carrick stood and looked into his friend's eyes. He could see in them only the same yearning he always felt. It was a yearning he understood, a yearning to try to put the past behind him. He took a deep breath and let it out slowly.

"I pushed too hard," he said, "taking you to a dark place. We are friends and friendship is a yoke by which our burdens are shared. It was not my attempt to probe into your soul. I do not need to do so because I already know what is there - the gnawing bitterness of guilt. It is the same that festers deep within my soul. In this regard, we are the same. My friend, please know that I would have done exactly as you did. Given the opportunity, I would have protected the Tar Shor."

Dalgaes looked down and away from Carrick. His face seemed softer than it had a moment before. But his eyes were different. There was a faraway look in them. He seemed to be withdrawing into himself.

"We have been friends for a long time. And we have seen the death and misery that war brings," he said. "But this was the first time we have seen each other frightened, each other's vulnerability. You must know I understand your actions with the warrior-queen, why you keep the truth hidden. There are too many who would not understand. Great discord would arise within the land." He paused, then returned his look to Carrick, his brow furrowed with a narrowness in his gaze. "Yes. It was she who aided us at the defile. She also visited with me later, to tell me of her visions, and warn of a new terror."

"Visions? A new terror?"

"She told me her reign was ending, that she was leaving the Harrow. She said another would come to lead the Tar Shor. But she also spoke of her visions, of unimaginable destruction, and of a mountain beast she called Dor Gordur, a creature of Drar Druul."

"It seems we may have yet another enemy to watch for."

"She told me that she felt the Si Jhys were most likely unaware of the beast, though, she was not sure about the Edainar. What worried her most was the Librarian, that perhaps his dark knowledge could awaken the evil. Carrick, if there is such a beast, I do not know how we can fight it with so much darkness upon the land."

Carrick was quick with the response.

"We cannot. We can only deal with what is before us right now," he said. "Fighting too many battles is not decisive in the long term. We must be careful, for victory on the day of battle is all too often followed by dark days of defeat, death, and brutal sacrifice."

"How many wretched, miserable, bloody affairs can we endure?"

"As many as need be," said Carrick with determination.

The Elf-King's thoughts turned to the Huntress and the Tar Shor.

"Throughout the tragedy of her race, she never wanted sympathy for the outrage, for the misfortune that beset them," he said. "There is a strength in her, grit, and a will that can never be denied. Those of the Tar Shor revere her, and she has always led them with a quiet but steely determination. Such is her faith, the belief that there is a purpose for everything."

Carrick hesitated a bit as a warmth came to his voice.

"I know she is special to you," he said. "To have survived for so many years, she has to be strong and courageous. I remember the words her followers spoke . . . by your life, no evil shall ever harm us. Such devotion."

Dalgaes smiled and thought of his friendship with Carrick. He thought of the burden of their secrets. Perhaps they could find something in this world, something that could help them overcome their guilt. Then he thought of the adventure that lay ahead of them not knowing what their future would hold. But there was one thing he did know - he would go with Carrick to the ends of the world.

He returned his hand to the tent's flap.

"The yoke of friendship," he told Carrick. "Those are good words. I have always taught myself that it is much easier to listen to the words of another if one steps back to rationally listen. Difficult to do, at times. As I have said, friendship is forever. We both have much to do before the night comes. As the great cat told us - let's be at it."

Carrick returned the smile.

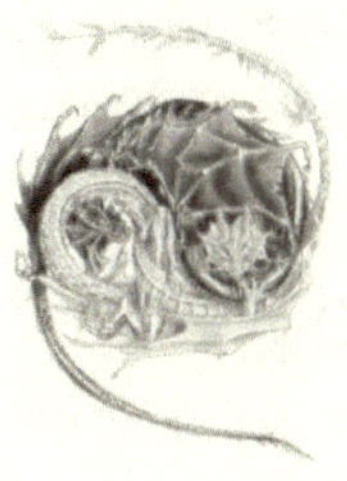

CHAPTER 15
CREEP

THE WIND GOT STRONGER and colder as the day wore on and the overall impression was of a frigid, miserable, windy day. The weather had turned especially foul across the eastern lands. As the wind gained strength, it brought heavy snows that swirled about the barrens, sometimes making it impossible to see. However, there were times when the gusts would slow. This made it difficult for the brood army. They could not tell if the gusts were foreshadowing a larger storm, but they would be prepared nonetheless. Grimsor issued orders that great fires be built to warm the thick hides of his wicked warriors. Rations of raw meat were increased, and great enclosures made of wood and pelts were quickly constructed to provide shelter. But the inclement weather would not slow the darkness as foul creatures continued to pour through the Dregec Kuul pass and onto the barrens.

Grimsor sat in a chair in his warm, well-lit lair on the flatlands, which was constructed of layers of pelts stretched over a timber frame with a sturdy westward-facing door. The floor was made of cob, a mixture of clay, sand, and straw. To let light in and smoke from a roaring fire escape, the very center of the lair's roof was left open.

He was content as he looked around his lair. It was spacious and a far cry from the dank caves and cold mountainsides he typically inhabited.

Befitting of an orc of my stature and power, he thought with a satisfied smirk.

He had been receiving updates from his many minions regarding the situation on the battlefield, and even though they had taken recent losses, he was pleased with what he was told.

Fools didn't follow orders. The En' Edan have been fortunate so far. But they are weak and foolish, and they will all bow before me and my might. More of us swarm from the darkness. It will only be a matter of time before we are victorious.

"May I enter?" came a deep voice from outside.

Grimsor recognized the voice as that of Darpulk, one of his commanders.

"You may do so," he growled.

A tall Urur Maw named Darpulk entered the lair. He removed his black leather mask and helmet revealing piercing orange eyes. As with all Urur Maws, Darpulk had a lean and well-muscled body, garbed in studded black steel plates covering his shoulders, upper body, and shins. He also had a long black cloak of armor weave and a short broad-bladed sword strapped to his back.

He bowed before Grimsor and looked about the lair. A fire in the hearth crackled merrily, casting a warm glow over the walls lined with maps. But then he flinched when he saw the decapitated head of Rotghoul rammed upon a spear. Rotghoul's one eye was bulged out of its socket, and his long tongue flapped over the side of an open mouth as if gasping for a last breath. The orc's face was battered, and dried blood crusted over his nose.

Darpulk was used to the sight of death and blood, but something was different with this. There was a feeling of power and dominance in the air. He could feel it emanating from Grimsor who was a fearsome sight.

Darpulk's eyes widened at Rotghoul's head and Grimsor was amused at the expression.

"Oh, you've noticed our friend here," he laughed.

He reached over and patted the top of Rotghoul's lifeless head, ever so gently.

"Did you know he lost a battle? Can you imagine that?" said Grimsor. "Not only did he lose a battle, but at the end of it, he crawled away like a coward, and he lost part of his sight to an enemy's blade, a female's blade at that. But that wasn't what sealed his fate. No. Do you know what it was?"

Darpulk gulped trying to swallow the saliva that was flooding his mouth. With a tremble, he shook his head.

"He didn't follow my orders," said Grimsor. "Sad really. They weren't difficult orders when you think about it. He thought he was smarter than me. But I guess he wasn't. Now, he's a decoration and a reminder, a reminder for all my commanders."

"Reminder?"

Grimsor stood and smiled a devious grin.

"Yes. A reminder to follow my orders or become a decoration like poor Rotghoul here," he told Darpulk. "Now, for why I summoned you. You'll replace our good friend here."

Darpulk took a deep breath, trying to focus his thoughts.

"And your orders, my master?" he asked.

"There'll be many more battles. More brood will flow over the barrens. They'll take up scattered positions. But whatever happens, those nearest the Heave must hold their position at all costs. Understand?"

"Yes, my master," said Darpulk with one last glance at Rotghoul's head. He bowed and placed his black leather mask and helmet back on and left the lair.

Alone again, Grimsor turned at Rotghoul's head and sneered. He reached over with his hand and gently brushed back some of the hair from Rotghoul's forehead.

Poor Rotghoul, don't worry, he thought. *Soon, you'll have friends. I'm afraid, there'll be others who'll join you.*

* * *

The tall and muscular Thondras Cendri tightened the straps of his horsehair crested helmet, and without words, looked back at about one hundred Basi Basu warriors on horseback, took his sword, and pointed it north. Through the darkness of night, he led them northward, west of the Old River.

The famed Basi Basu were well-versed in horsemanship, archery, unit tactics, formations, and rotations. They were also excellent swordsmen. They wore red, heavy, robe-like coats fastened at the waist by a leather belt. The long coats were doubled over, left breast over right, and secured by a button a few inches below the right armpit. The coats were lined with fur, and underneath the warriors wore shirt-like undergarments with long, wide sleeves. From their belts hung swords, several daggers, and for many an axe, or even a bow and quiver of arrows.

They were an independent lot and did not like to interact with others. They were fierce warriors, vicious, and feared for their bravery, known to invite death. Their tempers could rise as rapidly and unpredictably as a thunderstorm from the sea. Their lives were spent in warfare and war-frenzy, always engaged in the chase for blood and glory. They would never give up in a fight, and at times were wild and savage with extreme violence and barbarism. This was something that even the toughest of enemies feared and avoided. But the Basi Basu also had their code of honor, which they lived by. They would never attack women or children, nor would they ever kill an unarmed foe. They would only attack those who had themselves or their companions armed and prepared for war.

Led by Cendri, they traveled slowly until they came to a point where they would cross the river. It was here where Cendri raised his sword and halted the group. The Basi Basu quickly reconfigured into several triangular, wedge formations, one after the other. Cendri led them, slowly crossing the river onto the barrens, where they fanned out, first with two wedges, followed by three, and finally four.

In the distance, Cendri could hear the sounds of the brood milling about. He knew that they would soon be in the thick of it. He steeled himself for what was to come. He would not falter. He would not fail. He pointed his sword east and brought his horse to a full gallop. As he raced over the barrens, he heard the horses of the Basi Basu thundering behind him. They slashed their way through the bloodthirsty brood, swords, and arrows ripping through the cold air striking heads and bodies. Screams and curses rang forth as blood flew from the struggling mass of evil. They rode faster and faster until their pace was slowed by more brood surging at them.

Watching over the attack, Carrick immediately ordered those positioned in the Kaquena Kemen fields, south of Gortha Losh to engage the brood. Spearmen on horseback galloped north, followed by archers. The brood swiftly turned their attention south as the cavalry, also positioned in the Kaquena Kemen, both to the east and west, moved in a pincer manner, collapsing on the brood.

The brood became confused, and panic broke out. They were in disarray and started to scramble out across the barrens in all directions with most fleeing east.

"Hold your ground! Hold your ground!" yelled Darpulk from atop his muugaan, followed by the snap of his whip, which could be heard within the clanging of chaos. "Back to your positions! Back to your positions! Death to those who disobey!"

Carrick lifted a hand, and the banners were raised. The sound of drums could be heard, first faint and then louder and louder. Darpulk's orders were soon drowned out by the drumbeats of the Kyr Thysaer. Hearing the drums, cries of anguish and desperation came over the brood, as the massive army began to collapse upon itself. The mighty Kyr Thysaer made its way onto the barrens, thrashing through the enemy with incredible speed and ferocity.

From within the outcropping, Bran was watching the discord.

The time is right, he thought.

He gave a signal to the small group. They had already packed for the journey and were waiting. They quickly crossed the Old River unnoticed and into the marshlands of the Pas Shae. Bran led the way, followed by Molly, Elizabeth, Big Grey, Brows, An Van Au, Ug'ghi Otha, and lastly Ancorbow. As they entered the desolate Drueger, Brelaak and Chumsey ran south and with their fur ablaze joined with the surging feline beast that was the Kyr Thysaer.

The distraction worked.

"Do you think they made it?" asked Roundthaler as he and Carrick both overlooked the barrens and the fighting.

"I do not know," said Carrick, "but we have given them plenty of time."

They watched as the Kyr Thysaer cut through the brood at least three more times.

"Now. Sound the horn," Carrick told Roundthaler.

Roundthaler raised his hand and a series of blasts sounded from the winding horn. Upon hearing the horn, those on the Kaquena Kemen fields withdrew west across the Old River. To the north, Cendri felt a kind of visceral thrill shudder through him. He shouted orders to the Basi Basu to ride west, through what remained of the brood. He let out a great triumphant howl, raising his fist high into the air as he and the warriors raced through the bewildered brood, who could only pathetically flail sword and axe.

"The Maker wills it!" shouted the Basi Basu, each emboldened by their effort. "Hail to the Maker's glory."

When all had safely returned, Cendri went to Carrick.

"My liege, as I told you," he said, "if death is to have its way with me, it will do so when I am by your side."

* * *

Late into the night, the cold air became deeper, and a freezing rain quickly changed over to ice pellets. Dalgaes and Roundthaler trudged through the frigid night, ice pellets stinging their faces, driven by a gusty wind, making their way to Carrick's tent. When they arrived at the tent, they announced and upon entering found it to be warm and inviting. There was bread and dried meats on the table, as well as a large clap of butter and a decanter of mead. Candles on many tall brass stands lined the sides of the tent, the glowing red casting shadows on the canvas.

Carrick sat at the table, his hand to his head, staring at several maps.

"Too easy," he said with concern. "Much too easy. I simply do not understand."

Roundthaler pulled up a chair next to Carrick and poured a mug of mead.

"What is there to understand," he said as he tore into a piece of bread. "We were victorious yet again. Pass me the butter."

Carrick did so and Roundthaler slathered some on his bread.

"I mean, you En' Edan are always trying to understand things," said Roundthaler, his words muffled as he ate through the piece of bread. "Today, all there is to truly understand is that we were victorious. I am not sure what you are looking to find out, other than what is in front of you. Our fighters completed their work despite the odds that something could have gone terribly wrong. We were victorious. That is all that matters."

"Is that truly all that matters?" asked Carrick. He looked at Dalgaes. "What has your Vilyarok reported?"

"As you suspected," said Dalgaes who took a sip of mead. "The brood has returned to their scattered positions on the barrens, near the Heave."

Carrick leaned back in his chair and rubbed his beard in thought.

"But what does it matter," said Roundthaler taking another bite of bread, butter dripping from his beard. "I mean - let the beasts sit out in the open in whatever formation they like. Why should we care? It will only make for easy pickings."

"Always dealing with what is in front of you," said Carrick, smiling at his dwarf friend.

"Aye, so true. I only deal with what is in front of me, but I never worry much about it because I have the great equalizer, Mot Veorm."

As with all dwarves, Roundthaler gave his axe a name, Mot Veorm, which in the common tongue is *my beauty*. He gave a hearty laugh and swung the axe onto the table with a thump.

"But Carrick is right to be concerned," said Dalgaes. "There is something different here, something different with how the brood behaves. Yes, they are as bloodthirsty as ever, and yes, their emotions are easily played with, but they seem steadfast in their positions on the barrens. My friends, this is something very different and very disconcerting."

"It is strange, I will give you that. But what are we talking about here?" asked Roundthaler. "Are we now saying the beasts are intelligent?"

Carrick took a slice of dried meat and bit into it, then washed it down with a slug of mead.

"Let us keep our eyes out, ever vigilant," he said. He turned to Roundthaler. "Dispatch a messenger to the Ra Cath to express our gratitude to the Utine Heru. Ask if there has been word of those that passed into the Drueger."

"Aye," said Roundthaler with a nod. "As you command."

* * *

Prutmul was a smallish Urur Maw, as such beasts go, but what he lacked in size he made up for in muscle and ferocity and tenacity. He was known for his viciousness, notorious for killing brood who did not follow orders or perhaps looked at him in the wrong manner. He undertook such killing for amusement. Also known for his lechery of females, it was said he had spawned hundreds of beasts. Nothing frightened him. Nothing. No fear ever entered his mind, and therefore he neglected to make any provision in his dealings to prevent any fear of distress. But this did not make him reckless in his endeavors. The opposite was true. His fearlessness made him a force to be reckoned with, especially on the battlefield.

As he stormed through the brood, pushing and shoving the scum aside, he kept his orange eyes focused, staring intently ahead at Grimsor's lair. He did not know why he had summoned him. But it did not matter. Thinking of such a thing was a waste of time. True to his nature, his only thought was of his next killing, that is, who he would kill and where the killing would take place. Such were his thoughts, fond to him, as he confidently entered Grimsor's lair.

"Ah, there he is now," roared Grimsor who rose from his chair.

Prutmul looked up at Grimsor, unaware and uncaring, for that matter, that Rotghoul's and Darpulk's lifeless heads were nearby, rammed atop spears. Grimsor took notice of Prutmul's indifference.

"Don't you see them?" he asked.

“There are many times when I don’t care what my eyes show me,” said Prutmul. This is one of those times.”

“Aren’t you the least bit curious, about why they gave their heads to me?”

“I don’t know, and I don’t care.”

“Yes. Yes. You’ll do just fine,” said Grimsor with a smile. He laughed. “You’ll do just fine.”

“Why have you called for me?”

Grimsor neared the small Urur Maw. Slowly and tenderly, he patted Prutmul’s lifeless cheek with his fingertips.

“You’ll manage the worm to the north,” he told Prutmul. “You’ll make sure that they keep their positions and their eyes to the west, to the Heave. You’ll make sure that they understand that they’ll not engage in battle against our enemy, even if attacked. Their eyes must be focused on the dark forest. Understand?”

Prutmul’s face was filled with an unconcealed fierceness. He approached the decapitated heads and gave a glance at Grimsor. He then lifted Rotghoul’s head from its spear and started to feed on its flesh.

“The meat of the weak gives one strength,” he said, his words barely audible through the bits of flesh and saliva dripping from his mouth and down his chin.

Prutmul’s unexpected act brought a vicious beam to Grimsor. He was pleased and gave a howl that was half a gurgle.

* * *

Molly and the others stood before a small pathway, north of the river. Following the pathway east back to the mountain passage, they could make out a small, densely forested area between the river and mountains. But before they could get to the forest, they had to first pass through a marshland deep with water and heavily laden with reeds and brush. A curtain of fog drifted over the water towards them, and as desolate as the marshland seemed, it was not silent. A sound began to rise against the dry rustling of the brush - a strange sound, a wailing fraught with grief. It grew louder and more despondent until it rose to a shriek, then began again, a low, agonizing sound that became louder and more despairing. Then a second cry joined the first, and then another, until the wasteland echoed with a shrill, a relentless keening of unseen mourners.

"We didn't hear such horrible sounds before," said Elizabeth who shuddered in fear.

"We have awakened them," said Ug'ghi Otha.

"Who? Who did we awaken?" asked Molly.

"The spirits. Those who failed to escape the Pas Shae. Those who now make this place their home."

Bran looked south at the decimated brood and started down the path.

"Let us go," he said to the others. "We have little time before the worm gains its strength and notices us. We are easily seen until we can get to the forest and beyond."

He instructed Ancorbow and An Van Au to remain at the back of the group, as lookouts for anything that could approach from behind.

They soon found themselves at the path's end, standing before the marshland. The stink of it was pungent, the smell of ageless death and decay. It was a smell that made the back of their throats itch and their eyes water. But they dare not stop. They had to get across it.

"Such foulness! What a repulsive stench . . . too bad there is no other way!" said Brows. He brought a cloth up over his nose and mouth and unsheathed his blade.

"Orc, come here," summoned Bran. "Where is your friend?"

Ug'ghi Otha stood alongside Bran, as they both looked over the marshland. It lay like a dark stain on the landscape, damp and mysterious. Bran knew it was a sinister place, full of hidden dangers.

"He is here," said Ug'ghi Otha.

"What are we looking for?" asked Bran.

Ug'ghi Otha motioned with his hand as if asking the man to be quiet. A few moments passed when he saw movement in the water and pointed to it. They both looked down and saw what it was. It was a hand, pale and shriveled, with long fingers, reaching up from the water. It grasped gently upon the edge of the marsh where they stood.

"There. There. Do you see it?" whispered Ug'ghi Otha to Bran. "My friend knows we are here."

He bent to a knee and stroked the hand which responded with a feeble movement of the fingers.

"I call him Creep," he said. "He makes his way back and forth through the wetland, showing the many paths. But here, not all paths are safe."

"How do we know he will show us a safe passage?" asked Bran.

Again, Ug'ghi Otha gently stroked the strange hand, and again there came a feeble movement of its fingers.

"Do you see how his hand moves to my touch?" he said. "He knows it is me. Creep only shows a safe pathway to those who understand him. He will guide us safely."

"You keep on saying he. Do you know who he is?" asked Brows.

Ug'ghi Otha stood.

"Creep is a man, or should I say - was a man. He is but a spirit as all who inhabit the Pas Shae. In parts of the marshland, when the water is clear, you will see him. He wears a uniform of some sort."

Everyone watched intently as the hand moved away from them, disappeared briefly into the waters, then rose, softly touching areas of sod and brush ahead of them.

"He is showing the way," said Molly.

"Careful now," said Brows. "We do not want to drown in the waters or perish in the mud."

Led by Bran and Ug'ghi Otha, the group slowly threaded their way through the marshland, following the hand as it moved from fragments of silt, mud, and brush.

As they continued, a slight cold wind stirred. Molly could hear its angry murmuring over the wetland. She and Elizabeth were cold and shivering, but they both kept moving onward.

At one point, where the water was clear, a face came close to the surface.

Molly pointed.

"There he is," she said.

They could see a man's face with hollow, unshaven cheeks, a few wisps of hair falling across it, and open, round, pitch-black eyes fixed in an unsettling serenity.

Brows looked at him and recognized his garb.

"A warrior of the Mur' Edan. You can tell. Heavy woven cloak fastened around the neck with a simple metal brooch, long-sleeved tunic, trousers tied at the waist with a drawstring." Then, he enthusiastically pointed. "There, there, on his cloak - do you see it? A painted black circle, a rudimentary shape, the insignia of the caves of Gon Durth." Brows looked up at Ug'ghi Otha, a sense of sadness on his face. "I believe your friend fled from the extermination caves of the Ru Gwaith. He probably died here, in this wasteland, his soul captured by some form of dark magic."

"Can he be released from the spell?" asked Ug'ghi Otha.

Brows shook his head in grim disgust.

"The magic that imprisons him is powerful, more powerful than what the Edainar can conjure." He gave a deep sigh of dismay. "Here, in this place, wickedness has no limits."

Ug'ghi Otha bent to a knee and gently stroked Creep's hand.

"My dear friend," he whispered to Creep. "I am sorry. I will do whatever I can to free you. I will."

Molly overheard Ug'ghi Otha's whisper. She wanted to do something but knew that if she tried to use the Lia Fail it could give away their location.

There was more movement from Creep's long fingers, gentle, slow, and soft, as his face returned to the depths of the waters. Everyone looked out over the marshland watching for the hand to appear which it did, clutching a clump of sod and stone just ahead.

"Our next step," said Bran.

As they continued to follow Creep, Molly asked Brows about the caves he mentioned. She believed the more she knew about the Harrow, the more she would better understand how to help. She remembered what Bran told her about the Drueger, the bandits called Ru Gwaith, and their eternal struggle against the race of man that lived there. But she wanted to know about the caves.

"They are called the Gon Durth," said Brows. "Not too long ago, toward the end of the Gurtha Ahtar, the War of Death, and at the start of the Ra Ahtar, or Great War, the western races heard tales of massive caves in the ice mountains of the Drueger, caves where the Ru Gwaith would capture, torture, and kill those of the Mur' Edan clans. When the Great War was won, the west never ventured into the Drueger to cleanse the land of the Ru Gwaith. They had done what they had set out to do - Foulhand had been killed and the brood decimated. But the races of the righteous, well, they had lost so many lives. You see war is a great equalizer."

"Equalizer?" asked Molly.

"War brings death and destruction, to both sides who wage it. There was no more appetite for battle, especially one that would require venturing into the cold and inhospitable Drueger simply to help the Mur' Edan. Even though the Mur' Edan had forged alliances with its western brethren, they were always reclusive and never considered part of the Harrow."

"Was it a mistake, not going into the Drueger?"

"Mistakes are always made. I suppose you can say war itself is a mistake. But those who fight it will always tell you differently."

"Did Carrick want to go into the Drueger?"

"I do not know. But one thing I do know is Carrick always understands the context of war. I think he wanted to avoid a trap the Drueger presented. I think he believed that if they went into the ice lands the races could get discouraged."

"Discouraged?"

"A great leader, one like Carrick, understands the times in which war is fought. He knows the capabilities of both sides, but he also knows how others feel about it. He understands those rules that bind the races, that keep everything together. He knows a mother will always reluctantly give a child to war when the family is attacked. But he also knows that when war is over and the enemy is defeated, she will fight to keep her other children safe from battle. I am sure Carrick sensed this. He knew that going into the Drueger would be a very difficult endeavor and unpopular. Those of the good and righteous had endured so much pain and agony. I am sure he did not want to add to it."

Molly appreciated the history lesson and expressed her gratitude.

As with all lessons, you learn the "why", she thought. *Knowing the "why" helps to achieve understanding behind the "want." It gives a clear picture of reality.*

Creep kept them moving through the marshland. It was difficult going as their feet would sink deep into the accumulated layers of mud, held in place by old dead leaves and stems of the plants that had died back. The mud was dark and blackish and as they disturbed it, the scent of rot wafted up. When they came closer to where the marshland met the forest, Ug'ghi Otha put out his arm. He held back Bran who was about to move forward without Creep's guidance.

"Even though we are so close, we must be careful," he said looking for Creep's hand. "Mistakes are often made out of haste."

Bran nodded.

They were close to the edge of the marshland and could now see the forest stretching away like a huge wall. For the last time, the pale hand emerged from the water clasping a mound of sod and debris some distance to their right. Each would have to leap over the water to safety. It would not be easy for Molly, Elizabeth, or Brows. They were unsure if they could make it.

"What are we to do?" asked Molly.

Bran made the decision.

"My Queen, I will carry you while Ug'ghi Otha carries the Princess," he said.

Ug'ghi Otha agreed.

"I will come back for the bobbin," said Ug'ghi Otha. "He is heavier, and I am stronger."

Brows was indignant.

"Heavier!" he said. "What nonsense is this. I will show you. Get out of my way."

He pushed aside Ug'ghi Otha and Bran, took a few steps back, as far as he could, then ran as fast as he could forward and jumped. He barely hit the muddy ground and as he did his feet slogged in the mush, and he fell face-first among the brush. Everyone was concerned but when he lifted himself, they chuckled. There was black muck smeared on his clothes and face, but it was easily wiped clean. The others crossed safely, and they found themselves on dry ground and before the forest.

Ug'ghi Otha knelt to a knee. He reached for Creep's hand and softly stroked it.

"Remember. You have my word," he told his friend. "I will do what I can to free you from this misery."

Slowly, ever so slowly, the pale hand disappeared into the water, and barely a ripple was stirred.

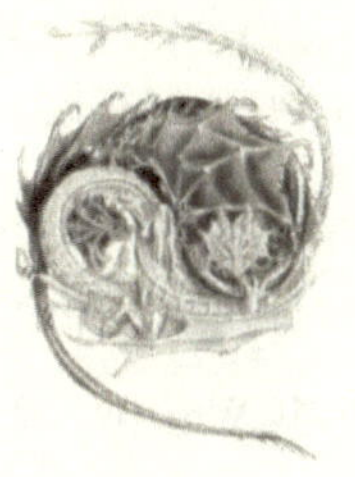

Chapter 16
The Pas Shae

AS THE NIGHT LINGERED, they rested for a while, taking care to stay hidden in the forest's shadow. When dawn crept over the rugged landscape, they awoke, still sleepy, and Bran instructed them to gather their belongings. They made their way into the forest. Bran and Ug'ghi Otha led the way. There were several paths within the dark forest, but the orc knew which one was best to take.

The forest was like most in the Harrow - it saw them perfectly, although they could not see it, and that gave them a haunting impression of isolation. It felt as if the shadows lurking within the trees were watching them, and it made them feel uncomfortable. Wherever they turned there were the shadows and trees, always there, a tall and impenetrable wall all around them. But they continued to walk, in the direction the Ug'ghi Otha took them.

It was a strange feeling, being enclosed in a forest like this, surrounded by trees that seemed to go on forever, in every direction. But it protected them from the wintry mix. It was a welcome relief, but even within the forest, the air was still cool and thick, and rarely did the sun find an opening through which to pour a splash of brightness. Everything seemed to fall into the shadows, a deep, black gloom. They started to see into its depth, but dimly, and the shadows became heavier as they traveled on. Then, just as it seemed as if the shadows were about to completely overcome them, the trees parted as Ug'ghi Otha brought them to the end of the woodland.

Upon leaving the forest behind, they came out onto land where grass flowed along a path that curved around a mountain, eastward, deeper into the Drueger. To the north, they saw a run-down cabin, and on a footpath leading to it were two bodies, barely identifiable. They had been severely burned, and the air reeked of death.

Bran looked over the charred bodies.

"Gulgulthra. Orcs," he said. "Most likely killed by the brood as they fled."

But Molly smelled something in the air. It was the smell of something dark and terrible, the smell of the unknown and the scary, the smell of the forbidden. It was the smell of things that would make others have nightmares.

"No, they were not killed by their kind," she said, taking several steps back. "Something else was at work here. We should leave."

It was then that three women came around from the back of the cabin.

"Witches!" said Brows.

The three women appeared to be normal at first glance. One was young and pretty, with long blonde hair, sweet blue eyes, and an enchanting smile. The second was a bit older in appearance than the first, with short brown hair and a darker complexion. The last was the tallest and oldest of the three. She had long grey hair and bright green eyes. All three wore long black robes and smiles that were both affectionate and malicious.

Then came a rustling sound from a small wooded area behind the cabin. A fourth woman appeared, and she was hideous. She was thin, without hair; her skin was grey and wrinkled; her eyes were pale; her body twisted and pulled in a manner that was almost impossible to describe, and she crawled about on her belly. Worms and other forest insects swarmed about her black robes, putrid things that had chewed their way through and now fed on her flesh. She joined the other three, propping herself up on her arms, and gave a sinister smile.

These were the Dree Dunn der and they feasted on the weak-minded.

Bran and Ug'ghi Otha backed away from the bodies, motioning the others to do the same.

"Oh, how sweet you are," said the oldest witch, staring at Molly. "So radiant."

"Pretty as pretty can be," said another. "Sweet as the sweetest fruit. Skin as soft as the down of a baby bird. Hair like the finest silk."

"And the sister. Oh, my! Look at her!" said the youngest. "How pretty she is. Eyes like the clearest sky. Such a glow!"

"Oh yes, much prettier than her older sister," said the deformed one. "The youngest one is so beautiful. I don't believe I have ever seen anyone as beautiful as she."

Elizabeth remembered the warning about the witches, about how their polite and friendly words would quickly change to torment. But strangely, she found herself delighted to hear the compliments. It was not just the words themselves, but how they were spoken. She felt there was sincerity in them. She grew cold, and her thoughts began to change. They turned dark and filled her with hate. She looked at Molly with pure loathing. All she could think about was how much she wanted to hurt her, to make her feel pain.

She is so jealous of me, she thought. *I am so much better than her. I am so much better than everyone. If I could just hurt her, she would be nothing. She would disappear and I would be Queen.*

Molly saw Elizabeth glaring at her with anger in her eyes. She had no idea what she had done to deserve such a look, but she did not like it one bit. She began to feel uneasy. She decided to confront her sister.

"What is it? Why are you looking at me like that?" she asked, staring back at her sister.

But Elizabeth just glaring at her, her face expressionless, and Molly began to feel uncomfortable. She was about to say something else when Elizabeth finally spoke.

"I'm tired of you always being the favorite," she said. "It's not fair. I'm more beautiful than you. I should be the one getting all the attention. I should be the Queen!"

Molly felt a cold chill go down her spine, an aching feeling. It was as if her whole body was being slowly consumed by an unseen force. A terrible sadness swept through her.

The witches! Their words, she thought.

It was not simply that their words were evil; their souls were evil; they were evil, and from such a source, nothing but evil could flow. But her thoughts started to change, and fear came over her. She could not stop what was happening to her. It felt like she was losing her mind. Anger and hatred filled her thoughts. She wanted to lash out and hurt Elizabeth. She continued to stare at her, the rage of hatred in her eyes growing. They faced each other, eye to eye, for a moment, each with a burning desire to kill the other.

But there would be more horror. As the witches spewed forth their torment, their bodies began to tremble and their heads began to turn. Slowly and painfully, their heads wrenched, the sound of bone cracking into bone and breaking until a second face revealed itself. The vision of the four new faces was horrific – each was dark, blue-skinned, gnarled, with eyes of pure white and mouths with cracked black lips, pustules leaking from the corners. From their vile lips came corrupt words.

"You and your sister have come here to die," said the oldest to Molly, blue slime oozing from its mouth. "You know this. Let me ease your worry. Let me help you. I can ease your pain. Kill your sister, so you can feast on her flesh."

"Do it, child. Listen to her," said the youngest to Molly as she scratched an itch on her face, tearing through the blue skin of her face. “Her soul is dark, comfortless, and cold. Death waits for such a soul.”

Molly tried to fight back against her thoughts. She grabbed the Lia Fail, her hand shaking.

“The stone you have is meaningless,” said one of the witches. “It will not end the corruption of the land. No. It will only bring corruption to your soul, and it has already started. Hasn’t it?”

“But she already knows this. Don’t you, my dear?” said another. “You struggle with your dreams. Or are they nightmares? Nightmares are about fear. Yes, that’s it. They are not dreams. They are nightmares that address questions and conflicts you meet in your pitiful waking life. You look to them to help you make sense of it all. Don’t you? Oh, it’s all very precarious. Very precarious indeed. Isn’t it, my dear?”

The hateful words tore at Molly. She stared at the witch and a rush of warmth came over her, its foundation, a terrible fear. She felt as if she was burning up inside.

Yes. Their words make sense. All of this is folly. I have struggled with my dreams. I should return home and enjoy my birthday.

The witches continued with their despicable words. Everyone stared at them as if willing them on, entranced by their words; entranced by a warmth that grew hotter within their bodies. Ug’ghi Otha fell to his knees and covered his ears. He shouted out to the others.

“Their words are a spell! Stop! Turn away! Turn away!”

But the hateful words of the witches flowed, now coming in short bursts, faster, stronger, breaking with emotion as they spoke.

Ug'ghi Otha looked at the girls, their faces were red with anger and rage. He turned to the others. They too had fallen under the spell of the vile words. A weakness came over him. He felt helpless.

Big Grey saw the anger and hatred in the girls.

"Do not listen to them!" he shouted at them.

But his words could not be distinguished from the cadence of evil words and moans from the witches.

"Vermin feline," said the oldest witch. "You are as fat as a cat can be. Not even an orc would want to chew on your greasy meat. Why are you with these thoughtless, heartless humans? Is not your race superior?"

Big Grey's mind began to whirl. He closed his eyes, trying not to think of the witches, trying to tune out their words. But then he started to feel sick. His head throbbed in pain, and his stomach twisted and turned.

"But the sweet little girls," said the oldest witch, "are not what they appear to be. Are they now."

Another cackled, "No, not at all. There is darkness in their souls."

"Oh, yes. I see it," chimed the youngest. "It is black as night and as ugly as sin. They are not what they appear to be. No. Not at all."

"They are distorted inside as I am on the outside," laughed the twisted one. "They are sick and full of decay. They rot from within. I do not know what all the others see in them. They are not even human. They are just things. Thoughtless things. Heartless things. Oh, but the youngest! My! She is most pretty! Prettier than her sister!"

Big Grey hunched low to the ground, cringing, his ears back. He had not succumbed to the witches' words but was ill most likely caused by his attempt to fend off the wickedness. Yet surprisingly, Brows stood steadfast and strong.

"Close your mind to their words!" he shouted. He drew his sword turning his attention to the witches. "Pathetic scum. You were banished by your families to live in the shadows of the Crag and spew hatred through words. But your words cannot harm me."

The malformed witch rushed at him, crawling on her belly, her eyes blazing, and her face contorted with rage.

"Puny man," she gurgled, almost choking. "Such a little one does not have it in him. No. Its diminutive height means that everyone towers over it. A physical weakness."

She lifted herself but before she could attack Brows brought his sword to her face.

"Ah, such a reminder is humiliating, is it not, puny one?" another gurgle from the witch. "You do not have the strength to wield your sword. If only you could."

"If it is villainy you wish for, so be it!" he screamed.

He swung the sword back and placing two hands on its hilt thrust it forward, through the head of the repulsive creature.

The witch wriggled a bit, then collapsed in death.

"They have little magic to wield!" he shouted to the others. "Through the power of their words, they look to debase you into a maddening death! The only way to stop their power is to mute their words!"

The three remaining Dree Dunn der hissed at Brows. He charged at them, slashing with his blade, cutting each down with a single stroke. They fell to the ground in a confused tangle.

With the words finally silenced, the others began to shake off the spell as best they could. Molly and Elizabeth hugged each other in relief.

"Why were you not overcome by their words?" Molly asked Brows.

He gave a smile.

"I am a historian. For a historian, only the written word has any meaning," he said. "The spoken word cannot harm me; it can never be my foundation because it will fail and turn sour. Give me something I can stand on, the knowledge and facts that can only come from the written word. When you understand the spoken word is fodder for deceit, you ignore it."

"But cannot the written word be false?" she asked.

"Of course, but you put what you read in perspective, against what you know to be true based on experiences. That is more difficult to do with the spoken word especially those that are reckless. Always remember - reckless words that are spoken are meant to attack. They pierce like a sword and more easily stoke emotion and change behavior. They get the better of you."

Molly looked down at the Lia Fail.

"Why did it not protect me? Should it not have saved me and us from the witches?" she asked.

"It cannot protect one alone," said Big Grey.

Molly could feel a seriousness to his words. It was clear that he was trying to tell her something.

"What do you mean?"

"The stone is more than a force to be used. It is alive," he said. "It senses your emotions, and these reflect your thoughts and influence your actions. It can sense happiness in you, love, and even anger. But it also can sense fear which is a weakness. You were frightened and the stone does not always help when it senses weakness. You must be strong. But you knew all this, did you not?"

Molly stood silent, alone, hurt. She nodded. There was truth in what he said, and it cut into her like ice needles. Elizabeth hugged her sister.

"We grow stronger each time we overcome adversity," Bran told the girls, a glimpse of a reassuring smile on his face. "I am afraid there will be more trials ahead. Come now. We must continue our journey."

Molly realized she must be stronger than ever. She would not let the darkness ever control her again. She would face it, and she would win. She had to be brave, for the sake of the others.

They pushed eastward, away from the forest and cabin, the path ahead becoming marked by tracks of brood. They stopped at midday to eat a meager meal, then continued at Bran's order.

***

They came to a pass where some large loose rocky fragments in the pathway impeded their progress and caused some difficulty in passing as walking turned into clambering. After some time of challenging work among slatted shelves and threatening crags, they found themselves in a trough-like hollow that meandered north. Rock piled on rock, and slippery stone channels scooped by torrents of cold and tempestuous winds, stretched as far as the eye could see until they came to a clearing.

Ahead, they saw dark smoke bellowing from a line of fires, slow and stalking, bringing a horrid stench. There were several shelters made of logs, bits of rawhide and skins, and heavy stones. Near the structures, they saw iron cages, the bars of which were thick, rust-caked, and covered with grime. Inside the cages were skeleton fragments, bits of bone that looked strange since the marrow had been extracted. Flesh still clung to some fragments, dried and for the most part blackened, starting to flake away. But in one cage, there was an orc, barely alive, its legs had been bitten away at the knees. It was an awful sight.

"Ask the orc what happened here," Bran told Ug'ghi Otha.

Ug'ghi Otha ran to the caged orc.

"Avell alnej whavv hafunt?" he asked in their native tongue.

The creature could hardly speak through the pain and anguish.

"Kulknej eukcapun avhw avowas," replied the orc, "buav ukuccumbun avo mubullat oneuk. Ukave yourukelveuk! Ukave yourukelveuk!"

Ug'ghi Otha returned to the group.

"What did it say?" asked Bran.

"He was with other orcs. They escaped the tower but could not escape the dark ones, the Nnar' Vasa. He told us to run and save ourselves."

"And how do you suppose we can save ourselves from the Nnar' Vasa?" asked Brows.

Ug'ghi Otha stared off blankly, fearful of the truth he would speak.

"There is only one way I know of," he said. "If you are in a group, you run, and let them have the slowest and weakest."

"We don't run," said Ancorbow. "We fight!"

The men unsheathed their swords as An Van Au set an arrow in her bow. The group turned to the end of the clearing where the smoke grew larger, thick black, flooding the ground like fog. From out of the smoke there came a sound, like a roar, and a great shout. Large figures began to emerge like ghosts, stumbling forward, beasts four times the size of an orc but more man-like. They were badly burned, and their skin was peeling off. They fell forward onto their faces, dead, as the ground shook under the group's feet.

"What are they?" asked Molly.

"The Nnar' Vasa," Ug'ghi Otha told her.

The group breathed a sigh of relief. They sheathed their swords and An Van Au returned the arrow to its quiver.

"Strange," said Ug'ghi Otha. "But what could have killed them."

Then the caged orc started to laugh. It was a convulsive and exaggerated laugh that shook the beast's body, twisting its mouth. It was a diabolic laugh that never stopped.

"Avhe avrap iuk ukprung!" it cackled, shrilly and loudly. "Avhe avrap iuk ukprung!"

Hearing the words, Ug'ghi Otha became fearful. He looked about the clearing, a look of dread coming over him.

Bran sensed something was wrong.

"What did it say?" he asked. "What did it say?"

"Trap! It is a trap!"

From out of the dark smoke in front of them rushed sword-wielding figures, horrid, rotting and decomposing creatures. Their clothing hung like rags, tattered, burned, and torn, barely clinging to their bodies. They were puss-filled beings of flesh and bone, of moldy tissue and exposed muscle and sinew, hideous in appearance, repellant, and bloodthirsty.

"The Ru Gwaith! Take arms! Take arms!" shouted Bran.

But there was no time. The demons came upon them like a plague, a terrible clicking sound filling the air. Ancorbow was instantly killed, torn in half by the monsters, while Bran had his legs slashed by swords, falling in a heap of blood. Brows was picked up and thrown into rock, and with a mighty swing from one of the beasts, An Van Au was tossed aside against a cage. Ug'ghi Otha struggled as best he could but was beaten into unconsciousness. Big Grey ran to a rock behind one of the cages, wedging himself between it and the cage. A Ru Gwaith reached for him, but he hissed and clawed at its hand and arm, drawing greenish blood. This did not slow the attack, and just as the beast was about to grab him a loud clicking sound echoed.

Hearing the sound, the creatures stopped their brutality, turning instead to the tallest and most formidable of them. It was pointing to Molly who was running away. The beast who was attacking Big Grey ran after Molly quickly overcoming her. Elizabeth attempted to protect her sister, wildly punching at the demon, but she was easily pushed away. The beast then threw Molly over its shoulder. She resisted at first but she fainted under the stress, her eyes rolling back in her head.

Within her darkness, the words from the Guardian came to her, like they were blown on the winds.

Search for the voice that is silent . . . Search for the voice that is silent . . .

With Molly captured, the Ru Gwaith plunged back into the cold blackness of the Drueger. But they were not alone. Big Grey was following them, carefully trailing behind.

***

As night slowly came, the sounds of the cold and bitter Drueger surrounded them. Dazed by the attack Elizabeth, who was dazed by the attack, rubbed the back of her head which was sore. She stood and looked about the mayhem. Her sister was gone. And Big Grey? She did not see him but saw paw prints racing north in the fresh snow, and strangely, small twigs marking his path. The cat was smart. He knew more snow would cover his tracks, but the twigs would help to point the way.

Elizabeth felt a profound sadness begin to creep up on her, but she took a deep sigh.

I cannot be sad, she thought. *There's no time for it.*

How alone she now felt, yet it pushed her forward to take control, to take action. As much as she wanted to go after and rescue her sister, she knew they would first need to regroup and devise a plan. She was the Princess of Ahlgren and she had to be strong. She saw the bloodied corpse of Ancorbow. It was a devastating sight. She closed her eyes as a lone tear fell.

No. I cannot be sad. Emotions are the enemy of reason. We must help the others.

She rushed to Brows and An Van Au, helping them to their feet. Both were weary and sore and could hardly walk. They wanted only the chance to rest but they quickly checked on Bran and Ug'ghi Otha. Both were alive, their breathing strong and steady, but unconscious.

"We must tend to Bran," said Elizabeth.

"What about the orc?" asked Brows.

"He is large and strong," she replied. "I'll quickly wipe his head wounds."

She did not care much for Ug'ghi Otha. She did not trust him and was afraid he would hurt her sister. But she listened to Molly and over time understood that he was important to her plan.

I will keep a watchful eye on him, she thought, feeling her new sense of strength.

As they made Bran as comfortable as possible, loosely wrapping his leg where it was badly cut, they realized their next undertaking was the grim task to gather stones and entomb Ancorbow.

Elizabeth looked away. She did not want to look upon him again in such a grisly state. She remembered when they first met, in the Garden Courtyard at Blackstone Keep, when she and Molly first met those of the Edainar. She wondered how fate could be so cruel, to have ended his life in such a manner.

"I am sure he would not want to rest in this place," said An Van Au to Brows.

"There is no other choice," Brows told her.

The two went about collecting stones.

As Ug'ghi Otha awoke, he rolled to one side and brought himself to his knees, straightening as he lifted himself upright. His vision was blurry; the head wounds had released a large amount of blood. He closed his eyes to gather strength then opened them, stood, and steadied himself. He saw Brows and An Van Au gathering and placing stones. He knew why and helped them.

When the burial mound was complete, the final, private, act of remembrance took place. Now joined by Elizabeth, the four stood near the mound, and Brows spoke these words:

"A deep peace of the running wave to you,
A deep peace of the flowing air to you,
A deep peace of the quiet land to you,
A deep peace of the shining stars to you,

A deep peace of the Maker to you.
May the road lift to meet you;
May the wind be always at your back;
May the sun shine warm upon your face;
May the rains fall softly upon your fields.
Until we meet again,
May the Maker hold you in the hollow of his hand."

There was a moment of silence as Elizabeth desperately tried to come to terms with Ancorbow's ghastly death. She had a thought. She found a small branch on the ground, and brushing away the snow, took a small stone and dug a shallow hole. She stood the branch upright in the hole, mounding what soil she could around its base.

"What kind of wood is it?" she asked Ug'ghi Otha.

He bent down and looked at the stick. He was in pain but able to speak.

"In my language, it is called adh avree," he said. "I am surprised it is here." He looked about, paying attention to what shrubbery and trees were nearby. He turned back to Elizabeth. "I do not see any such trees. I do not know how it came to be here. Very strange."

"Tell me about the tree?" she asked.

"It is magnificent in appearance when fully grown. It grows to a very tall height, and during the warm season blooms with large red and orange flowers. When the flowers drop, red fruit emerges. The fruit is sweet and very delicate in flavor. But I do not think it will grow in this place. It is much too cold here."

There were tears in her eyes.

"What matters is that it's placed into the ground with a warm hand," she said.

She looked into Ug'ghi Otha's eyes but did not seem to be looking at him. It was more like she was looking through him, and saw misery and suffering. She wondered if this was how Molly understood him.

Ug'ghi Otha gave her a heartfelt grin. It was as if he knew her anguish. A sudden warmth spread through her.

I will still be watchful, she thought returning his smile.

Brows felt her deep sadness as well. He wanted to erase it, smooth it over, heal it, even though he knew that was impossible. There was nothing he could do, other than to keep her and everyone focused on one thing - survival. But there was something he needed to tell her.

"Your sister is fine," he told Elizabeth. "Of this I am sure."

She turned to him and gave a smile. Somehow she knew he was right.

"Thank you," she said.

Brows then turned to the others and said, "We are badly hurt, but not destroyed. Come now, there is much to be done. We need to make a fire and heal before moving on."

With a long sigh, Elizabeth shook off her sadness and knew what was needed. Survival was paramount; they must survive to rescue Molly. She reached for Molly's satchel. She opened it and rummaged through it, removing small, dried twigs, and several bundled rags, each with writing on them.

"Here, for you, to make a fire," she said to Brows, pushing the twigs in front of him.

She then focused on the bundles of cloth looking for something specific.

"Here it is," she said, unwrapping one of the bundles, revealing several long, green leaves. "This should work." She gave An Van Au a handful of the leaves. "Use some of your water and warm it over the fire that Mr. Brows will make, then put in some of the leaves."

"Ah, yes. We can mash them and apply the poultice to help with the pain and swelling," said Brows.

"I would like to tend to him," said An Van Au. "If you will show me how."

Brows nodded to the young woman.

"Of course."

He started a small fire and she put some water in a small pot.

Elizabeth took the satchel and ran to Bran.

As Brows watched her, he whispered to An Van Au, "The girl is new to our land. Where do you think she learned all this?"

Ug'ghi Otha overheard him.

"From her sister," he said, "from the lessons I gave the Queen."

The three looked at Elizabeth as she gently placed the satchel under Bran's head for a pillow. She saw how the back of his legs had been deeply slashed by the Ru Gwaith's swords.

She waved her hands to the others.

"We need more long pieces of cloth," she said. "We must stop the bleeding."

Brows took his short sword and cut several long pieces from a blanket. He brought them to her and they tightly wrapped them around Bran's legs.

"That will stop the bleeding until we warm the leaves," he said. He looked at Ug'ghi Otha. "Move the burned Nnar' Vasa beasts away," he told him. "Take Bran's sword and keep watch. You are all we have for the moment."

"But the Queen - we must go after her," said Ug'ghi Otha.

"We are in no condition," said Brows, his voice stern, and level. "Look around you. We are going nowhere until we can heal."

Ug'ghi Otha did as he was instructed.

"Are you sure he should have a weapon?" Elizabeth asked Brows.

"We need his strength," he said. "I do not like it but our choices are few."

Elizabeth understood.

"It's going to get very cold. We must shelter if we have any chance to help Molly," she said. She looked up into the night sky as the snowfall became heavier. She pointed north. "While we've been busy, we've forgotten to take notice that Big Grey has left us."

Everyone looked about.

"There," said An Van Au noticing small tracks in the snow. "Yes. He makes his way north and leaves us signs."

There was excitement in her voice and her eyes. In the distance, she saw the cat's paw prints and small branches in the snow, the tips of which were bent north.

"Yes. He will follow those wicked creatures to the very end of this world," said Elizabeth, staring at the small branches in the distance. Her voice was determined, and her delicate jaw hardened. "He will not stop, and neither will we."

She wandered away and to the rusted cages.

"I wonder if we should have made this fire," said An Van Au as she prepared the poultice. "It could give away our location."

"The witches and the Nnar' Vasa are dead," said Ug'ghi Otha. "The only brood that enters this place flees from the dark madness. We are protected by the mountains. But we must be vigilant. When we can, we should move higher into the mountains where we can find more cover, to avoid the Ru Gwaith."

"I agree," said Brows in a hushed tone so Elizabeth could not hear. "I do not think they will be back any time soon. It saddens me to say - they got what they came for."

"Over here!" shouted Elizabeth back to them. She was pointing to one of the cages, the one that held the legless orc. "Something is different here! The cage is empty. Where is he?"

Ug'ghi Otha took Bran's sword in both hands. He pointed it forward and slowly walked over to the cage, its door ajar. He surveyed the area and saw shallow furrows, where the orc was pulling himself through the snow. The furrows went southeast for a bit until he saw something strange. Gone were the shallow furrows, replaced by large footprints in the snow, like that of an orc, clearly fresh. A terrible thought came to him.

"What do you see?" called out An Van Au.

Ug'ghi Otha turned back.

"The creature makes its way from the Pas Shae to the towers," he said pointing the sword southeast. "He does so on two feet. I am afraid he was part of a deception, to help deliver us to the Ru Gwaith."

"Shapechanger," Brows angrily muttered.

"What's that?" asked Elizabeth.

"A creature of the Ure Vorru, given of the dark spirit. The Ure Vorru can take many forms, but they are unable to control the form for too long. It is given to them for a particular purpose by the one who has bred them. When the purpose is fulfilled, they return for a new one."

Elizabeth closed her eyes and slowly shook her head.

"Without any choice, we're in a cauldron that boils with evil," she said.

They continued their work. When the poultice was ready, Brows showed An Van Au how to apply it to Bran's wounds. She felt the need to be close to him. She knew this was important, for she was his Caedaes. As she gently applied the remedy to his legs, she thought of Molly's Caedaes, Big Grey, and how he was alone in the dark lands, trying to rejoin with the Queen. Now, to her, it seemed a frightful thought to be separated from him.

We cannot become separated, nor can we escape from the commanding influence of your stone, she thought as she carefully applied the poultice to his wounds. *Only as one are we strong enough to defeat the darkness.*

While she tended to Bran, Brows took the first watch, while Ug'ghi Otha used his brute strength and took logs and stones from the ramshackle shelters across the pathway and constructed a shelter at the fire. He did not take the rawhide and skins for they were greenish and most likely made from orcs. The shelter was sturdy and warm while cold winds and storms of snow swirled around them.

As the night deepened, Elizabeth was overly exhausted, and she found it difficult to sleep, her mind restless and flitting. She thought of Molly and wondered if she was fine. She was tense and her mind raced in confusion. There were so many questions to answer. She calmed herself, eventually, with great effort, recognizing it would be a few days before they were strong enough to search for Molly. As the wintry wind howled loudly, she closed her eyes, and hesitantly fell asleep.

* * *

Drogur Vorn sat in a large wooden chair, resting his massive hands on a stone table in front of him. The towering beast was growing impatient. He glanced over his shoulder. Behind him was Kralin Morg, a small orc, or Ai Orqu, sometimes called by the derogatory word Mool. The Ai Orqu were offspring of orcs and captured dwarf females, bred to serve larger orcs. Morg's duties included dressing Vorn in his armament, serving him his meals, cleaning his weapons, and most importantly, cleaning and caring for the Dol Goran when Vorn was not wearing it.

Vorn closed his eyes as anger swept through him. He pounded his fist on the table.

"What's taking you so long?" he asked in a rage-filled voice.

The small orc shook in fear but continued to wipe down the Dol Goran with a cloth.

"I'm doing my best," said Morg. "It's so magnificent. I care for it as I care for my life. In it is held a power of life and death – life for my master, death for his enemies."

"Mool, you talk too much. I don't have time to listen to your stupid words."

"Yes, my master."

Morg dragged over a small wooden bench, and standing on it, lifted the Dol Goran and fastened it to Vorn's face.

"Now, bring the creature to me," bellowed Vorn.

"I don't like that thing, my master. Ever since you brought it here, something in it has changed."

"Not only don't I care to hear your words, but I despise even more to know your thoughts. Bring the creature to me!"

The small orc went to a stone ledge where the terrible creature sat. It was a head made of shiny metal. He trembled as he reached for it, lifting it slowly from the ledge and bringing it to the table. He set it down with its eyes staring straight ahead and directly at Vorn.

Morg shrunk into the room's greyish darkness knowing what would happen next.

The metallic creature sensed Vorn's presence and came to life.

Click! Clack!

Vorn hissed at the sound of gears whirring loudly.

The creature opened its eyes and looked at Vorn, a faint blue light glowing at the back of its eyes.

"Two of youth, the females will arrive. A jewel of red, one will revive," it said in a mechanical voice, going on. "Carefully tread the halls of sanity."

Morg shrank and covered his ears in fear, for the creature's words were haunting.

"Are these the only words you can speak?" growled Vorn at the burnished head.

Click! Clack!

The head twitched, and a sound of liquid gurgling in small tubes from inside its head could be heard.

"A task to rattle, painful news to tell. To the west a battle, the evil will swell," said the creature.

Vorn laughed grimly but then his face darkened into a savage scowl.

"Finally, new words from it, words that make sense." He turned to Morg. "Bring me a pack. I'll take the creature with me."

Fully armored and with the pack and swords strapped to his shoulders, Vorn wended his way through the labyrinth of the demon tower Urth' Goroth with Morg scrambling behind. They went all the way to the front gates. It was night and large flakes of snow were falling, blinding them to anything that was not in the immediate area. The snow was accumulating quickly and the throngs of brood that were surging from the depths of the evil tower's forges were barely seen.

Vorn trudged through the snow until he came up to an Urur Maw on a muugaan. He knocked the Urur Maw from the beast and swiftly mounted it and without a word spurred the brute westward, onto the barrens and to the Heave.

Morg struggled through the snow as he fought to keep up. He stopped to catch his breath, barely making out Vorn in the distance.

Why west? Why toward the forest? We cannot pass there, he thought.

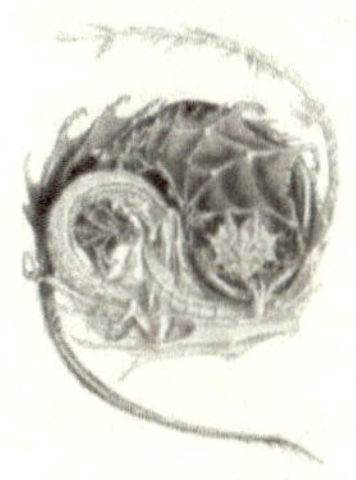

CHAPTER 17
THE OTHER SIDE OF TIME

"I DO WHAT I DO and that's the best I can do," said the white cat gleefully, scampering down the forest path.

Ras Amon smiled at Ridley Harwell.

"Shaer is excited. What about you? Are you prepared?" he asked.

"I am not sure," said Harwell. "I have not seen him since he sent me to the castle. What about you?"

"It has been ages. I cannot even remember when exactly. That is how long ago it has been."

"I do not know what to expect," said Harwell.

"One never knows what to expect from Ra Istar."

They had traveled within the shadows of the Merka 'Las forest for many days. When they had first entered the forest, the shadows deepened all around, that was, until they reached a small clearing and lake. There, the sunlight once again streamed upon them, in a rich and golden warmth, helping Ras Amon to heal and gain strength. Upon leaving the lake area, they continued their travels through the forest.

It had been ages since they had ventured through the Merka 'Las and they could not help but be amazed by how lively everything was. The forest was luscious, thick, and cool, and the leaves were brilliant shades of green. Wildlife constantly popped up as they traveled by, but unlike in other forests, here the animals were not afraid of the wizards or Shaer Thol. They merely raised their heads before returning to whatever they were doing. It was as if they were used to the sound or even the presence of wizards, and indeed the forest creatures were, for the Merka 'Las was the domain of the master, Ra Istar, the Great Conjurer, or as many in the Edainar called him, Windainn the Green.

"He always liked you," Ras Amon told Harwell. "He respected you for who you were, what you did. He told me so in later years."

Harwell's shoulders rose in a deeply drawn breath.

"And he expected you to respect him for who he was," Harwell said with a reluctance in his voice, "for what he was, what he did."

Ras Amon sensed consternation in his friend.

"What do you mean by that?" he asked.

"He was the one who told me to travel west, to learn new lessons," said Harwell shaking his head in dismay. "I was young and trusted him, but I was wrong. It was he, he that delivered me to the clutches of darkness where I was taught how to kill using my magic, how to disarm an enemy, and how to use his emotions against him. And I was taught how to kill using weapons, how to silently approach someone from behind, and how to stick a dagger in just the right place to rupture their lungs so they suffocated instantly. Sometimes I think it was he, he who defamed us, those of us who became Hulnur Istare. He made us into monsters even though he was not there."

Ras Amon saw concern in Harwell's face. He took his arm with his long fingers and firmly held him.

"My friend, let me remind you that the past is just that, the past," he said. "The past is not for us to live in, but to learn from. It is not nearly as important as today or tomorrow. You know this."

But Ras Amon's words did not help Harwell at all. His thoughts turned to his brother who had been killed by the brood. Anger and resentment floated within his mind, his thoughts.

Death always seems to follow me, he thought. *Try as I might, it seems I cannot avoid the darkness.*

He relinquished his mind to the images of battle and death, which fed the animal he thought he was. Emotions tore at him - sorrow for his brother, anger toward the brood, a betrayal of trust by Windainn, and a desperate longing to forget it all. Within this maelstrom of emotions and thoughts swirling in his mind, one thought emerged as a beacon of clarity.

What of revenge? Shall I become what I once was and seek revenge for my brother?

He wanted to lash out, to hurt someone - anyone - as badly as he had been hurt. But he knew that would only bring more pain, and so he forced himself to calm down.

He took a deep breath and tried to clear his mind, but the anger was still there, lurking just below the surface. He left his thoughts dangling, unspoken. He looked down at Ras Amon's grip and then into his friend's eyes.

"Your words tell a tale of forgiveness," he told Ras Amon. "I know you wish for me to forgive him for what I became, to forgive the past and begin anew. The problem with forgiveness is that it still focuses on the very thing I am trying to get away from."

Ras Amon shook him, with an anxious look.

"And what is that? Tell me! What is it you are trying to escape? Do you think you are the only one who has ever been hurt?" he asked.

But Harwell remained angry and pushed Ras Amon away.

Ras Amon sighed. He looked at his friend with a sad and troubled eye.

"Do you believe that no one else has ever had anguish so excruciating that they felt lifeless inside? And you are not alone in your feelings of betrayal. We each have burdens we have to live with. No matter who we are, what we do, or where we go, we will have difficulties. Problems are part of mortality."

"You are not of the Hulnur Istare, are you!" said Harwell with clenched teeth and lips barely parting. "You have no idea what they transformed us into, what we became. They inflamed a thirst for blood in us, and our sole purpose in life became death. We were but weapons of war, to be used as the Edainar saw fit. And when they were done with us, we were discarded like gnawed chicken bones, leaving most subdued and depressed. For many of us, the past was so haunting and vivid, so biting and raw, there could be no present, no future, ever again."

Ras Amon lowered his head in utter sadness. He realized his friend was consumed in deep resignation over something he could not understand. He looked up into the forest canopy.

"The past is always lurking in the present," he said, a calmness to his voice. "While we each have burdens to bear, one of the great advantages of being a part of the Maker's family is that we do not have to bear our burdens alone. I do not pretend to understand the hardships you faced. And I know you do not pretend to understand mine. We have both been through trials. Yet, here we are, fumbling through a trial at this very moment. Can you imagine the trials he has faced during his time? Can you?"

"He relished death in the same ecstatic way others enjoy a cup of tea."

"No, my friend. No. It was the Edainar who lessoned you in death. They were the ones who instructed you in the art of war, the use of magic as a weapon, and the powerful feeling one gets by killing another. No. He has never savored the darkness of death. He taught you as he taught me, to distinguish between what is good and what is evil, to better understand our self, and to live our life's purpose. He gave us that foundation, not the Edainar. You must understand this. He, like so many of us, was a victim of a most horrid malady."

The look on Harwell's face was curious.

"Malady? What malady do you speak of?" he asked.

"The sickness of circumstances, circumstances of time and place. The Hulnur Istare always spoke of darkness, about how prevalent it was, and how darkness could only be destroyed with darkness. But you forget what he taught you, that without darkness, there can be no light. This is the duality of all in existence. Listen to me. Why are we here, in this moment, in the now? It is because you aided a family as best you could. And who do you now turn to for help? You turn to him, to Ra Istar. Why? Because deep down you know that only he can help because only he can see the light in each of us. You did not even think of turning to the Edainar, because you know that what we face is much larger than any of us." He moved closer to Harwell, placing a hand on his shoulder. "You cannot continue to live inside the past when the future only demands your future. Do not flounder and drown outside the dictates of this reality. You must let the past be just that, the past."

But Harwell could not let go.

Let the past be just that, the past? he thought. *No. It is who I am. Best if I embrace it if I assuage my demons. Revenge. Yes. It will exact revenge for my brother's death, that any brood I face will suffer mightily before their death. I will let go of the anger seething in my mind and put it to good use. But I must have the Learned One believe my intentions are pure. Is this deceit? No. It is survival. It is learning how to turn my mistakes into intelligence.*

Tranquility washed over Harwell. It was the peacefulness born of past sorrow and strong determination to overcome it. He would let the past be his present and future. He would tell his friend what he wanted to hear.

"You are wise," he told Ras Amon. "The past is behind me, and the future, the future is what I shall make of it. The strong individual is the one who asks for help when it is most needed."

Ras Amon nodded, believing his words helpful. But he was unaware of Harwell's true motive.

They stood in silence as the forest remained as breathtakingly beautiful as ever, its sounds soothing. A slight breeze blew between the trees and the forest creatures continually chattered to each other. Now and then a bird would flutter overhead, uttering a high-pitched call. In this moment of calm, there came a voice, and not any voice, but a voice both strange and familiar, that at first seemed distant then rushed upon them like a heavy wind.

"Ah Vaeler, what fate brings you to me?"

They looked down the forest path, following the voice, where they saw the white cat rubbing up against the legs of a short, old man, wearing green.

* * *

The old man wore an old green swallowtail coat, tattered green wool trousers tucked into muddy boots, and a straw hat tied under his chin with a scrap of brown leather. He held a wooden staff, pale brown, made of highly polished wood. Along the shaft were several symbols carved into it, all a deep black against the pale brown. His face was like parchment, dried, and creased. His hands were weathered, calloused, and strong, and his eyes were lively, dark, and darting. There was no doubt that here was a man, rough to his foes and tender to his friends. Unsubtle maybe, but sure of himself and deeply learned. As the two looked at the old man, they were surprised.

"Strange how he looks," said Ras Amon to Harwell. "It is as if he has not aged one moment, nor has he changed in any other outward way."

"There was always a strangeness to him," said Harwell with a squint of his eyes that was showing concern. "Remember, we must always be cautious with the master."

As they appeared from the forest their sight brought a smile to the old man's face.

"Ah, do my eyes deceive me?" he said cheerfully with a wave. "Two of my finest students, Ras Amon and An Ranqu. It is good to see you both."

"He called you An Ranqu," Ras Amon told Harwell, under his breath. "That is a name I have not heard spoken in ages."

Harwell looked at his friend but did not smile.

He whispered back, "It is a name I have chosen to forget."

As they came closer to the old man, they kept their senses sharply attuned to the possibility of danger, always cautious.

"My master, Ra Istar, Windainn the Green," said Ras Amon.

They gave a gentle bow of the head in greeting.

"And what fate brings you to me?" asked Windainn. "Ah, but I know the answer. It is the darkness, is it not?"

They were quiet. Their facial expressions spoke more than the words they did not speak.

"I see. In time, we will speak to this then," said Windainn. He lifted Shaer Thol into his arms, whereupon the cat rubbed his head against Windainn's and began to purr like a swarm of bees. "Let us go to the house so you can play in the gardens with Twitcher. You remember Twitcher, eh?" he asked the white cat.

"I do what I do and that's the best I can do," said the cat, the words barely noticeable through the gurgling purr.

They continued down the path as it meandered between brush and tall trees, down a hill, and up the next. At the top of the second rise, when they stopped for a bit, to catch their breath, they came to another clearing, a valley below the gently sloping hills, abounding in rills and shady with trees.

In the valley, there was a homestead, a series of structures made of wood and stone, with walls packed with earth, flowers, and moss sprouting from its thatch. It stood isolated in a clearing, large, and lonely, surrounded by great oak and ash trees, near a river, and not far from the forest path. At the front were ferns and sharp-branched raspberry bushes, and moss that had grown over fallen tree trunks, and among the weeds and grass, wild strawberry plants were in white flower. To the back was a garden, a tangle of vegetables, herbs, weeds, and fruit trees, that needed tending. Surrounding it all were hedgerows, earthen banks with thick hedges and trees growing in them.

Ras Amon and Harwell saw how the place had changed. The house was larger than they remembered, and the farm, once brimming with neat rows of barley and corn, was now replaced by a disheveled garden, overgrown with tangled weeds and vines. Gone were the livestock and the sounds of the working day.

"Different, is it not?" said Windainn. "Everything is different. Everything changes. Everything changes, but at the same time, nothing changes."

They nodded at him. Everything about the place was older, more worn, more used, and the land more unruly. But everything they saw told stories long forgotten. A wooden chair near the front door caught their eye. Memories of Windainn sitting in the chair for hours, looking over the farmlands, and telling stories, flooded back to them.

"As more came to me, I built more rooms," said Windainn. "Over time though, slowly, they stopped coming." He paused and looked at the two, studying their reaction. "I guess no more were needed. Do you know the last time I had a visitor? Do you know?"

They shook their heads.

"I cannot even remember. I suppose, since I learned to step to the other side of time, everything changed." Then he whispered, mouthing the words so delicately, ". . . but at the same time nothing changes."

"What do you mean by *the other side of time*?" asked Ras Amon.

"I am sure you noticed – I have only aged a bit, but everything around me is still moving forward. I discovered a way to hold back time. The easiest way to describe it is that I step to the other side of time; I stay in my dimension while everything else continues moving on. I discovered this magic, held deep within the forest. But as with all magic, there is a trap."

"And what trap is that?" asked Ras Amon.

"If I were to leave the Merka 'Las, time would catch me. I would instantly perish in a heap of dust and bones. So, here I remain, in a prison of the mind, as the world moves all around me, just waiting for the right time."

"The right time?" asked Harwell. "The right time for what?"

"The time when I can leave, when all has been set right."

"I am confused. Did you not teach us that immortality is not a sufficient condition for the meaningfulness of life? So, why would you use this magic?"

"Yes, of course. Immortality is indeed folly. But I used the magic because I knew I would need to speak with you both, here, in this moment in time."

"You foresaw this event? But how?" asked Ras Amon

Windainn did not answer the question, and instead paused, a great smile on his face.

"Did I say I am so glad to see both of you?" he asked.

The two wizards looked at each other, perplexed. They did not pursue the issue. It was clear that neither could comprehend how Windainn could possess such foresight.

As they neared the homestead, Shaer Thol began to wriggle in Windainn's arms.

"I do what I do and that's the best I can do," said the white cat in a forceful tone.

"What is this? You want to get down?"

Windainn set the cat down, who darted off, into and through hedgerows to the back gardens.

"You will find him there, or maybe he will find you first," shouted Windainn with a chuckle in his voice. "Be careful with that Twitcher. You never know with him!" He turned to the two and asked, "How has our little friend been?"

"He is doing well, but there are times when he struggles," said Ras Amon. "It is the words in his mind."

"There are so many who find it difficult to find the right words," said Windainn, "but he knows exactly the right words to speak, all the time. How so few words can say so much. But even that takes an emotional toll." He looked at the two, a look on his face as if he knew their secret nightmares. "Unlike our friend, others use many words yet say so little - their words are meant to mask underlying motives, emotions, and pain. But in the end, everything becomes transparent and light."

Windainn's eyes fixed on them, unmoving, unwinking. His words tore into them like daggers. For an instant, their thoughts were synchronous.

He knows of our demons.

Then a few blinks and a smile, as Windainn asked, "And Shaer, his power? Is it as forceful as ever?"

"He has saved me more times than can ever be imagined," said Ras Amon. "Just a few days ago, against the magic of a Dark Wizard."

"Ah, the resurrected Foulhand. Your curse. Am I correct?"

Ras Amon nodded.

Windainn cocked an eyebrow at Harwell and said, "An Ranqu, who is your curse? Perhaps, it is me."

Harwell felt Windainn was trying to anger him, to push him to the edge of self-control. He became incensed and moved toward him, but instead stumbled into Ras Amon who nudged him back.

"What misery I have is not your concern," Harwell told Windainn over Ras Amon's shoulder.

"You do not want to do this," Ras Amon told Harwell in a hushed voice. "This is not the time."

But Windainn heard what Ras Amon had said and fixed Harwell with now icy eyes as a strange, peculiar smile came to him.

"All we have is time. All we will ever have is time," he said. "Until, of course, when time is no more. Am I correct, An Ranqu?"

"My name is not An Ranqu," said Harwell quietly but sternly. "You know my name is Ridley Harwell, and I would very much appreciate it if you would use it."

Windainn shrugged his shoulders.

"Still lessons to be learned, I see," he said. "With you, there are always lessons to be learned, often the hard way. Anger makes you careless. It makes you react without thinking. Let us continue, shall we? We will go to the house and talk over tea and sweets."

Harwell took a deep sigh and leaned slightly to the side to see Windainn's face. He could see that his look had not changed, the cold eyes and slight smile remained. Windainn gave a slow nod and started down the path to the homestead, his wooden staff helping to steady him.

Harwell tightly closed his eyes, trying hard to suppress his emotions. He reflected on how foolish he felt at that moment. With all the advice and help that Ras Amon had given him over the years, he always seemed at a loss at how to handle his feelings toward Windainn.

"He is right," Ras Amon told him. "Anger sometimes gets the better of you."

"It has served me well at times," said Harwell sarcastically, a tone laced with a bit of frustration.

Ras Amon gently patted his friend's shoulder.

"Have strength and patience," he said.

They continued down the path, following Windainn to the house, as the clouds began to move with strange speed. A slight breeze gave the forest movement and brought a chill to the air, while the day's light faded.

* * *

As they neared the homestead, in the now crisp forest air, the two wizards smelled wood smoke wafting from the fireplace chimneys. Windainn held the front door open for them as they walked into a small room lit by a cheerful fire in a fireplace. The furniture consisted of two large armchairs facing the fire and a small table under a window, on which a lighted lamp had been placed.

Windainn removed his hat and placed it on the table and, with the back of his hand, wiped his forehead.

"These days even short walks tire me out," said Windainn. He pointed down a narrow hallway. "That way. If you remember the library is to the right. I will return shortly with tea and sweets."

Down the hallway, past several doors and a large kitchen, Ras Amon and Harwell came to the library. It was as they remembered. The room was intimate, colorful, and cozy. There was a crackling fire in yet another fireplace, a desk, and a snug sitting area, surrounded by dark wood paneling and shelves. At one end of the room were glass doors that brought in views of the lush landscape.

Walking into the library was like walking into another dimension, an almost forgotten world, where light, furnishings, and scented books held the collective key to diving into unique experiences of the mind. It was a place of wonder, where imaginations could soar. It was also a place of loneliness, a place of learning, a place of purging disbelief, heeding the untrue, and accepting the unreal.

The two did not sit. Instead, they perused the volumes of tomes, many of them different, and strange. All around were old books and manuscripts, some of them moldy, worm-eaten, and most indecipherable, written in ancient languages, with unfamiliar symbols. There were many books whose exquisite illuminations and splendid bindings made manifest their value, even to those illiterate in the strange languages in which they were written. These books, some of them jewel-encrusted and edged with gold, were often locked in special boxes or chained to the shelves on which they rested. But many held a different value. These were unlike the medicinal, theological, or magical tomes. They had the power to impress and intimidate even those who could read them. These volumes spoke of special magic, of the kind associated for the most part with unpleasant events, both past, and future. Lesser creatures would have grasped those volumes with teeth and claws and hence would have understood why others, those of a clever nature, might desire them.

"It appears he has added to his collection," said Harwell.

"So many words to be read," said Ras Amon, "within a backyard garden of paradise. I believe that is what he had once said."

"It is," came Windainn's voice. He stood at the doorway holding a platter on which sat three cups of tea and a small dish of tempting sweets. "Please sit."

"Rosehip tea, I imagine," said Ras Amon.

"Of course. Freshly picked and dried."

Ras Amon and Harwell sat, each taking a sip of tea. It had been many years since they had tasted Windainn's rosehip tea. At first, it tasted a bit peculiar, until, after a few more sips, the flavor came through as they had remembered, sweet and tarty.

Windainn settled into his chair, sat back, and sipped his cup of tea. He gently set the cup down on a side table, atop an old dark, brown leather book. Ras Amon saw the book's spine was cracked, and many of its pages were frayed, with some coming loose. He could not make out the lettering on the spine for it was worn and faded. He thought little of the old book, telling himself it was of slight value, a nice place to rest a cup of tea.

"Now, for why you are both here," started Windainn. He looked at Ras Amon. "One is here because he needs to dispose of a Dark Wizard and his minion. While the other," his stare turning to Harwell, "is here to undo the wickedness of the Soran Cath. It seems the Deep Thicket could no longer hold the Grand Denier."

"Will you help us?" asked Ras Amon.

Windainn rubbed his chin with his thumb, deep in thought.

"Of course, but in time," he told them. "As I have said, I have been waiting for this moment to speak with you. First, you need to understand what has happened here. I suppose it is best to start at the beginning. You see, when there were no more younglings to shape, I was at a loss. I did not hear from the Edainar. So, I decided to travel to Blackstone to find out what had occurred. As I traveled west through the Merka 'Las, along a pathway known to me, I came upon something most strange in the forest. It was something I had never seen before, something surprising and extraordinary."

"What was it?" asked Ras Amon.

"It was a wooden door, right there in the forest, standing upright, with no frame, just standing there amongst the trees. It was old and beautiful and stout and thick, with a solid gold handle. It reminded me of the many doors in the Aina Dur. I sensed magic around it so I was careful as I approached. I peeked around the strange and saw the forest behind it. But the forest was blurred. It was as if I had water in my eyes. It looked like a green cloth, waving in the wind, but lost to me.

"I asked myself, what if I were to open the door? What would happen? Where would it take me? I thought and thought and tried to reason through the occurrence, to understand the door, and why it was there. I used my magic on it, those spells I thought related. But my magic did not help me to understand it, and yet there the door was, in my mind. So, I had no recourse, none at all, but to open the door and step through it. I put my hand on the door handle and pushed slowly. It gave a low-pitched creak. I continued to carefully open it, not knowing what would happen, or what was on the other side. Then I saw it - a long narrow passage, on the other side. I stepped through and the door closed behind me with a muffled thud."

Harwell was entranced with the story.

"Where were you?" he asked. "Where did the passage lead?"

"To a library in some far-away place, another time, another reality, I think. It was an enormous structure, warm and comfortable. But the air was heavy and thick, and unnaturally still and calm. At first, it was a bit difficult for me to breathe. So, I took a few deep breaths which helped. I looked around. There were books everywhere, very disorderly, mind you, but everywhere. Some were on shelves while others were on the floor, stacked in tall columns. There was a little maze through the books, so I started through it, and eventually, ahead I saw movement within the stacks.

"It was a small man. He was different in appearance from us. His features were strange. He was rugged, with wrinkled grey skin, and he had a massive head fronted by a pair of smallish horns and small bright eyes. I am sure I was as strange to him as he was to me. My presence startled him. He looked at me with a quizzical look as if to judge my reaction to words he then spoke, words in a strange language. Not understanding what he said, I responded by introducing myself. But he again spoke in a strange tongue. Realizing the problem we had in understanding each other, he shook his head rather quickly, as if to clear his mind. He started again, but this time in a different language. Once more, I did not understand him. Again, he shook his head quickly and tried yet another strange language. This happened a few times until he came to the old tongue. It was then when we could communicate."

Windainn took a sip of tea. He reached for a long-stemmed pipe, packed the bowl with some dark leaf, and lit it. The smell of the pipe was strong but warm and comforting and conjured memories in the two wizards of their time with the master. A few more puffs of his pipe and Windainn's voice crackled with age as he continued his story.

"He called himself Thecarius and referred to me as Book Hunter. He said he had been waiting for me and asked me to follow him to a smaller room which I did. The room was filled with books as well, but unlike the previous room, the books here were neat and elegant. My eyes were caught by their colorful bindings, and they were expertly arranged on silvery black wooden shelves. In the center of the room, I saw a wooden lectern with a rather large book perched on it. My new friend walked to the lectern and gripped it with both hands. He smiled at me and told me the book was for me. He opened it precisely where a tassel bookmark was set. He then motioned for me to join him which I did.

"As I looked over his shoulder at the tome, I saw that it was illuminated, its text supplemented with such decorations as colorful borders and miniature illustrations, one of which, to my astonishment, was an illustration of a man in my very likeness. Using a steady finger, Thecarius moved across words written in a strange language, and read the text aloud - Ra Istar, the Great Conjurer, Windainn the Green, Book Hunter. He looked up at me with a smile. That is you, he said. I asked, Me? Book Hunter? He blinked with surprise. Yes, he said, and all this is yours. He asked, isn't that why you are here? He told me the books had been collected over the ages, brought by the Great Synhadrin. Take them with you, he said. I asked, who is the Great Synhadrin? He responded, not a who but a what."

The light in Windainn's pipe went out and the bowl turned cold. He shifted in his chair; stood up, knocked out the pipe ashes into the hearth gate, and sucked on it a few times to clear out the bowl. He sat down and proceeded to again pack the pipe and light it.

"I asked him to explain about the Great Synhadrin, but he waved me off. He said there was no time for that. He went to a shelf and removed a book. He brought it to me. The book was old and worn. Its dark brown leather cover was torn and some of the pages were falling out. I asked, what is this? He laughed at me and asked, can't you see? It's a book for you, a book for you to read. I rubbed my hand over the title, a series of strange characters embossed in gold leaf. I asked, what is the book called? His look became serious. He said, the book's title is Hinge, and it wold help me to learn the many languages in the other books. I told him that Hinge is a rather strange title for a book. He said there was nothing strange about it. He asked, isn't a hinge something that connects things? I told him it was."

Ras Amon looked at the old book beneath Windainn's cup of tea.

"Is that the book?" he asked.

"Why yes, it is." Windainn's old hand gently caressed the book's tattered spine. "I do not know where I would be without Hinge. Books have a life and energy all their own, and like us, they have their destinies."

"Many of the books in this room do seem different," said Ras Amon. "Are they from that library?"

"It took me years to bring them here."

"There are so many questions to ask."

"None of which will I answer," said Windainn taking a couple of puffs of his pipe.

"I do not understand."

"Answers are unimportant, including mine. They contain mostly interpretations and perceptions. You should always approach answers given to you with great forethought. Answers are a pit where monsters lay."

"A pit where monsters lay," Harwell whispered to Ras Amon. "Yet, another trap."

He leaned forward and shook his head in annoyance.

"There are traps everywhere with you," he told Windainn. "Magic is a trap. Answers are a trap. Is not everything in this life a trap?"

"Exactly," said Windainn. "In that which is visible, everything is a trap."

"And the invisible? That which cannot be seen?"

"In that which cannot be seen," said Windainn with icy eyes, "you are the bait, wriggling on a hook, waiting to be devoured."

Harwell sat back in his chair and tried to relax. He was very untrusting of Windainn. He released a deep sigh

"Enough with all this storytelling," he said. "With your new power, you knew we would seek your counsel. You were aware of the dire situations we were going to face, and what we are now in. Why did you wait for us instead of first seeking us out? Because of this, lives have been lost and threatened."

"Again, seeking answers. Best to discover your own answers," said Windainn. "Because of these books, I have been able to foresee events and step across the other side of time, again and again, patiently waiting for you, for this exact moment. But you have to understand that some things just are. They are part of the natural occurrence of events."

He stood and stretched, a few more puffs of his pipe. He pointed to a large book sitting alone on a shelf.

"That is the first book I was able to read. Its title is Coil. From its pages, I learned how to," he paused looking for the right words, "I guess you could say, I learned how to unfold time, how to look into the many futures, bringing them closer to me. The future is like gazing at clouds. They come at you, and as they move, they change shape and color. But they are still just clouds, and you know they are, but when you stare at them long enough you begin to see things - a tree, or an animal, or maybe an image that resembles a close friend. There are many futures, always changing, moving, each desperately trying to become the present and past."

He returned to his chair and leaned forward with an intensity the other two had not previously felt.

"Coil allowed me to see my many futures," he said, "my many deaths in countless clouds, all within darkness so thick, so grievous, so intolerable that even those of great faith in the Maker would attenuate themselves to shadow. But of all the many futures, there was only one future that had any glimmer of hope. With Coil's help, I selected it and decided to remain here, protected by the Merka 'Las. But age was creeping up on me. I did not have much time. Coil also showed me how to use the power of the forest, how to step to the other side of time, over and over again, to hold back time."

He leaned back with a sigh and gave them an ominous look.

"We are now in the future I chose, the only future with a flicker of light," he said. "A darkness has come to the land, a darkness that will cause so much suffering that is darker than its soul. Little light will pierce through the darkness of this fallen world. Death will not come easily or smoothly, but it will come and when it does it will roar swiftly. There will be pain. There will be blood. But there is still light in this future."

"What are we to do?" asked Ras Amon.

Windainn shook his head and said, "Again, seeking answers from others. The answer is within you. Men suffer the worst evils for the sake of the strangest desires. They neglect the most necessary appetites as if they were strangers to our reality. Learned One, you have no choice but to face that which haunts you."

Although the words were difficult to hear, Ras Amon caught them.

Windainn looked at Harwell.

"And as for you," he said with slight hesitation, "you - Ridley Harwell – you are just dabbling at things, a toe in the water of a massive sea. One must live to one's purpose in life, even though the purpose is ever-changing. This is the truth of the self. If I can step to the other side of time, you can also step forward and back again, living that purpose. Become who you were and who you are."

At first, Harwell was not sure he understood what Windainn was trying to tell him. He gave a curious look. Windainn, as stoic as Harwell had ever seen him, returned the look with a slight nod.

Harwell did not speak. Thoughts were tugging at his mind. He looked at Windainn when it suddenly made sense to him. Windainn had given Harwell what he wanted.

Become who you were and who you are, Windainn's words rang through his mind. *Become who you were and who you are.*

But there was a matter of importance remaining, a matter Harwell had not forgotten.

"What about the family, the children?" he asked. "I must help them."

A smile came to Windainn, and he had a warm look in his eyes.

"They will be helped by another," he said, "one more powerful than you. The strength will come upon them at the right time. I have seen this and more. But for now, you both must get some rest, for tomorrow morning you and Shaer will leave the Merka 'Las. The future rolls forward, ever onward."

Harwell was not sure what to make of his words, but he knew he was right. That evening they ate a hearty meal in silence. Later, they spent time in the library, sipped tea, and smoked their pipes, as Windainn read them passages from a book entitled Clarity. Later, they would finalize their travel plans with Windainn's guidance.

As the beauty of night became their possession, Ras Amon and Harwell each lay in bed, each on their own. They thought of each other, dreamy thoughts, tormented by recent remembrances. They thought of Windainn's stories and struggled to determine their meaning. After some time, they closed their eyes and surrendered to wistful dreams of clouds, and futures undiscovered. They slept restfully and at peace as understanding came to them, an awareness of the path ahead. In the morning, after a small meal, they along with Shaer Thol bid their farewell and expressed their deepest appreciation to Windainn the Green.

Windainn gave Ras Amon his staff for he no longer needed it, and for each, he gave a final gift, words of wisdom: "The strength of magic is limited by the capacity of its vessel."

The three left Windainn and walked down a meandering forest pathway, deeper into the dark forest, in a setting unfamiliar, stopping when the pathway branched out in two different directions.

"He knows what will happen, how this will all end," said Harwell. "Why does he not tell us?"

"Maybe he does not want us to know," said Ras Amon. "Maybe he is afraid we will lose hope. Best to be kept in the dark, I suppose."

"Will we see him again?"

"I do not think so," said Ras Amon. "Why? Was there something you wished to tell him?"

Harwell looked at his friend and shook his head.

"No. But what about us? Do you believe we will again see each other?"

"Perhaps, we will," said Ras Amon, his eyes brilliant and clear. "Perhaps, on the other side of time, my friend."

"I do what I do and that's the best I can do," said Shaer Thol as he rubbed up against them, purring softly.

Harwell reached down and stroked the cat's back with his palm.

"Did I say how glad I was to see both of you?" he asked, harkening back to Windainn's words.

They smiled at each other and then took their separate paths.

A short bit of time passed, and the Merka 'Las became still, and the air filled with uncertainty. The trees grew so close together that the sun could hardly shine through the thick leafy roof. Harwell turned to see if he could catch one last glimpse of his friends. But the forest had swallowed them and erased their trail.

On the other side of time, thought Harwell. Then he remembered the teachings of the Hulnur Istare. *Be strong for the flood of death is upon us once again. When the whirlwind of fury comes from the Maker and the senses are shaken, and the soul is driven to madness, only the strong shall stand.*

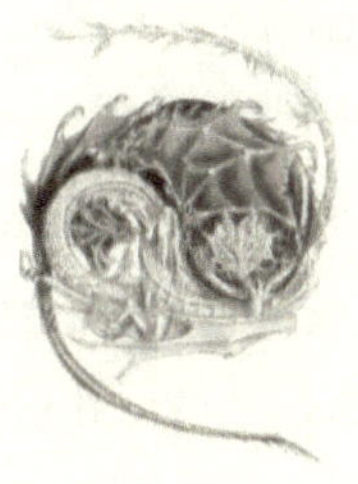

Chapter 18
An Ajatar's Nest

WITH AN VAN AU'S treatment, Bran's legs healed quickly. The young woman continued to apply the poultice on alternate days, still using tight strapping. The deep gashes mended seamlessly and soon, Bran was able to stand and walk, though not very far at first. But each time he went a little further and felt a sense of accomplishment. He was getting stronger and as determined as ever to keep going. For Ug'ghi Otha, the marks on his face, bruises, and scratches also healed quickly, leaving slight scar tissue.

While they healed, growing more and more anxious to set out and find Molly, the frigid weather continued to assault the place with ice, snow, and rain. They had plenty of firewood but had to carefully ration their food and water. None of the hardship, though, had deterred Elizabeth's resolve.

Molly, we are coming for you, she often thought. *Nothing will stop us!*

As they sheltered, she insisted they use the time to make plans. Ug'ghi Otha, Bran, and Brows shared what they knew of the northern reaches of the Drueger. The mountains would be treacherous to climb and traverse, with many paths impassable at times because of the heavy snow. Their journey would be a rugged task, one which would require courage as well as physical strength.

"The land north is called 'Shk Ndor," said Ug'ghi Otha. "We will run afoul of the cold weather and will need to find shelter in the mountains. There are caves, some deep, others shallow that will protect us from the cold and wind. In some places, there are rock formations that provide cover. But it is a cruel place, and the Ru Gwaith lurks in hideaways. We will need to be careful."

"What about the men of the land?" asked An Van Au. "Surely, they can be helpful."

"You speak of the Mur' Edan, those who live in the mountains. There are few if there are any left," said Brows. He lit a bowlful in his pipe and sat smoking stolidly, blowing out great clouds of smoke, a sweet, smelling aroma. "Doubtful any exist at all," he said between puffs. "The persecution of the Mur' Edan has occurred for ages."

"There is one the Ru Gwaith speak of, the one called I' Ereb," said Ug'ghi Otha. "Tales are told that he is of great force and intensity."

Brows shook his head, a few more puffs from his pipe.

"Intensity? More like madness," he said. "I have not met him nor do I know of him personally. But I have heard many tales, none of which tells us definitively who he is and how he acts, other than he has succumbed to rage."

"All I know of him came from a friend who fought beside him," said Bran. "My friend simply said this – he has been cast adrift from the past."

"I think we should stay clear of him," said Brows.

"But it would be helpful to have friends, to help in our travels," said Ug'ghi Otha, "to be able to push open the black gate, for the mountains are full of foes."

Brows chuckled. "Push open the black gate? We are far from that possibility."

"We are closer than you think, much closer," Ug'ghi Otha told him with a cold stare. "Remember our goal."

But Brows met Ug'ghi Otha's gaze and said, "I have not forgotten why we are in this wretched place. And remember, you are with us, to help guide us through the mountains and to the black gate - friends or no friends."

While the two continued to stare at each, Elizabeth stood.

"We've no time for such back and forth," she said. "We'll deal with what's thrown our way because we've no other choice." She turned to Bran. "Are you well enough to travel?"

He was impressed with her leadership and smiled at her with a nod.

"Good," said Elizabeth. "We'll leave in the morning."

But a flash of sadness suddenly washed over Bran as he looked upon Elizabeth. It was unsettling, deep, and penetrating, aligned with a thought: *Does the young girl know she will become Queen if her sister has perished?*

* * *

The large grey cat followed Molly's captors day and night. When they stopped to rest, he did the same. But he always kept his distance, not wanting to draw notice to himself. He knew attacking the Ru Gwaith was pointless, for as Caedaes, he had to protect Molly but also himself. There was little he could do but follow, with stern determination, and wait to embrace the earliest opportunity for events to unfold where a plan could take shape. Only if the beasts harmed her would he act. All this frustrated him, of course, but great care, flexibility, and patience were required.

As he followed the Ru Gwaith, he was an opportunistic hunter. When time allowed, he would prowl for moles and other vermin, catching them as they raced through the snow. He also dined on Ru Gwaith scraps which consisted mostly of dried hides, the ends of hooves, legs, and intestines of slaughtered animals, and even dry bread. The bread was simple, made of bitter flour, water, salt, and dried. It was difficult to eat and tasted horrible, but it provided some nutrition. When there was time to rest, he would burrow deep within the snow and into the ground for warmth and protection. He also foraged for small branches, and sprigs of wood, keeping them in his mouth as he traveled. These became his markers. He hoped that those he left behind would see them and follow.

Though his journey was difficult, he was determined to persevere. He held to his routines while always surveying the land nearby for foe or friend. Of interest, he saw an eagle who soared high above, unheeded by the Ru Gwaith. For leagues, the great bird had followed, making no sound at all. Its bill was yellow and its feathers black. He did not recognize the bird and could not take his eyes off its gorgeous, strong wings.

Does the En' Raama keep watch? he thought.

He knew the En' Raama made their home over the many places of the Harrow and met within the great mountain hall of Muul'duul Durra. He wondered if the steward of the winged creatures had sent the eagle.

Doubtful, he answered himself. *The Shori Orn, master of the owls, is no longer steward. The time when all those who took to flight garnered great respect by the races of the Harrow is ended. Time passes too quickly, as it does, and change occurs. The new stewards, the falcons, the wasps and bees, the mayflies, the hawks, and the harriers, have been mostly weak, not concerned with the trials of the other races.*

He was spellbound by the eagle as it circled until he saw that something caught the great bird's eye: more Ru Gwaith movement. The beasts were off into the mountains at full cry. Quickly, he dug through the snow until he struck the ground, clawing through it. He then placed a sprig upright into the ground and bent its top pointing in the direction of the Ru Gwaith. He pushed the ground and snow around the sprig's base.

Patience. Follow carefully.

He watched the Ru Gwaith as they ran off, trying to catch a glimpse of Molly. He saw her. She had been lifted, thrown over the shoulders of a beast, her arms dangling listlessly. This brought him great sadness, but anger as well. He calmed his anger, and pushing away the frustration, reminded himself.

Patience. Follow carefully.

***

Fairfax, Glaeynd, Thurir, and his pack, had successfully made it across the Aldpine River. They were now deep within the mountains of Ragmorok where the wintry winds wailed loud and dismally. Thurir led the way because he and the other Fenri were familiar with the many mountain passages. They traveled day and night, taking shelter in small mountain caves for a few moments at a time. Their bodies and minds were exhausted, but Thurir pushed them forward, on a winding path north.

It was then when Glaeynd sensed a presence along the path.

"Something is out there," she said.

"Tell me, what do you feel?" asked Fairfax.

"That someone follows."

"Someone? Or something?" snickered Thurir.

"It is someone," she said. "A person. Perhaps more than one. Of the En' Edan."

She closed her eyes. At the same time, she was careful to disguise her thoughts from Fairfax.

Twain? Is it you? I have missed you.

Slowly, she opened her eyes.

"What did you see? Is the presence clearer in your mind's eye?" asked Fairfax.

She shook her head. She did not want to raise her hopes, only to be disappointed if it was not her good friend Twain Boggans. She would be cautious.

"I am unsure," she said.

Fairfax felt she was keeping something from him, but he could not be certain.

Thurir instructed additional members of his pack to stand back and watch their rear flank.

"We do not know who it could be," he told them. "If you see anything, or if there is a strange scent about, immediately tell us."

As they continued their journey within the mountains, Fairfax kept a watchful eye on the skies. He knew they were close to the devil's hive of 'Ksh Nierwes, the home of the black ajatars, Mori Mengel's Lok Tumu. But Thurir did not need to watch the skies. Instead, he and his pack leaders, Janru and Talro, used their keen sense of smell, periodically sniffing the air for the scent of smoldering ashes and rot.

At one point, high atop a snowy peak, Fairfax turned south where he could see the mountain 'Ksh Nierwes, the black ajatar hive. But the mountain's presence was mysteriously blurred. On the one side was an impenetrable mist; on the other was smoke from a mountain of fire. But through the mountain's haze, Fairfax could see the shadows of hundreds of caves, nests on the sides of the great rock, and the nests of the Lok Tumu. Above, circling the place was the Tura himself, Mori Mengel.

Something tells me, we are not finished with the evil beast, he thought.

They traveled farther north, up a jagged and narrow mountain path, before they came to rest on a ledge. They stood overlooking a crevice that stretched forward, decreasing in width as it entered a large cave.

Looking at the cave, Fairfax became concerned. There was a heavy presence.

Ajatar nest?

He carefully observed the surroundings. The mouth of the cave was low and wide, a narrow horizontal gash in the rock, and protected by a barricade of closely woven branches. From the many claw markings, he could see that the crevice had been created by an ajatar continually using the edge to push its massive weight off the mountain to take flight.

"I do not like what I see here," he told the others.

Thurir moved forward along the ledge, closer to the cave.

"Do not fear," he said. "It is an old hive, one that hasn't been used by the Lok Tumu for ages. No evil ajatar would ever use this hive again."

"You want us to journey into this cave?" asked Fairfax.

"The cave provides a secret way to the Rakl. It is not been used by my kind for some time now. But I believe it is safe."

"How far does it go?" asked Glaeynd.

"The ancient hive is rather deep. At the back are a series of tunnels. Many link to storage chambers and lookout posts. But there is one chamber that links all tunnels to the low hills of the mountains. They have been there for ages. Those who dug the tunnels were, well, no one knows exactly what happened to them."

"Do you know your way through the maze?" asked Glaeynd.

"Of course." Thurir's response was immediate. He turned to Janru and Talro and gave them a firm order. "Lead the way."

But something was wrong. Fairfax could sense it.

Janru and Talro did not respond to Thurir's order. Instead, they stood silent, in fear and dread of the cave.

"Asht Bur," snarled Janru, baring his teeth and taking several steps back from the cave.

Fairfax turned to him.

"What was that? What was it you said?" he asked.

"Asht Bur," again snarled Janru.

"There are some who say that those who enter the tunnels are seized and devoured by an evil spirit," said Talro, his tone ominous. "Asht Bur - in your tongue, it's called *bone man.*"

Fairfax leaned on his staff and stared at Thurir.

"Now I understand why the tunnels are no longer used by the Lok Tumu," he told Thurir.

"What's this? Is a wizard of the Edainar afraid of a spirit?" mocked Thurir. His voice took on a treacly wickedness. Again, he ordered Janru and Talro, "Lead the way. Now! We've not a moment to waste."

But the pack leads did not move, nor did others of his pack.

"My friend, you hid something from us, something important for us to know about this place," said Fairfax. "What else are you hiding?"

Thurir became anxious and began to pace.

"My race bleeds!" he roared. "Too many have been deluded and made instrumental to evil by the Dark Wizard, and all you care about is . . ."

Fairfax interrupted with a mighty thump of his staff.

"All I care about is knowing what we may be up against," he said, an edge of anger to his voice. "I know we will face a Dark Wizard, and I know there will be Fenri and brood who will support the evil darkness. What I do not know is what is in those tunnels you want us to so freely enter . . ."

Thurir spun around with fury in his eyes. It was his turn to interrupt Fairfax.

"Enough!" he thundered. "I will tell you what we may face. A Lok Tumu once lived in the nest. It was said he rebelled against the Tura, Mengel himself. They viciously fought. The renegade ajatar returned to his nest, badly injured. It was unknown what happened to the beast. Time passed and there was little activity from the nest. So, we entered the cave. We found the beast dead. We believed the rebel died of his injuries at the talons of the Tura. A few days later, when some went back they found the beast had been devoured. All that remained were its bones - even the marrow had been ravened. We thought the culprits were raavs, large mountain vermin. It was only later when we began to map the vast array of tunnels and use them, that many of our very own began to die under suspicious circumstances.

"At first, the deaths were few, but soon the losses quickly accumulated. There were supposed sightings of a strange creature in the tunnels. Some described the creature as a more deformed and demented Ru Gwaith if there could be such a thing. Others described what they saw as a distorted man, perhaps an outcast of what remained of the Mur' Edan. But, others depicted the creature as a spirit, able to appear out of thin air and as quickly vanish into the darkness. It is this spirit, the Asht Bur that my leads speak of. But in all my travels within the labyrinth, I have never laid eyes on the creature, and I would venture a guess that neither have they."

Thurir turned to Janru and Talro. Both nodded in agreement.

Fairfax was deep in thought, placing the point of an index finger stiffly against his forehead, and with the other hand stroking his long beard. He was making mental notes of what he had heard.

"I tell you, there is nothing in the cave. But what does it matter?" said Thurir in a low, deep tone. "You have the stone. What worries should we have?"

Fairfax raised an eyebrow in disbelief.

"Did you not hear the words of the Paragon? His warning?" he said. "The use of the stone will give away our location. We can ill afford to do this. If I were to use the stone, there will be no surprise going forward. We will become transparent to the Dark Wizard, who will unleash a wrath unlike any seen before."

"Then why did you get the stone, if not to use it to defend us?" asked Thurir.

Fairfax became dark, his face frowning and fierce.

"Such power is not to be used so easily and especially in defense. It is to be used for one thing, and one thing alone - to crush the foe. Magic of any kind must be carefully used. Do you understand?"

Thurir clenched his teeth and hung his head down.

"Then what are we to do?" he asked.

"We have the dwarven sword," said Fairfax looking at Glaeynd, a smile to his face. "And we have the mighty roar of the Fenri."

Glaeynd was shaken by his words.

"But the Paragon also had a warning for me," she said. "Remember?"

Fairfax's smile widened.

"Oh, I remember. I remember it very well," he said. "The Paragon spoke of how the use of the sword would feast off the soul of the one who wields it. He warned it would quickly corrupt its wielder."

Glaeynd was frantic with confusion and worry.

"Then what are you saying?" she asked. "Are you saying I should sacrifice myself?"

Fairfax was still smiling. He brought a gentle hand over hers.

"I know two things," he told her. "First, your use of the sword will not reveal our location and it will be a most powerful weapon against whatever we may face. Secondly, you misunderstood the Paragon, his meaning."

"How so?" she asked, her eyes watering.

"The Paragon provided you not with one but with two gifts. He gave you the mighty Varekan Ithrun. But he also gave you the ability to connect to me in a way unknown to either of us. For him to grant you such powerful gifts, he knew that you had the strength to overcome those troubles that would try to hold you down. It is the strength to believe in yourself. He knew you had the favor of the Maker." There was now a reverence in his voice as he finished. "Do you not see, the sword only feeds on those who are weak. The Paragon was telling you to be strong. I must ask you, my sweet lady of the mists, what service is your purpose?"

She became overcome with emotion, trying not to cry.

You must not cry, she thought.

But her eyes filled with tears.

"Go ahead. Put your hand on the sword," he told her.

She trembled slightly as she placed her hand on the sword's hilt. It was cold to her palm but quickly warmed as the sword began to glow orange.

"Do you feel its warmth?" he asked.

"Why yes."

"It does not feed on you. No. It gives you strength. The sword senses the character of its wielder. There is no magic in it. No. It is very different. For you see, my lady, it is a living thing."

She lifted Varekan Ithrun from its sheathing. It was fully aglow, bathed in a deep orange. It felt light in her hand. She waved it in the air, cutting at wisps of nothing, and brought it down with a powerful blow. She felt its power, its rage. But she quickly sheathed it, a suggestion of fright on her face.

"Was the power disconcerting?" asked Fairfax.

"There was a strangeness to it, almost a seduction, calling to me. If I am not careful, I will be lured into an arrogant meanness. The power is corruptible. It can change my foundational beliefs."

"Now you understand. Such power can inflict an extraordinary amount of damage, and if not used carefully, corrupt its user, but only if its user is of weak mind and character."

She closed her eyes and took a deep breath. She felt a strength rise within her, a strength that she had not felt before, almost a peace.

"I will lead us through the cave," she said.

"And I will be by your side, my lady," said Fairfax.

They pulled aside the branches and entered the mouth of the cave. It was dark and damp, not the kind of place where one would want to spend much time. Dripstone hung from the roof, covered with feathery grass and roots that slowly seemed to stir in the air. Ajatar bones littered the floor - a large skull with a gaping crystalline jaw, serrated fangs as long as an arm, a massive rib cage splintered apart in places, huge leg bones as thick as logs, and a long tapering tail. Dried claws groped the ground like scythes. The bones were white and dried out, most of them half-buried in the soil. Glaeynd was astonished at the size of the remains, yet still, they seemed smaller than the Tura.

They moved deeper into the cave. Fairfax opened the palm of a hand and brought forth with magic a small orb shining a dull blue light, enough to travel by. As they slowly walked, Glaeynd kept one hand on the sword's hilt. She knew she needed to be ready. At one point, she put her hand out and touched something that slithered away under her fingers. She gasped. Fairfax swung the orb around, a weak ring of the blue light revealing that the walls were covered in heaving black fur, and alive.

Bats!

Fairfax directed his light at the ceiling where more bats hung, thousands of them, from the many dripstones. As the blue light swept over them, they raised their tiny faces, wet pink gums, and white fangs, all jabbering in fear. He did not want to disturb them further. So, he focused the light on the floor so that they stood, disconnected feet and legs, in the dull pool of light. He then motioned with a hand for everyone to continue but slowly and quietly.

"Keep straight," whispered Thurir.

Soon, they came to a massive cavern large enough to hold the ajatar that once lived there. It was partially lit from the surface far above, a small opening that brought a beam of light stabbing down into the center of the dark. Where the light faded Fairfax could make out several tunnels, bored into the rock, circular in shape, easily able to fit man and Fenri. But they were strange and magical. He remembered seeing such tunnels in his many travels throughout the Harrow. He knew the stories of a race of malevolent ancients, a race born and bred to hunt and kill others, those that burrowed deep within stone and rock, part of the I' Ksh. But the creatures were long since dead and extinct, at least that was what was thought. The beasts were feared by many, even after their extinction. But fear is easily washed away by time.

Cautiously, ever so cautiously, Fairfax approached one of the tunnels, reaching out to feel its side. The rock was smooth under his hand, but a slimy residue was left on his fingertips. He sniffed the slime. It was stale and smelled of mildew.

"Hush now," he said. He turned to Glaeynd. "Ready your sword."

She gripped the sword's hilt tighter and gave him a faint nod. She could feel its strength flow through her.

"Asht Bur," whispered some of the Fenri. "Asht Bur."

Fairfax slowly backed away from the mouth of the tunnel. The others followed.

"There is a creature within this place, an ancient creature of darkness," he said. "But it is no spirit, nor is it of the Ru Gwaith or Mur' Edan." He turned to Thurir. "We must make our way from this place. Which tunnel provides the quickest route from here?"

Thurir pointed to a tunnel at the other side of the cavern.

"That one," he said. "It leads to an area protected by rocks, close to the tower."

"Keep a watchful eye," Fairfax told Glaeynd. "We will hasten our journey through this maze."

Glaeynd brought Varekan Ithrun from its sheathing. The blade glowed a delicate orange.

"Only if you have to," Fairfax told her.

She understood what he meant and again gave a nod.

They walked at a quickened pace, to the other side of the cavern and into a tunnel, and down the narrow stretches of its twisting length. They came upon smaller caverns and passed innumerable tunnels and entrances to other subterranean chambers, at last coming to a stone stairway that seemed familiar to Thurir. They moved swiftly up the stairway and soon found themselves outside in the bitter cold, edged around by several rocks.

Still high in the mountains, they overlooked a long valley below; vast mists were rising from the rivers which ran from the surrounding ice-capped mountains and glaciers. To the east, nestled within the frozen peaks was the Rakl, a myriad of ice-huts dotted about the valley's long arms, while in the center of it all stood the dark blue death tower of Ur' Morir. Succumbed to the deep darkness of shadow, the wicked place was composed of three pillars of many-sided rock, its walls and tower windows weeping, countless dark holes of emptiness.

Their gaze followed along the riverbanks and pathways that found their way to the tower. There they saw hundreds of wood boards thrust into the frozen ground, to which Fenri, those who disavowed the tower's ruler, or others who constituted a threat to the new dark order were nailed. On some boards, only nails remained, what was left of the dead in heaps on the ground. On others dangled bones, muscle and tissue picked over by vultures. And on others, the slow rot of decay had started. Horrifically, there were many Fenri still alive, wriggling on the boards much like a dying fish. Cries, moans, pleading, and gasping lent a horrifying motif to the disease of death that transpired. As the frigid wind blew, a noisome exhalation of decay brought the stench of a most offensive description. This was a place where life seized in surrender to the black abyss of death.

Fairfax looked at Thurir and saw great sadness in the wolf-beast's eyes, and then something else he thought he would never see from the Fenri Prince - despair.

"We will drag ourselves forward, through the depths of evil," said Fairfax. "Every step may be reluctant, and time may seem to slow our pace. But though our pace will be slow, we will raise each foot and set it down with care and forethought. Let this be our last journey in this endeavor, a journey of hope, healing, and the restoration of freedom."

* * *

But their presence was not unnoticed.

Deep within Ur' Morir, the Dark Wizard Varul Teardash smiled; his master had told him of the newcomers' arrival. He was of a tall and slender form, pale and gaunt, his mouth thin and cruel set, and had large black eyes. He was shrouded in a long black robe, a sword hanging from his waist. He took the sword and spoke words in an ancient tongue long-since forgotten, lifting the black steel blade high into the air. It came to life bursting into flame. He thrashed it through the air a few times then thrust it into the stone floor bringing a swirling sphere of fire that encased him as if fed by the bellows of an ajatar's breath.

The sound of the fire created a powerful vibration, a hypnotic rhythm like a harmonic invocation. He found himself entranced by the heat and light. Around him, an image danced within the tangle of flame and smoke, a demon calling to him, begging him to enter its prison of fire. His hand shook. He took a long slow breath, trapping the hot air deep within him, burning his lungs. With all his might he pulled the sword from the stone floor. The flames ended and the sword returned to its original state.

What beauty it is for the eye to see, he thought, his black-gloved hand sliding over the sword's smooth surface, *for within the shadow in the flame lives eternal death.*

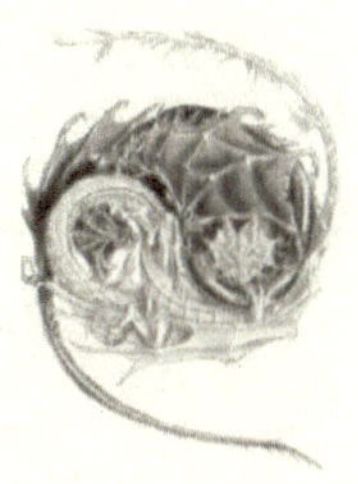

CHAPTER 19
I' EREB

MOLLY AWOKE TO A strangeness and remoteness that seemed like something more, something eery. She was alone, in an unfamiliar place, in an unfamiliar mind. She tried to orient herself, to remember how she got to this place, but her memories were foggy and elusive. She was disoriented and confused. But then a thought came to her.

I must not panic. I must not panic. I must stay in control.

Her hands were numb and raised above her head, bound with a black rope, and although she could not see them, her legs and feet were also secured by rope. She looked down at her body. Her clothes were a bit torn and soiled with a reddish slime that smelled like death. She felt sore and as she looked over her arms, she could see bruises. Then another thought came to her.

The stone?

She again looked down. It was there, tucked away.

I must not panic. I must stay in control.

She looked around the strange room and tried to get her bearings. Everything was still. The only sound was her breathing.

What happened?

Slowly her memories began to surface from the dark shadows of her mind. What she had thought was a nightmare must have been real. She remembered being chased by a horrific creature, frightened, finding it very hard to breathe, then punching at the creature, and becoming lightheaded.

I must have passed out.

Glimpses of consciousness, of what had happened flashed in her mind, including how she had been lifted into the arms of a disgusting creature and then thrown over its shoulders, how she had jounced along on its back as it ran through the wasteland, and how the other repulsive creatures kept pace, how they growled at her, and how the stench of rot and decay filled the air. She remembered the creature's body that carried her, that it seemed very strange as if it had been modified and scarred. She remembered that its skin was peeling away, and in some places, it was cut away from most of the flesh and fat. She remembered seeing exposed tendons, muscle, and threaded veins. And she remembered how its face was severely disfigured, and how its lips were peeled back exposing its teeth, which could only click together as a means of communication.

Click-click-click-click.

The dreadful sound blared through her mind. It was all around her, more visceral now, more painful, and felt more like an intense wave of air stinging her.

Click-click-click-click.

She closed her eyes.

Go away! Go away!

The sound went silent. She opened her eyes.

Where am I? What is this place?

She looked around. She was in a chamber, damp, dark, and appropriately foreboding. It smelled of fear, putrid and complex, of feces and urine and rotting flesh. She knew this was a place where others had been kept, trapped in desperation, spending days and nights in darkness and silence until their demise.

Then there came a sound that she immediately recognized.

Spiders!

The sound was unmistakable. It was the sound of tiny legs scratching against the cold stone walls, and of the scurrying across a maze of broken flagstones, dead roots, and withered vines. They were everywhere. She squirmed, but some were already on her. They were not so much alive as they were active and hungry. More came, climbing on her and crawling about, and they started to bite and nibble at her flesh. There was nothing she could do.

She looked up to a faint light shining through the iron grating of a small window, casting twisted shadows upon the floor. The chamber seemed to be getting brighter. In front of her, she could make out a door made of what looked like iron, cold, pitted, and in some spots rust weeping down its surface.

But the stinging sensation of spiders gnawing at her was starting to overwhelm her. More spiders were biting and she could feel the stings; they hurt like a little sharp knife.

I must not panic. I must stay in control.

She wriggled knocking a few from her. She tried pulling down on the rope, but she could not break free.

She looked around the room searching for something, anything that she could use to swat at the creatures, to keep them away. But the walls closed in on her consciousness, smothering and stifling her. Fear clutched at her throat and unwanted tears started to flow unbidden and unstoppable. She was lost.

This is what alone feels like, hopelessness.

Then there came another sound, a sound from outside the door that scattered the spiders.

She had heard the sound before. It was the sound of death, the sound of a blade being drawn, cutting, and singing through the air, into flesh and bone, and the spattering of blood like rain. The air was rent with the echoes of muted gasps, the gush of bleeding, and the thud of bodies hitting the ground. But it was only for a few moments. Then everything was still again.

Fear struck at her. She sighed and curled up.

All is certainly lost.

The door flung open. She could see the shadow of a man standing in front of her. He was tall, black-robed with a hood, his face lost in its darkness. He held a sword pointing down, blood dripping from its razor-sharp edges. He stood motionless except for the rhythm of his chest; then he took a step towards her, and another, and yet another. She could make out his eyes now. They were cold and intimidating in their stare. He moved closer to her, her eyes darting from his to the sword which was now inches from her body. It glinted in the light.

Fear began to ensnare her thoughts, but she ignored it. Her moment of fear was quickly replaced by something else, an indefinable something that seemed to give her strength and courage.

I am ready to die.

As he stood over her, she pleaded with her eyes.

"If you are going to kill me, be swift about it," she said.

He did not say anything. Instead, he bent to a knee and reached out and took her hair into his fingers, studying the long grey strands. His movement made her cringe and she gulped in worry.

She stared into his hooded darkness and felt deep misery inside. Suddenly, a little butterfly with a ripped wing appeared and fluttered about him, then slowly faded. It was a vision in her mind's eye. She remembered the butterfly. It came to her as a vision when she visited the tomb of Ra Carathor, the Prime Heru. She remembered that she thought the butterfly was the Heru's soul.

He seemed to meet her stare, his fingers continuing to move gently across her hair. He did not speak, but his words came into her mind.

Angel with a broken wing.

He then gently drew the back of his hand alongside her neck to her shoulders. She writhed against him, trying to back away. From her shoulders, his hand found its way to the pendant's chain around her neck. Placing his hand gently upon hers, he took the pendant from her neck into his other hand and examined it. The Lia Fail turned red and began to warm and throb.

The words from the Guardian came rushing to her, like an answer, and her anxiety stirred greater.

Search for the voice that is silent . . . Search for the voice that is silent . . .

Her heart pounded relentlessly in her chest and thundered in her ears, and she wanted to scream but was frightful that more of the disgusting creatures would come. She felt quite drawn to the man, although she did not understand this emotion. She again looked into his hooded darkness and now knew for a certainty that he meant no harm.

"What is your name, good sir?" she asked.

He released the Lia Fail and looked at her. His mind again spoke to her with his words.

The one who is lost must become the seeker.

She did not understand him, but somehow she felt she could trust him. He swiftly drew a small knife from a leather bracer and cut the ropes that bound her hands and feet. As he did this, she reached out to him with her mind. She sensed a hardness about him, a determination, an air of patience and confidence, a great strength that could not be denied or ignored. But she also sensed heartlessness. Here was a man who had seen death, wielded death, and did not fear death.

More of his thoughts entered her mind.

You have been imprisoned by the Ru Gwaith of 'Shk Ndor. The one who brought you here is their leader, and he is called I' Mor

Ba. He owes no allegiance to the brood of the Drueger. But he would sell your soul for the right price.

From outside, there came a sudden series of high-pitched whistling or piping notes, almost like a cackling type of laugh. It was not the clicking or clattering sounds from the creatures, but the sounds frightened her, and she shivered. He drew his gaze to the window, listening intently to the sounds as if they had meaning.

He turned to her, a look of determination in his eyes, raw and savage.

Do not fear. What you hear is a signal from my companion, a great eagle. It is a warning. We must leave.

He reached down and swept her up into his arms. She wrapped her arms around his neck and rested her head on his shoulder. She held on tightly as he carried her from the chamber. Where she pressed against him, she could feel that his body was solid and muscular, honed over the years with purpose. He walked resolutely down a hallway thickly strewn with the corpses of the Ru Gwaith he had killed. The stench of death was everywhere. When they were outside, she took a deep breath hoping for fresh air. But the air was stale and reeked of decay. There was little light, and a greyish mist lifted over the place.

She felt a rush of air as they were greeted by a great eagle who swooped and perched upon the man's shoulder and near her. The eagle was enormous and commanding, his eyes larger than hers, a bright yellow, the same color as its powerful bill. Its head was snowy-feathered and its tail white, while its wings, and body, were a deep black.

The eagle announced itself.

"Kee-yep! Kee-yep! Seeeeeeeeeeee-chk! Tiri Thoron! Tiri Thoron!" it screeched.

The great bird raised its head and spread its wings. It looked down at Molly, and tilted its head, focusing one eye on her. It then lifted itself, gave a melodious shriek, and flew high into the air, circling above.

The man stopped and looked up to the eagle and then to the north.

They are coming, his thoughts told her. *Hold on tight!*

Over a series of bleak hills rushed a band of hideous Ru Gwaith. She saw them and buried her head into his shoulder and held tightly. Still holding her, he brandished his sword and ran into the oncoming wave of brutes. He spun and twirled, his sword slashing and stabbing, cutting deep. His momentum diverted the evil, sending dozens rippling back along their path. They were ugly things of more bone and muscle than flesh, and they chattered madly as they were so easily ripped apart by his blade.

"I' Ereb, fighavu duukav!" they cried in their death throes. "I' Ereb fighavu duukav!"

The fight was soon over and without losing a step he continued his stride as the eagle soared high above, ever vigilant, on the lookout for more Ru Gwaith. In time, they came upon a vast mountain range that was lost from sight in a thick blanket of cloud. Rain started to slash down in great diagonal sweeps, and the wind battered against them in frantic gusts.

They made their way to a trail that was barely noticeable at first, shrouded with rocks and boulders and brush. The trail twisted and turned as it wound its way up a mountainside, stones falling and cutting them off from the other sides. It was a treacherous climb. There were times when they came across rock that had fallen across the path, but they continued onward, she still in his arms. Gradually the trail evened out, and they came to a cave opening, partially obscured by rock and brush. The eagle swooped onto the man's shoulders as they entered the opening.

But outside in the cold and cheerless dark, not very far away, within the shadows, two unwinking eyes were watching her.

* * *

Everything was dark, gloomy, and silent. Molly could scarcely see where they were going. They kept moving forward, deeper into the darkness until, ahead, she saw a glimmer of light, what looked like a yellow flame far off; and she could hear what sounded like the crackle of a fire, which pleased her. She thought of warmth from the rain and dampness.

As they neared the light, she could make out a fire and felt a rush of warm, fresh air. They entered what appeared to be a large cavern. The fire was crackling, and the light danced off the walls, revealing a female elf holding an infant to her bosom, and close by was a black-furred Fenri, whose eyes shined white.

The man gently put her down near the fire, wrapping her snugly in thick fur-lined blankets. He sat near her with the eagle still perched on his shoulder. He pushed back his hood, revealing a face chiseled and handsome, giving him a rugged look. Thin wisps of black hair swept over and around his face as deep brown eyes stared back at her, full of secrets. She was mesmerized by him. She could not help but wonder what secrets he was hiding. But for the time being, she felt safe and protected, wrapped in the blankets, with the fire crackling nearby.

As she looked at him, trying to understand who he was and what he was doing here in this wasteland, she saw sadness, anger, and pain in his eyes, the kind that she had never seen before. But there was something in the way he looked at her that drew her in. It was as if he had been through something she could never imagine. Her hands went up to touch his face, but she quickly brought them back to her side.

He leaned a little towards her. An ominous seriousness masked him, but a calmness came to her, for with him, she felt safe.

"The Fenri you see is a friend named Curdas, and the great eagle is Tiri Thoron," he told her, a sharp tone in his voice, unruffled, yet betraying an inward sorrow. "The child is my daughter. Her name is Alvida Ase. Her mother is of the En' Edhel and she is called Ar' Lhaineth. My child and I are the last of the Mur' Edan. I am called I' Ereb by those who wish me dead. It means the *last man.* But you may call me by the name given to me at birth – Ruin Thatch. This is my home, and you are welcome here."

She smiled at him, letting his soothing hand push her hair from her face. Sore and exhausted, she fell asleep in an instant.

* * *

When Molly awoke the next day, she rubbed her eyes, yawned deeply, and stretched. She looked around groggily, a little disoriented. She sat quietly, trying to understand her surroundings. It was the same place where the strange man had brought her, a large cavern, wide and lofty.

She saw the child, Alvida Ase, swaddled in fur wraps and wool blankets, asleep near the fire, her small face flushed scarlet. The Fenri was near the tunnel leading to the cavern, and the great eagle was perched on a stone ledge, pecking at the carcass of a small animal. She felt the warmth of the fire, and she could smell a morning meal waiting for her. But the meal was not alone in its wait. She felt a presence. It was Ruin Thatch sitting beside her.

She was startled and let out a little gasp.

"I did not mean to frighten you," he said. "Are you well?"

She took a deep breath and looked into his eyes. Again, she felt a sense of misery in him, something unsettling. There was a mystery about him, something strange that she did not yet understand.

Search for the voice that is silent . . . Search for the voice that is silent . . . The Guardian's words resounded in her mind, as clearly as if they had been spoken aloud.

"Are you well?" he again asked.

She regained her composure.

"Why yes, Mr. Thatch is it?" she said. "I am well and appreciative of yesterday, for saving me from those creatures."

His expression became dark, and his brow twisted as if something she said bothered him.

"They are the Ru Gwaith and they are not creatures," he said. "No, they are below creatures, for even a creature will listen when another of their kind speaks to him. They have no souls. Do you understand? Their want is the flesh of others." She felt anger and venom beginning to take hold of him, and it frightened her. "They have exterminated my people. For ages, I have fought the ghouls without the help of those from the west. They did not fight in my war or offer support when I needed it most. They think me and my people to be lesser in the eyes of the Maker. But oh, oh, when they required hardened fighters, they came begging for me and my people to help them wage war. And when they asked for our blood on the battlefield . . . "

He stopped as he felt a hand grip his shoulder from behind.

The hand was pale, the long fingers beautifully tapered. Molly looked up. It was the elven woman, Ar' Lhaineth.

She was tall, elegant, and poised, with long white hair that she wore parted down the middle with two long braids on each side. Her eyes were round and black, and she appeared young. Her dress was white, long, and demure, clinging to her curves, a subtle hint at the beauty beneath.

"Your words become tempestuous," she told him, her voice resonant and clear. He put his head down, and a slight tremble came over him. "Revisiting the past serves no useful purpose. Doing so only reopens painful wounds. We have discussed this. Have we not?"

He placed a hand over hers, turned, and gave it a gentle kiss.

"Lhainey, what would I be without you?" he said with a sigh of affectionate relief.

She bent down and kissed the top of his head.

"My beloved, we are one as the Maker intends," she said. "No man or woman ever stands alone; we must not deceive ourselves."

Molly gave a slight smile. She sensed love between the two, as powerful as any force in the world yet as ordinary as breathing.

"I am sure our guest is famished. We do not have much, but what we have is yours," Ar' Lhaineth told Molly, her voice pure and bright. "Come now."

Molly followed her to a large stone slab on the cavern's floor. In the middle were small portions of salted meats and fish, with a few slices of bread and a brownish slurry in a small stone cup. Water was served in metal mugs. Ruin Thatch joined them, and the three sat on the floor, legs folded. Not seeing plates or utensils, Molly hesitated until she realized they ate with their hands.

Thatch brought some fish from the center, placing a small portion in front of her.

"Try some," he told her. "It is very good. Caught from deep mountain waters, fresh and tasty. Trust me. As Lhainey said, it is not much, but what is ours is yours. Please, try some."

She took a small amount and cautiously nibbled at it. The texture of the fish was light, flaky, and soft, and its taste was sweet and buttery. Her eyes widened in delight. She ate more and more, and she especially liked the brownish slurry in which she dipped pieces of bread. It tasted like honey.

This brought a small smile to Thatch. He and Ar' Lhaineth were glad that Molly enjoyed the meal.

They were quiet as they ate; no one felt the need to speak. Molly thought of her rescue from the Ru Gwaith, but her thoughts quickly turned to her sister and the others, and she wondered if they had survived. If they had, she did not know where they were. Worry beset her.

"I was with others. Do you know what has become of them?" she asked Thatch.

He shook his head.

"I am sorry," he said. "I do not know about those you traveled with. When I saw you being taken into the Ru Gwaith's stronghold, I felt a strong presence in you, something powerful, something good. I knew it was the stone you wore."

She reached for the Lia Fail and held it tightly. It warmed to her touch.

What about my plans, my plans to save the Harrow? she thought to herself, not allowing him to enter her mind. *And this savior, this man who rescued me, who is he? Why did he deliver me from those beasts?*

She glanced at him. The truth was she did not really know much about him, even though feelings pulled at her, that he was just what she needed. She stole another glance, the power of the stone allowing a glimpse into him. Again, she felt anger in him and an unbound tension of hopelessness, under which he felt suffocated. But she also felt there was strength in him, to keep going even when everything seemed lost.

A tortured soul, she thought. *He casts a cold eye on life, and only the elven woman knows him. His mind is a storm as cold and dark, as the deepest sea. He is troubled by everyday things in life, where the smallest of problems cause emotions to run wild. I must be careful with him. There is so much volatility. But his thoughts spoke to me, and there is goodness in him still. He has a gift of some kind. I will need to find out more.*

Her thoughts then turned to the stone.

Does he want it?

She looked at him, her eyes wide, questioning. She reached out to him with her mind.

You can hear my thoughts when I allow it, and you have the power to do the same. Do you want the stone as yours?

He looked at her, a sadness in his eyes.

No. I do not have the power to control it. It would instead control me and that would not be a good thing for this land.

She knew what he meant.

Power corrupts and the pursuit of power is in itself evil, her thoughts to him. *It is easy to become the mirror image of the evil one wishes to overcome.*

He did not return the thought. He simply brought his eyes down and away from her.

She felt relief. It seemed he knew his strengths, but more importantly, he knew his demons and wrestled with them.

Yes, a tortured soul, she thought to herself.

"I will need to reunite with my friends," she told him. "It is urgent that I do so."

"This land is treacherous and not easily navigated," he said. "You will not be able to reach them without my help. It will be dangerous."

"I must try," she said. "I cannot give up hope."

"Hope is something that can get you killed in this place," he warned her, his face solemn. "I will send Tiri Thoron to scour the land from above. He will help to find your friends, that is if they can be found."

"I am most grateful," she said.

She did not want to think about the possibility of having lost her sister and the others. It was too painful. But she was hopeful that with his help and that of the bird, she might just stand a chance. She needed to think of something else so she then turned her thoughts to the cavern. She looked about the place, now from a different perspective. It had an amazing depth that extended into an unsearchable distance, and on its walls were circles, crudely scratched into the rock and faded in color. She remembered the circle on Creep's vestments and thought of the tale of the Mur' Edan, the genocide of a race of people.

The insignia of the death caves, she thought. *What did Brows call the caves?* The words came to her. *Yes. Gon Durth.*

Images of death flooded her mind and a low, dismal, terrible feeling swept over her. She could not think, could not begin to see what she should do next, other than to stare at the circles carved into the walls.

"What is this place?" she asked with a quiver of fear in her voice.

He was somewhat surprised by her question.

"Why, this is my home, as I told you. Is there something wrong?" he asked.

But Ar' Lhaineth understood Molly's question. She looked at Molly, tracing her vision to the circles, then back to a terrified expression that flickered in her eyes before she had closed them tightly shut. The elven woman turned to Thatch, her eyes calling to him, as clearly as words sounding upon his ear, and he nodded to her in answer.

"So, you know of this place, from the ones you traveled with," he said, words escaping his throat. "You have heard the stories."

Molly continued her stare, fixed on the circles in front of her. She then turned to him; her face serious.

I know of the death that came from this place. This cave is part of the Gon Durth. She allowed her thoughts to resonate in his mind. *But you have powers most men do not. You can sense things. You can hear thoughts and speak with thoughts. What power do you have? And why did you rescue me?*

He nodded slightly.

"Tell her everything," Ar' Lhaineth told him. "She needs to know."

"As I said before, I rescued you because I felt your presence," he said. "And my power, my power is the power to kill. I am of the Hulnur Istare, a sect of the Edainar. I am a warrior wizard."

"So, you are a wizard," she said. "But I have not heard of warrior wizards. Fairfax and Ras Amon did not say anything about this type of wizard."

"They would not say anything about us. Why would they?" he said, his face stormy with conflict. "After all, we are different from them. We are killing instruments, trained to destroy, pure and simple." He looked away from her. "After the great war, they forced us out, many to the most remote parts of the land. We were outcasts, shunned by them, no longer needed. Even the brood seemed more at peace than we were. We Hulnur Istare have a saying - one can only combat the darkness by using darkness."

"How many of your kind remain?"

"I do not know. Some never made it beyond the training, their minds ravaged by insanity. Those who survived the training fought on the many battlefields of the great war, where many were killed. And, those of us who endured the great war were, as I have already said, abandoned by the Edainar. Most had nowhere to go. Their homes and families had been lost to the ravages of war. It is said that some, those unable to control their power, those who only found purpose in war and death, ended their lives by their own hands. They reclaimed some elements of the good death in the process while denying another war the power to randomly and savagely pluck them from this place. The weight is too heavy a burden and difficult. The road from anger and hatred is often too long to travel."

Molly now understood his pain, his anguish.

"So, you have magic?"

"Magic is an abomination in the eyes of the Maker and do not think otherwise. The Edainar will tell you differently. But all magic is unnatural, and for that reason, it is to be feared and avoided."

"But you did not answer me," she said, firm and resolute. "You can communicate using thoughts. Do you have magic?"

He relented.

"Yes, I possess magic," he said. "All Hulnare Istare have magic. My magic was honed by one of the Edainar, from the one called Argannon the Canonical. He has deep knowledge of enchantments and a long experience in casting magic spells. He is very contemplative, spending a lot of time in reflection. I learned much from him."

She remembered the name and she remembered the wizard when she met with the Edainar, at the start of her journey. She also remembered the worry she had with him, an instinct that came to her from the stone.

"Fairfax and Ras Amon use magic to help those that need help. What about you?" she asked. "Do you do the same?"

He became incensed with the question. The tension was palpable. His anger was building and she felt it.

"Do they? Do they? Do they help others?" he said, clenching his teeth. "Let me ask you - does harming one person to help another bring balance to this reality? Or does it simply make one feel better about himself? Few are unwilling to admit that in the equation of good and evil, we are far more evil than good."

She shook her head in disappointment.

"I am not here to argue with you over such things," she said. "I am only trying to understand everything about this place and how I can help to fight the darkness."

He felt her frustration.

"I have suffered to grow wild," he said. "Evil has lived here, in this part of the land for what seems like an eternity. And I, I have fought it for the better part of my life. I know what it is like, how the battle can damage a person, how it can consume him, make him one with the darkness." He stopped and looked at Ar' Lhaineth with loving eyes. "She has brought me from the abyss into which I have repeatedly plunged. I cannot repay her for all she has added to my life." He kept his eyes on her. "My dear Lhainey, if my destiny is to again enter the black chasm, will you follow?"

Ar' Lhaineth looked at him with loving eyes. She saw into the depths of his soul.

"Yes, my love," she said to him. "I will always follow."

Her words seemed to soothe him. He turned to Molly.

"And the equation of good and evil, that which I have suffered," he said to her, "it will change again and again, hopefully to what is best."

Molly felt compassion for him. So much had happened to him. He fought in terrible wars, lost friends, was cast out by the Edainar, and his people decimated by evil. It seemed his life was a prison with no hope of escape.

But there was a strength to him, an assurance that he knew of his prison, that his mission would always be to escape.

Prison. These stone walls. The Ru Gwaith. We must move on, she thought to herself.

"I understand and I am most thankful for everything you have done for me," she said. "But the Ru Gwaith, will they not follow us here? Should we not seek refuge somewhere else?"

"It is unlikely they will enter the caves. I' Mor Ba does not crave my life. Instead, he craves my anguish, my torture. He prefers me alive so he may bask in my suffering."

She placed a hand over his and squeezed.

"But it is different now," she said. "It is not about you. It is about me. It is me he wants. I carry the stone. He is most likely in service to others, to those of the darkness in the Drueger."

He looked away in thought.

"How wrong of me to not have considered that," he said. "You are right. He will come for you. We can use the Gon Durth. It is vast and complex, with mazes and passages. We can evade their chase and make our way south, to the depths of the Drueger, to the black towers. That is where you wish to go."

He knows, she kept the thought to herself. *He knows of my plans.*

"But what about your family?" she asked.

He smiled and climbed to his feet. He stood behind Ar' Lhaineth and lovingly wrapped his arms around her shoulders and neck.

"We will be fine. This is the life we have chosen, the risks we take," he said. "Danger is always a step away."

Ar' Lhaineth dropped her head to the side.

"Vanim ilya ro valur," she said in the elvish tongue.

His eyes gleamed in tears.

"It means, I go with him in love," he told Molly. He took a deep breath. "It is settled then. We will leave tomorrow. Tiri Thoron will let us know if he is able to find your friends."

Molly felt the Lia Fail warm against her skin. She remembered his thoughts.

The one who is lost must become the seeker.

As the day waned, they prepared for their journey. They told stories and Molly learned about how Thatch and Ar' Lhaineth met, and about the Mur' Edan and their struggle with the Ru Gwaith. Later, they shared a small meal of cheese, dried meats, bread, and Curdas made tea from the roots of high mountain grasses.

"It will help you sleep," he told them in a beastly voice, passing cups to the others.

Molly and Ar' Lhaineth sipped on the tea, reveling in its warmth and sweetness.

"I will have some a bit later," Thatch told his Fenri friend. "I will take the first watch. You will follow."

Curdas nodded.

Thatch instructed Tiri Thoron to leave the cavern and scout the surrounding area for Molly's friends and the Ru Gwaith.

"Later, tomorrow morning, we will meet up at the Avhe Greaav Ukae," he told the great eagle.

Molly did not know the words, but she felt she understood their meaning, as a place where they would rejoin with Thoron.

"Kee-yep! Kee-yep! Tirrrr-chk! Meets when light in sky," said the eagle.

He lifted himself from his ledge and into the air and flew off down one of the tunnels.

After their tea, it was time to sleep. Ar' Lhaineth fed Alvida Ase. When the child finished, she held her against her chest and patted her back until she brought up wind. She then wrapped her in several blankets, placed her on a thick fur, and they cuddled. Thatch took a hand and gently smoothed over Ar' Lhaineth's hair. He bent down and kissed her cheek.

"Good night my love," he whispered. "Rest now. Paint the night sky with stars."

She closed her eyes and cooed.

He then sipped on his tea and stoked the large fire with more wood, while Molly curled up in the warmth of a heavy blanket. She stared at the fire, watching a shadow in the flame dance.

The man is a prisoner within himself, she thought, hiding her thoughts from him. *He is been unable or unwilling to deal with the death that has swirled around him. Difficult. But he speaks of a mentor who he believes is reflective. But he is not. Who is this Argannon?*

Gradually her eyes became heavy and slowly closed to the darkness of sleep. Within the shadows, watching it all, the Fenri lay still, his white eyes shimmering strangely.

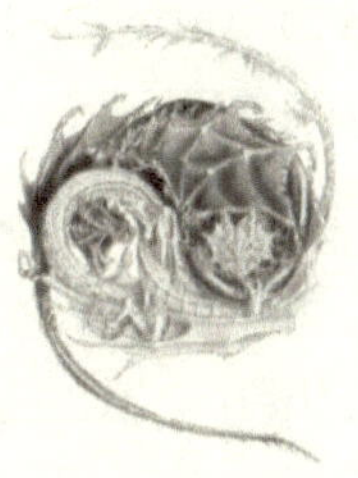

CHAPTER 20
THE MEANING OF BLACK

SINCE THE DEPARTURE OF the Huntress from Zheu Zhullus, there was great strife amongst the Tar Shor felines. The grand high-priestess Shamma became aware of an uprising and made every effort to put an end to it. She spoke to the others of what the Huntress told her, of the great turmoil that would befall the land, and of a darkness greater than any darkness in their history, one that could enter their sanctuary forest. She told them that they needed to prepare, to gather their strength against the gloom. But she quickly learned that some would only listen when the words suited their needs. She found it difficult, if not impossible, to lead because she lacked what the Huntress had, the En' Calin Kalina, the power of the green light.

She heard a shout.

"Come quickly!"

Running toward her was a high-priestess, a cat called Brielle. She was brown-furred and was distinctive in the Tar

Shor for her rounded ears. She had large paws and was strong and cunning.

"We've not much time," she told Shamma. "I'm afraid of what may happen."

"What? What is it?" asked Shamma.

"It has started. The darkness is here."

They ran from Zheu Zhullus and into the Gagdash toward the noise of shouts and screams. Crashing through the thick brush, they ran wildly, blindly, the undergrowth tearing at their fur. When they reached a clearing, they saw the Tar Shor felines, their eyes ablaze with hatred and fear, circling the black cat Nott who stood triumphantly over Tessia. The small cat had suffered a vicious beating, and Nott was pressing a paw down on her throat. Scattered about the clearing were the bodies of the other high priestesses, desecrated by maniacal savagery. The air was thick with the smell of their blood and rotting flesh.

"We're too late," sighed Brielle.

Shamma was filled with dread, not wanting to believe what her eyes told her. She had never seen such wickedness. She stood frozen, wallowing in the evil now in front of her. She looked down at the weak Tessia. The little cat was barely alive; her eyes were open but creepily vacant. Shamma could see that her breathing was shallow and that her mouth was open slightly, her pink tongue, and her whiskers quivering with each inhalation.

Nott hissed at Shamma.

"Ah, if it isn't the Laurn Cora," she said, her voice deep and venomous, so deadly that it stopped Shamma. Nott pressed down harder on Tessia's neck, and the little cat helplessly wriggled. "Why are you here? To save this little one? To save us all? You and the others are so pathetic."

All Shamma heard in Nott's words was evil; all she saw around her was death. She felt her body grow tense as an inner strength erupted in her, pushed along by anger. She wanted to scream and rip into those around her, but she knew this was a battle she could not win.

"Let her go," she told Nott. "Let her go, and you and your followers will be allowed to leave the Gagdash."

But Nott gave a horrible laugh that became a wild shriek.

"You stupid creature," she screeched. "Have you not looked around? Do your eyes not show you the new truth?" She pressed down even harder on Tessia who squirmed. "Look around you. Don't you see it? The death of the others? The end of what was? The whole of the Tar Shor is behind me. You are blind to the new truth. It is here, right in front of you but yet you cannot see it. Or, do you refuse to see it?"

Shamma began to slowly pace, her eyes never leaving the many Tar Shor felines that stared back at her. She could feel their distrust and hostility, but she did not back down. She met their gaze with her own, unblinking and unafraid.

"I see your new truth," she shouted out with conviction. "I see it. I see it as clear as day. I see it in your faces. But what I see is different from what your eyes show you. What I see is death brought about by the absence of the spirit of Si Kur, that which was given to us by the I' Ra

Heru. There is but death and emptiness in this new truth, a great void that aches and aches. It is a void that hatred cannot fill."

"Keep your words to yourself," growled Nott. "The Huntress was old and weak, and now she's gone. We are N'alaquel and we are strong. We no longer require her protection. And why should we have faith in the Si Kur, in words written so long ago? For too long, we have been enslaved by those words and their meaningless principles of what is right and what is wrong. It is time to change our world, shape our destiny, and bring to it the new truth. We will take what is rightfully ours, and no one will stop us."

"Tell me! Tell me!" sneered Shamma. "What will you do?"

"We will leave the Gagdash and travel to Dagda," said Nott, an evil smile on her face. "We will take the sacred citadel of Katzhu Pu and all its riches in battle. We will dominate the Si Jhys, freeing them to join with the I' Ra Heru, much like we freed the high-priestesses you see before you. We will change our world."

"You are no match for the Balor," said Shamma. "They will tear through you over and over again. Any survivors will be tortured, enslaved, and used for other purposes."

Nott applied more pressure to Tessia's neck; the little cat was now laboring, gasping for air.

"We do not fear the Balor," Nott hissed. "Those who do not see the new truth will fail! Fool! We will change our world, with or without you!"

The evil in Nott was cold, dark, and horrifying. Shamma knew this. There was little she or Brielle could do.

But Brielle had a thought. She rushed on Nott, knocked her down, and ripped at her with her enormous paws. It was a desperate move, but it worked.

"Take the little one and run!" she yelled to Shamma.

Shamma took Tessia by the scruff and dashed off. Many of the Tar Shor took chase, but she was swift and knew the many hiding places within the Gagdash. They found a small place, a hole in the ground, partially covered by moss and rock. They burrowed within the dampness as the Tar Shor ran by.

"We are safe," Shamma whispered to Tessia. "They will not find us here."

"I tried. I tried to stop them," said Tessia, her voice faint and faltering. "But I am too small."

"Quiet now. You must rest."

Shamma reached for some of the moss and applied it to Tessia's many wounds. She then cuddled with her, providing healing warmth. Tessia started to breathe more easily as she slowly started to purr. Shamma closed her eyes and considered returning to help Brielle, but she was certain that her friend had been killed. She wondered where the Huntress was and thought about the darkness and how far it had spread. She then considered her next course of action. She thought about all these things until, finally, she was too tired to think about anything else. Weariness overtook her, and she slept through the night and well into the next day before venturing west with Tessia.

* * *

Along the northern countryside, men worked stolidly, clearing their land of the fertile alluvial deposit, and preparing their fields for the next planting. The landscape was beautiful and the silence was peaceful. But war was afoot and the Nur' Edan army was on the march, shattering the tranquility. On the roads, the warriors' voices were harsh and excited. They talked of the war to come, of the promise of glory, and their power. As they marched through villages and towns, children gathered to stare, open-mouthed and awestruck, but their faces quickly grew sad as their fathers left to join the march. Women rushed to their men, trying to pull them from the march, but they could only resort to throwing stones and yelling as the army trudged on. They would then turn to their children and grab them in their arms, shielding them with their vulnerable bodies.

Watching over this was the malformed Lord Drow. He watched with great delight as frail old men hobbled after the women who sought shelter in their homes. But their homes provided little protection from the army, for Drow's men pillaged food and goods, burned villages, and brutalized the land. Those who complained were met with retribution and certain death. Yet the army would not be slowed. They marched on, growing in numbers and power, their songs filling the air, continuing south along the Aldpine River, closer to Mistmere and the Forest Heave.

As night encroached and with Mistmere in reach, general Virl Voracious and Grimshade stood on a rocky ledge that broke off into a lofty cliff. They anxiously awaited a meeting with Lord Drow, to talk over their plans. A sound startled them as from within the night shadows, Vrong Kav emerged, carrying Drow on his back. The brutish, tall, and strong Kav, was gentle in his handling of Drow, slowly placing him on the rocks, safely away from the cliff. But the miscreant leader, his clothes torn and tattered, discolored where open sores oozed pus and blood, used his muscular arms to drag his distorted body across the rock and to the very edge. He looked down at the white-stoned city of Mistmere cradled within the valley below. There he saw many fires burning inside the city and outside its walls. He saw its fountains and waterways dry, its formal gardens burned, and its grand promenades and courtyards, broad walks, and wide avenues empty. He could see through the flickering shadows that much of the city's walls had crumbled away under the recent battle, and in many places, the once lavish white walls were now a smoke-tinged black. Mistmere was a torn city, a maze of destruction; it bore little resemblance to its glorious past.

Drow's hollow, soulless eyes sunk into his bulbous head as he looked up at the three. He smiled, drool dripping from the corners of his mouth.

"Death reeks over the city," he laughed. "And where there is death there will be the Nur' Edan. This should be easy for the picking."

"Perhaps not as easy as my Lord thinks," said Voracious with some emphasis. "We've seen Vilyarok and elements of the White Star."

"Their numbers?" asked Drow.

"Difficult to tell, my Lord. We could very well have the advantage in size, but they have the winged horses."

Grimshade, pale and gaunt, stroking the fur trim on his leather coat drew closer.

"My Lord, we do have an advantage," he said, "one which the elven scum may not know of."

"And what is that?" asked Drow.

Grimshade had an evil smile playing across his lips.

"Catacombs. There are catacombs beneath the city," he said, "a vast labyrinth of rues, passages, and turnings, in which there is the danger of becoming bewildered, that is, if one does not know their way. I know of several entrances. The element of surprise and the chance to disguise attacks would be most advantageous."

"Voracious, your thoughts?" asked Drow.

"Very effective. We'd catch them off guard."

Grimshade's smile grew.

"My Lord, the great hall, Ewellinoth," he said, "it still stands with the crystal throne."

Drow looked up at Grimshade, wiping drool from his chin.

"I know you covet the throne," he said. "But once the city is taken the throne is mine by rights. Yet, I will grant you lordship of the city. Voracious will give you what you require. Use the catacombs and destroy the elves. Enslave its people, kill those who oppose you. Plunder its riches. All in my name." He lifted a clenched fist. "How I long to have those of the south in my palm, to squeeze them, to see them wriggle in pain. Gurandurm, when you are done, when you have squeezed until there is nothing left to squeeze, then, and only then, may you sit on the Cryuk Avhro, in praise of your Lord Drow."

Grimshade let out a sigh and bowed his head. His smile grew even wider, sinister, and terrifying.

Drow motioned to Kav who lifted him and carefully secured him to his back.

"Voracious, let us continue on our path to the Heave. Destiny awaits the Nur' Edan," he said, his words gurgling in his throat, forcing greyish spittle to froth from his lips.

* * *

The night air cooled and the Forest Heave seemed to freeze up in anticipation of something vile. There was absolute stillness within the richly green darkness; not a shadow moved about the thick trees. There were no animals in sight that called one to another. The scene was dark and creepy, the trees seemed to grow and shrink as the brood army's torches glimmered from the east. But there was indeed life in the forest, strange and evil. Yellow eyes danced like candle flames, and there were whispers, voices of the mind that spoke to one another.

He comes to us.

Yes. He makes his way.

Do you sense his presence?

Yes. His presence is strong.

Very strong, his presence is.

It has been such a long time.

It has been a very long time.

Yes, much too long since he graced us.

Indeed, much too long.

What will he do?

Whatever he is told to do.

Yes, from the great book.

Ah, the Sanye e' Soran Cath.

He knows the great book.

He lives the great book.

Its words sustain us.

Yes, living words give.

Food for the body and soul.

Do you think he will release us?

Oh, that would be grand.

Yes, very grand indeed.

He has the power to do so.

Yes, he has such great power.

Incredible power he has.

Oh, and the looking glass!

Yes, the looking glass!

He will gaze into the looking glass!

We should speak to him.

Yes, to welcome him home.

To welcome the Grand One.

Then, we will speak as one.

Always we will speak as one.

Strong when we speak as one.

And the creatures did speak, joining as one, one loud voice of the mind. Their master, his journey in a northerly direction, still several leagues away, heard the voice, and it brought a most conniving smile to slink across his face. Soon he would approach the vastness of the Thorndell Fields.

* * *

The small, scraggly black cat, fur tufted in many places, with a back leg twisted and deformed, had traveled for days and days, pacing his way carefully, hiding within forested areas, and keeping a distance from other creatures. When he happened upon a stream, he would drink and then recede into the darkness of the countryside. Only when hunger took him did he eat. He would raise a paw, and from it would emerge a fleeting flash of magic that would snatch a scrap of whatever was closest to him, usually vermin. His thoughts were varied and inconsistent, cold, and distant from the world, as they always were. But they were clear, always returning to one theme: pain and suffering. He had not forgotten the terrible grief and anguish he caused to the Bucklorn family and the memory made him smile; the torture that the family suffered pleased him. He loved to play with his victims, and the anguish of despair that they endured had something exciting in it. It was a source of great satisfaction to him, the knowledge that they had no hope of escape filled him with a perverse pleasure.

As he continued, he came upon the rugged valley of the Thorndell Fields, with its outcroppings of jagged rock, patches of wildflowers, and tall golden grasses that waved in the wind. He knew the history of the place. He knew that where he now stood great battles had been fought, that blood had poured like rain. He took a deep breath and smelled death. It was undeniable and final. He stared south and saw the thousands of grave mounds resting undisturbed. He could feel the souls of the dead trapped in the earthworks. They were wailing, crying to him, pleading to get out. But their howls only brought him joy and gladness.

He then turned his stare east where he saw vast fields of grass stretch as far as the eye could see, broken here and there by thickets of tough cottonwood. He was looking for something.

Now, where is it?

He adjusted his eyes and squinted. A shape emerged out of the tall grasses in the distance, barely discernible. A skull was perched atop an upright wooden pole.

Ah, there it is.

He picked his way through the grass, sidestepping smaller rocks and climbing over larger ones. Slowly he approached the wooden pole and skull.

His monument. Pity the skull is not his.

He lifted a paw, closed his eyes, and muttered a few words in the old tongue. Overhead dark clouds quickly formed. A wind kicked up, whipping the grasses about wildly. A peculiar feeling filled the air, an unnaturalness. A furious crash of thunder followed shaking the ground. There was a flash of lightning, violent, a jagged white streak that pierced the strange air. It struck the skull and wooden pole, the sound of the impact booming deeper than any thunder. A sudden heat washed down and around the place, leaving behind only scorched earth that emitted grey smoke. Untouched by the heat and flame, he grinned and continued his journey north.

But the noise and lightning flash did not go unheeded by the forces of the good and righteous. Many leagues away, Carrick bolted from the command tent with Roundthaler following.

They looked west just above the tree line where they could see the dark clouds dissipate.

"A storm," said Carrick. "Strange don't you think?"

"Disconcerting strangeness abounds," said Roundthaler.

"Do you think it was magic?" asked Carrick.

"I am a dwarf. What do I know of such magic? But in this land full of unknown ways and secrets, such magic would hardly surprise me."

"Speak with Dalgaes. Send the Vilyarok. Let us see what the winged elven eyes see."

Roundthaler nodded.

***

As the cat continued his travels north, he came to a small village, just south of Tollford Farthing. There were fields of wild wheat and vines, and among the trees there were maples. There were a few farmsteads, and one, a small barn and house close to a spring, had a few fields of grass for its farm animals, and fields of corn, greens, and potatoes for the family's use. The fields were separated by rows of grape vines and fruit trees and other trees that were bounded by narrow ditches, difficult for him to traverse. But he pushed his way through one ditch and into a field of lettuce when a boy spotted him limping slowly along.

Concerned that the cat was injured or sickly, and out of kindness, the boy called to his mother.

"Mother, look. A cat in the fields. It can barely walk. We must help," he said running from the barn to aid the cat.

The cat turned to the boy and cocked his head to one side.

What is this? A pathetic human child. Inquisitive it is.

The boy's mother watched as he ran from the barn. She saw the cat, its yellow eyes narrow in anger, its front claws kneading the soil. She knew that there was an evil spirit in the cat which fed on death. Fearing for her child, she hurried to him, grabbed him, and held him in her arms, just steps from the cat.

"No, my son," she whispered in the boy's ear, kissing him to calm him. "No. There's no helping this abomination."

She pushed the boy off to the house.

"Run home!" she told him. "Run home! Go now!"

The cat stared at the woman and using the common tongue spoke to her.

"Foolish human," he said. "You would sacrifice yourself to save something so small, so insignificant?"

"A mother will always protect her child," she said with a clenched jaw.

She reached for a stick for protection. But there was no protecting her from his magic.

He lifted a paw, closed his eyes, and summoned a demented spell. The woman's eyes widened in intense pain. She stiffened, dropped the stick, and croaked a moan of deep grief. He sensed her fear, her pain, her suffering, and it pleased him. With a slow blink of his eyes, her body began to twist, over and over again, spasms with the sickening sound of bones snapping and crunching as they changed and lengthened.

Her body had been forever altered into the shape of an insect with two large compound eyes, ferocious mandibles, and spindly legs. With a shriek, she crawled off like a four-legged insect, darting through the fields, and back to the barn and house.

There. Much better. Now, who is the abomination?

He smiled at the corrupted woman and her twisted movements, the sound of her bones crunching, and her screech.

Now when the child looks at his mother, all he shall see is a nightmare. It is how it should be.

* * *

The hills and trees were darkening even more in the night shadows as the scraggly cat came west of the Old River. He started to follow the river's bank north, dragging himself through light snow. To the east, he could see the brood army forming into a series of columns facing west, to the Heave. He paid little attention to their activities for he had foreseen this.

The brood force was enormous, and it reached far east into the darkness of the Drueger, column after column of firbolgs, cu sith, orcs, and other cruel beasts of fright. The brutes pounded their weapons against their shields and hollered wordlessly. Horns sounded from among them, blaring in a low, ominous tone that echoed over the land. And within the demon horde there stood a staggering number of mighty siege engines of war. The siege engines were massive, towering constructs of wood and metal, with great boulders strapped to their sides. They were pulled by teams of massive beasts, and they were flanked by rows upon rows of brood.

At the lead of the evil army was Drogur Vorn upon a great beast, the cloth pack holding the metallic head to one side. He lifted a massive arm signaling the brood to hold its position. To the north, he could see the Nur' Edan army now gathered. He could see Virl Voracious at its lead with Lord Drow strapped to Vrong Kav's back.

Voracious saw Vorn and the brood army to the east. He raised his shining sword, a signal to his army. In response, the thousands of Nur' Edan warriors drew their swords and lifted them high above their heads in a show of power. They stood in formation, close together, arranged for the tactical concentration of force - infantry in large squares to the front with cavalry and rows of archers in the rear.

Both armies watched as the small cat approached, looking across the way where the river neared the Heave. Silence descended upon the land as the evil throngs watched the cat make its way toward the edge of the large woodland. A dense fog from the dark forest began to swirl, painted by the pale light of the broken moon. There was an eeriness about the place.

But the silence was broken. The sound of a single Vilyarok, sent by Dalgaes at Carrick's instruction, flew overhead. The elven archer had followed the small cat along the river and now he sensed impending doom. He grabbed his bow, notched an arrow, and aimed it at the small cat.

Without looking up, the cat nestled on his back legs, stumbling a bit. He raised his front paws into the air and spoke a few words in the old tongue. A strong, cold wind began to gust blowing itself back and forth through the forest. The forest trees emerged from the darkness with limbs stretching high into the sky, like gnarled-fingered hands. They grabbed the elven archer and winged horse, swallowing them into the blackness of the Heave.

The cat paused and drew a deep breath. He spoke more words in the old tongue, along with a fiendish howl. The trees began to wave and sway, radiating outward from the center, like ripples in a pond. They bent and opened revealing an ornate, weather-worn, stone archway that framed a golden pathway through the Forest Heave to the western lands. Climbing red roses clung to the stone like greedy ivy plants, and on either side were lighted red candles. Silhouetted near the archway were the yellow-eyed shadows of contorted creatures.

Magic was in the air, thick and pungent. Vorn motioned his army forward, westward, through the archway, and into the Heave. The ground trembled from the dark hollows, deep and strange. It was deafening, the thud of hooves and clank of armor and weapons, joining the dull thump of a brutish chant.

You can never destroy the seed of evil for it grows within all creatures, thought Vorn. *Take pleasure in the harvest.*

Far away, Carrick and Roundthaler stood alone, as Dalgaes raced from his tent to join them. Their stares fixed to the north. They could feel the evil armies marching in cadence and it chilled every bone and every soul.

Carrick squeezed his eyes shut as if to drive the horrid sound away.

"It can only be the Grand Denier," he said. "He has opened the Forest Heave. How could I have not seen this? How could I have been so wrong?"

Roundthaler stood unflinching and firm, every trace of emotion drained from his face.

"Despair not at the sound of evil, for our fathers will never let our blood flow on the land," he said, the words from the ancient writings of Paragon Driado Aldril. "Let there be light even in the depths of darkness."

His words fell from all ears. Fear now gripped the armies of the good and righteous, and as the last of the brood and Nur' Edan entered the Heave, the ever-diminishing echo of death trampling over the land faded.

But as the sounds from the north waned, did there grow different sounds, sounds from the east, garbled and inhuman. What remained of the massive brood army was readying to battle Carrick's forces, a plan to thwart any pursuit westward. The sounds swelled clearer and louder, the clashing of arms, the steady throb of movement.

How could I have been so wrong? thought Carrick.

Then there came the sound of a galloping horse, a sound that drowned out all the other sounds. Through the mists of despair came a massive and muscular black horse. It was Saraanth of the Ure Rokko, and his rider the young Elban Miragrin, who reached behind and unsheathed the great black sword Zi Gurut. He lifted the sword high into the air.

"With the Maker's breath shall we rid the land of the dark minions!" he bellowed victoriously.

At that very moment did the hearts and souls of the good and righteous lift, and a great cheer resounded over the land. But for Carrick there was sadness. He clutched Gallia's vial knowing these would be his last days.

* * *

As Molly slept, again the dreams of death and the continual debasement and destruction of the land came to her. Only this time, they included the deaths of those she had met, and those she had befriended, which added a new dimension of emotional pain to her suffering. She was frightened because everything seemed so real and vivid. She tried to leave her dreams but could not.

Then she felt a biting coldness descend upon her. She let out a breath, the last gasp, and all her dreams fluttered away with it. She struggled to open her eyes, but it was as though they were made of lead. Searing pain shot through her, then the deepest gloom.

There would be no more dreams, no more light, only darkness.

* * *

A strangeness came to Thatch as he slept. He started to awake, feeling a warm pressure, then an uncomfortable slicing, stinging cold. He opened his eyes to find Curdas, the black-furred Fenri, white eyes ablaze, biting at his neck. Instinctively, he summoned the magic of the Hulnur Istare, throwing the beast against the stone.

"What are you doing?" he yelled at Curdas.

"You and the others must die," growled the Fenri. "The master has deemed it so. You have no choice in the matter. Your deaths will serve a purpose, even if you do not understand it."

Curdas then lunged at him, but he was ready. He grabbed his sword, the one he called Avhe Killas, and drove it into the beast's chest, and then with great might, twisted it as if hunting for the heart. He then yanked the sword out from Curdas in a wash of gore causing Curdas to collapse on his stomach with a shriek. He tried to raise himself, but Thatch plunged the sword through his skull.

Curdas fell in a heap of death. In an instant, there was a flash of light as the body began to transform into a large, brown, and scaly beast, with a round head and fiendish black eyes.

Thatch sensed magic as it washed over the creature.

Shape changer! he thought.

Then came a horrid thought: *The others!*

Bleeding from his neck but still tightly gripping his sword, he turned to see death staring at him. His beloved Ar' Lhaineth had been killed, her body mangled, teeth and claw marks ripped through her flesh, flowing blood and swelling around the gaping, angry-looking edges of each gash. Her eyes were open in a dead stare that was frightening. He turned to Molly and saw that her neck had been slashed; her head was cocked to one side and her eyes were closed. The necklace was covered with blood that had spilled from her neck but he could see a faint glimmer from the stone.

The Lia Fail remains!

There was blood all over, oily dark red lines flowing slick, and all he saw was death. He could not think straight. His thoughts were a jumbled mess as he tried to make sense of what had happened. He dropped his sword and fell to his knees. Anger and remorse raged through his veins as he pounded his fists on the stone floor, screaming in anguish. He pounded and pounded until his hands were raw and bleeding, but it did not matter. Nothing mattered anymore except for the pain he felt. It was as if his entire body was on fire, and he could do nothing to stop it. He cried out until his chest ached, and his throat was sore. When it seemed like he would never stop, he finally did. That is when his mind suddenly cleared and a thought shook him.

Alvida? Where are you?

He then heard a sound, a soft, slight whimper.

"Alvida!" he cried out.

There came another whimper.

"Alvida!"

To one side of Ar' Lhaineth, beneath several layers of thick fur blankets, he saw movement. It was the child wriggling. He crouched and carefully lifted her into his arms, smiling at her tiny fists flailing in the air. He held her close to his chest and she was content, her eyes half-closed as she nuzzled into him. He looked down at her and his heart swelled with love. And within the flickering shadows of the fire he then gazed upon his beloved Ar' Lhaineth, her face completely pale. He leaned over and kissed her forehead, tears falling from his eyes. He thought of the words he would say to her each morning when they woke.

My love, the morning is upon us yet again. And as the light clasps the land, it shall brighten our love, a love which is brighter than any star.

Now those words brought him a great sorrow that washed over him like a wave. He closed his eyes in tears knowing she was gone forever. A sweat of agony drenched his forehead. He could have screamed aloud with the horror and agony of it all, but he dared not make a sound. He barely dared to breathe, because of his shame and loathing of himself, that he was alive.

He turned to look at Molly's lifeless face through tearful eyes. It had been a long time since he had cried, but the tears came unbidden now.

Angel with a broken wing. It was not supposed to be this way.

His mind churned in madness.

Why does death haunt me so?

He sat near the fire, cuddling his child, and began to rock, humming a Mur' Edan lullaby. As she slowly closed her eyes to sleep, he continued the lullaby while gazing into the fire. He watched it burn away, felt it dissolve into ashes, and with it a shadow in the flame that faded.

He immediately knew what he had to do.

So ends the second part of the history of the Second Shadow War as written by Tollen Popperdock . . .

www.ingramcontent.com/pod-product-compliance
Lightning Source LLC
LaVergne TN
LVHW050910080826
845145LV00001B/41

* 9 7 8 0 9 9 7 7 1 0 9 1 5 *